I0638301

# A Spark
# Of Heavenly Fire

## By

# Pat Bertram

Deep Indigo Books
Published by Indigo Sea Press
Kernersville

Deep Indigo Books
Indigo Sea Press
PO Box 26701
Winston-Salem NC 27114

Second Deep Indigo Books edition
published February, 2017.
Deep Indigo Books, Moon Sailor, and all production design are trademarks of Indigo Sea Press, used under license.

For information regarding bulk purchases of this book, digital purchase and special discounts, please contact the publisher at indigoseapress.com

Cover design by Pat Bertram

Manufactured in the United States of America
ISBN 978-1630663667

For Jeff

Always

# 1

*Friday, December 2*

Kate Cummings counted backward from one hundred, though she knew it wouldn't help her sleep. Dead people didn't slumber, and she hadn't felt alive for a long time. Not since before Joe's funeral, anyway.

*Three. Two. One.* She raised her head, squinted at the illuminated face of the alarm clock, and flopped back against the pillow. Five-fifteen. Six hours of thrashing around in bed. She blinked away the sting in her eyes. All she wanted was one good night's sleep. Was that too much to ask?

*One hundred. Ninety-nine. Ninety-six. . . .* A sound startled her awake. A siren's scream, fading now. She checked the time. Five-thirty. Even if she could doze off again, she'd have to rise in less than an hour. Not worth the effort.

She hauled herself upright and groped for her eyeglasses. After sitting on the edge of the bed for a moment, gathering her strength, she dressed and wandered through the house. She hesitated by the closed door of the second bedroom where her husband had lived during the last years of his protracted illness, touched the knob with her fingertips. Yanked her hand away.

*This is ridiculous. Joe's been gone for thirteen months.*

Taking a deep breath, she grasped the knob, but could not force herself to turn it. She rested her forehead on the door for a minute, wondering if she'd ever be able to face the ghosts of sorrow and regret locked inside, then squared her shoulders and headed for the front closet to grab a coat and hat.

She trudged the seven blocks to Cheesman Park. A dozen hardy souls had braved the frigid early morning air, but as the hematite sky softened to pearl gray, others joined the parade of exercisers rounding the paths.

An elderly couple swaddled in layers of heavy clothing marched in front of her, their arms pumping faster than their legs.

A young man jogged toward her. With his beard stubble, ancient gray sweats, and tousled hair, he looked as if he were one step away from being a street person.

Coming up behind the jogger was a man in a cropped tee shirt and skimpy nylon shorts, a rapturous smile on his face. He passed the jogger, moving so swiftly and lightly his feet barely touched the ground.

As he neared Kate, he stumbled, and his smile faltered. He held out his hands, a beseeching look in his bright-red eyes. All at once an impossible torrent of blood gushed from his mouth, soaking her, and he toppled into her arms. She tried to steady him, but she slipped on a patch of blood, and they both fell.

"Are you all right?" two quavering voices asked in unison.

Kate turned her head so she could look out of the one clean spot on her glasses. The elderly couple peered down at her, their faces creased in concern.

"I'm fine." The stench of the blood and the weight of the runner made it difficult for her to breathe, and her buttocks felt sore and cold, but she didn't seem to be injured.

She struggled to scoot out from beneath the runner.

"Let me help." The voice sounded young, male, and had a pleasing timber. Catching a glimpse of gray fabric, Kate realized the voice belonged to the disreputable-looking jogger.

After rolling the body off her, he extended a sturdy hand. Clutching it, she lumbered to her feet.

She reached into her coat pocket for a wad of tissues, wiped her face, hands, and glasses the best she could. Then, squatting next to the runner, she checked his pulse, listened to his chest. No sign of life.

She passed a palm over the runner's eyes to close them.

Her knees creaked as she pushed herself upright. Four or five people, still breathing heavily from their exercise, stopped and gawked at her. "What happened?" one bystander asked "Was he shot?"

Not shot, Kate wanted to say, but she couldn't summon

the energy to speak aloud.

A redhead in a pink and lime green warm-up suit jogged by while pressing buttons on a cell phone. "I've been calling nine-one-one," she said without slowing her pace, "but the lines are busy."

"Something's going on," the old woman commented. "I heard sirens all night long."

Kate cocked her head to listen. Off in the distance, underlying the sounds of the wakening city, was a cacophony of sirens. Too many sirens.

She tried to hug herself to ward off a sudden chill, but the freezing blood stiffened her coat sleeves. She thought about going home, peeling off her ruined clothes, and taking a long hot shower, but she didn't feel right about walking away from the unknown man lying dead at her feet. Besides, she had to wait until the police or the paramedics arrived.

"You go get cleaned up," the old woman said. "We'll wait for the police."

Kate shivered. Her hands and feet felt cold, and her heart beat too fast. Perhaps she should leave; it wouldn't help anyone if she collapsed. As she turned to depart, she heard the woman whisper, "Someone ought to go with her. I think she's in shock."

"I'll go." The voice was that of the man who had helped her up.

"I'm fine," Kate managed to say. "I don't need anyone."

He fell into step beside her. "If I remember correctly, there's a city ordinance prohibiting a woman covered in blood from walking the streets unescorted."

She slanted a glance at him. The compassionate look and the hint of mischief in his brown eyes warmed her, and she gave him a flicker of a smile. "In that case, I have no choice. I wouldn't want to attract any further attention."

They set out for her house on Elizabeth Street. She concentrated on putting one foot in front of the other, and after a few minutes, the worst effects of the shock wore off.

"I'm Greg Pullman," he said, breaking the long silence.

"Kate Cummings."

"So tell me, Kate, do you work for a living, or do you hang around parks all day waiting for men to fall on you?"

She scrabbled about in her mind for a witty response, but when the pause dragged into awkwardness, she said simply, "I work at the Bowers Clinic."

"Isn't that the converted mansion on Seventh Avenue where the rich people go?"

"Yes."

He raised an eyebrow.

"We like rich people," she said. "They have money."

"Are you a doctor?"

"No. A patient's representative. I take medical histories, deal with any grievances patients might have, and listen if they need someone to talk to." Trying to match his light tone, she added, "What about you? Do you work for a living, or do you hang around parks all day rescuing women who have men fall on them?"

"I'm a reporter for The Denver News."

Kate stopped and slapped herself on the forehead with the heel of a palm. "I am so stupid. Here I thought you were being nice, and all you want is a story."

"No story. I promise."

She glanced into his guileless eyes. "You don't look like a reporter."

"I don't?"

"Reporters are hard-eyed, weary-faced people, beaten down by the low-level types they have to deal with."

He smiled at her. "Funny you should mention that. I go to a bar downtown—The Lucky Star. It's close to the central fire station, police headquarters, The Denver News, and Channel Ten, so it's filled at all hours with hard-eyed men and women. I used to try to imitate their stare, but I looked ridiculous."

"Good."

He seemed bemused by her response. "Why do you say that?"

"All the hard stare means is that they no longer have the desire to care. You do."

\*   \*   \*

Kate shifted uneasily in her seat. She tried to focus on Rachel Abrams's play-by-play description of this past Sunday's Broncos game, but it reminded her of the dead runner in the park; he had been wearing a Broncos tee shirt.

Rachel's shoulders twitched, and an arm flailed out. She stopped in the middle of a rambling account of a pass interception and announced, "There's something terribly wrong with me. I feel great. I never feel well, you know that."

Kate studied the elegantly dressed woman sitting across from her. With a rosy glow brightening her normally sallow cheeks, Rachel did indeed look healthy. Or she would have if not for her twitching muscles and blood-shot eyes.

"Have you been experimenting with your insulin dosage again?"

"No. I've been following Dr. Hart's orders."

"What about the spasms? How long have you had them?"

Rachel's head bobbed, one of her feet kicked the desk, and her fingers kneaded nonexistent dough.

"What spasms?"

Kate made a quick notation on the medical form: Patient seems unaware of muscle spasms. When she looked up, she saw Rachel bending forward, clutching her midsection.

Dropping the pen, she jumped to her feet. "What's wrong?"

Rachel's body jerked upright.

Kate hit the panic button to summon a doctor. Rachel's mouth opened and bloody vomit burst out with such force it arced over the desk and hit Kate full in the chest.

Gagging on the smell of so much blood in such a small room, she rushed to Rachel's side. She was bending over the inert woman when a lanky blonde wearing a pristine lab coat, linen slacks, and an ecru silk blouse came charging into Kate's office.

"Oh, Kate. Now what have you done?"

Kate stepped aside to make room for the doctor. "She

acted fine, then she vomited blood."

Dr. Hart looked Kate up and down. "Wait in the examination room next door. I'll check you over when I'm finished here."

With an odd sense of detachment, Kate obeyed.

She was staring at the white tiled floor, wondering how she could have seen two people die in the same manner within such a short time, when she heard a familiar voice.

"Exactly how many times a day do you do this?"

She looked up. An attractive clean-shaven man in his early thirties lounged in the doorway. Dressed in dark slacks, a tan trench coat belted at the waist, and a battered fedora perched rakishly on his chestnut curls, he bore little resemblance to the scruffy individual who had walked her home a few hours earlier.

She gave him a sheepish smile.

"Okay," Greg said. "Time for me to take you home again. Let's go."

Kate finally found her voice. "What are you doing here?"

"I came to see if you're all right. But look at you."

"Don't remind me. I need to get my coat." She went into the locker room off the women's restroom and came out holding her old blue coat at arm's length. "You better carry this. I don't want to soil it. It's the only coat I have left."

Dr. Hart exited Kate's office and stood with hands on hips, narrowing her eyes first at Kate then at the reporter.

"What's going on here?"

"I'm going home to get changed. I can't work looking like this."

"And who is he?"

Kate glanced at Greg. The mischievous gleam in his eyes encouraged her.

"He's an experienced escort. Every time someone vomits blood on me, he's there to escort me home."

"What do you mean, 'every time'? Has this happened to you before?"

"This morning when I took a walk in Cheesman Park."

Dr. Hart studied Kate for a moment. Apparently deciding the preposterous story was true, she flicked a wrist.

"Take the afternoon off, Kate. You've had enough for one day. Let me know if you need me."

When Kate and Greg stepped outside, he asked, "Yours or mine?"

"Yours. I don't have a car."

He ushered her toward a battered red Honda Accord that looked as if it could have been one of the first models off the assembly line.

"It has close to two hundred thousand miles on it," he said proudly, opening the door for her.

To her relief, the heater worked.

They headed down the long sweeping driveway and waited for a break in the unusually heavy traffic. After several minutes, Greg slipped his car between a Volkswagen and a Porsche.

"Are you married?" he asked.

Kate shook her head. "What about you?"

"No, but I think I'm going to be."

Kate's lips twitched. "You're not sure?"

"My girlfriend has been hinting at marriage for months now, but when I proposed, she said she'd think about it." He smiled at Kate. "What's with you women, anyway? Some of you can't make up your minds, and some of you are always covered in blood."

Kate glanced ruefully down at her beige suit. She had thrown away everything she'd worn to the park; now she'd have to throw away this set of clothes, too.

"At the rate I'm going," she said, "I'll need to get a whole new wardrobe."

"You say that as if it's a bad thing."

"I hate shopping."

"A woman after my own heart," he teased.

She turned her head toward the window to hide a sudden flush, and noticed they'd progressed only a few blocks.

Slanting a glance at him, she took a deep breath. "You found out something, didn't you?"

"What makes you say that?"

"Your eyes. I see a reticence in them now I didn't see earlier."

"I talked to my contact in the medical examiner's office."

When he didn't offer anything more, she said, "And?"

"And they don't know what causes the red death."

"The red death?" She swallowed. "They've named it already?"

"Unofficially."

"Do they know how many have died?"

"Hundreds, possibly thousands."

Kate stared straight ahead, trying to imagine so many people dying the same horrific death as Rachel Abrams and the runner in the park. Remembering the woman's description of the game and the man's tee shirt, she mentioned a possible Broncos connection.

Greg gave her a thoughtful look. "Interesting coincidence."

They drove in silence for another couple of blocks, then Kate said softly, "It isn't going to end any time soon, is it?"

His response was as subdued. "I don't think so. The death rate is rising."

The driver of the green Jeep Grand Cherokee behind Greg edged closer, revved his engine, and honked his horn. It had no effect on the stalled traffic, but the driver of the white Subaru ahead of Greg thrust an arm out the window and extended a middle finger.

Greg double-checked his doors to make sure he'd locked them. Any minute now, it seemed, the two drivers would be resorting to violence, and he had enough problems.

He glanced at his watch. Half an hour late. His editor wouldn't be pleased he'd missed his deadline, but he couldn't help it. All afternoon, ever since he had dropped Kate off at her house, he'd been caught in one traffic jam after another.

He called the newspaper again but still could not get

through. He tossed the phone onto the seat next to him, then folded his arms across the top of his steering wheel, and rested his chin on them.

In the end, it didn't matter that he couldn't reach the newspaper—he had been unable to complete his assignment.

His contact at the medical examiner's office had supplied him with the names of the first victims of the red death. He'd interviewed the families of three of them. They were too grief-stricken to tell him much, though they did confirm Kate's surmise of a Broncos connection. Those three victims had all been at Sunday's game.

Another early victim had been John Takamura, a professor at the State University Extension. Greg hoped the man's wife, a professor herself, would be able to give him a newsworthy statement. She had not been at her campus office, and when she didn't answer her phone, he headed for her house in University Hills, but it looked as if he wouldn't get there.

Movement jarred him out of his contemplation. The driver of the Jeep had closed the gap between them and was nudging Greg's car toward the white Subaru.

The Subaru pulled out of the line of traffic, drove over the median, and made a U-turn. As it passed Greg, the driver—a white-haired, apple-cheeked woman who had to be seventy—once again displayed a middle finger.

So much for sweet little old ladies.

But she had the right idea.

He crossed the median and headed back to The Denver News.

Two blocks later, Greg noticed the white Subaru zigzagging. Suddenly the windshield of the vehicle turned crimson; the old woman fell forward and collapsed onto her steering wheel. Then, midst the clamor of honking horns and screeching tires, the Subaru veered across the next lane and crashed into a parked car.

As Greg slammed on his brakes, he found himself looking around for Kate, but didn't see her. This time, at least, she wasn't involved.

# 2

*Saturday, December 3*

Kate was standing by the meat counter at the grocery store, picking out a package of ground beef, when a sharp-featured woman about her own age approached her.

"You're not going to buy that, are you?" the woman demanded.

"Why? Do you want it?" Kate offered the woman the package of meat she had been about to put in the shopping cart.

The woman recoiled. "No, I don't want it. Haven't you heard? The meat's tainted."

"She's right." An older, pleasant-faced woman parked her cart next to Kate's. "There is something wrong with the beef. I heard it on the news last night. Several people have died from it."

A dimple-chinned man, accompanied by a boy who looked exactly like him, joined the group. "Seventy-five dead so far."

The boy made exaggerated retching sounds. "A man hurled blood. It was awesome."

"Oh, Billy." Exasperation tinged the man's voice, but his eyes shone with pride as he regarded the child.

Kate dumped the package of ground beef into her cart. Whatever else the red death might be, it was not a reaction to bad beef; Rachel Abrams had been a zealous vegetarian.

She moved away from the meat counter and headed for the dairy case. She made slow progress; groups of people discussing the catastrophe blocked most of the aisles. Everyone, it seemed, knew someone who had died or knew someone who knew someone, yet no one questioned the reported count of seventy-five fatalities.

Listening to the excited voices, Kate felt terribly alone. Didn't they know what was happening? Couldn't they feel it? Then she thought of Greg and drew comfort from the knowledge that he too knew the truth.

\* \* \*

Greg met Peter Jensen at the usual place: Washington Park next to a tree surrounded by a wrought iron fence.

Peter, a gaunt forty-seven-year-old wearing thick eyeglasses and discount store clothing, smelled faintly of formaldehyde and death. He worked at the medical examiner's, preparing bodies for autopsies and cleaning up afterward.

"I've always loved this place," Peter said, gazing at the tree. "There used to be an elm here, the scion of a tree George Washington stood under when he took command of the Continental Army. Isn't that incredible? The very tree."

"What happened to the elm?" Greg asked.

"It died in 1983 from Dutch elm disease and the parks department planted this oak in its place."

Peter continued to contemplate the tree a few minutes longer. "The death toll is continuing to climb," he said finally. "There have been isolated outbreaks all over the country—all over the world, actually—but it seems to be centered in Colorado. They're estimating fifteen thousand dead in Denver alone."

"Where are they putting all those bodies?" Greg asked, keeping his tone professional.

"In an old meat locker on Wazee Street. They're not releasing any of them until they know for sure what they're dealing with."

"So they still don't know what the red death is?"

"No. Because of the conjunctival hemorrhages that turn the eyes red and the fever that gives the face a ruddy glow, they thought it might be a viral hemorrhagic fever like Ebola, but now they're leaning toward a virus/bacteria combination."

"Is that possible?" Greg asked, jotting down the information.

"It's rare, but it does happen. A combination of the swine flu virus and Pfeiffer's bacillus probably caused the flu pandemic in the early years of the twentieth century. More than two percent of the entire world's population died in that pandemic. If the red death is equally lethal, one hundred sixty million people could die. One way or another, they're going to have to do whatever it takes to stop it."

"Like a vaccine?"

"Could be, but until the toxicology reports come in, there's not much to go on. It would help if they could find the index case. Because so many people died simultaneously, no one knows where it started."

"I do."

Peter jerked his gaze from the tree and stared at Greg. "You do?"

"Yes. The Broncos game last Sunday."

"How on earth did you find that out?"

"I *am* an investigative reporter."

Peter turned back to the tree. "They do know one thing about the red death. It sends hormone levels soaring, particularly endorphins and adrenaline, so people are still able to function and feel good while they're bleeding to death internally."

"That's probably what caused all the road rage yesterday," Greg said.

"Right. Then the perpetrators died. Instant retribution."

Greg eyed the other man curiously. "You don't act at all bothered by any of this."

Peter shrugged. "It's not my world. It has nothing to do with me."

"You could still catch the red death."

"You don't get it, do you?" Peter said with an uncharacteristic harshness. "All my life I have done nothing but suffer. Now my body is wasting away for no reason the doctors can discover, I'm going blind, and I can't find a decent job. You think the red death scares me? I would welcome it. But I doubt I'll catch it. Life isn't finished tormenting me yet."

Greg opened his mouth to speak, but closed it again when he realized he had no idea what to say.

He finished writing his notes, then looked up. "Did you find anything on the guy I asked you about? The one who died in Cheesman Park yesterday morning?"

"Just his blood work."

"That's what I need."

"No AIDS, no hepatitis, nothing to worry about. He was perfectly healthy."

"Except for the red death."

"There is that."

Gripping the heavy grocery bag, Kate took a shortcut through Cheesman Park. She hadn't gone far when she noticed people clustered around a man in his late fifties who looked unbearably sad. Her stomach clenched. *Please, not another death.*

Ignoring hushed protests, she elbowed her way through the crowd, then stopped, confused. The man watched not a tragic scene but children at play. His eyes seemed focused on one in particular: a little girl wearing a pink jacket and a delighted grin, who chased after a yellow ball.

Kate became aware of the cameras and realized they were filming a movie. The man's ordinary face looked familiar. Could be Jeremy King. She had heard on the news he was in town for a few days.

As she watched the actor, his expression changed from sadness to bewilderment to horror.

"Cut. Cut," the young director shouted. He did a victory dance. "That was awesome."

But the look of horror still distorted the actor's face. Without even turning to see, Kate knew exactly what he witnessed.

Her eyes burned, but no tears came.

# 3

*Sunday, December 4*

Jeremy King was sitting on the edge of the hotel bed, rubbing his gritty eyes, when he got his wake-up call.

He stood, then quickly sat back down, breathing deeply to still a sudden nausea. It had taken the entire contents of the mini bar to remove the image of the little girl from his retinas. Who would have thought a child that small had so much blood in her?

Man, he hated Colorado. He must have been out of his mind when he agreed to do a film here.

After his stomach settled, he stood again and stretched. He had to do a few short scenes today, then he could head for home where he and not some punk kid barely out of school called the shots. Okay, so Mr. Big-Time Director Cameron Hoffman couldn't break away from his new picture to come direct a few measly last-minute scenes for *Cry of Hope*, but did he have to send a snot-nosed kid?

Jeremy went into the bathroom and stared blearily into the mirror. He tried to put on his trademark deprecating grin, the one that had won him two Oscars, but he couldn't manage it.

Man, with those bags as big as the Montana sky under his eyes, he looked old, really old. He tilted his head to see himself from several angles. Maybe he should get a facelift? No. He still looked more commanding and distinguished now, at fifty-eight, than he had ever looked before.

Except for the bags under his eyes. Good thing he had the tube of hemorrhoid ointment; it would shrink them in no time.

He ordered room service, then showered, shaved, and put on his hand-tooled cowboy boots, well-worn jeans, blue chambray work shirt, and western-style chamois sport coat. Once on the set he'd exchange his coat for his character's flannel-lined denim jacket, but otherwise he would wear his own clothes. That way, after the filming, he could go directly to the private airfield on the outskirts of Denver where his jet would be waiting, already refueled.

Then home to his vast Montana ranch.

By the time Jeremy dressed, his breakfast had arrived—a large pot of coffee and an order of toast. When the waiter left, Jeremy rummaged in his luggage for one of the cans of imported sardines he had brought with him.

He opened the can, laid the sardines side by side on the toast, and dribbled the olive oil over top as he had done as a child growing up in a trailer by the wrecking yard in Grand Junction. He didn't even like sardines—hated the damn things—but eating them had become a daily ritual, a reminder of how far he had come.

After Jeremy choked down his breakfast, he headed for Trinity Methodist Church, a block from his hotel, to begin his morning's work.

The film crew was set up outside the historic stone church when Jeremy arrived, but he made them wait a few minutes while he got into character.

*I am a rancher far from home. My son is dying. My cattle are dying. I feel as if God has forsaken me. I am standing here outside the church, watching people enter. I hang my head in despair, knowing I have been denied that simple solace.*

"Cut," the director yelled, earning frowns from the last few Methodists straggling into the church.

"I wasn't ready," Jeremy said. "Let's do it again."

"No. You did good. But be ready next time."

Jeremy smiled to himself. He knew he had been perfect, but if he had said so, the snot-nosed kid would have made him do it over and over again.

"Let's move to the next scene," the kid said.

One of the production assistants ran up to him and gasped out, "Have you heard? It's all over."

"What?" shouted the little snot. "The movie? It's been canceled?"

"No. The sickness. It's all over. All over Colorado. We're stuck here."

"Stuck here? What does that mean?"

"Colorado has been quarantined, and air space is restricted to military planes. No one's allowed in or out."

Jeremy stepped away from the crew gathered around the production assistant. Not allowed out of Colorado? We'll have to see about that.

Pippi O'Brien absently stirred her bowl of oatmeal sprinkled with flaxseed. Because she ate so little in her effort to maintain a model-thin figure, she needed her gruel, as she called it, to keep her colon working properly. This morning, though, she felt too queasy to eat. Maybe she shouldn't have drunk that entire bottle of Chablis last night, but she couldn't help it. Ever since Greg Pullman proposed, she had been on edge.

She had maneuvered him in the direction of marriage almost from the first day she'd met him. She'd even dragged him to a jewelry store and shown him the ring she wanted. So why, when he asked, had she panicked and said she'd think about it? She'd told the truth; she kept thinking about it, and there sure wasn't any fun in that.

A shrill scream ripped through the silence. Pippi clamped her hands over her ears until the machine answered the telephone.

"Pippi? You there?" A brief pause. "Call me, okay?" Another pause, then, "I love you."

Suddenly, like smog blown away by a quickening breeze, all doubt vanished. Of course she intended to marry him. She'd tell him soon.

Tomorrow, perhaps.

# 4

*Monday, December 5 (a.m.)*

Kate walked to work, choking on the exhaust from thousands upon thousands of idling engines. Used to the sight of stalled traffic, it took her a while to realize not a single car moved, not a single car could move.

The drivers acted strangely docile. A few people talked on cell phones; most stared out their windshields, hands resting on their steering wheels, waiting.

An attractive young woman in a pale gray business suit whizzed past Kate on a mountain bike. "Get off the sidewalk, you old bat," she screeched. Seconds later the bicycle careened into a parked car, setting off an alarm, and the woman went flying.

A quick glance told Kate the young woman was beyond help. The gray suit jacket had turned a sticky maroon and the woman's head tilted at an unnatural angle.

Kate wrapped her coat more firmly around herself, glad she hadn't been subjected to another bloodbath.

She arrived at the clinic before anyone else. While she was turning on the lights in the waiting room, the phone rang. She settled herself at the reception desk and picked up the receiver.

A woman cried hysterically. "He's dead! My baby's dead."

The wails continued for several minutes before they subsided into hiccupping sobs. "This is Gillian Grover," the woman finally managed to get out. "My son Eddie vomited blood and when I dialed nine-one-one, I got a busy signal. What am I supposed to do now?"

Eddie Grover dead? He'd been a favorite with the nurses at the clinic, a Dennis-the-Menace sort of child with an unruly cowlick and a propensity for getting into trouble.

"Keep calling nine-one-one," Kate said, though she knew it wouldn't help. If by some miracle an ambulance could get to the Grover's house, the boy would still be dead.

"Did Eddie go to the Broncos game a week ago?" she

17

asked over a fresh spate of sobs.

A moment of silence, as if the incongruous question had shocked the other woman out of her grief.

"No," she said at last. "He played hooky from school the Friday before the game, so my husband took our daughter Alice instead."

"How are they feeling?"

"Alice, you mean?"

"Yes. And your husband."

"They're fine now, but they both got sick a few days ago." She sounded defensive when she added, "I thought they had the twenty-four hour flu."

"You did the right thing," Kate said soothingly.

"But if I had taken them to the clinic, maybe Eddie wouldn't have got sick." Gillian started crying again. "It's all my fault."

"No, it's not—" Kate began, but Gillian had already hung up.

At ten o'clock Dr. Amanda Hart waltzed into the clinic and frowned at Kate. "What are you doing out here? Where's Joan?" She looked around the waiting room. "Where is everyone?"

"Stuck in traffic," Kate said.

Dr. Hart nodded. "Tell me about it."

"How did you manage to get through that gridlock?"

"I rode my old ten-speed." She tilted her head back and shook her pale hair. "Did any staff make it in yet?"

"No."

"Well, Dr. Bowers will be here soon. He's coming on foot. We couldn't even get out of our driveway this morning. Cars were packed bumper-to-bumper on Circle Drive. Where did they all come from? Not that many people live in the entire neighborhood."

Kate smiled at the outrage in Dr. Hart's voice. Amanda Hart had been born poor, but she had quickly adopted the supercilious attitude of the Bowers, the old-money family she had married into.

A loud rumble reverberated through the waiting room.

Kate looked out the window to see Joan Wheeler, the twenty-two-year-old receptionist, climbing off the back of a vintage Harley Davidson.

After the driver had roared down the driveway, Joan dashed into the clinic.

"Do you know who that was?" she asked excitedly. "Harley. Harley Reese."

Dr. Hart peered at her. "You know Harley Reese?"

"No. I hitchhiked—" Joan held up her hands as if warding off a blow. "I had to get to work, didn't I? When I couldn't get out of my apartment's parking lot this morning, I could have stayed home."

"Who's Harley Reese?" Kate asked.

"Only the richest man for his age in Colorado," Joan said. "He's on the news all the time. I don't understand half of what he says, but he's soooo good-looking." She sighed theatrically. "Money, looks, brains. What more could a girl want?"

"Enough of this foolishness," Dr. Hart said. "I'm sure you ladies can find some work to do."

Except for the computer, everything had been cleared off Kate's desk. The room smelled of the industrial-strength disinfectant the cleaners had used to scrub away Rachel's blood.

Breathing shallowly, Kate turned on her computer, pulled up her electronic daily planner, and stared at the date, wondering why it seemed so familiar. Then it hit her. Her birthday. The red death had pushed it out of her mind.

*Forty-two years old and alone. How sad is that?* Even sadder, the only person she wished to share the day with was a much younger, almost-engaged man.

Two hours later, she looked up from the files belonging to the few patients who had managed to keep their appointments. As if she had conjured him, there he stood, leaning against the doorjamb.

He gave her a slow, sweet smile, and her heart fluttered in response.

"I wanted to see what you looked like when you weren't red." He nodded approvingly. "You clean up nicely."

She felt a blush creep across her face. "That's all you came for?"

"That, and to take you to lunch."

She gave him a doubtful look. "Is any place open today?"

"I saw a lunch room that seemed to be doing a booming business. The Black Forest."

"I seldom pass up an opportunity to go to The Black Forest. Let me get my coat."

Outside, he gestured to the bicycle chained to one of the columns supporting the porch roof. "Sorry I can't give you a lift. Unless you want to ride on my handlebars."

"That's okay. We can walk. It's only three and a half blocks."

They had no trouble getting a table. Although the restaurant was busy, most of the customers were the drivers of the cars stalled out in front. The drivers rushed in to place orders, then returned later to pick them up.

Shaking his head, Greg turned to Kate. "This is not at all the way I expected people to act today—so quiet and subdued."

"People don't believe they're going to be inconvenienced for long. Life today is geared for things mostly working out the way they're supposed to. I think they're waiting, expecting things to return to normal any minute now."

"What are they going to do when they discover things aren't going to return to normal?"

She shivered. "I'm afraid we're going to find out. A boy died today. He didn't go to that Broncos game, but his father and sister did. They both had flu symptoms, but that's all."

He blinked. "So the red death is contagious."

"Seems like it."

They stared at each other for a long moment, and she knew he too pictured her covered with blood.

"I am so sorry," he said. "I came to tell you that you had

nothing to fear from the jogger's blood, but if the red death is contagious . . ."

"I know." She kept her voice level for his sake. "Maybe they'll discover a vaccine or a cure before I get it."

He nodded, but didn't look convinced.

A skinny young woman in jeans and a tee shirt, with six earrings climbing each ear and a vibrant streak of purple in her bleached hair, tossed two menus on the table as she scurried by.

"Back in a sec," she called over her shoulder.

Greg glanced at the menu.

Seeing the surprise on his face, Kate said, "I can pay for my own meal."

"It's not all that expensive, it's just . . . well, look at this place—ancient linoleum, mismatched tables and chairs, bright lights. For these prices, we should be served by buxom wenches in dirndls."

Kate smiled. "What The Black Forest lacks in atmosphere, it makes up for with good food. They use real butter and heavy cream, and it makes all the difference in the world."

"Yeah, but—turkey tetrazzini? Spaghetti? What kind of German restaurant is this?"

"It started out as a German bakery famous for its Black Forest cake. They did so well that when the catering service next door went up for sale, they bought it and combined the two businesses under one roof. A few years ago, they expanded even more to include lunch. Lottie Untermeyer, the owner, planned to redecorate, but she's been so busy she never got around to it."

"The owner's a friend of yours?"

"Lottie's daughter and my mother were close, so I became acquainted with most of the Untermeyers. You'd like Lottie. She's a character—almost ninety, and still going strong. If I see her, I'll introduce you to her."

The waitress skidded to a stop.

"I'll have the turkey tetrazzini," Kate said.

Greg handed the menu to the waitress. "Make that two."

When the food came, Greg took a tentative bite and nodded approvingly. "This is delicious."

After eating a few bites, he got a phone call. He reached into a pocket for his cell. "Do you mind if I take this?"

Kate waved her fork. "Go ahead." She tried not to eavesdrop, but couldn't help hearing his side of the conversation. He seemed to be speaking to his girlfriend.

He closed the phone, crammed it back in his pocket, and beamed at Kate.

"I'm going to get married. We're meeting tonight to set a date. I don't know if I mentioned, but she's Pippi O'Brien. You might have seen her on television. She works for Channel Ten."

Kate nodded. "She's a lovely young woman."

He slumped in his seat. "This isn't right, feeling so good when the world's going to hell."

"There's nothing wrong with being happy. There's enough misery in the world as it is. If there's one thing I've learned, it's that happiness is fleeting. You have to enjoy it while you can, regardless of the circumstances."

"It's hard to believe there could be worse circumstances."

"Believe it." Kate took a deep breath. "This morning when I couldn't sleep, I got up and looked out the window, and I saw a garbage truck pull up in front of the house across the street. Two people in biohazard suits got out of the truck, went inside the house, and came out carrying a woman's body. They threw it into the back of the truck, drove down a couple of houses, collected another body, and threw it in the truck, too. I stopped watching after that. I didn't want to know how many other stops they had to make."

# 5

*Monday, December 5 (p.m.)*

Jeremy ripped the phone out of the socket and threw it across the room hard enough to knock a chunk of plaster out of the far wall. The phone pinged in protest, then fell to the floor, and lay still.

He had been trying to get through to his wife, his agent, his lawyer, his publicist, anyone, but each time he made a call, he got a busy signal before he finished punching in the numbers.

Staring at the dead phone, it suddenly hit him that he knew someone here in Denver to contact. Gabriel Weiss, the lawyer who had acted as a liaison between the producers of *Cry of Hope* and the Colorado Film Commission. Weiss could find a way out of Colorado; he had a reputation as a man who got things done.

Jeremy searched through his wallet for the card the lawyer had pressed into his palm when they first met. He reached over and plucked his cell phone off the nightstand where he had dropped it after he found it could pick up no signal outside the state. After a few tries, he managed to get through to the lawyer.

"I need to get out of Colorado, Gabe."

"You and three million others," Weiss responded.

"Isn't there someone you can call? The governor, maybe, or the mayor?"

Weiss chuckled. "The governor left Saturday night before the quarantine went into effect, a special junket, he said, but rumor has it he's shacked up with a call girl in D.C. until the quarantine is lifted. And the mayor, who got left out of the loop, is barricaded in his mansion and refuses even to talk on the telephone in case the red death seeps through."

"There has to be someone who can get me out of here." Hearing his voice ascending into hysteria, Jeremy stopped and took a deep breath. "Money is no object," he said evenly.

"Let me see what I can do. Where can you be reached?"

Jeremy recited his cell phone number and the phone number for his suite.

"I'll get back to you as soon as possible, but be advised this could take days."

"I don't have days. I have to leave now." Fury, like bile, rose in his throat. "My plane is here, but I can't get off the ground. The National Guard wouldn't let me. And my rental car is stuck near Tiny Town. I tried to drive through the mountains yesterday morning, but the roads were clogged with people trying to escape."

"They weren't trying to escape. Hardly anyone knew about the red death or the quarantine yesterday morning. What you experienced was normal traffic brought to a standstill. I used to live in the mountains until I realized I spent more time in my car than in my house."

"I want to get out of here," Jeremy said.

"I understand. I'll get back to you."

After Jeremy hung up, he paced his rooms for what seemed like hours, willing the phone to ring. On one of his last passes around the suite, which shrank with every step, he tripped over the hotel's phone. He picked it up and replaced it on the bedside table, then took the elevator to the lobby.

"One of the phones in my suite is out of order," he told the young woman behind the desk.

"We'll get that fixed right away, Mr. King," she said breathlessly.

Jeremy checked his pocket to make sure he had his cell, then stepped outside.

He gagged as the putrid air filled his lungs. Coughing and sputtering, he threaded his way through the idling cars to the other side of the street, then set off down Broadway.

He entered the surplus store several blocks away to give his respiratory system a break, but as he wandered among the shelves, he realized how ill prepared he was for his escape. He scurried up and down the aisles, grabbing everything that caught his eye.

A sleeping bag. No, two. He was too old to sleep on the cold, hard ground without the extra padding. Camouflage fatigues. Rations. Canteens. A twenty-gallon receptacle for water. Water purifying tablets. A good hunting knife. A dusty case of sardines. (How did that get here?) A backpack.

He kept piling things on the counter, barely aware of what he was doing. The fever stayed with him until he paid for his purchases with his Platinum Visa.

He stared at the mound of merchandise, wondering how to get it back to the hotel.

"Do you want help out with that, sir?" the paunchy, middle-aged salesman asked. The suggestion of respect in his voice told Jeremy that the man had recognized him.

"I walked from my hotel downtown," he said.

"Jack!" the salesman roared.

A teenage boy slouched out of the back room. "What?"

"Box this stuff, load it on a couple of hand trucks, and help this gentleman take it wherever he wants."

Jack made no effort to comply.

"I'll pay you, of course," Jeremy said.

The boy disappeared into the back room and returned with an armful of empty boxes.

By eight o'clock, Jeremy was sick of the ever-shrinking hotel suite, sick of waiting for a call that didn't come, sick of his own company.

Wishing desperately for the wide-open spaces of his ranch, he went outside to roam the streets of Denver, which finally began to empty. He ended his journey at The Lucky Star, a place he had discovered last night during another spate of aimless wandering. The seedy bar normally wouldn't have appealed to him, but it fit his mood. Besides, after being a cop in more than a dozen films, and a firefighter in two, he felt as if he belonged.

He propped himself on a barstool.

"Scotch and soda," he said.

The bartender, a lank-haired individual with grooves of discontent etched on his otherwise nondescript face, continued to polish a glass. He held it to the light, squinted at it, then placed it in the rack with the clean glasses. Jeremy could clearly see a lipstick smear on the rim.

When Jeremy finally had his drink, he tossed it back, making a point not to look at it.

"Another," he said, banging the glass on the bar.

"Hey, Jeremy," someone called out. "Come join us."

Jeremy turned around to see a ruddy man beckoning to him. Who? Oh, right. Dick Whelan, a firefghter, one of his drinking buddies from last night.

He took his drink to the booth. Dick started to introduce him to his buddies, then stopped in mid-sentence and stared over Jeremy's left shoulder.

"Christ, that is one fine piece."

Jeremy craned his neck to see what caught Dick's attention, and the familiar pulse pounded in his groin.

Standing in the doorway, scanning the bar, was the most beautiful woman he had ever seen. Well, maybe not the most beautiful, but she'd do in a pinch.

"Who is that?" he asked, unable to take his eyes off the tall, model-thin redhead with the aquamarine eyes.

"Pippi O'Brien," Dick Whelan said.

"The Channel Ten weather girl," someone else chimed in.

"Greg Pullman's girlfriend," Dick added. "You met him last night. He's the reporter you talked to about the quarantine."

"The pretty boy?"

"That's the one."

Jeremy watched Pippi glide to the bar and perch on a stool. Without even a nod to Dick and the others, he hauled himself out of the booth and ambled straight for her.

Pippi rummaged in her purse for a mirror, more to take her mind off her upcoming date than because she needed to check her appearance. She had thought that after telling Greg she'd marry him everything would be fine, but she felt as confused as ever.

"What's a nice woman like you doing in a place like this?"

Pippi winced. Why couldn't men leave her alone? Or
come up with a more original line. She turned her back on
the man and busied herself with the mirror, hoping he would
take the hint and go away.

He moved closer, giving her a whiff of boozy breath. As
she leaned away, she caught a glimpse of him in her mirror.

Her heart stopped. Then it began beating wildly.

Jeremy King! Jeremy King was coming on to her!

Without moving, she said coolly, "Is that the best you
can do?"

"It's all I've ever needed."

*I'll bet it is.*

She turned to face him and practically fell off the stool
when she felt the full force of his personality. No wonder
they called it star-power; it was like being bathed in the light
of a thousand suns.

She batted her eyelashes. "Maybe it's not the line, ever
think of that?"

Jeremy smiled at her. "You're adorable. Where have you
been all my life?"

A wave of heat surged through her body. She dropped
her eyes. When she raised them a moment later, she
managed to speak calmly.

"Right here for part of it, but I've always dreamed of
going to Hollywood. What's it like being an actor?"

"Not much different from being a weather girl."

Her eyes widened. "How do you know what I am?"

He smiled at her as if to say he knew things about her
even she didn't know. She lost herself for a minute, but the
pain in her hands brought her back. She looked down to see
that she gripped the small mirror so tightly her knuckles had
turned white. She relaxed her hands and took a surreptitious
glance at her image. Her cheeks were pink and her eyes
bright.

"There are a lot of differences," she said, tucking the
mirror into her purse. "Doing what I do, I won't be able to
get my name in a star on the sidewalk in front of Grauman's
Chinese Theater like you did."

"That whole thing is so silly. You know how it got started?"

Pippi shook her head no.

"In 1927, an actress by the name of Norma Talmadge accidentally stumbled onto a freshly laid sidewalk outside the theater. The press, egged on by studio publicity agents, made a big deal about it, and it became a tradition."

She bit the inside of her cheek to keep from grinning. Jeremy King! It was as if he had stepped out of her plasma TV into her life.

"I watched *Mesa Grande* on television last night," she said. "The movie you did with Janet Richards. I envy her. She has it all—money, fame, great marriage."

"Money and fame, but not a great marriage. Her husband cheated on her."

"How could he look at another woman? Janet's so gorgeous."

Jeremy smiled. "It's one of those stories that could only happen in Hollywood. Janet accused her husband of seeing someone else. He swore he was faithful, but she hired a detective. When the detective sent her pictures of her husband having sex with a woman, she didn't know whether to be angry or relieved: the detective had taken pictures of her and her husband. Then she looked at them more closely and realized she didn't remember ever being in that particular hotel room. Turns out her husband met a lingerie salesperson who looked exactly like Janet. So, in a strange way, he was faithful—to her looks."

Pippi laughed. "Tell me another story."

"Okay. There's this actor who plays rough, tough guys, but he's so terrified of speaking in public he seldom makes appearances, not even on talk shows to promote his films. He has a reputation for being a nice guy, which he usually is, but there are times when it all gets too much for him, so he goes into a bar, the seedier the better, and picks a fight."

"Who is he?" Pippi asked.

Jeremy beckoned to her.

She leaned her head toward him. He put his lips to her

ear, but the sound of her raging blood drowned out the name he whispered.

He pulled back slightly. "You're thinking of becoming an actress?"

She could only nod.

"I have one of my agent's cards at my hotel suite. Why don't you come back with me, and I'll get it for you."

She giggled. "Is this one of those 'come up and see my etchings' things?"

"If you want," he said softly.

Suddenly all the air seemed to be sucked from the room. She looked at him. Their eyes met and held.

"What about your wife?" she said in a voice she barely recognized as her own.

"We have an understanding. As long as I'm discreet, I can do as I wish."

Pippi searched his eyes. She thought he lied, but she didn't care. There was something dangerous about him that thrilled her to the core of her being.

Greg hurried toward The Lucky Star, trotting in his eagerness to see Pippi.

He stopped abruptly.

The ring? Where was the ring?

He searched his pockets with increasing urgency.

Oh, there it was—safely stashed in his jacket pocket.

When he entered The Lucky Star, there was a sudden hush, and he thought he heard his name whispered.

Then someone yelled, "Hey, Pullman, seen Pippi lately?"

Several people snickered.

A man, so tall, muscular, and dark-skinned he seemed to block out all light, appeared by Greg's side.

Greg took an involuntary step backward. "Jeez, you startled me. I wish you'd make some kind of noise instead of sneaking up on a person."

Jim Clayton's lips twitched. Then the smile faded and his naturally menacing expression returned.

"Let's take a walk."

"I'm meeting Pippi. Can't it wait?"

"No. I have something to tell you."

Once outside, Jim didn't say anything.

"What?" Greg said. "You're scaring the heck out of me. Did something happen to Letisha or one of your kids?"

"They're fine. It's you I'm worried about."

"Me? Why would you be worried about me? I've never been better in my life. Pippi's agreed to marry me, and she's meeting me here at ten tonight to set the date." He checked his watch. "It's almost that now. She should be along any minute."

"She was already here. She and that actor, Jeremy King, left together."

Greg smiled complacently. "She'll be back."

Under the streetlight, Jim's balding head gleamed like bronze as he moved it from side to side. "Not tonight she won't. They were draped all over each other when they left, and everyone could tell what they were up to."

Greg's knees buckled. He took a step backward and slumped against a parked car.

"Look, Greg, if it's any consolation, I doubt it means anything. I know she loves you, but she's scared and confused and not at all sure what she wants."

"Poor Pippi," Greg said softly.

"You're taking this better than I thought you would."

Greg rubbed his eyes. "I'm too tired right now to feel much of anything."

"Would you like a ride home? The streets are mostly clear now."

"I noticed. What happened?"

"All of us on the job, including detectives, desk sergeants, secretaries, dispatchers, even some of the brass, have spent the past several hours directing traffic. We're under strict orders to have the streets cleared by midnight tonight. What a mess. Hundreds of vehicles abandoned and thousands totaled."

Greg pulled his notebook out of his shirt pocket. "What

did you do with them?"

"If we found room, we pushed them to the side of the road to be dealt with later, but most got towed outside the city someplace."

"Did you ever discover what caused the gridlock?"

"Isn't it obvious? Too many people died while driving to work today. And if that isn't enough, we have a mass mutilator to contend with. Can you believe it? Someone's going around beating corpses to a pulp. Three so far."

Hearing a strange note in Jim's voice, Greg said, "Are you okay? You don't sound like yourself."

Jim laughed humorlessly. "I'm not myself. I don't know what I am now. I don't know if I'm still a detective. I don't know if I'm still a cop. Hell, I don't even know if I'm still working for the good ol' U.S. of A."

"What are you talking about?"

"My bosses are still my bosses, but I've been advised that when I see someone from FEMA, I must take orders from them. I've been advised that when I see someone in a military uniform, I must take orders from them. I've been advised that when I see someone in a UN uniform, I must take orders from them, and if they're speaking a foreign language, I must find an interpreter to figure out what the hell they're trying to say."

Feeling as if he had been doused with a bucket of ice water, Greg jerked upright. "Who's really in charge here?"

"To the best of my understanding, it's the commanders of the UN troops. According to my bosses, every major emergency in the world now comes under the jurisdiction of the United Nations. Even FEMA and the U.S. military have to take their orders from them."

"I thought we were under quarantine. How did all those people get here?"

"Supposedly FEMA has a base of operations in Colorado Springs, and the UN troops were doing maneuvers at Fort Carson, so they were already here, but some Germans were flown in from their military base in California before the quarantine went into effect. That's right. *Their* military

31

base. The Germans have been deeded a base, the first permanent foreign military base in the United States, with no Americans in the chain of command."

"I know. Gorbachev sold it to them."

"Mikhail Gorbachev? The former premier of the Soviet Union?"

"He was part of a task force that oversaw the closure of unprofitable military bases in America. You didn't say if any of what you told me was off the record."

Jim shrugged. "On the record. Off the record. What difference does it make anymore? I'd better go. I'm still on duty, and I don't want to get shot as a deserter."

Greg started to smile, but the forbidding look on Jim's face told him it wasn't a joke.

The sound of weeping woke Jeremy. He turned his head toward his companion and saw one trembling shoulder and a tangle of gleaming hair.

He stretched luxuriously. The red hair hadn't lied. The girl had been all fire, kindling a passion in him he hadn't felt in years. The memory of it made him hard.

He reached over and pulled the girl into his arms. He smoothed back her hair and kissed away her tears, murmuring, "Honey," and "Sweetheart," and "Dear."

"I'm such a terrible person," she said, sobbing.

"Shh. Shh," he whispered between tiny kisses.

Her arms stole around his neck, and her lips sought his. In a surprisingly short time she bucked beneath him, calling out his name.

*You've still got it, King*, he thought exultantly. Then, after one final thrust, he tumbled into oblivion.

# 6

*Tuesday, December 6 (a.m.)*

So many people milled around outside the emergency room of Denver Health Medical Center, it took Greg longer to wheel his bicycle to the bike rack by the entrance than it had taken to pedal the six blocks from the newspaper.

He locked his bicycle, then tried to make his way to the door.

A big man with mean eyes blocked his way. "Beat it. We got here first."

"I'm from The Denver News—"

"I said beat it." The man put his paws on Greg's shoulders and pushed. Greg stumbled, but the press of bodies kept him from falling.

"He already hit two guys," whispered a young woman, sounding more thrilled than appalled.

Greg held up his palms and backed away. He had been on the wrestling team in high school and could still take care of himself, but getting in a senseless fight played no part in his immediate plans.

Ignoring the man's jeers, Greg made his way through the crowd and headed for the ambulance entrance where he entered the hospital unmolested. He had to slog through another crowd, but as soon as he passed the emergency room, the hospital became eerily quiet. Perhaps that was normal for four o'clock in the morning?

He yawned. Not wanting to think about Pippi and Jeremy King, he'd worked through the night. When he finished here, he'd go home and take a nap before starting the new day. If he could sleep.

He passed a deserted nurses' station. Where was everyone? Maybe on break.

He strode through empty corridors until he found the cafeteria. After purchasing hot chocolate and a sandwich— egg salad, he thought, but couldn't tell for sure—he stood and surveyed the room. He caught the eye of a plump young blonde sitting with three other women; all wore what looked like nurse's uniforms.

The blonde whispered to her companions, and one by one, they turned to watch his approach.

He gestured to an empty chair. "Mind if I sit here?"

The blonde giggled and shook her curls. "Not at all."

"Do you work here?" a pregnant woman asked when he was seated.

"He doesn't," the blonde said. "I would have known if he did."

Greg took a sip of the watery chocolate. "I'm a reporter for The Denver News."

The pregnant woman massaged her belly. "You visiting someone?"

"I'm here on assignment. May I ask you ladies some questions?"

The blonde edged her chair closer to his. "My name is Brandy. I'm twenty-six years old and available."

A heavy-set older woman sighed. "Oh, Brandy." Then she turned to Greg. "What do you want to know?"

"Mostly how the epidemic has affected the hospital."

They gave him blank stares.

"For instance," he added, "how are you dealing with the influx of new patients?"

"You mean the red death patients?" the pregnant woman asked.

"Yes."

The women looked at one another and burst into laughter.

Greg's brow furrowed. "What did I say?"

Brandy jumped up, clasped his hand, and hauled him out of the chair. "Come on. I'll show you." She dragged him out of the cafeteria to the bank of elevators.

Greg's stomach growled in protest at not having been fed, but he didn't mind leaving the unappetizing meal behind.

When they got off the elevator, Brandy opened a door and gestured for Greg to enter. "We're on the surgical ward," she said.

It took him only a moment to scan the room; both beds had been stripped.

They went up one hallway and down another, looking in all the rooms. Most were unoccupied.

"What's going on?" Greg asked.

"It's like this all over the hospital. Patients on life support are still here, but we discharged most of the others. We needed to make room for the red death patients. I mean, we are in the middle of an epidemic, aren't we? But we aren't admitting anyone. The ones who are really sick die, and the others aren't sick enough to need hospitalization."

"What about all those people in the emergency room?"

"Oh. Them. Most of them aren't even sick. They get the sniffles and think they're dying of the red death. Babies!"

They reached a door at the end of a corridor. When Greg pushed on it, he found it locked.

"What's this?"

"The infectious disease ward. TB, hepatitis B, typhoid, things like that. When these patients heard we planned to admit red death patients, they tried to escape, so we had to lock them in."

"You mean you're keeping them here against their will?"

"Sure. One epidemic is bad enough. What if we had a TB epidemic and a hepatitis epidemic, too?"

Greg suddenly felt so weary he wanted to drop right there and go to sleep, but somehow he summoned the strength to thank the nurse and return the way he had come.

Retrieving his bicycle, he found that the crowd outside the emergency room had disappeared. Two soldiers leaning against a Humvee stared at him until he left the area.

Huddling under the covers, Kate wrapped her arms around her abdomen to soothe the cramps that wracked her body. Until the advent of the red death, she had not understood how visceral fear was. Could a person die from fear? Another cramp seized her, forcing a moan to her lips.

She hated herself for the way she felt. Although her

mind told her fear was a physical reaction and had nothing to do with cowardice—hadn't she read that sometimes soldiers who had messed their pants before a battle had gone on to win medals of valor?—her body told her otherwise.

A squadron of fighter planes screamed overhead, and in the distance she heard the unmistakable sound of helicopters. Lots of helicopters.

Her stomach spasmed. Whoever said the only thing we have to fear is fear itself must have been an idiot. There were many things to fear in the dawn of this new world.

"Get a grip," she said aloud. "And get moving. You're not sleeping, anyway."

Still, several minutes passed before she could take her own advice. When she finally rose to get dressed, her body moved sluggishly, but by the time she'd walked a block or two, she tread briskly.

This isn't so bad, she thought. The cold air smelled clean, and she detected a hint of pine drifting down from the mountains. Or maybe it came from a Christmas tree lot.

Christmas! She'd forgotten about Christmas. Would there be a Christmas in Colorado this year? Not that it mattered to her—she hadn't celebrated the holiday in a long time—but it would be appalling if the red death hung on so long.

Seeing an open truck transporting armed soldiers, her stomach cramped. She wanted to go home and climb under the covers, but she forced herself to keep walking. Some day they would be gone. Until then she would have to endure. She blocked out the thought she might be dead before they left Colorado and stared at the ground in front of her feet until she reached Cheesman Park.

The park appeared deserted except for the jogger on the path ahead of her.

Hearing an unfamiliar rumble, she looked around. An army tank slowly rolled through the park. Tanks? This could not be happening.

When she glanced forward again, she noticed she was gaining on the jogger. Could he be sick? If so, he probably didn't have the red death. He showed none of the hyperactivity of the afflicted—quite the reverse, in fact.

She continued to gain on him. Recognizing the ancient gray sweats, she quickened her pace and soon caught up to him.

"You're jogging," she said, "and I'm walking, yet I'm moving faster than you. Does that tell you something?"

"Yes." Greg smiled at her. "I quit."

He stopped pumping his arms and legs, and lengthened his stride to match hers. "You're right. Walking is faster. What do you know."

"Are you okay? You seem out of it."

"I'm tired. I worked all night, then when I went home to take a nap, I couldn't sleep."

"Maybe you need some hot coffee. I have a pot brewing at home."

"Sounds good."

"Sure you can make it all the way to my place?"

"If I can't, I'll lean on you."

She found herself smiling, thinking how good it was to see him again.

Greg stepped into her living room and looked around. Following his gaze, Kate glanced at the off-white walls devoid of ornament, the old green upholstered couch and chairs, the nicked coffee table. Maybe it hadn't been such a good idea to bring him to this shabby and anonymous room.

"I like it," he said. "It looks lived in, comfortable." He sank onto the couch, and sighed. "This is nice."

She let out a breath she hadn't realized she'd been holding. "I'll get the coffee."

A few minutes later, she set the coffee cups on the table along with a plate of cinnamon rolls she'd warmed in the microwave.

He inhaled, and a smile lit his face. "My two favorite scents." He took a bite of cinnamon roll. "This is fabulous. Where did you ever get these?"

"Made them."

He took another bite. "Kate Cummings, woman of many talents."

She beamed. It really was good to see him again. "Don't you think it's odd we keep running into each other? I mean, until last Friday, I'd never seen you before."

"I've seen you."

Her eyes widened. "You have?"

"Yes. Out walking in the morning. You always look so—" He stopped abruptly.

"You can't leave it there. I always look so—what?"

"Sad."

"Maybe you do have reporter's eyes after all." She pushed the plate of cinnamon rolls toward him. "Have another."

"Aren't you going to eat?"

"I make the things. You don't expect me to eat them too?"

"Of course not. That's a job for a man."

When she finished her coffee, she stood. "Well, time for me to get ready for work, but you sit back and finish eating."

"I'd like that."

Showered and dressed in a rump-sprung navy blue suit, Kate went into the living room.

Greg slept on the couch.

She reached out a hand to smooth his furrowed brow, but drew it back. She felt as though she'd known him forever, but he was a stranger, after all. A stranger who planned to marry the beautiful Pippi O'Brien.

She stood and watched him sleep for a few minutes. Then she covered him with an afghan and quietly let herself out of the house.

The sun was streaming in the window when Pippi awoke. She glanced at the clock on the bedside table. Almost noon? How did it get so late?

Trying not to disturb Jeremy, she slipped from between the satin sheets, scooped her purse from the antique wingback chair, and went into the black marble bathroom. The tub seemed as big as a swimming pool, and had gold faucets. She gave a shiver of excitement. She'd been born to live this way.

She rummaged through her purse for her cell phone and called her producer. "I won't be in today. I think I'm coming down with something."

"That's all right," her producer responded heartily. "Julie will be glad to go on for you."

Julie? Who the hell was Julie? Oh, she must be that new young production assistant.

Pippi faced the mirror and studied the faint lines etched around her eyes. They looked more pronounced than usual—like troughs.

Her stomach churned at the thought of gorgeous, smooth-faced Julie taking her spot.

She fingered the redial button on her phone, intending to announce her miraculous recovery, when she remembered she would soon be embarking on a new career in Hollywood. She smiled at herself in the mirror.

Hearing Jeremy's voice, she stepped out of the bathroom. "I'll meet you in an hour," he said into the telephone receiver.

Pippi fought to keep her temper in check, but when he hung up, she lost it. "I called in sick so we could spend the day together, and you're making other plans?"

He rose and moved toward her, shaking his head as if at the folly of a child. "We'll still have the whole rest of the day to spend together, my lovely little hellcat."

She laughed huskily and raised her arms for a hug, but he turned her so her back nestled against his front.

As she leaned against him, he slowly massaged her breasts.

"Do you know where the Larimer Fish House and Bar is?" he murmured into her ear.

A sweet languor stole over her body. "Downtown. Not far from where I live."

His hands caressed her belly. "How do I get there?"

39

"I'll take you. Then I'll go home and—oh." She sucked in her breath as his hands slid lower. "Pick up some things," she finished in a strangled voice.

Jeremy stood outside the Fish House watching Pippi dance down the street. From any angle, she was a beautiful young woman.

Gabriel Weiss appeared by his side and smacked his lips. "I'd sure like to get me some of that." He heaved a sigh. "Too bad she's in a committed relationship."

Jeremy smiled. "So I've been told."

"Are you hungry? If not, it might be better if we took a walk. Fewer ears, if you know what I mean."

"A walk is fine," Jeremy said. He needed food, but he preferred not to eat with the lawyer. The one time they had dined together, Weiss had managed to squirt lemon juice in Jeremy's eyes, spray him with half-masticated food, and spill an entire glass of burgundy on his calfskin jacket and brand-new, hand-stitched, raw silk shirt.

While they walked, Weiss complained about the Broncos. What kind of season would they have next year when most had succumbed to the red death? After they reached a narrow, deserted park, the lawyer became all business.

"I'm sorry to have to tell you there is no legal way to get you or anyone else out of Colorado. I found plenty of people willing to have their palms greased, but if they knew a way out, they'd have taken it themselves."

"You said legal way. What about illegal ways?"

Weiss folded his arms across his chest. "All in good time, my man. Listen. The sensors around the perimeter of the state are set to detect movement from about two feet off the ground to about ten feet. That way they aren't triggered by small animals or large birds."

Jeremy brightened. "So all I have to do is get to the border and crawl out."

Weiss shook his head. "It's not that simple. The sensors are arranged in such a way they cover a swathe a quarter of a mile wide, but the swathe is not a straight line. It varies from a quarter of a mile on this side of the border to a quarter of a mile on the other side of the border. To be certain of safety, you'd have to crawl a half a mile without once raising any part of your body above two feet. And, even if you could do that, you'd be in the militarized zone so long you'd be spotted by one of the helicopters patrolling the border."

"How can they go after everyone in the border zone? Don't some people live there?"

"Not anymore. They've been relocated. Some were taken to a World War Two detainment center near Granada in the southeastern part of the state. Others were taken to a place outside Trinidad. The ones who fought the internment were killed."

"How could they have put border control into effect so quickly? Colorado's only been under quarantine a couple of days."

"People laugh at the bungling bureaucracy of the government, but the truth is, they can be exceedingly efficient and foresighted. They've been prepared for this eventuality for many years."

Jeremy clenched his hands into fists. "So there's no way out?"

"I didn't say that. There is a flaw in the electronic curtain. Radar doesn't detect anything below twenty feet."

"So?" Jeremy paced for a few seconds, then he stopped short. "That means someone flying at fifteen feet would be invisible!"

"Exactly."

Jeremy's eyes narrowed. "If there is a way out of this mess, how come you're still here?"

"Too risky. Anyone who tries to escape is shot on sight. No questions asked. You might be better off holing up in your hotel room and waiting out the quarantine."

Jeremy gripped the lawyer's shoulders. "No. Absolutely not."

Weiss shrugged off Jeremy's hand. "You're a pilot. You know how dangerous it is to fly that low."

The image of a stunt pilot who had crashed and burned during the filming of one of his movies flitted through Jeremy's head, but he ignored it.

"I can do it," he said.

"Even if you managed to fly at the proper altitude, you could be spotted by a helicopter pilot. And then there's satellite surveillance."

"What about it?" Jeremy asked impatiently when Weiss hesitated.

"That's the problem. I don't know much about it. I'm told there could be a lag between the time something shows on the computer monitor and the time it is identified and acted upon, but I don't know if it's seconds or minutes or what. Your only hope is to be in the air for as short a time as possible. The way I figure it is you head east, hop in a plane about a quarter of a mile from the Kansas border, fly across at fifteen feet, then land about a quarter of a mile on the other side, jump in a car, and get the hell away."

Jeremy laughed, feeling suddenly lighthearted. "What do you need me to do?"

"Wire me the money. I've been on the Internet all night, and I've got people watching the border patrol helicopters to try to find the best time to cross. I've lined up a plane in Colorado—talked them down to a hundred thousand—and I'm negotiating for a field where you can land. Also a car. As soon as the money's in my account, we can finalize the deal."

"How much you need?"

"A million."

"Done. When?"

"Now, if you want. My bank is around the corner. They should be able to take care of the wire transfer for you."

Drunk with the thought of leaving Colorado, Jeremy was barely aware of walking to the bank.

"Here we are," Weiss said, startling him.

"Wait a minute." Jeremy put a hand on the door to keep the lawyer from opening it. "You told me how to get across the state line, but you didn't say how to get to the plane."

Weiss smiled wolfishly. "Now that's a whole other story."

"Tell me."

"I'm working on a safe route, and I've found a used truck for you—a silver Toyota Tacoma. I'll need an additional fifty thousand for it."

"Fifty thousand for a used truck!"

"I can get the truck cheap. The gas is exorbitant. There's a shortage. Prices have gone sky high, and purchases are limited to two gallons at a time, but I managed to get you four twenty-gallon containers. Normally, that would be way more than you need, but these are not normal times and you have to be prepared for any eventuality. In an emergency, you might even be able to use it for currency."

"Good thinking," Jeremy said. "Anything else I'll need?"

"I won't know for sure until I've got the rest of the plans firmed, but I think we've covered everything. At any rate, you'll be hearing from me in a day or two." He rubbed his hands together. "Now let's go get my money."

Pat Bertram

# 7

*Tuesday, December 6 (p.m.)*

Pippi and Jeremy were heading back to the hotel after a lunch of scampi at the fish house, when the door to a chrome-fronted restaurant opened and out poured a group of thirty-somethings expensively attired in black business suits.

Pippi heard one of the women whisper, "That's Jeremy King."

The others turned to stare. Then, as one, they gathered around him. The crowd swelled when others became aware of his presence.

Pippi stood by his side, even signing a few autographs herself, and she saw their future: the charismatic king and his beautiful queen, loved by all.

"What's going on here?" an authoritative voice demanded.

"It's Jeremy King," someone answered.

"Well, move along." When no one obeyed, he thundered, "Move, I said!"

"Chill out, man, we aren't doing anything."

"Hey stop that, don't hit him!"

"Help! Oh, God, someone help."

Then pandemonium.

Jeremy seized Pippi's hand and pulled her to the edge of the crowd, but before they could escape, a white truck pulled up and men in white uniforms jumped out of the back. Holding their automatic weapons waist high, they leveled them at the crowd.

"Everybody down," one of the men bellowed. "On your faces. Now!"

Pippi stared at the men in confusion.

Jeremy yanked her to the ground.

"What are UN troops doing here?" she whispered. "When I've seen footage of them, they've been in places like Somalia and Bosnia."

"Down," the soldier roared.

Most of Jeremy's fans dropped to their bellies, but some

ran away and others, shouting defiance, remained standing.

The UN troops fired.

"Don't worry," Jeremy said into Pippi's ear. "I'm sure they're using rubber bullets."

As Pippi watched, hoping Jeremy was right, she saw the back of a man's head dissolve into a red mist. Blood and bits of gray matter rained on her.

She closed her eyes tightly and shoved her right fist into her mouth as far as it would go. She bit down hard, trying to hold back the screams welling inside her.

*Oh, please, please, please*, she begged silently.

Long after the last echo of gunfire had faded away, she raised her head.

The UN soldiers were gone.

Jeremy helped her to her feet. She looked around, unable to comprehend the carnage she saw.

One by one, the other survivors picked themselves up, but dozens of bullet-ridden bodies remained.

Eyes burning with unshed tears, Pippi gripped Jeremy's hand so tightly they'd need a crowbar to pry them apart.

"Let's get out of here," Jeremy said.

She let him tow her away, but every few steps she turned to look back.

As soon as they slammed the hotel suite door behind them, Pippi yanked off her clothes, threw them in the trash, then darted for the shower. She scrubbed her skin and washed her hair twice, but she still felt dirty.

Before she finished, Jeremy joined her, but his interest, it seemed, lay in getting clean.

Afterward, they came together in a furious coupling, and when she climaxed she screamed and screamed and screamed.

Peter Jensen was waiting by the oak tree in Washington Park when Greg arrived at five minutes to six.

"I have a question," Greg said. "Since you're a paranoid sort of guy—"

"Paranoid?" Peter interrupted. "What makes you say that?"

"You believe in all sorts of conspiracy theories . . ." Greg's voice trailed off, silenced by the other man's look of contempt.

"For a writer you don't choose your words well," Peter said. Then his look of contempt changed to one of profound weariness. "It's not your fault. The English language has no word for rational suspicion or rational fear. If you think a man—or a government—is plotting behind your back, and he's not, that's paranoia. But what if he is?"

Peter looked at Greg expectantly; Greg had no answer.

"But to use a phrase like 'conspiracy theory' is plain sloppy," Peter continued. "Being a journalist, you should know about words and phrases used to induce an emotional rather than an intellectual response. The more these words and phrases are used, the more the phrase itself becomes important, and not what it's describing. Most so-called conspiracies are merely plans our leaders make and don't bother to tell us. Future generations, I'm sure, will have all sorts of theories about what's happening in Colorado right now, but the way we're being treated is the result of leadership. Even if you don't like what's going on, it's still leadership."

Greg stepped back, feeling slightly battered by the onslaught of words. Hearing a dog yipping, he glanced around and saw a German shepherd nudging a man who lay crumpled on bloodstained ground. The dog's cries turned to whimpers; it lay down beside the fallen man and rested its head and paws on the man's chest.

Greg turned to Peter. "I don't know what to think anymore. It's not only the red death. It's everything. FEMA, UN troops, martial law. That's what I wanted to ask you about. I always had the impression of FEMA as a benevolent government agency that arrived after an emergency to help co-ordinate clean-up efforts, but they're here now. Do you know who they really are?"

"I do know FEMA is not a benevolent government

agency—there is no such thing. What people see is an agency empowered to throw a life preserver in times of natural catastrophes like hurricanes, but in reality, FEMA's latitude for control is vast. In an emergency, they have virtually unlimited command over every aspect of our lives. Energy, transportation, food, the economy, the government. Everything. Including us.

"Besides all else FEMA is, it seems to be a bureaucratic sleight of hand allowing the military, the military reserves, and the UN to police the United States. People talk about the New World Order, but what they don't realize is that it's already here."

"It's hard to come to grips with what's happening," Greg said.

Peter nodded. "I've been studying what you call 'conspiracy theories' for most of my life, but it's one thing to have an academic knowledge of government machinations and another to see it in action."

Peter turned his gaze to the oak tree and contemplated it in silence.

Greg watched Peter, wondering why the man had spent so much time ferreting out the nation's darkest secrets if the knowledge gave him so much pain. Perhaps when Peter had embarked on his voyage of discovery, he hadn't an inkling of where his search would lead him.

Without taking his eyes off the tree, Peter said, "They know what the red death is."

Excitement rippled through Greg. "What?"

"A chimera."

"The only chimera I know is a mythological fire-breathing monster with a goat's body, a lion's head, and a dragon's tail."

"It's also an organism that has a diverse genetic constitution, such as a grape vine grafted onto a genetically different root stock."

"Were they right about it being a virus and bacteria combination?"

"Partly. It also consists of a fungus and a few human

genes."

Greg's heart pounded. "How is that possible?" he asked, though he already knew the answer.

"It had to have been bio-engineered."

"Man-made!"

Peter nodded.

"Have they identified the individual parts?"

"No, and they won't be able to until they map the entire genome, and perhaps not even then. Someone did one heck of a lot of gene splicing. They do know that part of the virus segment comes from the green monkey virus, one of the most lethal viruses known to man, but while the monkey virus is not airborne, the red death is."

"Does anyone have any idea how the organism escaped?"

"Nothing official," Peter said. "Because no group claimed responsibility, they've temporarily ruled out terrorism. They think maybe it happened by accident."

"One good thing. Now that they've isolated the red death, they can develop a vaccine." Even before Greg finished speaking, Peter shook his head no.

"Why not?" Greg asked.

"Considering the mosaic-like structure of the organism, it's highly unlikely a vaccine could be developed. And even if it could be developed, the organism mutates so rapidly, by the time the vaccine would be ready, the disease would have altered so much the vaccine would be worthless."

"Jeez. The perfect biological weapon."

Peter's smile didn't reach his eyes. "It's not that perfect. There's no way to control it."

When Kate came home from work, she first noticed the afghan neatly folded on the back of the couch. Then she saw the note lying on the coffee table in place of the dirty dishes. It contained a simple thank you accompanied by Greg's phone numbers.

A smile twitched at the corners of her mouth, her only smile since leaving Greg in the morning. At the clinic, she'd been mobbed while trying to unlock the door, and if not for the action of the soldiers dispersing the crowd, she would have been trampled underfoot. Her suit had been torn in the scuffle, and Dr. Hart had provided a set of old surgical scrubs for her to change into.

She had no idea why the doctor wouldn't let her go home; after that first hectic rush, the clinic had been surprisingly slow.

Kate changed into her threadbare robe, picked up a novel she'd started days ago, and settled herself on the couch to read, but the words on the page refused to coalesce into sentences. She tossed the book aside and opened a newspaper to the crossword puzzle; unable to convince herself that deciphering it was worth the effort, she tossed that aside, too.

She hauled herself out of the sagging couch and paced the room. Minutes later, she found herself on the couch again.

She grabbed the remote and turned on the television to Channel Ten. The words moving across the bottom of the screen made it impossible for her to lose herself in the show.

In helpless fascination, she focused on the crawling message: *Attention Colorado Residents. To stop the spread of disease, all schools in the state are closed. All assembly is prohibited. All deaths must be reported by calling 222. Failure to do so will result in arrest, a $10,000 fine, and possible jail time. All residences where a death has occurred will be marked with a large fluorescent orange dot. Any attempt to remove the dot will result in arrest, a $10,000 fine, and possible jail time. All looters will be summarily dealt with.*

On his way back to The Denver News, Greg passed Jim Clayton's neat brick house on Clarkson Street, not far from Washington Park. Seeing Jim's car in the driveway, Greg rolled his bicycle to a stop.

Letisha, a tall, handsome, serene-faced woman, greeted him with a kiss. "We haven't seen you for a while, Greg.

Come to dinner tomorrow night."

"If I have time, I'd love to."

"Make time."

"Yes, ma'am."

They smiled at each other, then Letisha waved her hand toward the basement stairs. "He's in his den."

Several years ago, Jim had decided he needed a place of his own away from the noise and tumult of his growing family, so he had soundproofed a room in the basement and furnished it with comfortable chairs and shelves full of philosophy books. The one snag was that his family tended to gather round, and he didn't have the heart to throw them out.

Tonight, Kenesha, Jim's youngest daughter, and her best friend Joey, the freckle-faced boy who lived next door, lay in front of the muted television, crayons and coloring books strewn all around them.

Jim lounged in his recliner, eyes closed, listening to Sibelius' *Finlandia* playing on the stereo, with a well-thumbed copy of Schopenhauer's *The World as Will and Idea* resting on his knees.

Greg smiled at the sight of the book.

As a cub reporter, he had been assigned to interview Jim about a series of break-ins. He had found Jim in a diner on Colfax Avenue, perusing that very same book.

Greg's surprise at seeing someone actually reading Schopenhauer for fun must have shown on his face, because Jim had given him a hard stare.

"Never seen a knee-grow read, kid?" he had growled.

"Never seen a cop read," Greg had blurted out.

Jim had continued to stare at him for a few seconds, then had thrown his head back and let out a loud guffaw.

Still smiling at the memory, Greg crossed the room and collapsed into a chair.

Jim opened one eye, nodded, but didn't say anything.

Letting the music wash over him, Greg leaned back and watched the silent flow of news on CNN.

When he saw a jumble of bloody bodies lying on a

familiar street, he grabbed the remote, turning up the sound.

"Race riots broke out in Denver this afternoon," the talking head said, "and hundreds died."

Greg muted the television, but he had to raise his voice above the sounds of the now squabbling children. "I haven't heard anything about race riots today. Have you?"

Jim pointed to the two children. Kenesha, shrieking at the top of her lungs, pummeled Joey who was shouting and pulling her pigtails.

Jim stood, hoisted one enraged child in each hand, and held them out at arm's length. After a minute of thrashing around, trying to get at each other, the little black girl and the little white boy dissolved into giggles. Jim deposited the children back on the floor where, side by side, they continued to color.

"You want to know about race riots in Denver today?" Jim nodded toward the children. "That was it. As far as I know, that was the only racial altercation of any kind in the entire city today."

Greg smiled, but he couldn't hold it. "The wounds on those bodies looked like gunshot wounds. Do you know who killed them?"

"There was a crowd downtown today getting autographs from that actor—"

Heart pounding, Greg sat bolt upright in his chair. "Don't tell me something's happened to Pippi."

"She's fine. Really. A witness saw them walking away after it was all over."

Limp with relief, Greg leaned back.

"It all started when two cops, following orders, tried to disperse the crowd," Jim said. "A shoving match ensued, the crowd erupted. Then UN troops arrived. They mowed down everyone who didn't immediately drop to the ground, including both cops."

# 8

*Wednesday, December 7 (a.m.)*

Without any hope of getting it into print, Greg wrote and filed a story revealing the red death as a possible bio-weapon. Few of the stories he had written about the red death had appeared in the paper, but his editor still wanted him to pursue the investigation.

When he stood and stretched, he noticed a rotund little man making coffee. Bill Upton, a science reporter. The very man he wanted to see.

After a few minutes of idle chitchat, Greg asked, "Do you know anyone who would be willing to talk to me about bio-weapons and genetic engineering?"

Bill propped a shoulder against the wall. "You angling for my job, Greg?"

"I need some background information, is all."

"Let's see. Jack Thornton at the Reese Institute is usually willing to talk to me. Also John Takamura and Alice Polk at the State University Extension. And Charles Guest at GeneCo."

Greg jotted the names in his notebook. "Why does the Reese Institute sound so familiar?"

"It's owned by Harley Reese."

"Colorado's youngest billionaire?"

"Yes."

"I never did figure out how a guy goes from a lab in his garage to a multi-billion dollar corporation in a couple of years."

"The usual. Venture capitalists, investment bankers, government grants."

"Why would they give a kid all that money? He'd just gotten out of college, right?"

"Among other things, he developed a computer program that makes it possible to map the genetic code of any living organism in about a tenth of the time it once took."

"Is it that important?"

"Sure. Once you have the genetic code for Ebola, say,

you can manipulate the genes to make it benign."

"Or more deadly."

"That, too." Bill paused. "Are you thinking the red death is a biological warfare agent? Well, let me save you some trouble. I got off the phone with the medical examiner a minute ago, and she assures me the disease is a new, vicious strain of flu. No terrorism. Ergo, no bio-weapon."

Greg frowned. "I don't follow."

"Experimentation in biological and chemical warfare was banned in the U.S. in 1970 and all existing stockpiles were destroyed in 1975. Furthermore, all bio-weapons have been banned worldwide by the 1972 Biological Weapons Convention, and it's now been ratified by one hundred and forty nations. That means only terrorists use bio-weapons."

"So? Murder has been banned, but people still kill."

"You've got a point, but trust me, it's a dead end."

Jeremy heard a knock.

"Message for Mr. King," a voice rang out.

He rushed to the door, fumbled for a tip, and grabbed the envelope from the messenger.

As soon as he closed the door, he ripped open the envelope and scanned the contents. His pathway to freedom! Even Weiss's demand for more money couldn't dim his euphoria. Although the lawyer had sent all the instructions for the border crossing, he claimed he needed another half a million dollars in order to finalize the escape route from Denver to the border.

"Meet me at the same place at eleven o'clock," Weiss wrote.

Jeremy pocketed the key to the Toyota Tacoma along with the parking lot claim check, and stowed the envelope in the suite's safe. He had just finished repositioning the painting in front of the safe when Pippi wandered out of the bedroom.

Yawning, she said, "Is there any coffee?"

"No time for that now. Go get dressed. We have an errand to run."

They reached the Larimer Fish House and Bar a few minutes before eleven.

Pippi yanked on the door. "It's closed."

Jeremy shaded his eyes with a hand and peered down the street. No Weiss. He strode back and forth in front of the dark fish house, checking his watch and willing Weiss to appear.

Suddenly he stopped and slapped himself on the forehead. The bank! That must be where the lawyer planned to meet him.

He grabbed Pippi's hand and ran to the bank, but didn't see Weiss there, either. He dashed into the lobby and, spying the banker who had arranged the wire transfer, hurried over to him.

"I'm supposed to meet Gabriel Weiss here," he said, panting. "Have you seen him?"

"No, Mr. King. We had an appointment for eleven o'clock, but he didn't show."

*Damn that lawyer. What was he trying to pull?*

Jeremy dug the lawyer's card out of his pocket and handed it to Pippi. "Know where this is?"

"Sure. It's that new skyscraper down the block."

Five minutes later they stood in the lawyer's reception area. No one sat at the desk, and the place seemed eerily quiet.

"Weiss?" Jeremy yelled.

No response.

"Weiss, damn you! Where are you?"

Still not getting a response, he strode through the reception area to the small hallway and opened one door after another, looking for Weiss's office.

He had every right. He'd paid good money for an escape plan, and Weiss had dared to demand another half million. Even worse, Weiss had stood him up.

Ebullience gradually displaced his anger.

Soon he'd have the itinerary.

Soon, maybe even this afternoon, he'd be on his way out of this putrid state.

He opened one final door. His breath caught in his throat. Then he let out a cry of despair and fled the office.

Greg spent all morning on the phone, trying to get through to the four people Bill Upton had recommended. Unable to get beyond voice mail, answering machines, and uncaring receptionists, he left the building and bicycled the short distance to the Auraria campus. With a feeling of déjà vu, he strolled through the echoing halls of the State University Building. When he passed Dr. Ann Takamura's office, he realized he wasn't experiencing déjà vu at all—less than a week ago he had traveled this very corridor.

Cursing himself for a fool, he pulled his notebook out of his pocket and riffled through the pages.

There it was, on his list of the red death's first victims: Dr. John Takamura, husband of Dr. Ann Takamura.

He backtracked and entered Dr. Ann Takamura's office.

A girl frantically opened and closed desk drawers.

"Dr. Ann Takamura?"

The girl looked up. "She's not here."

"Do you know where I can reach her?" Greg asked.

"At home, probably. Dr. Takamura—Dr. John Takamura, I mean—died last week and she took some time off and who knows when she'll be back now that classes have been cancelled." She opened another drawer. "I need my thesis outline. It's got to be here someplace."

"Do you know where Alice Polk's office is?" Greg asked.

"Down the hall," the girl answered without looking up. "But she's not here, either. No one is."

After confirming the girl was right, Greg peddled for University Hills where the Takamuras lived.

This time no traffic jam impeded his progress. He did see cars, but they mostly waited in long lines at gas stations. Fuel was rationed, two gallons per customer each fill-up, and prices escalated hourly.

After an appreciative sniff of the clean air, he spent the rest of the trip thinking about Dr. John Takamura.

According to the profile Greg had constructed last week, Dr. Takamura had been a biogeneticist who taught a couple of classes to maintain his university status, but he had also spent two or three days a week working at a research facility in the Four Corners area.

Four Corners—where people had died from the mysterious Hanta virus.

Could that virus also be a bio-weapon someone had unwittingly released?

Peter Jensen had once proffered that same theory.

Thinking of Peter reminded Greg of the man's ominous comment that the red death could not be controlled.

Could its creator have been one of its earliest victims?

Auraria, where Dr. John Takamura taught, sat alarmingly close to the Broncos stadium, and the doctor had been one of the first to die . . .

# 9

*Wednesday, December 7 (p.m.)*

Jeremy scrubbed and scrubbed, but he could not wash away the sight of Gabriel Weiss draped over his blood-sodden desk and computer.

It was too much: first that little girl, then the crowd yesterday, now Weiss today.

He'd thought he was inured to death, having been in many films featuring bloody bodies, but the one thing separating those carefully arranged scenes from the real thing was the smell—the overwhelming stench of old pennies, feces, and urine, underlined by the promise of putrefaction.

At the memory, Jeremy's stomach heaved; he took deep breaths to still the nausea.

He thrust his face into the spray of water, trying to cleanse the smell out of his nose and the back of his throat, but he knew that, for as long as he lived, he'd never be able to get rid of it.

When he stepped out of the shower, he wrapped himself in the thick, white terry cloth robe supplied by the hotel, and went in search of Pippi.

He didn't find her in the bedroom or the sitting room.

Then he noticed that the door to the second bedroom, where he'd stashed his supplies, stood ajar. He strode to the door and banged it open.

"What the hell do you think you're doing?" he demanded.

"Nothing." Pippi hefted a pair of binoculars, and looked around at all the boxes. "What is this stuff? Where did it come from?"

"I found it here when I moved in," he said curtly.

Pippi shook her head, smiling, and regarded him with an expectant air.

"Hunting trip," he said.

Her smile broadened. She reached for a gas mask and dangled it from her fingers. "Hunting trip, huh?"

Despite himself, he returned her smile. "Movie props?"

She laughed. Suddenly she went still. Her eyes got huge. "You're going to try to escape, aren't you? Take me with you. Please? I won't be a burden, I promise, and maybe I can even help."

"Save your breath. It's off."

She gave him a penetrating glance. "That's why you needed the lawyer. To arrange your getaway."

He nodded wearily.

"But he died before he could give you the plan."

Another nod.

"Can we go back to his office and maybe break into his computer or something?"

He gagged as the image of the bloody computer impinged on his retinas. "Impossible."

"If he found a way out, maybe we could too."

"We don't have the contacts. And the whole thing is too dangerous." He reported some of what Weiss had told him, but instead of deflating her, as he had hoped, she grew more excited.

"He gave you part of the plan already, didn't he?" she asked, eyes feverishly bright.

"The last part. There's a plane waiting for me at a farm several miles southeast of Holly, but I don't have any safe way to get to it."

"I can help. I know the eastern plains. The plains have more weather than anyplace else in Colorado, so I've spent a lot of time out there doing remotes."

Their eyes locked; he could feel himself catching her excitement. Taking her into his arms, he thought maybe he'd get out of Colorado after all.

Dr. Ann Takamura had the timeless beauty of a Japanese doll, but she wore jeans and a sweatshirt, both items limp and faded from too many washings.

She and Greg perched on an undistinguished contemporary sofa, drinking jasmine tea out of fragile old cups.

"I don't know much about my husband's work," she

said.

Greg carefully set his cup and saucer on the coffee table. "Anything you can tell me about him would be helpful."

She didn't answer right away, and when she did, she sounded distracted. "He'd come to hate teaching—said kids nowadays had more interest in sex and drugs and potential salaries than in learning—so he kept cutting back his teaching schedule and spent most of his time in his laboratory at ARC, the Agricultural Research Center, near Cortez. I wanted him to work closer to home, maybe arrange for a lab at CU in Boulder, but he said he liked the autonomy he had at ARC.

"He felt disillusioned with the whole educational system. He said schools taught propaganda as fact in order to turn out 'right-thinking' citizens. 'Groupthink' he called it.

"But most of all he hated that despite the criminal behavior of the athletes and the low percentage of athlete graduates, the athletic programs got all the acclaim, all the attention, all the money."

"Can you tell me anything about ARC?" Greg asked.

"They're well-endowed, I know, and their equipment is top of the line."

"Do they do anything but plant research?"

"Animals, too. I know someone down there who's working with anthrax."

"Weapons-grade anthrax?"

Her laugh sounded low and musical. "Of course not. Experiments in bio-chemical warfare have been banned in the United States, as I'm sure you know. People forget that anthrax is primarily an animal disease. My friend is trying to find a way to eradicate it."

"What else can you tell me about your husband?"

"Not much," Dr. Takamura said, sounding bitter. "John came home so seldom, and when he did, he spent all his time in his office upstairs going over his lab notes and studying the papers in those boxes."

"What boxes?" Greg asked.

She waved a dainty hand toward two file boxes stacked

by the door. "Those boxes."

Do you know what's in them?"

"Junk, mostly. John found those boxes while cleaning out his mother's house after her funeral. They contain all sorts of worthless notes and receipts, including some papers belonging to his father. John's father died when John was very young, you see, so the papers meant something to him, but they have no intrinsic value."

"Do you mind if I go through the boxes?"

"You can have them. I planned to throw them away. You won't be able to read my father-in-law's papers. They're in Japanese."

"You speak Japanese?"

Dr. Takamura smiled. "No. Never could get the hang of it. My father knows a little, and he looked at the papers for me. He urged me to get rid of them. Said they were records of logs and lumber. Something to do with forestry, I imagine."

"Do you have any strong trash bags?" Greg asked, eyeing the boxes.

"Sure. Why?"

"I'm on my bike, and I don't think I'd be able to carry the boxes."

Dr. Takamura left the room and returned with two bags. She watched in evident amusement while Greg dumped the contents of the boxes into the two bags, tied them together forming a huge knot, and slung them around his shoulders so one hung down each side with the knot positioned between his shoulder blades.

He thanked the doctor, then staggered out to his bicycle.

Wobbling dangerously, he pedaled for home.

All day people complaining of imaginary flu symptoms had inundated the Bowers Clinic.

Between conducting patient interviews and pacifying distraught telephone callers, Kate could not keep up with her paperwork. Long after the last patient left, she remained in her office.

Dr. Hart entered. "Go home, Kate."

"In a minute. I still have more work to do."

The doctor sat and crossed one leg over the other; her dangling foot bobbed uncontrollably.

Feeling as if their roles were reversed, Kate studied the doctor; despite Dr. Hart's uncharacteristic twitchiness, she did not have the adrenaline high or the red eyes indicative of the red death.

Dr. Hart gave a laugh that sounded more tearful than amused. "So what's your diagnosis?"

Kate smiled. "Overwork."

"But that's the problem," Dr. Hart cried. "I'm not overworked. People all around me are dying of a terrible disease, and there's not a damn thing I can do about it. The medical examiner's office has issued a statement saying the red death is a flu virus, but when I see someone with actual flu symptoms, all I can do is issue a prescription for rimantidine which won't be filled."

"Why won't it?"

"There was a run on it after the ME's announcement, and now pharmacies are out of stock, with no chance of replacing it since nothing, not even prescription drugs, is being shipped into the state." She stopped, looking as if she had been slapped. "Oh, God, Kate. What's going to happen when all those patients who need their meds to survive can no longer get them? People with diabetes, heart disease, AIDS, mental illness."

At the rate people are dying—and being killed—I don't think that's going to be a problem, Kate wanted to say, but she held her tongue.

Dr. Hart banged her fist on Kate's desk. "Dammit! I didn't become a doctor to sit around and watch people die."

Kate reached out and touched the other woman's hand. "Dr. Hart—"

"Oh, for pete's sake, Kate, call me Amanda, at least outside of office hours. I mean, you are my oldest friend."

Kate stared at the doctor. They had known each other since grade school, but they had never been friends. Amanda had been popular and graceful, a gymnast whose hair fell into perfect waves even after executing a back flip or a cartwheel. Kate had been lonely and awkward, and no matter how much care she took, her knees had always been skinned, her elbows scraped, her hair a tangle. She did not know why Amanda had hired her, for the doctor still seemed to see her as that accident-prone little girl. Could she really have thought they were friends?

Dr. Hart stood. "Come on Kate, time to go." She went to the door and stood with one hand poised on the light switch, the other on her hip.

Kate had no choice but to obey.

The streets were empty. No cars, no people, no cats, no dogs. The tapping of Kate's heels sounded inordinately loud in the eerie quiet. Hearing a rustling in the shadows, she started to cut across the street. She'd made it halfway when a group of teenagers wearing World War Two gas masks, with black trench coats swirling about their bodies like wings, appeared out of the darkness and encircled her.

Heart pounding, she managed to take a few more steps before the circle tightened, forcing her to stop.

Suddenly the teenagers melted back into the shadows.

Kate looked behind her.

An olive drab truck approached.

She scurried to the sidewalk and continued on her way. The truck caught up with her and kept pace. She kept her eyes focused straight ahead, but she could feel the gaze of the soldiers on her.

She hadn't gone more than a half a block when she saw another group of teenagers, younger than the first, coming out of an unlit house, laughing and punching one another.

"Hey, cut it out," one said, giggling. "You'll make me drop the television."

The truck pulled ahead of Kate and stopped in front of the house. Two soldiers got out and eyed the youths.

"Having a bit of fun, boys?" the blond soldier asked.

The biggest of the teenagers, apparently the leader,

sneered. "What's it to ya?"

"All of you lie face down on the ground," the dark-haired soldier said conversationally. When no one obeyed, he bellowed, "On the ground. Now. Or we will shoot."

"Don't pay any attention," the leader said. "They can't shoot us. We're kids."

There was an abrupt burst of gunfire.

Kate froze. For a half of a second it looked as if the leader was doing a mad dance, then he collapsed.

The boys dived for the ground.

Within minutes, the soldiers had cuffed their hands and shackled their feet with plastic restraints. They herded the boys into the back of the truck, bundling them in like so much dirty laundry.

The boy who had been carrying the television started to cry. "I can't go to jail. My mom will kill me."

The dark-haired soldier rammed him in the side with his weapon, a monstrosity that looked to Kate like something from a science fiction movie.

The blond soldier grinned. "Hell, son, we're not taking you to jail. We're putting you to work."

"Work?" the boy yelped.

"Sure. We have orders to round up a work brigade. Looks like you people volunteered."

"What kind of work?" the boy asked in a quavering voice.

"Garbage collecting. You'll love it. You get to work with cadets from the Air Force Academy, and you get a fun-filled tour of all the rat-infested alleys in the city."

"You can't force us to work," one of the other youths said.

"Of course we can. We can do anything we damn well feel like."

"I'd rather go to prison," the teenager muttered.

"Not an option, kid. You are now an official member of the work brigade."

"What if I refuse to work, or run away?"

"Then I will shoot you right in the head."

No one spoke another word.

The blond soldier climbed into the driver's seat. The dark-haired soldier directed his weapon toward Kate.

She raised her hands, holding herself rigid under his cold-eyed scrutiny.

After an endless moment, he spun around and jumped into the back of the truck with the boys.

The vehicle drove a block before Kate could force herself to move.

The grocery store looked normal and solid and brightly lit. When Kate drew near, legs still shaky from her encounter with the soldiers, she saw that its appearance had deceived her. Armed soldiers patrolled both inside and outside the store. On the door hung a huge sign: *COMMODITIES DISTRIBUTION CENTER—LAST NAMES BEGINNING WITH A, B, C TODAY.*

She entered hesitantly.

Inside hung another sign: *REGISTRATION.* An arrow pointed to the right, where people were standing in long lines. At the head of each row, a grim young man or woman attired in civilian clothes sat at a table containing a complicated-looking computer system.

Kate turned to the left. Another sign confronted her: *NO ADMITTANCE WITHOUT REGISTRATION.* Beyond it, a tired-looking woman wheeled a sparsely filled grocery cart to the checkout counter.

"Hand," the clerk said.

The woman held out her trembling right hand.

The clerk grasped a wand that looked like a large remote control device with a tiny computer screen on it, and ran it over the back of the woman's hand. Using the same wand, she scanned the groceries.

After a series of dainty blips, the wand let out a loud screech.

The clerk looked at the screen, then shoved a carton of eggs off to the side.

"What are you doing?" the woman asked tremulously.

"You're allowed one dozen eggs." The clerk pointed to the computer printout clutched in the woman's hand. "It should say so on that."

Something poked Kate in the small of the back, making her jump. She turned. A soldier who looked as if he were too young to shave jabbed her with his rifle.

"Move along," he said, prodding her toward the registration area.

She joined the shortest line. In the next line over, an overweight woman with scraggly hair shouted at the computer operator.

"If you can't keep your voice down," he said, not taking his eyes off the computer screen, "you will be escorted out of here at gunpoint."

The woman lowered her voice but didn't sound any less angry. "What do you mean, I'm allowed rations for four? There are seven in my family—me, my husband, and our five children."

"Commodities are limited to two children per family."

"So what am I supposed to do?"

"I don't know. You're the one who had all those children. Didn't you ever hear of overpopulation? What made you think you had the right to a greater share of the world's resources than anyone else?"

The woman frowned. "Whether you approve or not, my kids have to eat."

The computer operator shrugged. "So feed them your share." He pointed to a slot in a large black box attached to the computer. "Put your right hand into the slot."

"Why?"

"Fingerprints."

"I don't want to be fingerprinted."

"No prints, no food."

The woman gingerly slid her hand into the slot. After a moment she yanked it out again. "Ow. That stung. What did you do to me?"

"Inserted a tiny microchip. The chips allow us to keep track of everyone getting commodities and make sure no one gets more than their share."

He snatched a piece of paper the computer had finished printing out, and handed it to the woman. "Here's a list of allowable commodities for your family. Your distribution day is Wednesday. Be sure to bring your husband and children next week so we can chip them. That way, if anything happens to you, they can still get their share."

He waved the woman away.

Another woman, this one very young and pretty, carrying a sleeping infant, stepped to the table.

"Identification?" the young man said.

She handed him her driver's license.

He handed it right back. "A, B, C today. You're M— come back Saturday."

Her eyes filled with tears. "But we don't have any food in the house."

"Some grocery stores still have food for sale. There's also an emergency commodity distribution site at Fourteenth and Krameria. Next."

The young woman didn't move.

The computer operator raised an arm; a soldier came and ushered the young woman out of the building.

An elderly man shuffled to the table and handed over his identification. The computer operator processed and chipped him.

Sick to her stomach, Kate stepped out of line and made her way to the door.

"Something wrong, Greg? All evening you've been acting like you've finished a job of hard labor."

"I have."

Jim Clayton raised his eyebrows. "I thought reporters didn't do anything more strenuous than lifting a pen."

Greg rotated his shoulders. "So did I. That's why I became a reporter. I did enough physical labor as a kid to last me a lifetime."

He proceeded to regale Jim with an intentionally amusing account of his torturous journey home with the garbage bags full of paper and how he had to stop every half-mile to ease his aching back.

Jim rewarded him with a hearty guffaw. Then, seriously, "What's so important about those papers?"

Greg shrugged, wincing at the stab of pain. "A story I'm working on."

Jim gave him a sharp look. "Anything I should know about?"

"I doubt it will amount to much."

Letisha entered the den with a big bowl of walnuts in the shell and a couple of nutcrackers. "Thought you boys might like a snack. Neither of you ate much at dinner."

Jim grimaced at the sight of the nuts. "It's Greg who's addicted to walnuts. I'd prefer potato chips and dip."

Letisha kissed the top of his head. "I know, but it's time you started eating healthy."

Jim winked at Greg. "We're all about to die from some godawful flu, and she's concerned about what I eat."

Greg laughed and reached for the nuts. He arranged three of them in his palm just so, then closed his hand. The shells cracked.

"I've never figured out how you do that." Jim grabbed three walnuts and closed his huge hand around them, but nothing happened.

"It's all in how they're arranged. Look."

Greg demonstrated the proper placement, but Jim still could not crack the nuts.

"Maybe your hand is too big."

Letisha laughed. "You boys have fun."

After she went back upstairs, Jim said quietly, "The mass mutilator struck again today."

Greg jerked up his head. "How many is that now? Four? Five?"

"Five."

"Jeez." Greg picked a bit of nutmeat from a shell. "Why is it that in the midst of an epidemic where hundreds of thousands have died, in the midst of martial law where thousands have been killed, the mutilation of a corpse stands out as being particularly horrendous?"

"Probably because it's so personal," Jim said. "The red death is impersonal, killing without deliberation."

"The soldiers are killing deliberately."

"It's still impersonal. Americans are so dang arrogant, they hate taking orders from anyone. The whole point of shooting those who don't immediately obey is to instill fear in the rest of us and to show us who's boss."

"Well, it's working."

"Tell me about it. I've never seen the city so quiet."

Jim ate a few nuts, then snagged the remote and turned on the television.

A commentator from CNN Headline News looked out at them with calculated gravity.

"The National Guard was called up today to quell the riots still raging in Denver and Colorado Springs.

"In Ames, Iowa, youths dragged two Colorado residents from their car and beat them to death. A bystander said, 'I didn't see who did it, but they deserve a medal.' The retired couple had been in Ames, visiting their daughter and son-in-law for the past month.

"In Cincinnati, a man drooling blood robbed The First Federal Bank. He told the teller he had the Colorado flu, and he threatened to vomit all over her if she didn't give him the money.

"In New York City, a man from Denver was shot and killed during a mugging. The alleged mugger said, 'Self-defense, man. When I saw his Colorado driver's license, I knew it was him or me.'"

# 10

*Thursday, December 8*

"Do you think I should pluck my eyebrows?" Pippi asked.

Jeremy blinked. "Now?"

Pippi laughed. "No, silly. It's almost time for us to leave. I mean, when I get to Hollywood."

"You have lovely eyebrows. Plucked eyebrows looked ugly in the thirties and forties, and they look ugly today."

"I think they're glamorous."

"Know what they remind me of? A prizefighter who got punched in the eye so hard the area over the orbital bone swelled, pushing up his eyebrow."

"Oh. Ick." Pippi sliced a muffin and smeared grape jelly on it.

Jeremy yawned. He and Pippi had stayed up late last night making plans, but they still awakened early to load the truck in relative privacy. Now they were back in the hotel suite, nibbling on the food they'd gathered from the hotel's meager breakfast bar and waiting for ten o'clock, their agreed upon departure time. He glanced at his watch. Nine-thirty. Maybe they could go now? No. Better stick to the plan. Once they started second-guessing themselves, they'd vacillate so much they'd never get out of Denver. Also, since the military showed their strongest presence in the early morning and early evening, by leaving at ten, they'd have a better chance of avoiding trouble.

"What does Pippi stand for?"

Pippi looked at him in surprise. "You know something? That's the first time you ever used my name. I didn't think you knew it."

"You're evading my question."

"It's silly. I wore pigtails when I was little, and they looked sort of carroty—"

Reaching over the table, Jeremy ran his fingers through her shoulder-length hair. "Not a carrot in sight now."

She caught his hand and kissed it.

Pat Bertram

He pulled away, laughing. "You're evading again."

"Do you know the Pippi Longstocking books? She had red hair and wore mismatched clothes. Well, besides my red hair, I had one blue eye and one green eye, so naturally everyone called me Pippi."

He leaned forward to study her. "Are you wearing colored contacts?"

"No. For some reason during puberty, my eyes changed color. The green got bluer, the blue got greener, and I ended up with aquamarine eyes, but I kept the name Pippi. It's better than Kathy. Kathleen is my real name."

"Are you from Denver?"

"No. Oshkosh. My parents and two sisters still live there, but I couldn't wait to get away. I went to Northwestern University and got a job in television right out of college. I had hoped for New York or even Chicago, but the best I could do was Denver."

"So there's nothing to keep you in Colorado."

"No."

"Not even your nice young man?"

Her eyes widened. "How do you know about him?"

Jeremy smiled.

"He asked me to marry him," Pippi said with a sigh.

"What's the problem—not enough spice in the nice?"

She nodded. "He's too nice. I do love him but I thought I'd get bored."

Jeremy rose and held out his hands to help Pippi to her feet. "Stick with me, babe. I promise you won't be bored."

"I'm bored," Pippi said. "I thought this would be exciting, but it isn't."

"Be glad it's not exciting. That means we're doing everything right." Jeremy kept his voice upbeat, but he too felt bored; he found stop-and-go driving tedious.

Because major thoroughfares were so well patrolled, they had kept to side streets. Even so, they had seen a military vehicle of some sort every few miles. Each time, he had pulled into the nearest parking space on the theory that a

70

parked vehicle would be of less interest to the military personnel than a moving one, and each time the soldiers had passed without giving them a second glance.

Seeing an open Jeep with two soldiers coming their way, Jeremy parked in front of a small white frame house. The Jeep stopped, and the soldiers stared at him.

"What do we do now?" Pippi asked.

"Pretend we live here."

They got out of the truck and marched up the walkway to the house. The soldiers continued to watch them.

Jeremy opened the screen door, then pulled Pippi into his arms as if he couldn't wait any longer to kiss her.

A curtain at the front of the house twitched, and Jeremy caught a glimpse of a pale face and two frightened dark eyes. Moments later, he heard the army vehicle moving down the street. To be safe, he waited another thirty seconds before returning to the truck.

Nothing else happened to relieve the monotony of their journey.

Suddenly Pippi jerked upright. "Oh, no!"

Jeremy slammed on the brakes. "What?"

"We're going the wrong way." She pointed to the reddening skies. "We should be driving away from the setting sun, not toward it."

Jeremy studied the compass he had installed on the dashboard. "We're heading east."

"You're sure?"

He nodded.

"Then what's that?"

"I don't know."

Pippi clutched his arm. "I don't like this."

The sight of the red skies made Jeremy uneasy too, but he patted her hand and said, trying to sound convincing, "I'm sure it's nothing. Probably a reflection of the sun on the clouds."

"You're probably right," Pippi said, but she didn't relax her grip on his biceps.

Jeremy moved his foot from the brake to the accelerator.

"We're coming up on the last subdivision, it looks like. Soon we'll hit open country. We'll find a place to camp out, fix something to eat, get some rest. We'll feel better in the morning."

"Can't we drive straight through?"

"No. We talked about that. Remember? Our headlights would make us too conspicuous."

Pippi sighed heavily and retreated into silence.

Greg was on his way back to the Denver News after interviewing Alice Polk in Littleton, when he passed by the Channel Ten building and noticed Pippi's white BMW in the parking lot.

He hopped off his bicycle, shoved it into the bike rack, and ran into the building.

Gus, the night security guard, greeted him with a nod.

"Okay if I go see Pippi?" Greg asked breathlessly.

"Sorry, Mr. Pullman. She ain't here."

Greg stared blankly at him. "But her car . . ."

"Her car's been here since Monday night but not her."

"Do you know where . . ."

"I overheard someone say she called in sick, but someone else said the two of you were probably together, celebrating your engagement."

"No. We aren't," Greg said, feeling old and tired. "Sorry to have bothered you, Gus."

He left quickly, needing to get away from the guard's sympathetic gaze. Did Gus know Pippi dumped him for Jeremy King but refrained from mentioning it out of kindness?

It didn't matter. He knew.

The last few blocks to the paper seemed to take forever, as if he lived a nightmare, peddling and peddling, but getting nowhere.

Finally reaching his desk, he sank into his chair, but could not figure out why he had worked so hard to attain that simple goal.

Oh yes—he needed to enter his interview notes into the

computer.

Alice Polk, a spare, silver-haired woman with widely spaced pale blue eyes, had been glacial at first, but had gradually thawed.

What kind of research did she do? None. She taught Biogenetics.

Yes, she had known John Takamura.

No, she didn't know what he had been working on.

If she had to guess? Plants, since his lab had been at ARC.

Yes, he had probably worked with chimeras; most agricultural research nowadays entailed combining the genes of disparate species—fish genes in tomatoes and all that.

No, she didn't know if he had worked with human genes.

John? Oh, he had been a good teacher, a conscientious researcher, a cordial, if distant, colleague.

Off the record? He had been greedy, self-centered, arrogant, and not above "borrowing" other people's research or going after their grants.

Greg reread his notes. Nothing here to connect Dr. John Takamura to the red death, but nothing to disconnect him from it, either. Even if the scientist had been experimenting with plants, he could have also been working on another project for himself, stealing lab time, perhaps, and pilfering supplies.

Greg tried to log onto the Internet to do a search on Takamura, but couldn't get a connection. He'd had no luck this morning, either. He suspected the telephone lines had been jammed to prevent Colorado residents from reaching the outside world and telling the truth about the quarantine, but he thought it an unnecessary precaution. The only thing people out there cared about was making sure the "Colorado flu" didn't affect them. Or infect them.

Belatedly, he remembered to check his voice mail. Kate Cummings at the Bowers Clinic wanted him to call her; she had some information for him.

# 11

*Thursday, December 8 (evening)*

Pippi lifted her head and sniffed. "What's that stink?"

"Something burning," Jeremy said.

She sniffed again. "It smells vaguely familiar, but I can't place it."

"Burnt pork roast?"

"That's it."

The wind shifted. Pippi coughed and gagged as the nauseating odor filled her nose and mouth. A few minutes later the wind shifted direction again. The stench lingered, but it didn't seem as strong, and she could catch her breath.

"Definitely not a burnt roast," she said, trying to laugh.

When Jeremy did not respond to her feeble attempt at humor, she glanced over at him. He stared straight ahead, and his hands gripped the steering wheel so hard his knuckles had turned white.

He mumbled something that sounded like "Nora's dream," then pulled the truck to the side of the road, turned off the engine, and jumped out. He ran up a small incline, the only distinctive feature of the otherwise flat and empty terrain.

More bewildered than fearful, Pippi climbed out of the truck and looked around. The setting sun looked like a blood-red ball of fire dropping behind the red mountains. As she topped the small rise, she saw that everything appeared red: the sky, the land, the smoky haze choking her, the cluster of unfinished houses—frameworks, actually—and the long line of trucks heading for a huge smoking crater.

Hysteria bubbled within her at the thought that perhaps an asteroid had crashed to earth.

All at once she knew where she was: Meadowlands, a housing development planned around an artificial lake. One of the first remotes she had done for Channel Ten had been about the development, a casualty of the drought. After the lake had been dug, water became scarce. By the time the snowpack returned to normal, the developers had defaulted on their loans, and Meadowlands became a ghost town before it had even been built.

The smoking crater the trucks dumped their loads into was the would-be lake.

Pippi crept closer, trying not to breathe the foul air.

The wind gusted. For a second she had a clear view of the pit.

She inhaled sharply. Before she could let out her breath in a long, mindless scream, someone seized her from behind and clamped her mouth shut.

She fought wildly, too panicked to remember anything she had learned in her self-defense classes.

She could feel herself being half-dragged, half-carried but, eyes watering from the smoke, she could not tell where she was being taken.

She renewed her struggle. Her captor's arms loosened. She fell to the ground, sobbing and retching.

Gradually she became aware of someone crouching next to her, stroking her hair and murmuring words of com-fort in her ear.

Jeremy. Oh, no, what had she done to him?

"Did I hurt you?" she asked contritely.

"Some, but don't worry about it."

He stood and helped her up.

"Jeremy," she said with a catch in her throat. "I saw—" But she could go no further.

He wrapped his arms around her and rocked her gently. "I know. I saw it too."

"But why?"

"Oh, honey. What did you think they're doing with all those dead bodies? How many have died in Denver alone? Two hundred thousand? Three hundred thousand? And no end in sight." His voice hardened. "That's one more reason I've got to get out of here. There's no way in hell I'm going to end up in that . . . that funeral pyre."

Greg arrived at the Bowers Clinic as Kate was leaving. By the light of the low-wattage bulb over the front door, he could see strands of light brown hair escaping from beneath a knitted cap that matched her blue coat. Her hazel eyes looked sad.

He hopped off his bicycle. "I didn't realize it was so late. Maybe I should come back tomorrow."

"I'd rather talk to you now," Kate said. "We could go back inside or . . ." She hesitated. "Maybe you could walk me home?"

"Glad to." Wheeling his bicycle, Greg fell into step beside her. "It's too dark for you to be walking home alone."

"I'm used to it. It's just that after last night . . ."

Kate shuddered visibly.

"Want to talk about it?"

"Actually, yes. That's why I called you."

After a few false starts, as if she didn't know how to tell her story, she launched into an account of her walk home the previous evening.

"Work brigades? Computer chip implants? It all sounds fantastic," Greg said.

Unexpectedly, Kate smiled. "I can't believe it. I almost said 'you've got to believe me.' Talk about a tired movie cliché."

"That's about as bad as 'trust me.' Whenever a character in a movie says that, you know it's one thing you shouldn't do."

"Or when they shine a flashlight in their eyes to see if it's working."

"My favorite, 'I have something to tell you, but I can't tell you over the phone.' A sure sign the person is going to get killed."

"What about when a bad guy's hands are cuffed in front? Big surprise—he escapes."

"You know what gets me? How they usually use saxophone music for sex scenes, as if they think it's called a sexaphone."

Kate chuckled then said, sounding surprised, "We're here already. Would you like to come in? I can fix us something to eat."

Greg shook his head, but his stomach growled in protest. Besides, talking to Kate would be much more enjoyable than going home and worrying about Pippi.

"That sounds nice," he said. "This time I promise not to fall asleep on your couch."

She smiled at him. "I didn't mind."

During the simple but delicious meal of homemade soup thick with barley and vegetables, and homemade bread and butter, Greg found himself telling Kate about Peter Jensen's revelation that someone had manufactured the organism.

"Do you believe him?" Kate asked. "I mean, everyone else is saying the red death is a virus."

"Interestingly enough, I do believe him." Greg paused, trying to find the right words. "Peter subscribes to all kinds of theories about conspiracies, lies, and cover-ups. I don't believe everything he says, but I know some of it is true. It's not just what we're going through now with the red death, the quarantine, martial law and all the rest of it that makes his theories sound plausible to me. Something happened when I was a kid."

He looked at Kate and laughed. "You must be good at your job. I'm not one of your patients, and I still always spill my guts to you."

Kate smiled and ladled more soup into his bowl.

Looking into her sympathetic eyes, Greg realized he felt ready—no, eager—to exhume his long buried secret.

"I never told this to anyone before, not even Pippi. I grew up on a ranch in Delta County on the western slope. There were five of us. My parents, my brother, my sister, and me. Like most kids, I didn't like going to school and doing chores afterward, but I was happy.

"Then the cattle mutilations started. Not many, one every few months, but we couldn't afford the loss. It drove my father nuts. He couldn't figure out why anyone would cut off the lips and other inedible body parts, and leave the rest of the animal to rot.

"One time we even found one of the mutilated cattle in a fork of an old cottonwood tree, as if it had been dropped from above.

"There were the inevitable stories about UFOs. My brother was excited about the possibility of meeting aliens, but my father didn't believe it. For one thing, he found traces of fluorescent paint on the backs of several of the mutilated cattle, as though they had been marked to aid in finding those specific animals in the dark. For another, he had toxicology tests done on the animals that showed large amounts of nicotine in the liver and blood of the animals. Nicotine is the most common ingredient in tranquilizer guns. The tests also showed that some of the cattle died from a disease of the Clostridia family.

"My father did some research and found that many such bacteria had been used in biochemical warfare experiments, which were supposedly banned. In 1976, a Senate Select Committee on Intelligence found that the CIA had not complied with the ban and had admitted to keeping stockpiled canisters of bacteria.

"My father didn't necessarily think the CIA had anything to do with the mutilations—why would the government be interested in his unimportant ranch, located in an unimportant county? But he knew it wasn't aliens, either.

"He decided to find out the truth.

"He took to roaming around our ranch most of the night, and he didn't see anyone or anything, but he did hear helicopters.

"Then one night he happened to be in the right spot—or wrong spot, as things turned out—and he saw a black helicopter with no identification markings hovering over a small group of cattle that had strayed from the herd.

"The helicopter pilot must have caught sight of my father because it came toward him, and suddenly a bright light, like a halogen work lamp, shone down on my father. He felt as if he were being cooked from the inside out. He fell to the ground and lay there, unable to move. The helicopter landed. Two men dressed in black, with black watch caps covering their hair, jumped out of the helicopter and went to my father. One man shone a light in my father's eyes, then stuck something cold far into my father's left ear. My father passed out. He woke alone at first light.

"He looked around and didn't see any mutilated cattle, but he did discover that one of the animals was missing.

"He never acted the same after that. He became weak and listless, and lost a lot of weight.

"My mother talked him into going to the doctor. The doctor discovered my father had breast cancer. None of us had any doubt the men in the black helicopter had caused the disease, but we couldn't do anything about it.

"My father's cancer did not respond to any of the so-called treatments. Finally, he refused to let the doctors play with him anymore. He came home and died a slow and painful death.

"After the funeral, Mother got rid of the cattle and planted fruit trees and vines. She said no one goes around mutilating apples, cherries, and grapes. She wasn't trying to be funny, either—she'd lost her sense of humor by then.

"She used to love to laugh more than anything. She always used to laugh, but after my father died, she never laughed again.

"My sister had been one of those vibrant, joyful girls everybody loved, but she became fearful and moody. She didn't go to college, didn't get married, just stayed home and worked in the orchards.

"Overnight, the world had gone from an orderly, predictable place to one so alien and chaotic neither my mother nor my sister wanted anything to do with it.

"One good thing, since they're so reclusive, the red death hasn't touched them."

"And your brother?" Kate asked.

"He changed most of all. He had been a studious, timid boy, but when he realized danger could come out of nowhere, he saw no point in avoiding it, so he met it head on. He bought a motorcycle and rode it without wearing a helmet, went rock climbing without using a rope, got involved with drugs, smoked, did anything that even hinted of danger."

Greg paused for a few seconds, then he said quietly, "Four years ago he died in a hang-gliding accident."

"I'm sorry," Kate said.

"Yeah, me too."

"You seem to have landed with your feet firmly on the ground."

"At first I felt angry *and* fearful *and* reckless, but somewhere along the line I got so fed up with all the lies the government tells and all the secrets it keeps that I decided to become an investigative reporter and reveal the truth."

"Is that why you dress like a secret agent?"

Greg pointed to his well-pressed chinos and his pale blue shirt. "Me? A secret agent?"

"The tan trench coat and the old fedora," Kate said.

"Oh, those. They belonged to my father. The summer after I graduated from college, I helped my mother clean out the attic, and I found them packed away. I started wearing them as a memorial to my father, and I kept it up when I discovered they made my job easier. A lot of people, especially older women, seem to be disarmed by them."

Kate smiled. "Well, this older woman was disarmed. And charmed."

"I wasn't referring to you," Greg said.

"Even if you were, that's okay. I didn't take offense. I am old." Kate sighed. "You know how people say you're as old as you feel? Well, I must be closing in on ninety. But this isn't about me."

She fell silent as if she knew he hadn't finished his story.

Greg drew a ragged breath. His throat felt like sandpaper, and when he spoke, his voice rasped.

"I idolized my father, but when I found out he had breast cancer, I forgot about the black helicopters and focused all my resentment on him. How could my hero do that to me? How could he be dying from a woman's disease? He died before my resentment left me. I never got a chance to tell him I loved him."

"I understand," Kate said softly. She reached over to

touch his hand, but he jerked it away.

"How can you possibly understand? I doubt you ever did anything shameful in your entire life."

Kate didn't answer.

When Greg stole a look at her, he saw a few tears trickling down her cheeks.

Instantly filled with remorse, he held out a hand.

She grasped it as if it were a lifeline thrown to a woman being submerged for the third time.

"You are so wrong," she said. She rose from her chair, led him to a closed door, and pointed. "There. There's my shame, locked away so I don't have to face it."

Jeremy peered through the windshield, trying to see the road. He drove without headlights, more fearful than ever of drawing attention to himself. If those people back at the burning pit knew he had discovered their filthy secret, he knew he wouldn't live to tell about it. Not that he ever would tell; he wanted to forget it as quickly as possible.

For the first several miles after they had left the funeral pyre, it had been easy to see the road for the fire in the pit had emitted a far-reaching glow.

Now, only the moon and stars lit the way. Once, perhaps, that would have been enough, but his eyes were not as young as they used to be.

Maybe Pippi should drive? He glanced at her. She huddled in the seat, knees drawn to her chest, arms wrapped around her legs, head resting on her knees. She shivered so hard her teeth rattled.

He smiled to himself, remembering a long ago argument with a director. The director had told him to show fear that very way, but he refused, calling it unrealistic. Well, what do you know, the director had been right after all.

Pippi whimpered.

Stifling a flash of irritation, Jeremy pressed harder on the accelerator. The sooner he got out of this mess, the better he'd like it.

"What did you mean back there when you said 'Nora's

dream'?" Pippi asked in a small voice.

Jeremy frowned at her but, to his surprise, found himself answering. Maybe he felt more shook up than he thought.

"Before I left, my wife Nora told me she dreamed about me and a girl in a desolate place. She said skeletons of buildings stood in the background and some trucks and bulldozers were parked haphazardly around an immense smoking pit. Because of the smoky haze, the setting sun looked red, like the sun of a dying planet, and it made everything else look red, too. Blood red."

He hadn't paid much attention when his wife had told him about it; she often had dreams. Once she called him on location in Mozambique, all frantic because she dreamed he would be tortured. And he had been tortured—in the movie they were filming. Another time she dreamed he would be hit by a car and end up in a coma; that scene also came from a movie set.

But what about when she accused him of having an affair with his co-star Janet Richards during the filming of *Mesa Grande*? He had managed to sidestep a battle by swearing the affair happened only onscreen, but he had not understood how she found out about it. Had she really dreamed of them making love as she had claimed?

A pair of blinding headlights appeared in his lane.

He veered to the left. Too late, he realized the headlights belonged to a semi turning onto the road, and the trailer blocked the left lane.

Heart pounding, hands sweating, he slammed on the brakes and turned the wheel sharply to the left. He missed the trailer by inches and came to a skidding halt next to a ditch.

The semi—a cattle truck, he now saw—straightened itself and disappeared down the road.

He crossed his arms on the steering wheel and rested his head on them. He breathed evenly, hoping the steady rhythm would slow his heart, but his heart continued to pound so rapidly against his rib cage that his chest hurt.

Something thudded against the truck.

Pippi let out a squeal.

Jeremy lifted his head.

A second thud.

When an object hurtled by his window, and another struck the windshield and bounced off, it dawned on him someone was throwing rocks at them.

"Do something," Pippi said in a tiny voice.

"What?"

"I don't know."

A face, a gargoyle's face, loomed in front of the truck.

Pippi squealed again and clutched Jeremy's arm.

He shook it off and rolled down the window a couple of inches.

"You've already got everything," the gargoyle screamed. "There's nothing left. You hear me? Nothing!"

"We don't want anything," Jeremy called out. What did one say in a situation like this? We mean no harm? We come in peace? Take me to your leader?

The gargoyle moved closer, and Jeremy saw a woman about his own age. She might even be attractive when rage didn't contort her face.

"I don't care if you are from the government," the woman screamed. "It's still murder. It's still theft."

"We're not from the government. I'm Jeremy King, the actor."

"Jeremy King?"

"Yes."

"You're trying to trick me," the woman shouted, hefting another rock.

"No trick. Wait. I'll show you my driver's license."

He got out his driver's license and turned on the light inside the truck so the woman could see it.

"What are you doing here?" the woman asked, sounding uncertain.

"Short version? I was filming a movie when the quarantine went into effect."

"But what are you doing here on my property?" The woman sighed wearily and dropped the rock she held.

"Never mind. Maybe it's better if I don't know."

"Can I come out?" Jeremy asked.

"Use the passenger door. I have enough problems without you falling into my irrigation ditch and breaking a leg."

When they had climbed out of the truck, the woman said to Pippi, "I know you. You're the Channel Ten weather girl."

Pippi nodded.

"What did you mean about the government?" Jeremy asked.

"They came and stole our cows and our grain, said they had the right. Even had a copy of something they called an executive order signed by the president saying they could take possession of food supplies. Doesn't make it right."

"No, it doesn't," Jeremy said.

"When my husband objected, they shot him." The woman's hands clenched into fists. "I suppose they had an executive order for that, too, but they didn't show it to me."

"Why did they take your cows and grain?" Pippi asked.

"To feed the people in the cities, of course. They don't care about us in rural areas, there's not enough of us to cause any trouble. They don't care about the city folk, either, but hungry people in cities riot."

"The soldiers have guns," Pippi said.

"Believe me, child, if you have millions of starving people, you need more than a few thousand guns to control them." She turned to Jeremy. "Will you help me carry my husband into the house? I couldn't bear leaving him out here."

Jeremy's stomach heaved at the thought of coming face to face with yet another dead body, but he agreed to help.

After they had laid her husband to rest in the spare bedroom, the woman looked at them helplessly. "I'm sorry. I can't offer you anything to eat. They cleaned out my pantry, too."

"We've got food," Pippi said. "You can eat with us."

Jeremy glared at her. Didn't she know enough to keep

her big mouth shut?

"Thanks, child, but no. I don't think I can eat tonight."

"Is there anyplace around here we can camp?" Jeremy asked.

"You can stay in the barn if you want. It's not as if I have a use for it anymore."

Jeremy and Pippi ate a silent meal of cold, unidentifiable C rations, then they got into their individual sleeping bags.

"I'm freezing," Pippi said after a while.

"So am I."

They zipped the two sleeping bags together and fell asleep in each other's arms.


"I'm going to make some hot chocolate," Kate said. "Want some?"

"Please."

Greg cleared the dishes off the table while Kate busied herself at the stove.

Back at the table, with steaming mugs of hot chocolate in front of them, Greg gave Kate a quizzical glance.

"You still haven't told me what's behind the closed door."

"I shouldn't have said anything."

"Hey," Greg protested. "I told you my whole life history."

"You're right." She took a sip of her hot chocolate, but still could not bring herself to begin.

"Start with the simple things. I know you're not married now, but were you ever?"

"Once." A dam she had built deep inside herself suddenly burst, and a flood of memories washed over her. She closed her eyes against the pain, but still the memories came.

"His name was Joe," she said. "He was tall and wide-shouldered, with thick, dark wavy hair, and eyes as clear and blue as the September sky.

"He owned an antiquarian book store that did so well he needed an assistant. I answered the ad. At first he seemed

85

forbidding, so I decided not to take the job if he offered it to me. I didn't think he'd be an easy man to work for. Well, we got to talking about books. An hour later he offered me the job. I planned to refuse, but then he smiled at me, and I was lost. It took him a year or so to realize he loved me too. Shortly after that, we were married.

"About a month or so after the wedding, he lost his grip, couldn't hold on to anything. Then his vision dimmed. He made appointments with a physician and an ophthalmologist, but he canceled them when both his grip and his vision returned. We worried about it awhile, but we figured the stress of the wedding caused the problem, so we forgot about it.

"A year later, Joe had another attack. This time the right side of his face went numb, he suffered from dizziness and double vision, and he tripped over his own feet. He made an appointment with the doctor, and again when his appointment rolled around he felt fine, but this time he kept the appointment.

"The doctor didn't appear concerned, just said to let him know if Joe experienced any further problems.

"Six months later, Joe had another attack. After weeks of tests to rule out every other possibility, the doctor told us Joe had multiple sclerosis but that we had every reason to be hopeful. He said Joe's expected life span probably would remain the same and remissions could last for many years.

"Within two years, Joe was disabled more often than not, and since his remissions were so short, he couldn't recover his strength before his next attack began. Even though he had to sell his store, he maintained a positive outlook. He kept the best of his stock, turned the second bedroom into an office, and sold his books on the Internet.

"Our friends acted supportive at first, but after a while they stopped calling. I didn't blame them. Humans are conditioned to believe in progress, to believe things will get better, and when things don't get better, they can't handle it. And it didn't help that they saw healthy-looking celebrities on TV talk about having MS. It made them think Joe was malingering.

"Joe began sleeping in the second bedroom, and unless he needed my help, he preferred to be alone.

"He continued to deteriorate, both mentally and physically.

"We muddled along in this way for years, then a little over a year ago, during one of Joe's rare remissions, I mentioned we were coming up on our fifteenth wedding anniversary. When he ignored me, I asked, 'Would it kill you to be nice to me once in a while?'

"He didn't answer.

"I went out for a walk. When I returned, he was gone."

"Dead?" Greg asked.

"No. Not then. He'd taken our car, an old Volvo, and left. I didn't know he felt strong enough to drive. He could barely walk and had a hard time gripping so much as a glass of water.

"When the state patrol called to tell me Joe had been in an accident, that he'd driven off a cliff in the mountains and had died instantly, I wasn't surprised. It did surprise me when they ruled it an accident. It seemed so obvious to me he'd taken his own life that I was sure everyone else could see it, too."

Kate gave an unamused laugh. "I never did buy another car."

Greg looked at her, a frown wrinkling his brow. "I don't see that you did anything shameful."

Kate toyed with her empty cup. "I'm not proud of what I said, and I hate knowing those were the last words I ever spoke to my husband, but I don't think it had anything to do with his suicide. I doubt he even heard me.

"About two weeks after the funeral, I decided to clean Joe's room. I didn't feel up to sorting out his things, but I thought I should dust and vacuum in there. I cracked opened the door, as if expecting Joe, or at least his spirit, to inhabit the room. I stepped inside, but seconds later I scrambled out again and slammed the door.

"Memories of all the shameful, petty, inconsiderate

things I had done over the years haunted the room, and I couldn't bear to face my own mean spirit. Too many times I snapped at him or purposely waited a few minutes before going to see what he wanted when he called out. Other times I felt so angry at the way life had treated us, I stomped around the house, slamming doors and kicking furniture. Usually, though, I pounded my pillow, or cried. I'm embarrassed to admit how many times I cried, wishing I had a normal life with healthy children to take care of instead of an uncommunicative and disabled man. Sometimes I even hated him for what he had become, as if he chose to get sick. Can you believe that?"

She didn't pause for a response, but hurried on, wanting to get it all out.

"Worst of all, I realized I was not a strong woman who had shouldered her burden with courage, but a weak woman who lacked generosity of spirit."

Greg reached across the table and put a hand over hers. "We are a sad pair, aren't we?"

She gave him a wistful smile.

A full minute went by without either of them speaking, then she asked, "Would you like some more hot chocolate?"

"No. It's getting late. I should go."

He rose, put on his trench coat, tucked his hat under his arm, and headed for the front of the house.

They stood at the door, shifting from foot to foot.

Kate couldn't think of anything to say, and when Greg too remained silent, she wondered if he was having as much trouble as she in striking the right parting note.

Their eyes happened to meet. Then, awkwardly, they leaned toward each other, and they hugged.

# 12

*Friday, December 9 (a.m.)*

Jeremy woke to an unnatural stillness.

Even the vast quiet of his ranch never seemed this silent. Though there would be no birds singing or insects chirping at this time of year, there would still be the sounds of distant neighs or barks, a few words carried on the breeze, maybe a noisy motor or two.

But now, huddled in a sleeping bag on the floor of an unfamiliar barn, he heard only a soft whiffling from the young woman lying next to him.

He sat up, took a deep breath, and immediately wished he hadn't. Underlying the barn's odor of fresh hay and stale animal droppings he detected the stench of the far away funeral pyre.

Wide-awake now, he staggered to his feet, put on his coat, and went out behind the barn to relieve himself.

Back inside, he ran in place for a few minutes to get warm, then he rummaged in his supplies for a can of sardines and a piece of bread.

He had just finished eating when Pippi awoke.

She staggered to her feet and looked around, frowning. "Where . . ."

"Toilet facilities?"

She nodded.

Jeremy jerked his head toward the door. "Nearest bush."

She grabbed her purse, slung the strap across a shoulder, and hurried from the barn.

The sight of her—rumpled clothes, tousled hair, and all—made his pulse quicken, and suddenly the crotch of his pants felt uncomfortably tight.

He went over to the sleeping bags and rolled them, refusing to let anything, even his own hormones, impede his quest for freedom.

"I'm hungry," Pippi announced upon her return.

"Then fix yourself something to eat, but hurry. We're behind schedule."

She went into her bags and brought out a packet of instant oatmeal, a bag of flaxseed, and a jar of instant coffee.

"I need some hot water," she said.

"Can't you use cold?"

"No."

"You go find some twigs for a fire while I dig out the saucepan," he said peevishly, but secretly he felt glad he would not have to forego his morning jolt of caffeine.

Before they left, Pippi stacked several cans of food on the floor in the middle of the barn.

"What the hell are you doing?" Jeremy demanded.

"Oh, don't be such an old grump," Pippi said. "The woman who let us stay here has nothing, and you have enough to feed an army. You won't miss a few cans."

"They're my cans." But, not wanting to waste time arguing, he left the food.

They drove away from the ranch. Pippi chattered, apparently in high spirits.

Jeremy was trying to figure out how long it would take them to get to Holly and the plane when he realized she had asked him a question.

He turned his head to look at her. "What?"

She pouted. "I knew you weren't listening."

He rolled his eyes and directed his attention back to the road.

"I wondered why you're alone," she said after a moment. "I mean, don't celebrities usually travel with huge entourages?"

"I used to, but it got old after a while."

"I would have thought you'd at least have a bodyguard."

He laughed shortly. "It's not like I'm the president."

"I know, but still . . ."

"I didn't need one. No one could get close to me because someone on my staff was always around. Tax attorneys, accountants, personal assistants, publicists, an agent, a contract attorney, secretaries to handle my fan mail, and others I don't remember. I was a corporation with hundreds of employees and one product to sell—me."

"What happened?"

"One day it dawned on me I had so many employees trying to figure out ways to keep my money out of government hands, that it cost me more for their salaries than I saved on taxes, so I got rid of the lot of them. Now I have one attorney, one CPA, my agent, my publicist, a ranch foreman and a few ranch hands, a high school boy to maintain my website, and a couple of old women to deal with my correspondence. I don't even need a pilot anymore, since I prefer to fly solo."

"What do you do with your money?" Pippi asked, then all in a rush, "I'm sorry, that slipped out. I don't mean to pry."

"It's no secret. As everyone who reads the tabloids knows, I put it in the bank so I can get to it whenever property near my ranch becomes available. I am one of the largest landowners in Montana."

"What do you do with it all?"

"I have a lot of cattle, but mostly I turn it back to nature."

"You mean wild animals?" Pippi asked, sounding awed.

"Yes. Rabbits, coyotes, bears, a mountain lion, even a couple of wolves."

"Wolves! Wow! But don't they steal your cattle?"

Jeremy shrugged. "Occasionally, if they have nothing else to eat, but I don't mind. It's a small price to pay to have wolves still roaming the face of the earth."

He was envisioning himself in old clothes at his ranch, on the back of his favorite horse, racing across the long sweep of his land, when Pippi let out a squeal.

"Look," she said, pointing a trembling finger at the sky.

Jeremy leaned forward and squinted through the windshield.

What appeared at first to be a dark cloud, turned out on closer inspection, to be dozens of huge birds circling above a small town.

"Are they hawks?" Pippi asked.

"No. Hawks fly alone."

"Then what?"

"Vultures."

Seeing the panic in her eyes, he took pity on her. "Is there a bypass around the town?"

Her voice sounded faint. "No."

"What about a turnoff before we get there?"

He caught the negative shake of her head out of the corner of his eye, and gave a mental shrug. They had passed a crossroads several miles back, but he did not intend to retrace his route. She'd have to be satisfied with his driving through town as quickly as possible.

As they approached the town, Jeremy fought a sudden urge to laugh. The place looked like a set for a film crossing a spaghetti western with a horror movie: Sergio Leone meets Alfred Hitchcock.

Squat buildings in need of paint lined both sides of the street. Prairie winds blew mournfully, loose shingles flapped, an unlatched screen banged.

Several vehicles were parked haphazardly in front of the buildings. Three cars were stopped in the middle of the road, doors open, drivers sprawling half in, half out, with crusted brown blood pooled beneath them.

Between two buildings, a pack of dogs fought; a victor emerged, carrying his spoils—a bloody foot with a shoe still attached.

The vultures descended and pecked at the victims of the red death who lay in crumpled heaps in the street. The birds looked up as Jeremy neared, stared balefully at him, but didn't move until the truck came within inches of running them over. As one, they took to the air, escorted the truck out of town, then swooped back to their meal.

When Jeremy heard Pippi gagging, he slowed down.

"No, no. Keep going," she cried. "For God's sake, don't stop!"

"You sure you're okay?"

"I'm fine. Go. Get us out of here."

Neither spoke for several miles, then Pippi said, "I don't get it."

"Don't get what?"

"Back there—all those dead people. I mean, that was a small place. Denver's huge, and hundreds of thousands have died there, but we didn't see many dead bodies at all."

"That's because they've been clearing them away in Denver. Apparently, they're not concerned about a place as small as that town."

"I didn't see many dogs running loose in Denver, either. Wouldn't you think with so many people dying, there'd be a lot of abandoned dogs?"

Jeremy didn't want to answer; voicing the truth would make it even more real, but when Pippi looked at him expectantly with those incredible aquamarine eyes, he gave in.

"I think they're being killed by the people collecting the dead bodies. Last night at that burning pit I saw them throwing the bodies of dogs and cats into the fire, too."

Pippi's eyes filled with tears. "Who would do such a thing?"

"I don't think they have much choice. If the epidemic continues much longer, there won't be enough food for all the people. And things are bad enough without packs of wild dogs terrorizing the city."

They had passed several more miles of endless flat farmlands when Jeremy eased up on the accelerator.

Ahead appeared another town, much larger and in better repair than the one they had just passed. Behind the town lay an extensive subdivision of new houses, each surrounded by several acres of winter-brown grass. It looked peaceful, but something felt wrong.

"Get me the binoculars, will you?" Jeremy said quietly.

Pippi turned and poked around in the back seat.

"Here," she said, handing him the binoculars. Then, "What do you see?"

"A roadblock." And men with guns, he added silently.

As he drove toward the town, a loudspeaker suddenly blared, "Turn back. You are not wanted here."

Jeremy continued to approach.

"Go away," the loudspeaker blared.

Jeremy heard the unmistakable, amplified sound of several shotguns being pumped.

He braked.

"Leave now," the voice ordered, "or we will shoot."

"Are you going to do what they say?" Pippi asked.

"Do you have a better suggestion?"

"Ram them?"

"Yeah, right. How far do you think we'd get before they killed us?"

"They're not going to kill us."

"You sure about that?"

"No."

Jeremy drummed his fingers on the steering wheel. After a moment, feeling sick to his stomach, he turned the truck around.

He hadn't driven far when he noticed a gravel road angling off their paved one. Minutes after he turned onto the gravel, the first snowflakes fell.

Greg reached halfway to Broomfield to keep his appointment with Jack Thornton, when it began to snow.

In his youth, the first lazy flakes of a new storm had promised magic, but when his father had died, so had the wonder. Now, pedaling through the deserted streets, a feeling of well-being washed over him, as if he were that child again. Laughing aloud, he pedaled faster. Within a remarkably short time, he coasted toward the entrance of the Reese Institute.

The simple brick building, long and low, nestled in a park-like setting where paved paths meandered through stands of mature trees. A blacktopped parking lot bordered the property.

The half-full lot surprised Greg, as did the building blazing with lights; most other businesses in the metro area had closed.

He locked his bike and entered the building.

A woman in her forties sat behind a huge horseshoe-shaped desk, which took up most of the small reception area.

The woman's eyes looked red. When she dabbed at them with a shredded tissue, he realized she was heartbroken, not sick.

"I'm Greg Pullman, here to see Jack Thornton."

The woman glanced up, but didn't meet his eyes. "Yes," she said sniveling, "Dr. Thornton is expecting you. Upstairs. Room 203."

"You okay?" Greg asked.

The woman nodded.

"Anything I can help you with?"

"No. No one can help."

He moved away from the reception desk but turned back when the woman said, sobbing, "They're dead."

"Who's dead?" he asked gently.

"My husband and daughter. They came and got them this morning." She looked up at Greg. "Do you know where they're taking them?"

Greg shook his head no.

She let out a loud wail. "They're dead and I can't even have a funeral and bury them properly. All that's left of them are two large fluorescent dots on my front door."

"I'm sorry," Greg said.

The woman blew her nose, then squared her shoulders. "You better go. Dr. Thornton is waiting for you."

As Greg headed for the doctor's office, he realized his feeling of well being had evaporated.

Dr. Jack Thornton was tall and slim with touches of silver at his temples, but because of his snub nose and twinkling blue eyes, he looked more impish than distinguished.

"Call me Jack," he said, grasping Greg's hand. "A doctor is a physician, and I'd as soon not be associated with that particular loathsome species. And Mr. Thornton is my father.

"Sorry I took so long to return your call. We've been busy around here. It's good of you to come on such short notice, though why I'm grateful to you, I don't know. You're the one who wanted to see me. You weren't doing anything important, I hope."

Greg shook his head. He'd spent a tedious morning sorting through Dr. Takamura's papers and had been glad of the interruption.

"That's good." Jack twinkled at him. "So what can I do you for?"

Greg winced. He hated that expression; it made him think of calculatingly hearty used car salesmen.

"I notice the parking lot here is half full," he said, "and a lot of the offices are occupied. Most people in the metro area have stopped going to work, too afraid of the red death to venture out of their homes except for emergencies."

"The red death?" Jack asked, looking bemused. "Is that what they're calling it?"

Greg nodded.

"Interesting. I didn't know." Then, "You're wondering what makes us different?"

"Yes."

"We're scientists. If you check, I'm sure you'll find people still working at most of the research labs in the area."

"Are you saying scientists are less prone to fear than everyone else?"

"No, of course not. But this is an exciting time for science."

"Exciting?" Greg could think of a few words to describe the red death: tragic, horrifying, frightening. But exciting? No.

"Of course it's exciting—from a purely scientific point of view. I wouldn't expect you, a non-scientist, to understand."

"Explain it to me."

"Modern medical techniques—vaccines, early diagnoses, antibiotics—prevent alien organisms from running their natural course, but now we're being given a rare opportunity to observe the effects of one such organism moving freely through a human population."

"By alien organism do you mean something from another planet?"

Jack's eyes twinkled. "No, though it has been theorized that some viruses do come from outer space. By alien I meant not us, not connected to us."

"But it is connected to us." Greg stopped, not certain how much he should reveal.

"You're referring to the human genes in the chimera?" Jack asked.

Greg had been taking notes, but now he focused his attention on the scientist. "How do you know it's a chimera?"

Jack smiled. "Well, this is the Reese Institute."

Greg thought the man deliberately obtuse until he remembered that Bill Upton, the science reporter, had said the Reese Institute mapped genetic codes.

"What can you tell me about the chimera?" he asked.

Jack shrugged. "Not much. We have the genetic blueprint, but most of the individual gene sequences have yet to be identified."

"Why would someone splice human genes onto an organism like the chimera?"

"To see what would happen, I imagine."

"Do you know Dr. John Takamura?"

"No."

"Have you heard of ARC?"

"The Agricultural Research Center in the Four Corners area?"

Greg nodded.

"Nope. Never heard of them." Jack chuckled. "Yes, of course I know who they are. They're the ones trying to create things like disease- and insect-resistant vegetables."

"Are they involved in research other than agricultural?"

"Like what?"

"Biochemical warfare."

Jack snorted. "Of course not. That sort of research has been banned."

"But someone created the chimera that's causing the red

death."

"Doesn't mean they created it to be a weapon."

"Why else would someone make such an organism?"

"To learn. A biogeneticist isn't solely interested in studying genes, you know. We're primarily concerned with the development of life from pre-existing life. By breaking down genes and recombining them, we can discover the very essence of creation."

"Playing God, in other words."

"We don't call it playing God. We call it progress."

"You keep saying we."

"Meaning us biogeneticists as a group, not me personally. That kind of cutting edge research is a young scientist's game."

"Everyone keeps reminding me that biochemical warfare experiments have been banned, but isn't it possible some experiments are being done in secret?"

Jack looked skeptical. "Anything's possible."

"Could the Hanta virus be a bio-weapon that escaped from a lab? It originated down in the Four Corners area where ARC is located."

Jack shook his head, smiling at Greg as if he were a child who had said the darnedest thing. "Doctors treating U.S. troops during the Korean War first noted the Hanta virus. They named it after the South Korean river where they discovered it."

Undaunted, Greg said, "I've heard that AIDS began as a bio-weapon tested in Africa and Haiti but it evolved away from its parent virus, and now there's no way to stop it."

For the first time during the interview, Jack's eyes lost their twinkle. "That's just another conspiracy theory."

Greg tried to hide his smile at the scientist's use of the term, but he must not have been successful, because Jack said caustically, "You think that's funny? I'll tell you what's funny. If the AIDS virus hadn't appeared on its own, someone probably would have created it. Because of AIDS, we know things about the human immune system that would have taken us decades to learn. Now, if you have no more serious questions, I have work to do."

By the time Greg left Jack Thornton's office, snow had begun to accumulate. He lifted his face to the descending flakes, but could not recapture the lightheartedness he had felt before entering the Reese Institute.

He hesitated for a moment, trying to decide what to do next. He wanted to see if he could find Charles Guest at GeneCo, but he also wanted to go to the Buddhist temple downtown in Sakura Square, and he wouldn't have time for both before the streets became too slick for bike riding.

The temple won.

While he had been going through Takamura's papers that morning, he had found a book bound in leather embossed with cherry blossoms. Many of the handwritten pages had doodles in the margins—lovely and deceptively simple drawings of samurai, geishas, flowers—which had aroused his curiosity.

The writing appeared to be Japanese and he hoped someone at the Buddhist temple would be willing to translate some of it for him.

To that end, before he had left his apartment, he had tucked the book into his backpack, along with some papers on official-looking stationery.

Outside the temple, a man dressed in a bright green parka with a blue and green knitted hat pulled over his ears swept away the snow. He looked up as Greg approached.

Greg could not tell the man's age—his face appeared smooth and unlined, but his eyes looked ancient and wise. Nor could he figure out who the man was. A monk? A custodian?

The man's eyes, more rounded than slanted, held a faint glint of amusement, as if he knew Greg's thoughts. "May I help you?" he asked.

Greg removed a sheaf of papers from his backpack. "Is there anyone here who can tell me what these papers are about?"

"Perhaps I could help," the man said, holding out a

chapped hand.

The man looked at the papers for a moment, then gave them back. "They're official requisitions for logs and lumber."

Greg pointed to the letterhead. "Can you tell me what this means?"

"*Boeki Kyusuibu.* Anti-Epidemic Water Supply Unit."

Shrugging philosophically—well, Takamura's wife had warned him the papers contained nothing of importance—he stuffed them back in his pack and pulled out the leather-bound book.

"What about this? Can you tell me anything about it?"

The man accepted the book and lightly ran his fingers over the cherry blossoms on the cover. He opened it randomly to a page containing a tiny drawing of a lotus blossom floating in a reed-rimmed pool. He touched the lotus, then scanned the rest of the page. After looking at a few more pages, he closed the book and handed it back to Greg.

"I do not know how to read this," he said, face impassive.

Greg stared at him in consternation. "Do you know Japanese?"

"Yes."

"And the book is written in Japanese, right?"

"Yes, but I do not know how to read it." The man turned his back and resumed his sweeping.

"Is there anyone here who could read it?" When the man remained silent, Greg asked, "Could you tell me what the book is? A journal, maybe? Or a diary?"

The swish of the broom was the man's only response.

# 13

*Friday, December 9 (p.m.)*

The snowfall on the eastern plains wasn't heavy, but strong winds kept it in the air, making it seem like a major blizzard.

At three o'clock, unable to see more than a few feet ahead of him, Jeremy pulled to the side of the road and turned off the engine.

The sick feeling that had overtaken him when he had turned away from the roadblock returned ten-fold. Not only did the storm force him to stop; due to the hazardous driving conditions, he had made little progress.

He banged his head a couple of times on the steering wheel. Getting out of this hell called Colorado seemed like an impossible task.

He banged his head once more for good measure, then sat up straight. He lifted his chin and brandished one arm. "As God is my witness, I will succeed!"

The young woman sitting next to him laughed. Clapping her hands, she said, "That was great."

Startled, Jeremy turned his head; he had forgotten all about his companion.

"You really are a good actor," Pippi said, sounding half-admiring and half-envious.

"Well, thank you, kind lady," he said, bowing as gracefully as he could in the cramped cab of the truck. Then, ironically, "I suppose you'll be wanting my autograph next."

She snuggled into his arms. "I don't need it. I have you." She pulled his head down and kissed him.

As he felt the first twinges of arousal, she drew away.

"Do you think I'll ever be as good an actor as you?"

"Yeah, sure," he said, seeking her lips again.

"Do you think I'll be successful?"

He reached beneath her coat and caressed her breast. "Yeah, sure."

Panting slightly, she said, "Truthfully?"

"Yeah, sure."

101

She pulled away from him. "You're not taking me seriously."

He heaved a sigh. "What do you want from me?"

"The truth."

His lips curled in a sardonic smile. "You couldn't handle the truth."

She sniffed. Despite the dim light, he could see the sparkle of tears in her eyes. He reached for her, but she turned her back on him.

"You want the truth?" he asked.

"Yes," she said, wiping away her tears with the heels of her palms, like a little girl.

"Then, no. I don't think you'll be successful."

Her chin trembled, but when she spoke, she sounded defiant and a bit curious. "Why not?"

"You don't have it in you."

"What makes you say that?" she demanded.

"I know you." When she opened her mouth to speak, he held up a hand to silence her. "I'm not an actor who works on instinct. I study people—their strengths and weaknesses, their mannerisms, their motivations—so when I say it's not in you, I know what I'm talking about. Do you know who Alan Mead is?"

"He's the hunk who played George Sharp in that old movie, *A Life Forsaken.*"

"Right. That film had two directors. They fired the first one because he could not get along with Alan, probably because he knew Alan's secret."

"What secret?"

"Until Alan could break into the movies, he worked as a streetwalker on Hollywood Boulevard. I'm not telling you this to put him down or to arouse your prurient interest. I'm trying to explain that a winner, like Alan, is someone who will do anything, *anything* to succeed. He denigrated himself, destroyed his pride, dignity, and respect so he could gain greater pride, dignity, and respect. That takes a special drive, a killer instinct, and frankly, my dear, you don't have it."

"Yes I do."

"No. Here's a for instance. Supposing somebody breaks into your house. He points a gun at you. You happen to be in the kitchen, so you grab a knife. A noise distracts him. You have one second to act. What do you do?"

"Run."

"And like the bimbos in horror movies, you'd probably run upstairs where there's no way out. This is what I'm talking about. How can you ever claw your way to the top when you don't even care enough about yourself to kill someone to save your life? A true winner would not have hesitated for even a moment."

"But what if I had gotten close enough to knife him, but the knife slipped and I nicked him. Then he'd really come after me."

"You could have stuck it in his eye."

"Oh, ick."

Not trying to hide his irritation, Jeremy said, "Fine. Change the scene. He has the knife. You have the gun. Do you shoot?"

"I don't know if I could."

"Being a winner is not just about winning, it's about whether or not you try."

"But you didn't try," she said. "This morning at the roadblock you turned around and drove away."

"That was different."

"You're saying that because you don't want to admit you acted like a coward."

"I did not act like a coward," he said through gritted teeth. "It took all the courage I had to drive away. Confronting them would have gained us nothing."

"So?"

"It's not enough to fight. You have to choose your battles. The strength of your enemy determines your own strength. Which one becomes stronger, a person who vanquishes teddy bears or a person who vanquishes dragons?"

"They're both the same," she said saucily, "because

neither enemy is real."

He squinted at her. "Have you understood a word I said?"

She sat staring ahead of her for several moments. "Yes. All of it. I just didn't realize how little respect you had for me."

He touched her hand. "I do respect you, sweetheart. I think you're special. But you asked so I explained the situation. In Hollywood, you're considered nice if you manipulate someone else into stabbing your best friend in the back instead of doing it yourself."

Her eyebrows drew together. "I don't believe that."

"Fine. If that's the way you want it . . . I was trying to keep you from getting hurt."

She gave him a level stare. "I can take care of myself. No one helped me get where I am. I did it all on my own."

"And where, precisely, are you? A weather girl on a third rate television station, whose contract will not be renewed."

"You don't know that."

"Yes I do." Suddenly weary of the whole conversation, he said, "Forget it."

"No. Tell me."

"You're what? Thirty now? And you have the first signs of age on your face." He ignored her indignant gasp and continued, not caring if he sounded cruel. "There are hundreds of younger girls out there who would willingly kill to take your place. One of them is probably sleeping with your boss right now."

"My boss is a woman."

"What difference does that make?"

Pippi turned away from him without answering.

"Look," he said. "Can't we forget the whole thing? This is a small truck, and we have a long night ahead of us. It's also going to get exceedingly cold, and two bodies wrapped in a sleeping bag can keep a heck of a lot warmer than one."

A long while later she scooted toward him. "Okay, I'll forgive you, but only for tonight."

As he wrapped his arms around her and probed her lips with his, he couldn't help feeling complacent. After a night of his tender ministrations, she would forget she had ever been upset with him.

Kate locked the front door of the clinic, then stood on the porch, waiting.

After a minute, laughing at her folly, she hurried down the snow-covered driveway. Of course Greg wouldn't be coming; any rapport she'd felt last night existed solely in her own mind. Why would a young man be interested in her? And besides, he planned to marry the delectable Pippi O'Brien, though something seemed off-kilter there. He'd lost the radiance he'd had when he announced his engagement and, unlike other besotted men, he'd failed to mention his beloved. Perhaps he was simply worried about the red death, but she didn't think so.

Well, if he ever wanted to talk, he knew where to find her.

Deep in thought, she set out on a route that would take her through Cheesman Park. When she noticed her heading, she hesitated; she didn't like going through the park at night. Then, deciding it couldn't be any more treacherous than the streets, she continued on her way.

She had almost made it through the park when she heard a long, low, wordless cry. Her eyes burned with unshed tears, and her heart felt as if it were breaking; in all her life, she had never heard such a mournful sound.

She tilted her head, trying to find where it came from, but it was all around her, seeping into her. After quiet sobs replaced the ululation, she located the source.

A woman huddled on the ground beneath a tree, an ancient grocery cart filled with clothes and aluminum cans parked nearby. Kate recognized her as a one of the homeless women who roamed the area.

Not wanting to alarm her, Kate approached slowly. She reached out her arms to comfort, then drew back. Perhaps the woman would not appreciate the intrusion on her grief.

The woman moved slightly, giving Kate a glimpse of a frail man lying in bloodstained snow. She crouched to examine him.

"He's been beaten to death!" Though she spoke softly, her voice seemed to fill the park.

The homeless woman nodded.

"Who did this?"

"Insect boys," the homeless woman said in a raspy voice, as if she hadn't spoken in a long time.

Kate knew instantly to whom the woman referred: the same boys who had accosted her two days ago. In their outdated gas masks and long black trench coats, they did look like insects.

The woman smoothed the man's wispy hair and stroked his cheek with the back of her hand.

"I didn't know his name," she said, barely above a whisper. "He was my friend, and I never knew his name. We called him Totter."

Sensing the woman's need to pay tribute to her fallen comrade, Kate asked softly, "Why Totter?"

"His toes curled under, so he had poor balance. He tottered as he walked, and the smallest shove would topple him."

Kate ached for the man, imagining the torment he had endured; his handicap would have provided great entertainment for those who delighted in the misfortunes of others.

The homeless woman bent over to kiss Totter's forehead. "He was such a gentle man. He deserved more than life gave him."

"Why, you're shivering," Kate said. "It's much too cold for you to be out on a night like this. Come home with me. I can give you a bowl of hot soup."

When the woman hesitated, Kate added, "There's nothing you can do for Totter. He's in a better place now."

"Do you really believe that?" the woman asked scornfully.

"Yes, I do," Kate said. "Even if there is no life after

death, oblivion has to be better than this."

The homeless woman, who had introduced herself as Dee Allenby, neatly spooned soup into her mouth. Kate nibbled on a piece of bread with butter and worried about having invited a complete stranger into her house.

Dee looked up and gave Kate a knowing smile.

Unnerved, Kate averted her eyes.

"Do you want to know why you're so afraid of me?" Dee asked.

Kate flushed, embarrassed at having been so transparent.

"It's because we're alike, you and I. You know it wouldn't take much, just the merest shift in the kaleidoscope of life, and you would be where I am."

Kate shook her head, but something deep inside her acknowledged the truth of the woman's words.

"You're not at all what I expected," Kate said.

"Smart people have bad luck, too." Dee ate another spoonful of soup. "People don't believe in luck anymore, either bad or good. They think they control their own destinies. I know I did. I'd see homeless people, and I felt sorry for them, but I also felt contempt, knowing I'd never be one of them."

"What happened?"

"I got a terrible cold that kept getting worse and worse. My doctor finally admitted it hung on much too long to be a cold or the flu, and he put me through the whole gamut of tests. When he could find nothing wrong, he told me I had Chronic Fatigue Syndrome. He acted as if I should be grateful to have a name for my illness, but it didn't change anything since there's no cure for Chronic Fatigue Syndrome.

"I had bad days and worse days, but no good days. Because I couldn't work, I had to quit my job as office manager of a trucking company. As I watched my savings disappear, I got more and more frightened, not knowing what would happen to me. After a long, hard struggle with myself, I finally conceded defeat and went to apply for welfare." She laughed bitterly. "Oh, silly me. You know what I discovered? There is no welfare in this country, at least not for a middle-aged man or woman without dependent children. They have individual programs like AFDC and Section Eight, but I wasn't eligible for any of them."

"What about food stamps?" Kate asked. "I thought everyone below a certain income level was eligible."

"Not me. I could get them if I had a job. Or if I joined their works program, attending meetings and doing volunteer work while I applied for a job, but if I could have done any of that, I wouldn't have needed them in the first place. The woman at the food stamp office told me I had a third choice—apply at the Social Security Administration for disability benefits. I did, but they rejected me. I had expected it, but it still shocked me, and I burst out, 'I can't work and my money's almost gone. What am I supposed to do now?' She said, 'There are soup kitchens.' I looked in her uncaring eyes. 'Are you telling me I have no option but to live on the streets?' She shrugged and said, 'It happens.' Then she added, 'The system isn't perfect. People do fall through the cracks.' As if that should make me feel better."

"Don't you have family or friends who could have helped out?" Kate asked.

"No friends."

Dee's clipped words and pained expression told Kate the whole story. At first, Dee's friends would have been solicitous but, one by one, they would have stopped calling. Only the truest of friends would have persevered through the protracted illness; Kate never had such a friend and, apparently, neither had Dee.

Dee finished her soup and pushed the bowl aside. "I don't have any brothers or sisters. My mother's gone and my father's living in a home for Alzheimer's patients. He doesn't know I exist, not that he ever paid much attention to me. I was just a girl, you see. I do have a cousin, but with a wife and five kids, he doesn't have money to spare or the room to offer me a place to stay."

"I'm sorry," Kate said.

"I know you are. I wish I could say it helps, but it comes too late to make any difference. Perhaps it was too late then, I don't know. I just knew I didn't want to end up on the streets like so much garbage." Dee laughed mirthlessly. "The ultimate throw-away society—even human beings are tossed in the trash like apple cores, old magazines, and obsolete computers." She paused, then added quietly, "I had no idea there were so many losees in the world."

"So many what?" Kate asked.

"Losees. It's a word I made up. To me, losers are people who brought their misfortunes on themselves, like addicts who refuse to get help or kids who run away because their parents won't buy them an expensive pair of sneakers. Losees are people who have misfortune thrust upon them, like poor Totter.

"After I got evicted, I lived in my car until two guys stole it. They broke in while I slept, and they threw me out on the street. Totter found me and took care of me, showed me where to sleep, where to find food. He even scrounged some blankets for me."

"How long have you been living on the streets?" Kate asked.

"Nine months. I was surprised I lasted that long, considering my illness, but the irony of the whole situation is that I got better on the streets. Thinking back, I realize I took sick around the time the owners started remodeling the apartment building where I lived. I doubt I had Chronic Fatigue Syndrome. I think all those harsh chemicals in the building materials poisoned me."

"Once you got well, why didn't you—" Kate stopped, not sure how to put her thoughts into words.

"Get a home? A job? A life?" Dee supplied.

Kate nodded.

"Fury. I wanted nothing to do with the world that had repudiated me." After a minute or two of silence, Dee said softly, "The adage is wrong. Misery doesn't love company. It just wants not to be miserable anymore, but then you know that."

Kate stared at her. "What do you mean?"

"I see the same emptiness in you I see in many people living on the streets. What's your story?"

"His name was Joe," Kate began, thinking that after a year of keeping her pain to herself, she was opening up for the second time in as many nights.

As she neared the end of her tale, it surprised her to discover she felt so nauseated. Wasn't talking about one's troubles supposed to bring about a catharsis? A purification and renewal?

Her stomach heaved spasmodically. She stood so quickly, her chair crashed to the floor behind her. She rushed to the bathroom, closed the door, and leaned against it, taking deep breaths. When her stomach settled, she went to the sink and splashed cold water on her face.

Catching a glimpse of herself in the mirror, she gasped.

Her eyes were bright red.

Her stomach heaved again, and she felt dizzy.

Disoriented, she reached out a hand; suddenly her head exploded with pain.

Everything went black.

Thinking of Dee and Totter, of Greg and his father, of her and Joe, thinking of all the pain in living, Kate let herself slip away.

# 14

*Saturday, December 10*

Jeremy climbed out of the Toyota Tacoma to stretch his cramped legs and ease his aching back. When he could stand upright, he looked around in satisfaction. The day was sunny and still, and everything glistened with pristine whiteness like a Christmas card. Though four-foot drifts dotted the landscape, only an inch or two of snow remained on the wind-swept roads. If they were lucky and had no more delays, they should reach Holly by mid-afternoon.

He frowned, realizing there would be no coffee this morning—snow blanketed any potential firewood. His brow cleared when he remembered buying a couple of ancient cans of Sterno at the surplus store.

He was unloading the back seat, when Pippi awoke.

"What's all the noise?" she asked sleepily.

"I'm looking for the canned heat so I can make some coffee."

"Coffee? Awesome."

She untangled herself from the sleeping bags, grabbed her purse, and hung it over her shoulder as she hopped down from the truck. Unzipping her jeans, she shuffled behind a snowdrift, the closest thing to a bush on that desolate land.

Jeremy found the Sterno, but discovered that their canteens were empty. He went to the back of the truck where he'd stashed the twenty-gallon container of water, filled the saucepan and refilled the canteens.

While the water heated, he checked the oil, dumped more gas into the tank, then refastened the tarp.

Congratulating himself for a job well done, he fixed himself a cup of instant coffee.

He and Pippi each ate their customary breakfasts but, still ravenous, they tore into their food supplies, stuffing themselves with canned fruit, tapioca pudding, and hot dogs and beans.

"I can't believe they actually fed this stuff to soldiers at war," Pippi said.

Jeremy laughed. "It is strange—feeding them children's food, then sending them off to kill."

He ate the last bit of his pudding. "You ready to go?"

"Sure."

They repacked the back seat, then headed off down the road.

Pippi acted as lookout. She wore the binoculars around her neck; every time they saw something suspicious, she would raise them to her eyes and take a closer look.

They had to detour around more towns with road-blocks, but they made good time—there was almost no traffic, and the snow was quickly melting.

Morning turned into afternoon. The flat, featureless plain gave way to gently undulating inclines and a scattering of trees.

Less than an hour away from Holly, they topped a small rise and saw a green sport utility vehicle angled to block both lanes of the road.

"Uh-oh," Pippi said.

"Can you see what's gong on?" Jeremy asked, decelerating.

Pippi peered through the binoculars. "They're sitting, watching us."

"How many?"

"Four. They look like kids. Boys."

"Car trouble?"

"I don't think so."

While Jeremy hesitated, a red SUV, also filled with boys, pulled up behind them.

Hemmed in by the SUVs and two deep ditches flanking the road, all Jeremy could do was move over to give the vehicle behind room to pass.

It stayed right on his tail.

"What are they doing?" Pippi asked in a small voice.

"I don't know. Playing games, maybe."

The windshield cracked, accompanied by a sound like a car backfiring.

"Down," Jeremy yelled. "They're shooting at us."

A second bullet tore off the side-view mirror.

"Fuck this," he said, stomping on the accelerator. He veered left, heading for the field on the other side of the ditch. He only had time to register that the ditch was steeper than it looked, then the truck hit a huge rock. The engine stalled.

Another bullet shattered the cracked windshield, missing him by inches. Seizing Pippi's hand, he pulled her from the truck. He scrambled out of the ditch, then helped her up.

They raced across the field. He slipped in the mud and fell.

Pippi stopped and looked back at him.

"Run," he yelled. "Head for those trees."

He struggled to his feet and reached the stand of trees seconds after Pippi.

Trying to catch his breath, he took a moment to check behind them. The boys whooped and hollered, and swarmed all over his truck.

"Look at all this gas," one boy yelled. "We won us the lottery."

Jeremy hoped that maybe the truck would satisfy the boys, but two of them, rifles in hand, loped toward him and Pippi.

Pippi watched the two boys come nearer. With their eyes alit with laughter, they looked young and innocent, like children playing a game.

The larger boy stopped, raised his rifle to shoulder height. All at the same time, she felt something whizzing by her face, heard the crack of the rifle, and saw a piece of bark flying off the tree next to where she stood.

She stayed rooted to the spot. She knew she should run, wanted desperately to run, but her body refused to cooperate.

Jeremy grabbed her coat and yanked her behind a thicket of bushes, where they stood ankle-deep in leaves.

"Listen," he said urgently. He tugged at her coat. "Are you listening?"

With robotic jerkiness, she turned her head to look at

him.

"Yes," she answered, marveling at how far away her voice sounded.

He lay face down on the ground. "Cover me with leaves."

She gazed at him, not comprehending.

"Cover me with leaves," he said harshly. "Now! Do it now."

She dropped to her knees.

As she scooped the wet, soggy leaves over him, he said, "As soon as you're done, I want you to start running. Zigzag through the trees. Make a lot of noise so they think we're both running away. And whatever you do, don't look back." He turned his head and looked up at her. "Got it?"

Pippi nodded, but refused to meet his eyes. How could he talk to her like that? Blinded by tears, she finished covering him with leaves, then took off running.

The binoculars banged against her chest, branches tore at her hair, rocks tripped her, and still she ran.

She stopped for a moment to massage a stitch in her side. To her horror, she saw the boys up ahead, coming straight at her.

She looked around in confusion. Seeing the thicket of bushes and the mound of leaves covering Jeremy, she realized she had come full circle.

She glanced at the boys; they leered at her and licked their lips.

Her skin prickled.

The smaller boy, whose hair had been dyed a deep crayon blue, thrust his pelvis forward and cupped his crotch with his hand. The larger boy, blond ponytail swinging, flailed his arms and legs in a gross burlesque of a woman running.

The boys convulsed with laughter.

Still laughing, the blond boy raised his rifle. With his finger crooked on the trigger, he aimed it at her.

Suddenly the mound of leaves at the base of the bushes erupted. A creature—barely recognizable as Jeremy, with his tensed body and his rage-distorted face—sprang toward the young blond rifleman.

The boy didn't even have time to turn his head.

Dressed in camouflage clothes as Jeremy was, it looked as if the very leaves reached out, grabbed the blond ponytail, pulled the boy close, and made three rapid sawing motions across his throat.

Blood spurted in a bright red arc from the boy's neck.

It happened so fast that when Jeremy tossed the blond aside, the blue-haired boy was still cupping his crotch and laughing.

Jeremy turned to confront him. The grin slid off the boy's face. He dropped his rifle and raised his hands. His eyes, the irises rimmed with white, were riveted on the bloody knife.

"Hey, man," he said, voice cracking. "It wasn't me. I didn't do nothing."

He backed away, but with frightening speed, Jeremy lunged and thrust the knife into his stomach.

The boy's jaw dropped in surprise; his hands reached out in supplication.

He raised his head.

The man and boy stared at each other.

Jeremy withdrew the knife.

His eyes still locked on the boy's, Jeremy plunged the knife into the boy's stomach again, and ripped upwards.

As the boy crumpled, Jeremy jerked out the knife. He bent over and wiped it on the boy's coat. Then, face expressionless, he tucked it into his boot.

He grabbed both rifles. With one in each hand, he headed back across the field.

Unable to breathe, to move, Pippi watched him go. She shook her head to clear it. Had Jeremy—her Jeremy—knifed two boys? She hadn't even known he carried a knife.

She took a quick peek at the fallen boys, wondering if she should check to see if they were still alive. She shuddered. No way was she going to touch them.

Averting her gaze while she detoured around the bodies,

115

she hurried after Jeremy.

Relief washed over her when she saw Jeremy's truck back on the road and exhaust coming out of the tail pipe.

As quickly as it had come, her relief vanished. In fascinated horror, she watched two boys snatch their rifles and turn them on Jeremy.

Jeremy dropped to the ground. Lying prone, he positioned a rifle on his shoulder. He took aim and fired.

The two boys returned fire. The others scrambled for the vehicles.

A bullet whizzed by Pippi's chest. She yelped and threw herself down on her belly.

"Come on. Let's go," shouted the boy sitting in the driver's seat of the Toyota. The two with rifles jumped into the truck bed, and the three vehicles took off.

When Pippi saw the silver Toyota disappear over the hill, she wanted to cry. More than transportation, it had been a place of refuge, a means of survival, a home of sorts.

And now it was gone.

*Come back, come back*, she screamed silently. But she hoped she'd never see those boys again.

She remained on her belly, weighted down by the enormity of the loss, until she saw Jeremy staggering to his feet.

Rising also, she tried to swallow the lump lodged in her throat. For a minute, seeing him lying so still, she thought he'd been wounded. Or worse.

She ran to him and put her arms around him.

He jerked away.

White and wild-eyed, he stared at her.

Then, without a word, he scooped up the rifles and walked back to the slain boys.

He searched their pockets, pulling out a wad of bills, a handful of bullets, several candy bars. He divided the cash into two piles and handed one to Pippi, along with half of the candy bars.

She put her hands behind her back.

He reached over and tucked them in her coat pocket.

"I never eat candy," she said, but she couldn't force herself to touch the bloody things in order to give them back.

Jeremy walked away, then stopped.

He returned to the boys, squatted beside them, and took off the blue-haired boy's belt.

"What are you doing?" Pippi asked.

He regarded her with cold, hard eyes. "Help me."

She bent down. Together they undressed the boy, then took off the blonde's coat, jeans, shirt.

Pippi gazed in consternation at the pubic mound visible through lace panties, the budding breasts encased in a black bra.

"It's a girl," she said.

Jeremy shrugged. "So what?"

In silence, they removed the girl's shoes and socks.

Jeremy rolled everything into a bundle, which he fastened with the belts. Carrying the bundle and the two rifles, he headed for the road.

They'd been hiking through one field after another for the past hour. Pippi's feet were wet and icy from trudging through patches of slush, and she was exhausted from her unsuccessful struggles to keep up with Jeremy's long strides.

As if finally becoming aware of her, his steps slowed, allowing her to catch up to him.

"You did good today," he said.

She still hurt from the way he had treated her but, recognizing the compliment as an apology, she smiled at him. Though his answering smile did little more than bare his teeth, she took it to mean he had returned to himself, that the terrifying stranger had disappeared.

"Do you think they will come after us?" she asked.

"Could be. By now they've probably convinced themselves they're the victims, and they may want to retaliate. That's why we're staying out of sight of the road."

"Oh." Her stomach clenched. She hadn't even thought of that. "I meant the cops. Do you think they'll come after us?"

"I doubt it. If those kids went to the sheriff, they'd have

to admit to carjacking, and I'm sure they wouldn't want to do that."

"But what if they got caught? Then they wouldn't have anything to lose by telling on us."

He turned and walked backward for a few steps. Looking her in the eyes, he said, "That's the least of our worries. With as blatant as those kids were, I have a hunch there aren't any law enforcement officers around here right now. In case you've forgotten, there's an epidemic going on."

She swallowed and said faintly, "Oh, right," but, in truth, the experiences of the afternoon had pushed all thoughts of the red death out of her mind.

"The only two who got close enough to see us are dead, and nothing in the truck can be traced to us. The license plates, the registration—none of that is in my name."

"They have my purse. It has all my identification in it."

"What's that?" he asked, pointing.

Puzzled, she looked down. "Binoculars."

"No. This." He tugged at the bag dangling by her hip.

She looked at her purse as if she'd never seen it before. "How did that get there?"

"You probably grabbed it when I pulled you from the truck."

She hugged her purse to her chest. "I don't remember." Nor could she remember Jeremy pulling her from the truck.

Jeremy shook his head. "You women and your purses. If you were in a burning house, the first thing you'd do is grab your purse. It's in your genetics or something."

"What about fingerprints?"

He looked befuddled. "Fingerprints? On your purse?"

"The truck," she said impatiently. "They could trace us from our fingerprints on the truck."

He took a deep breath and let it out slowly. "I keep telling you there's nothing to worry about. If it ever got to that point, which it won't, it's a clear case of self-defense."

The image of Jeremy stabbing the boy a second time and savagely ripping upwards rose unbidden in her mind.

"Why did you . . ."

Jeremy's eyes hardened. "They shot at us first. They set the rules. I just played by them."

She shivered. Not wanting him to know he scared her, she said, "I'm cold."

"Yeah, well, you'll have to get used to it."

He strode ahead of her.

Later, when he once again matched his pace to hers, she asked, "What's going to happen to us?"

"We are going to get to that plane. Even if we have to walk all the way, we will get there."

Hearing the steel in his voice, she didn't doubt him, but the thought of having to walk fifty miles—fifty miles in a cold, wet, windy December—appalled her.

They'd gone what? Three miles? And already she'd had enough. She was freezing in her inadequate coat. Her uncovered ears ached. And a heel blister was forming beneath her wet socks and running shoes.

As if reading her mind, Jeremy said, "Let me know if the cold gets too unbearable."

She smiled. "What? You'll give me your coat?"

"No. Not mine."

She stopped short. Oh, no. He couldn't mean what she thought he meant.

She hurried to catch up to him. When he turned to her with raised eyebrows and hefted the bundle of clothes taken from the dead kids, she realized he did mean it.

She shuddered. No. No way was she going to wear any of that stuff. She'd rather die.

# 15

*Sunday, December 11*

In the early morning hours, when the temperature dropped to its lowest with dawn still a faint hope, when Pippi could not stand being cold for even one minute longer, she reached for the bundle of bloodstained clothes.

She took off her damp shoes and icy socks, massaged her feet until the sharp pains told her circulation had returned, then put on both pairs of borrowed socks.

With a frisson of distaste, she tied one shirt over her aching ears and the other around her neck, and pulled on the girl's jeans over her own.

She would gladly have wrapped both coats around her, but Jeremy had spread them beneath the sleeping bags for a modicum of protection from the frozen ground.

Still shivering, Pippi huddled against Jeremy.

Afraid of nightmares, she resisted falling asleep, but when she finally passed out from sheer exhaustion, she dreamed of being back in Denver, safe at home in her Lower Downtown loft.

Kate swam up through the darkness. Seeing the tunnel of light and the angel limned in gold, awe washed over her. It was exactly as those near-death people had described it.

The harsh light blurred her eyes, but she could not look away.

The angel had his back to her. He turned.

Disappointed to find that even in the afterlife she had poor vision, she watched the angel approach. Her heart leapt when he drew close enough for her to see, then tears stung her eyes for the young life cut short.

"Greg? You're dead, too?"

"I'm not dead," he said, laughter tingeing his voice, "and neither are you, though you did give us a scare."

Kate frowned, remembering how her red eyes had stared back at her from the mirror, remembering, too, how she had surrendered to the darkness.

"I thought I died of the red death."

"No. You fainted from hunger and exhaustion."

Still confused, she looked around and recognized her bedroom. The partly drawn drapes created the illusion of a tunnel of light.

"When I visited the other night, scarfing your food," Greg said, sounding chagrined, "I didn't even notice you weren't eating."

"I ate. Bread and butter."

"Had you been getting any sleep?"

"No. Couldn't."

He patted her hand. "You've had plenty of sleep now—thirty-six hours worth."

Her head ached, making it hard to concentrate. "How come I've been out so long?"

"You hit your head on the toilet bowl. Dr. Hart said to let you sleep it off."

"Dr. Hart?" Kate asked, not certain she had heard correctly.

"Yes. A doctor from the clinic. After you fell, Dee didn't know who to call, so when she found my name and number by your phone, she called me."

Tears sprang to Kate's eyes. "And you came?"

"Yes, of course."

Kate mulled that over for a moment, then she asked, "Who's Dee?"

"The woman staying with you."

"Oh, right. The homeless woman." Kate smiled contentedly. "Well, she's not homeless now."

"I guess not," Greg said, smiling in return.

"Then what?" Kate asked.

"I found you unconscious and called the Bowers Clinic. I got the answering service, but Dr. Hart called right back. She seemed concerned about you."

"She did?"

"Yes. She came and examined you and acted relieved when she found nothing seriously wrong."

The effort of trying to make sense of it all exhausted

Kate; she drifted off to sleep.

When she awoke, Dee smiled down at her.

Kate was wondering if she had only dreamed that Greg had been there, when Dee said, "Greg had to leave, but he said he'd come back later."

Kate struggled to sit up—she hated the thought of Greg seeing her as such a weakling—but she fell back on the pillows.

"Are you ready to eat something?" Dee asked.

Suddenly feeling famished, Kate nodded.

The soup Dee brought came from the same batch Kate had served to both of her visitors.

Kate ate a small spoonful, then greedily shoveled the rest into her mouth. Never had anything tasted so delicious.

Greg propped his elbows on his desk and rested his face in his hands. The brief uplift in spirits he had experienced when he'd seen that Kate would be okay had drained away; now he felt old and spent. He'd better be careful, or he'd end up flat on his back like Kate.

When had he last slept? Or eaten? He couldn't remember.

Oh, yes. He'd had a handful of walnuts and raisins last night before falling into a short, fitful sleep.

He rubbed his gritty eyes. Maybe he should forget about working today and go home, get some rest. If John Takamura had been the one to unleash the red death, he didn't need to hurry and prove it—the man was beyond human retribution.

And the publishers weren't paying him to work so hard; payday had come and gone, and he hadn't received a check.

Right now he didn't care about the money. He had paid his rent on the first of the month as usual, and since mail deliveries had ceased, he received no bills. Few stores or restaurants remained open, so he couldn't spend the money he still had.

But he did care about finding the secret behind the red death.

He took the leather-bound book out of his backpack, opened it, and lightly ran the tips of his fingers down a page like a blind man reading Braille. But the book kept its own counsel.

Something flew over his right shoulder and plopped on the desk in front of him.

The first section of today's paper.

He turned around and saw his boss looming over him. In his late fifties, Don Olaf was still a powerful man with little fat on his thick body. Even his wrists and forearms were thick, making him look more like a lumberjack than a newspaper editor. Greg had been surprised when Olaf began spending time with him every day. A dour Norwegian, Don Olaf seldom smiled, never laughed, and spoke as little as possible. Lately, though, he acted downright chatty.

The man felt lonely, Greg thought. Few people bothered to show up for work anymore: some because they lived too far away to make the daily commute; some because they were afraid of leaving their houses; some because they didn't like working without pay. Some because they were dead.

Greg didn't know how many of his colleagues had died; he and Olaf talked of numerous things, but they didn't mention the dead.

Greg leafed through the paper. "Twenty pages?" he asked. "That's slim for a first section on a Sunday."

Olaf sank heavily into the extra chair he'd brought into Greg's cubicle the first time he'd come to talk. "It's not the first section," he said. "It's the entire paper."

Shocked, Greg said, "The entire paper?"

Olaf winced. "Yes."

Greg looked through the paper. He found no advertisements, no press releases, no fluff articles, no inserts. He saw few national and fewer international news items. Financial news, reduced to half a page, recapped Friday's rise in the stock market, due to the containment of the red death.

Greg looked up. "Containment?"

"Meaning no deaths outside of quarantine areas."

"I was afraid that's what it meant."

Greg continued to leaf through the paper, finding both of his articles, the one about the computer chip implants, and the other one about the work brigades.

Again he looked up at Olaf. "I'm surprised they allowed you to print these."

Olaf shrugged. "By now everyone knows about the computer chips, and apparently FEMA doesn't care if people know about the work programs."

Greg turned back to the newspaper. He'd already scanned everything but the classified ad section: a single page of ads, all of which consisted of pleas for information about missing persons.

Olaf's restless gaze settled on the leather-bound book atop Greg's desk. "What's that?"

Greg handed it to him. "Your guess is as good as mine."

Olaf opened it. "Japanese?"

"Supposedly."

Greg told Olaf about his visit to the Buddhist temple. At the end of the recital, the editor raised his eyebrows.

"Cryptic," he said.

Greg nodded. "I thought so."

As Olaf studied the book, Greg asked, "Do you know anyone who can read Japanese?"

"Clara D'Onofrio."

"The financial news reporter?"

"Sure. Smart woman. Back in the eighties when the Japanese were buying the whole damn country, she figured she ought to learn. So she did."

Greg didn't know why he felt surprised. Clara looked capable of doing anything she set her mind to, even demolishing a small country if she so desired. She was a big woman—tall and broad, though not fat—with a look of determination on her square-jawed face, and more silver than black in her thick head of hair.

Despite her undainty appearance, or perhaps because of it, she wore flared skirts with frilly blouses and soft challis dresses cut on the bias. Interestingly, the frivolous clothes made her seem even more intimidating, rather than less.

"I'll be seeing Clara later," Olaf said diffidently.

Greg smiled to himself. So the rumor about the recently divorced Olaf and the long divorced Clara having an affair proved true.

"If you wish," Olaf continued, "I could show the book to her."

Greg hesitated. He hated letting the book out of his sight, but even more, he hated the thought of having to confront the woman. Whenever their paths had crossed, her deep-set steely gray eyes had regarded him with disapproval, though he didn't know what he had done to offend her.

In the end, realizing Clara would probably be more willing to do the translation for Olaf than for him, he let Olaf take the book.

Pippi awoke. Still in the throes of her dream, she thought she was home. Without warning, full consciousness slammed into her.

Stomach lurching, she sat up and stared at the empty fields, then at Jeremy nibbling on a piece of chocolate.

She cringed. He looked so foolish sitting there with the boy's jeans wrapped around his neck like a shawl.

Then she glanced down at herself, at the bloody clothes she'd put on during the night.

She closed her eyes. This could not be happening.

Suddenly her eyes flew open.

*Chocolate!*

She scrabbled around in her pockets and triumphantly pulled out a candy bar. She ripped off the wrapper, broke off a chunk, and crammed it into her mouth.

The chocolate stuck to her palate; she couldn't find enough saliva to swallow it.

"You're dehydrated," Jeremy said. "Eat some snow."

She shook her head, thinking about dysentery and typhoid and malaria—no, wait; malaria came from mosquitoes, didn't it?

She tried to ignore her thirst, but images of lakes, of

rivers, of waterfalls, of drinking fountains, of tall glasses of water, pushed everything else out of her mind.

With a whimper, like a mewling kitten, she jumped to her feet, rushed to the nearest snowdrift, and scooped up a handful of snow.

"Take it from the center," Jeremy said. "It's safer."

She threw a resentful glance at him, but obeyed. She took a mouthful of the snow and let it melt before swallowing it. She closed her eyes, savoring the feel of the cold liquid trickling down her parched throat. She rubbed some snow on her chapped lips, then took another mouthful.

"Don't eat too much," Jeremy said. "You don't want to lower your body temperature."

Gritting her teeth, she squeezed the snow into a ball, but then she dropped it, unable to muster the energy to throw it at him.

She returned to the outspread coats and sat facing away from him. What right did he have to keep telling her what to do? He wasn't the boss of her.

She finished eating her chocolate bar, making it last as long as possible.

"Time to go," Jeremy said. He stood and tugged at the coats she sat on.

She got to her feet, grabbed one of the coats, and tied it around her waist. She stared defiantly at him, but he nodded in approval.

The field where they spent the night had been flat and even, but the farther they had traveled, the bumpier the fields had become.

The field they now hiked across had been disked and the soil lay in huge frozen clods. Pippi kept tripping, and even Jeremy stumbled once or twice.

When her left foot slipped between two of the rock-like clumps of dirt, she fell.

Jeremy held out his hand to help her up, but she batted it away.

"I can't do this anymore," she said, massaging her ankle.

"Yes, you can." Then he added, "What other choice do you have?"

"We could walk along the road."

He shook his head.

"Why not?"

"Three vehicles passed us about a mile back. I didn't get a clear look at them, but one was green, one was red, and one was silver."

She stared at him for a moment, then looked away. "You're making that up."

"I wish I were," he said quietly.

"How come you didn't tell me before?"

"I didn't want to alarm you."

She bit her lip. "Do you think they're looking for us?"

"Could be. Could be they're just looking for any kind of trouble."

She remained silent for a long while, but she wasn't thinking things over; her mind was a complete blank.

Finally, she rose. They continued to hike across the field.

"What's that?" Jeremy asked, squinting at the fortress-like structure on the horizon.

Pippi raised the binoculars to her eyes. "Looks like a cornfield."

"Let me see." Jeremy held out a hand for the binoculars, but she held them out of reach.

*What had gotten into her?* "For cripes sake," he said. "I'll give them right back."

She eyed him for a moment, then removed the binoculars from around her neck and handed them to him.

Peering through the binoculars, he could see the cornfield clearly. The brown desiccated stalks seemed dense and covered many acres. A river ran along the right rim of the field, the road ran along the left, and a second field lay on the other side of the road.

He lowered the binoculars to get a panoramic view, then raised them to his eyes again.

Because traveling on the road was not an option, they

would have to fight their way through the cornfield, but he didn't like it. The stalks should have been cut down during harvest, plowed under, or baled; they should not still be standing.

When he handed the binoculars back to Pippi, he kept his eyes focused on the strange field.

The closer they got to the corn, the more his sense of foreboding grew.

Maybe the road would be safer after all? No. Better to choose an imagined threat over a real one any day.

When he entered the cornfield and saw the stalks closing in over his head, his heart beat faster and icy beads of sweat chilled his brow. He wiped his clammy hands on his pants and forced himself to relax.

He looked around. A wide path cut through the corn, and the tall stalks afforded some protection from the incessant wind.

He stopped short. What was that?

He listened, but did not hear anything out of the ordinary.

*Man, you've got yourself spooked. Get your head straight!*

As he hurried to catch up to Pippi, he heard the noise once more.

Was something shuffling through the corn?

He stopped.

Listened.

Heard only the wind rustling the dry corn stalks.

He started walking again. Straining his ears, he thought he could hear the sound of footsteps, not in sync with his but a fraction of a second later, like an echo.

Maybe it was an echo? It couldn't be. He barely made any noise.

He moved faster; so did the furtive footsteps.

Pippi stopped and waited for him. "Did you hear something?" she asked. "I thought I heard footsteps."

"Me too."

She shivered. "It's like *The Children of the Corn.*"

He heard a metallic thunk. A rifle being cocked?

Without warning, Pippi took off running.

He hesitated a moment, then he trotted after her.

The first time Greg had stepped into the vacant apartment in the art deco building on Pennsylvania Street, he had felt right at home. The thick walls created an oasis of quiet in the noisy Capitol Hill neighborhood, and the high ceilings and large windows had made the small rooms appear spacious.

He had furnished his new home simply.

The bedroom contained a dresser, his grandmother's cane-seated rocker, and a double bed covered with the burgundy and green comforter his mother had made for him.

The dining alcove served as an office.

In the living room, two recliners with a small table between them sat before a large-screen television. Several framed photographs of his family and a studio portrait of Pippi adorned the walls, along with a picture of a clown's face—a remnant of his childhood.

Greg had never liked that picture—the clown's knowing leer seemed to say, "If you think things are bad now, just you wait." In fact, when he was very young, he had been so afraid of the clown he had slept with his back to it. He had no idea why he had kept it all these years.

His high school wrestling trophies resided on top of a bookcase crammed with review copies of books from work. The newspaper received more books to review than the book section editor and her staff could possibly peruse. They dumped the ones they couldn't get to on a table for anyone working at the newspaper to read then write about. As a neophyte reporter, Greg had latched onto many of the volumes, finding a special joy in reading books not yet available in stores.

The apartment had fit Greg like a comfortable pair of slippers, but now it pinched. He lay on the neatly made bed, knowing he needed to get some rest. He bobbed up.

Maybe he should eat first.

He went into the tiny kitchen, opened the refrigerator. Closed it. Opened the freezer. Closed it. Both were still well stocked with food, which pleased him since he couldn't bear the idea of having a computer chip stuck in him, but nothing caught his fancy.

Maybe he should rest first.

On the way back to bed, he stopped in the living room and surveyed the piles of paper covering the floor.

He still hadn't sorted through all the papers Ann Takamura had given him, but he had looked at enough of them to know she'd been right—they were worthless, though apparently they had meant something to John's mother.

Besides saving her husband's papers with the Anti-Epidemic Water Supply Unit letterhead, John's mother had kept the bits and pieces marking her son's growth: essays, drawings, tests, and elementary school report cards (studies hard, they all said, but doesn't get along well with others), as well as the greeting cards he had sent her over the years.

She had also kept cash register receipts, thousands of them, some so yellowed and faded with age they were unreadable. Why had she kept them? Had someone once told her to save all her receipts, without telling her why or for how long?

Unable to help himself, Greg picked his way through the piles of paper and knelt beside the trash bag he had yet to empty. He stuck his hand into the bag and pulled out a wad of paper.

More receipts.

He went through them one by one, then dropped them on the pile of receipts he had already examined.

He leaned back on his heels and once again studied the papers spread out before him.

The truth or the link to the truth lay there; he could feel it reaching out to him.

"You think you're so smart," he said to the clown, "you tell me where it is."

The clown leered at him.

\* \* \*

When they reached a small clearing in the cornfield, Jeremy stopped and turned to look behind him. He tilted his head, as if listening.

"Do you think they're still after us?" Pippi asked. She could hear the panic in her voice, and she hoped Jeremy hadn't noticed, though why she cared, she didn't know. He already thought she was a loser, so what difference did it make?

"I don't hear anyone," Jeremy said, "or anything. It could have been an animal."

Pippi shook her head. The image she had of evil children silently moving among the corn stalks was too vivid for her to be able to believe anything else.

Frowning, Jeremy looked around again.

"What's wrong?" she asked.

"We've been running for so long, we should have been out of this field by now." He jumped, jumped again. "It's no use. I can't see over the damn stalks. Come here."

She stepped back, eyeing him with suspicion.

"Oh, for cripes sake," he said. "I only want to lift you so you can see where we are."

Feeling foolish, she moved toward him. He bent his knees, grasped her beneath her buttocks, and lifted her. Steadying herself with her hands on his shoulders, she strained to look.

"What do you see?" he asked.

"Corn stalks. Looks like we're in the center of the field."

"Can you see a way out?"

"I see the path, but it meanders all over the place." Then she gasped. "I know where we are, and if you're depending on me to get us out, we're dead."

He let her down none too gently. Seizing her arms, he looked her in the eyes and demanded, "What are you talking about?"

"We're in a maze," she said.

"We're amazed?" he asked. "What does that mean?"

"We are in a maze," she repeated, punctuating each word with a giggle.

"A maze? You mean like a labyrinth?"

"Yep." She giggled again. "That must have been the Minotaur coming after us."

He grasped her arms again and shook her. "You're not making any sense."

She wrenched away and glared at him. "Ow. That hurt."

"At least you're not hysterical anymore."

"I was not hysterical," she said. "I thought it was funny."

"Explain it to me. I could do with a good laugh."

In a sing-song voice, as if telling a story to a small child, she said, "The people who own this farm got fed up with all the government controls and price-fixing, so one year they decided to do a field of dreams sort of thing, only instead of a baseball field, they built a maze. It became so successful they do it every year now. It's unbelievable. People come from all over the country, even from other countries, just to go through this silly maze. The owners make a fortune. They even have a gift shop now and sell all sorts of corn and maze related items."

Pippi giggled again. "I wonder if that's what gave them the idea—maize and maze, get it?"

Jeremy bared his teeth in a mock smile. "I get it. Very funny."

"That wasn't the joke," Pippi said. "The joke is I can't do mazes. Even if you could hold me up to study the paths for a thousand years, I still wouldn't be able to find the way out of here."

"If I lift you again, would you be able to see which direction we were traveling before we got lost in this field?"

"I already saw." Pointing at each direction in turn, she said, "That's where we came in. That's the road. That's the house." She stopped and stared at Jeremy. "The house! We can go to the house. I'm sure they'd help us. I got along with the old man when we filmed his maze." Then her excitement faded. "We still have to get out of here." .

"No problem," Jeremy said. "It's not as if these are brick walls."

He spread the stalks apart and disappeared into the corn.

A few seconds later, he poked his head out.

"You coming?"

She hesitated. Then, with the image of the evil children still filling her head, she followed.

After a while, Jeremy said, "These people may have made a fortune off their maze, but they still harvested their corn. There aren't any ears left on the stalks."

The thought of piping hot corn on the cob slathered with butter made Pippi's mouth water. As if her hunger had conjured it up, a lone ear of corn appeared on a stalk ahead of her.

"Food," she exclaimed, pouncing on it. She ripped off the husks and bit down, almost breaking her teeth on the desiccated corn. Sick with disappointment, she flung it to the ground.

"Are you nuts?" Jeremy said, retrieving the ear of corn and sticking it in his pocket. "That might keep us from starving to death."

By the time they finished crashing through the maze, they had found two more ears of corn, several empty beer and pop cans, and a plastic bottle containing an inch of water. Jeremy acted pleased with the treasure, but Pippi felt like a bag lady—probably looked like one, too.

As they approached the house, the farmer's wife came out onto the porch and pointed a shotgun at them.

"Stay where you are," she called out.

Pippi and Jeremy stopped and raised their hands.

"Who are you?" the old woman demanded. "What do you want?"

"I'm Pippi O'Brien from Channel Ten in Denver, and this is—"

The old woman pumped the shotgun. "I know who you are, you hussy. We don't want the likes of you around here. Now go on, git."

"Our car got stolen," Pippi said. "We don't have any food—"

"I said git." The old woman waved them away with the gun. "There's no law around these parts—red death got them all—so I can pump you full of lead if you don't go, and no one will care. Hell, I might do it anyway."

"I'm Jeremy King," Jeremy said. "I—"

"I don't care who you are." The woman raised the gun as if to shoot.

Pippi and Jeremy were well outside of shotgun range when they stopped running.

"What did you do?" Jeremy asked. "Flirt with her husband?"

"Of course not. The old goat came on to me."

Jeremy laughed. "So, do you have any more bright ideas?"

"You're one to talk," Pippi said crossly. "You stood there and didn't do a damn thing. You could have shot the old hag."

"No, no," he said chuckling. "You did fine all on your own, you hussy."

At dusk, they set up camp by a stand of trees that provided a windbreak. They found some dry twigs and made a fire using a mostly empty book of matches Pippi found at the bottom of her purse.

Jeremy cut the tops off the cans they had scrounged, filled them with snow, and put them on the fire to boil.

He cut the dry kernels of corn off the cobs and dropped them in three of the cans.

He cleaned the water bottle with boiling water that had cooled enough not to melt the plastic, then filled it with more of the water, and set it aside for tomorrow's journey.

When the corn had plumped, they ate it along with the pot liquor. It didn't have the flavor of fresh corn on the cob with butter, but it tasted mighty fine, especially with a chocolate bar for dessert.

# 16

*Monday, December 12 (a.m.)*

Kate lay still, feeling her heart beat, feeling the blood pulse through her body. She stretched, and felt her muscles respond.

So it was true: she really was alive.

*Alive!*

Joy bubbled up from a well deep within her, and suddenly all things seemed possible.

She jumped out of bed like a child on Christmas morning, ran to the window, and opened the drapes.

It looked as dim as dusk. The sunless sky embraced heavy dark clouds that hung so low she was sure she could reach out and touch them. The howling wind blew a few snowflakes around and rattled her leaky window. The icy draft made her shiver.

She laughed aloud.

*What a lovely day!*

"You shouldn't be up."

Kate turned and smiled radiantly at Dee. "I feel great."

"But Dr. Hart said—"

Kate chuckled. "Don't tell me you believe in doctors, after all they put you through."

"No, but—"

"Don't worry. I'll be sure to tell Dr. Hart you tried your best to keep me in bed."

Dee shook her head, but made no further protest.

Kate peered at her. "You okay?"

Dee shrugged.

Frowning, Kate continued to study her.

The woman, who had looked so old and shriveled in the park had expanded into a fiftyish, big-boned woman with a pleasant face, but now she appeared shriveled again.

All at once, Kate understood. "Don't go," she said. "Stay here and keep me company."

Hating the idea of Dee being back on the streets but not wanting the woman to know of her concern, Kate had blurted out the first thing that popped into her mind. The more she considered it, though, the more she liked the idea. It had been years since she'd had a friend, and perhaps she and Dee needed each other.

When Dee remained silent, Kate said, laughing, "I need you. What if I fall and hit my head on the toilet bowl again?"

Dee smiled noncommittally and said, "Oatmeal for breakfast?"

While Dee fixed the oatmeal, Kate showered and got dressed for work.

They ate in silence, and when Kate left to go to the clinic, she still didn't know whether Dee would be there when she got home.

Dr. Hart stormed into Kate's office, stood with her hands on her hips, and glared. "I couldn't believe it when Joan told me you came to work today. I gave those friends of yours strict orders you were to stay in bed for several days."

Kate opened her mouth, but the doctor didn't give her a chance to speak.

"What did you do to yourself?" She bent forward, regarded Kate with narrowed eyes, then jerked back and stared at her in astonishment. "You're wearing make-up!"

"Lipstick," Kate said self-consciously.

Dr. Hart smirked.

"What?" Kate said.

"He is gorgeous, your young man."

"Who? You mean Greg? He's just a friend."

"Sure," Dr. Hart said with an exaggerated wink. "Just a friend."

Kate laughed. "You always did have a dirty mind, Amanda. If you must know, he's engaged to Pippi O'Brien."

Dr. Hart nodded reflectively. "That makes more sense than . . ."

"Than me and Greg," Kate finished.

"To be honest, yes." Her eyebrows drew together. "If it's not your gorgeous young man, who is it? Who's the guy?"

"What guy?" Kate asked, not bothering to keep the

exasperation out of her voice.

"The one who put the twinkle back in your eyes."

Kate smiled. "There is no guy. I made an important discovery this morning, is all."

"What discovery?" The doctor's pager beeped. She looked at it, then ran off without waiting for Kate's response.

Kate answered anyway, wanting to proclaim the miraculous truth.

"I am alive."

Greg arrived at the newspaper earlier than usual, anxious to see if Clara D'Onofrio had translated the leather-bound book, but he didn't find her in the office.

When Don Olaf stopped by Greg's cubicle for his morning chat, Greg pumped him for information, but Olaf didn't know if Clara planned to work today, didn't know if she translated the book, didn't know if she had even looked at it.

Alone again, Greg sat with his feet propped on his desk, cracking walnuts and eating the meat while he waited for Clara. When ten o'clock rolled around and the woman still hadn't appeared, he decided he needed to stop wasting time.

He dropped his feet to the floor and called GeneCo. A female who sounded young and sullen answered the phone. She connected him to Charles Guest's voice mail.

When he called Guest's home phone, a machine greeted him.

He called GeneCo back and asked the sullen female if she knew whether Charles Guest had come to work. She didn't say anything but rang him through to Guest's voice mail again.

Remembering Jack Thornton's enthusiasm for the red death and his certainty that most research labs in the area were busy because of it, Greg thought Guest might be too engrossed to answer the phone.

Perhaps if he went to the lab in person, he could entice the man away from his work for a short interview.

\* \* \*

GeneCo took up an entire block on Federal Boulevard where once a crumbling strip shopping center had stood. The cinderblock exterior had been painted a blinding white, but even so, the huge building with its tiny windows had the forbidding appearance of a county jail. The razor wire topping the fence and the guard booth by the gate made the place look impregnable, but no one attended the booth or stopped Greg from entering the building.

The receptionist looked exactly as Greg had pictured—young, sullen-faced, lank-haired, and pierced in places too painful to contemplate. She did not fit in with the severe aspect of the building. Considering the havoc the red death had wreaked on Denver's work force, the company had probably counted itself lucky to find anyone willing to answer the phones.

The girl—no way could Greg call her a woman—smacked her chewing gum and studied the elaborate designs painted on her fingernails.

She did not look up at his approach, not even when he pointedly cleared his throat and announced, "I have an appointment with Charles Guest."

She held one hand out at arms length, scrutinized it, then, frowning, brought it in close again. She raised the hem of her cropped tee shirt to buff her nails, giving Greg an inadvertent view of the three small moles on her breasts.

After repositioning her shirt, she glanced at him. Her eyes widened and her lips parted.

"Who are you?" she asked, locking her gaze onto his.

"Greg Pullman. I'm a journalist."

"TV?" she asked eagerly.

"Newspaper."

"Oh." She tilted her head to one side and touched a finger to her lips, obviously trying to look coy, but only managing to look childish. "You should be on TV," she said, as if imparting words of great wisdom.

Greg forced himself to smile. "Would you please tell me where I can find Charles Guest?"

The girl's face scrunched, like a child getting ready to

cry. "I can't."

"Then would you get him on the phone for me?"

She looked at him with large doe eyes; after a moment of visible indecision, she crooked a finger at him.

He leaned across the counter.

"I'm not supposed to tell," she said in a loud whisper. "My boss doesn't want anyone to know that some of the scientists have died." Then, in a deep voice, as if imitating someone, she added, "It's bad for business."

Greg straightened. "Are you saying Charles Guest is dead?"

She pointed to the center of the bleak reception area. "Right there. That's where Dr. Guest got the red death."

So, another biogeneticist killed by the chimera. And GeneCo lay even closer to the Broncos stadium where the red death originated than did Takamura's office in Auraria.

Greg frowned. Maybe the red death had nothing to do with Takamura. A mere hunch had made him focus on Takamura in the first place.

"Do you know what Dr. Guest worked on?" he asked.

She shook her head. "I only know he worked in the restricted area."

"Did he have a partner? Or a lab assistant?"

"Matt Baxter."

"Is he here today?"

"I think so."

"Will you see if he'll speak to me?" Greg asked trying to remain patient. Talking to this girl felt like wading through a pool filled with gelatin.

She hesitated a moment, then reached for the phone.

"He'll be right down," she said, hanging up. She looked at Greg, then glanced away. "Can I ask you some-thing?"

"Sure."

"Will you go out with me sometime?"

"No," he said, hoping she didn't notice his involuntary recoil. Then, remembering how terrifying it could be to ask for a date, he added gently, "I'm engaged, but I appreciate the invitation."

She pouted and turned her back on him.

He had to put up with a few minutes of her surreptitious dirty looks before a stocky man who looked like a linebacker charged into the reception area.

"Dr. Baxter," he said, grasping Greg's hand, "but everyone calls me Matt."

"I had an appointment with Charles Guest," Greg said, sticking with his lie. "I'm told he's not here today. Perhaps you could help me."

"With what?"

"Well, for starters, what he's working on."

Matt giggled, an incongruous sound coming from such a large man. "Boy, you don't beat around the bush, do you?"

Greg smiled and waited for him to get to the point.

"I'm surprised Charles agreed to see you," he said. "It's too early to publicize our results in the daily press. Usually we're published in a scientific journal first, and we're not ready for that yet."

"Charles said he'd talk off the record."

"Well, then," Matt said, sounding doubtful. "Come. It's probably best if I show you."

Greg followed him down a welter of corridors. They passed through two doors containing retina scanners and one with an airlock before reaching Matt's laboratory. The scientist unlocked the door with a key card and turned to face Greg. "You're the first outsider ever to see this." He opened the door and, with a flourish, ushered Greg inside.

Greg stood and stared. Green mice? *That's* what this was all about?

"This is one of the greatest breakthroughs in energy the world has ever seen," Matt proclaimed. "We have managed to enhance these mice with chlorophyll-creating genes." He pointed to a glass-enclosed cage where mice of varying shades of green scampered about. "How long do you think it's been since these little guys have eaten?"

Looking at the lively creatures, Greg shrugged. "I don't know. A couple of hours maybe."

"Three weeks. See these lights above the cage? They're

full spectrum fluorescent lights, which simulate sunlight. The mice create all the energy they need directly from the light. All we feed them is water. Just think, in the future humans will be able to forego eating."

Trying to picture a world full of green people, Greg asked, "What about fall and winter? Wouldn't they have to eat then?"

"Good question. Unfortunately, I don't have the answer yet. That's why this is off the record. It's premature."

"I understand," Greg said, wondering if Matt was hoaxing him.

"Considering that most people spend all their time indoors," Matt said, "I don't foresee any problems as long as they use full spectrum lights. I think we're through here. I'll take you back to reception now."

As Greg followed the scientist, he asked his standard questions. Matt said he'd known Takamura, didn't know anything about bio-weapons or the red death. He delivered these terse answers in a bored monotone, but as soon as he started speaking about his green mice again, his voice became reanimated.

Listening to the man talk about his work gave Greg a new awareness of the scientific mind. It chilled him to think the creator of the red death was probably as ordinary as Matt. And as obsessed.

For the second time that morning, someone charged into Kate's office and stood before her desk with hands on hips. Greg, however, didn't glare; he looked at her in concern.

"Weren't you supposed to stay at home today?" he asked. "I stopped by your house to see how you felt, but no one answered the door."

Kate felt a pang of disappointment that Dee hadn't accepted her offer of a place to live, but she consoled herself with the thought that she had tried to help.

She brushed her hair off her forehead and smiled at Greg. "You don't need to scold me. Amanda—Dr. Hart— already did that. And anyway, I feel great."

"You look great," Greg said, then added with a hint of surprise in his voice, "really great."

Kate flushed under his intent gaze, but managed a lighthearted laugh. "I bet you say that to all the middle-aged women you snatch from the brink of death."

He pursed his lips in a silent whistle. "Middle-aged? Today you don't look a day over twenty-five."

"Yeah, right."

"Okay, twenty-six."

They sparkled at each other, then Kate said softly, "I didn't thank you for helping me and for being there when I woke. So, thank you. It meant more to me than you can ever imagine."

He shrugged. "I didn't do much."

"But you came. I still can't get over that."

"I was glad to do it. Now you can do a favor for me."

"Anything."

"Come to lunch with me."

"Where? No place is open."

He smiled.

Her eyes widened. "You mean The Black Forest is still open for business?"

He nodded. "Unbelievable, isn't it?"

"I told you Lottie was an amazing woman, but even I didn't realize how amazing." She jumped up from her chair. "Come on, what are we waiting for?"

Compared to the rest of the moribund city, The Black Forest teemed with activity. Kate and Greg had to wait a few minutes before someone noticed they needed a seat.

Lottie, who had been making coffee, was the first to glance their way. She dropped the filters and hurried toward them.

Though people often used spry to describe active octogenarians, it never came to mind when Kate thought of Lottie. The woman was as wrinkled as an apple-headed doll, but she moved about on sturdy legs that showed little sign of their great age.

Her still strong hands gripped Kate's. "Good to see you," she said with a complacent air, as if, despite living in a city where so many had died, she had somehow known Kate would survive.

Kate laughed and shook her head. "Leave it to you to still be open for business in the midst of an epidemic."

"Well, I have to be," Lottie said. "My regulars depend on me. They know eating good, hearty food, made with fresh, wholesome ingredients, like butter and eggs, is the way to stay healthy."

"Do many of your regulars still come in?" Kate asked, making conversation.

"All of them," Lottie answered.

Kate blinked. "All?" She turned to Greg; he shrugged as if to say he didn't understand it either.

Lottie sighed. "George Pappado died, but that's because his wife made him stop coming here—said he had to watch his weight. Now they're both gone. And Lucy, my waitress who poked all those holes in her ears, died too. She wouldn't eat here, even though she earned a free meal. She preferred to waste her money at those fast food places."

"Anyone else?" Kate asked.

"Heather, the teenage daughter of one of my regulars, but she refused to eat when she came here. You're young, Kate. Tell me, why do these skinny girls think they need to get even skinnier?"

"Maybe because it's all they feel they have any control over," Kate said absently, her mind still focused on the regulars.

Lottie nodded. "Makes sense. It's a hard world out there."

"What about your regulars—the ones who actually eat here," Kate asked. "Did any of them die?"

"None that I know of."

Kate didn't know what to make of Lottie's declaration, and when her eyes met Greg's, she could tell he felt at a loss, too.

"Well," Lottie said briskly, putting an end to the

Pat Bertram

conversation, "I'm sure you young people would rather talk to each other than to an old woman like me. There's a nice private table over there in the corner you can have."

"May we sit at that table by the window?" Greg asked, pointing to the table where he and Kate had eaten the previous week.

Lottie's eyes twinkled. "He speaks."

Kate flushed. "I'm sorry. Lottie, this is Greg Pullman. Greg, Lottie."

"Pleased to meet you," Lottie said. Bright-eyed, she looked from one to the other.

Kate laughed. "It's not what you think. We're friends."

The old woman smiled and nodded, as if to say she knew better.

"Don't mind Lottie," Kate said after the old woman had shown them to their table and left them alone with their menus. "She has three interests in life—food, her family, and romance. Trouble is, she thinks she can detect romance, but it's often only in her own mind."

"I thought she was cute," Greg said. Looking around, he added, "A lot of people are working here today, way more than last week."

Kate smiled at a little girl who, with unwavering concentration, carried two glasses of water. The girl carefully set the glasses on their table, then ran off, giggling.

"That was Jennifer, Sally's daughter. Sally is that woman taking that old man's order. She's one of Lottie's grandchildren and works for a software company. The waiter is Ben, a tax consultant." The man turned, giving Kate a better look at his face. "No, wait. I think that's Rick." She laughed. "All the Untermeyers look alike to me."

"They do all look alike," Greg said. "It's amazing how some genes are passed from generation to generation without any discernable change."

Watching Lottie grin as she hugged her great-granddaughter, Kate said, "No wonder Lottie's so happy. She always wanted her family, especially the younger generations, to be a part of the business, but so many of them

144

had other plans."

Turning to look at Greg, she said, "It seems wrong to be happy at a time like this."

He gave her a puzzled glance. "It doesn't sound like you to begrudge Lottie her happiness."

Confused, Kate stared back at him. "Lottie? You think I—? Oh, no. I didn't mean that. Lottie deserves all the happiness she can get. I meant me."

"You don't think you deserve to be happy?" Greg asked.

"Well, yes, but not now. It's making me inured to all the suffering. I didn't get choked up or anything when Lottie told us about those people who died."

"Did you know them?"

"Not by name. Maybe by sight."

"You can't cry over every single person who's died in the past ten days. No one has enough tears for that. A wise woman once told me 'there's nothing wrong with being happy. There's enough misery in the world as it is.' Then she said, 'Happiness is fleeting. You have to enjoy it while you can, regardless of circumstances.'"

Kate nodded. "Good advice. Who said that?"

"You don't remember?"

"No."

Greg laughed. "You did. Last week. Sitting at this very table."

His laughter faded. As he turned to look out the window, Kate caught a glimpse of the bleakness in his eyes, and she knew he was thinking about Pippi. Would he consider it intrusive of her to ask what had happened?

Before she could open her mouth, he said, "It's so different today from last week. Then traffic clogged the streets. Now they're practically empty."

"It feels like a lifetime ago," Kate said.

A smiling woman, who looked like a slightly younger version of Lottie, came to the table and held out her arms. "Kate, my dear, it's so nice to see you."

Kate stood and submitted to the embrace, uncomfortable as always with the woman's exuberant shows of affection;

but then, all at once, her self-consciousness evaporated, and she hugged the woman back.

It really was good to be alive.

She turned to Greg and said, "I'd like you to meet my mother's friend, Elspeth Landrum. Lottie's daughter."

Greg rose and held out a hand, but Elspeth grabbed him and gave him a hug.

"Be good to her," she whispered, loud enough for Kate to hear. "She's had a rough time of it."

Then, like her mother, Elspeth glanced from one to the other with twinkling eyes. After a moment, she asked, "What will you kids have? There's a great chicken soup. You should start with that. Then how about roast beef, mashed potatoes and gravy, corn with lima beans, and cherry torte for dessert. I think that should do it for you. Also a nice, hot cup of tea. Anything else?"

"No," Greg said, looking dazed. When Elspeth hurried off, he asked Kate, "What are you going to order?"

Kate laughed. "I think I'll have the roast beef."

"Me too," he said. Then, "Jeez, is the whole family like that?"

"Pretty much. Lottie's husband was quiet and re-served, but he claimed the energy of his wife and offspring kept him feeling young. He died last year at the age of ninety-three."

"I didn't see Elspeth last week. Is she helping out temporarily, like Sally and the others?"

"No. She usually works in the office here, ordering supplies, scheduling catering jobs, things like that. Oh! Now I understand how they can still be in business in spite of the food shortage. A catering service makes all its arrangements well in advance; they'd have all the food they ordered for the Christmas parties and banquets that aren't taking place because of the red death."

Greg took a sip of water. "How can Lottie know that none of her customers have died?"

"She didn't mean all of her customers, just her regulars—the ones who come in every day or almost every day. She knows their names, what time they come, and what they like to eat. She would notice if one went missing. What I find interesting is that she's so sure it's good food that's preventing them from dying."

"Do you think there's any truth to that?"

"I don't know, but something's keeping them alive."

"You're alive too," Greg said. "And we know you were exposed to the red death at least twice. What do you have in common with her regulars?"

"Not much. I haven't been eating any good meals at all."

"But you do eat butter."

"True. About all I've been able to eat since this whole thing started is bread and butter. What about you?"

"I don't usually eat butter."

"What do you eat?"

"Lately? Mostly walnuts and raisins." He smiled at her. "I'm a good cook, thanks to my mother, but I haven't felt like taking the time."

"Butter and walnuts both contain fat. I wonder if fat has some inhibiting factor on the red death." She looked off into the distance, thinking about it. "Can't be just any fat. Rachel Abrams, the first woman I saw die, was such a strict vegetarian, she wouldn't even touch butter, and she had an allergy to nuts. She did use vegetable oils, though not olive oil—couldn't stand the taste. And the Grover boy ate a lot of fried foods."

"Who's the Grover boy?"

"I think I told you about the Grovers. The father and sister went to that Broncos game, but they came down with something resembling the twenty-four hour flu. The boy caught the red death from them and died."

"Didn't the whole family eat the same meals?"

"The boy would only eat foods he could pick up with his fingers, like french fries, chicken nuggets, fish sticks, so Gillian microwaved a separate meal for him."

"Do you know what the father and sister ate?"

"Typical meals, I think, but I do know they were addicted to buttered popcorn, real buttered popcorn, not the microwave kind. Gillian once mentioned they'd burned out their popper, and had a hard time finding a replacement."

"What did Gillian herself eat?"

"She's been on a high protein diet and eats a lot of fish, including fatty fish like water-packed tuna and sardines in olive oil or tomato sauce. Another man I knew claimed he'd live forever because he exercised, ate mostly fruits and vegetables, used no fat. He ridiculed his wife's love of homemade cookies made with butter. He used to tell her about the young chicks he intended to boink—his word— when she was dead. She cried when he died. I don't know why."

Elspeth brought their soup and tea, gave them a knowing look, and left.

With obvious appreciation, Greg concentrated on eating his soup. When he finished, he pushed the bowl away. "Setting aside for the moment the possibility that some people have an innate immunity to the red death, what we have learned so far is people who eat vegetable oils, fried foods or, conversely, no fat, die when exposed to the red death, but people who eat butter, walnuts, and sardines in olive oil or tomato sauce survive."

"It's not conclusive," Kate said, "but there's a pattern."

"So what do walnuts, butter, and sardines have in common?"

"Boy, it's hard to say other than that they're all unmodified fats."

Greg laughed. "Well, jeez, why didn't I think of that? What the heck is an unmodified fat, anyway?"

"As I understand it, when fats are heated, particularly vegetable oils, they change and are no longer simple oils. They form carcinogenic solids. For some reason, butter doesn't have the same effect. When animals were fed heated oils and heated butter to note the effect on their health, all the oil-fed animals developed tumors, but none of the butter-fed animals did."

"Aren't vegetable oils good for us?"

"Only if you think cholesterol is a bad thing."

"It isn't?"

"No. If you don't eat dietary cholesterol, your body manufactures it."

He smiled at her. "How do you know all this?"

"I used to read a lot of nutrition and health books, trying to find ways to help Joe. We experimented with various diets and supplements, but nothing helped. I stopped using vegetable oil long before I ever read about the different kinds of fats. I used to oil my cookie sheets when I made French bread, and the oil baked on so hard I found it difficult to clean off. I figured since our bodies are slow-burning ovens, the oil would do the same thing to me it did to my cookie sheet, so I switched back to butter."

"What other foods contain unmodified fats?" Greg asked.

"Anything you eat raw, of course, such as nuts and seeds, and maybe fatty fish and fish oil supplements such as Omega 3."

"Pippi uses flaxseed."

"Then, if we're correct, she should be safe, too."

Elspeth bustled to the table with their entrees, told them they would enjoy their meal, scooped up the empty soup bowls, and hurried off again.

Greg pulled out his notebook and wrote in it while he ate. When he finished writing, he glanced up and gave a start, as if he had forgotten her.

Kate laughed. "Very flattering."

Looking sheepish, he slipped the notebook back in his pocket. "I tend to get carried away when I'm writing, but I wanted to make sure I got it all. It's worth looking into."

"I didn't mind," Kate said. "Anyway, I was teasing."

A gleam appeared in Greg's eyes, as if at a sudden memory. "I saw something today you might get a kick out of—green mice."

Kate swallowed her mouthful of roast beef too quickly. Choking, she said, "Green mice?"

"A scientist I interviewed told me he had added chlorophyll-producing genes to rodent DNA. Supposedly the mice haven't eaten in three weeks—they get all their energy from full spectrum lights. He thinks that in the future human DNA will be enhanced in the same way."

"Green people. Should be interesting. Did he happen to mention if they will breathe carbon dioxide?"

"No. He seemed long on enthusiasm, short on information."

"Well, considering the increasing carbon dioxide in the air, it might not be a bad thing if humans were less oxygen dependent. It sounds so fantastic. Do you think it's possible?"

"I don't know, but a few days ago I wouldn't have thought the red death possible, either."

Kate sighed. "It always comes down to that, doesn't it?"

"You know what I keep thinking?" Greg said. "Fifty or seventy-five years from now, the red death will have been forgotten."

"You think so?"

"I know so. In the last few years, there's been a resurgence of interest in the flu pandemic that occurred in the early part of the twentieth century, but before that, who ever heard about it? A staggering number of people died in that pandemic, too many to count, actually, but few mentioned it in literature or movies or even history books. And the red death doesn't even rate as a pandemic. It has spread as far as it's going to. The only people dying are those of us contained in quarantined areas, and I get the impression everyone else has already forgotten we exist."

"Do you think the whole story will ever be told?" Kate asked. "I don't mean just about the red death, but all of it— the martial law, the senseless slaughters, the—" She stopped, silenced by his shaking head.

"Half of what I write isn't getting into print now," he said. "Why would it be any different later? Oh, I'm sure a spate of books will be published giving sanitized versions of the whole ordeal, but even if the truth did manage to get out, the majority will not believe it because they won't want to believe it. Most people have this strange idea that if they believe something doesn't exist, then it doesn't exist. As if their opinion counts."

He looked at Kate and laughed. "Jeez, where did that come from? I'm the one who listens to other people's homegrown philosophies. I don't sprout my own."

"Sprout away," Kate said. "I don't often get to listen to someone philosophize. Mostly I get to listen to people talk about their aches and pains."

"I can talk about aches and pains, too," he assured her. He twisted his arm so it hung at an awkward angle. "It hurts when I do this."

Kate laughed at his antics. "Well then, don't do that."

# 17

*Monday, December 12 (p.m.)*

Greg walked Kate back to the Bowers Clinic after lunch. While they stood on the porch chatting, Joan came charging out and gave them a dirty look before hurrying down the street.

"This seems to be my day for getting dirty looks from young women," Greg said.

Kate waved her hand dismissively. "It's not you. She's angry that I have a date—well, you know what I mean—and she doesn't. Poor girl's been in a terrible mood lately. Last week Harley Reese picked her up hitchhiking. When he came by for her again after work, she had visions of living a life of luxury, but then he didn't call her, even though he said he would."

"Harley Reese? The billionaire?"

"The one and the same."

Greg looked thoughtful. "Interesting how his name keeps popping up."

Kate laughed. "I wouldn't know. I never heard of him until last week. I have to go," she added reluctantly. "I'm supposed to answer the phone while Joan's away."

Greg unlocked his bicycle, but didn't leave. They continued to talk until the ringing phone called Kate inside.

Kate answered the phone. "Bowers Clinic."

"I'd like to make an appointment," a tired-sounding woman said.

"What is the nature of your complaint?"

"Complaint? I don't have a complaint. It's my kids who have the complaint."

"You're making the appointment for your children?"

"No. For me."

Trying to make it as simple as possible for the harried woman, Kate asked, "Is this an emergency? Or do you need a check-up?"

"Yes," the woman said.

"Which?"

"Both. I'm calling to make an appointment for a check-up, but it's an emergency. I haven't been sleeping well, what with the worry over the red death and all, and I've been real tired lately since the kids are underfoot all day—there's no school, and they can't go out and play with their friends." She paused.

"Yes?" Kate said encouragingly.

The woman drew a ragged breath. "When I got up this morning my eyes were red. The kids thought I had the red death, so they took my keys, pushed me out of the house, and locked the door."

"Your kids locked you out of your house because they thought you have the red death?" Kate asked, shocked.

"Yes. They said I can't go back unless I get a note from my doctor saying I don't have the red death, but my doctor's dead and no one else can see me today."

"One of the doctors here will see you. Will two o'clock today be okay?"

"Fine."

"And your name?"

The woman hesitated for so long Kate wondered if they'd been disconnected.

"On second thought," the woman said. "Forget it. If those kids think they can do without me, let them try. I need a break, and the house is insured. I think I'll go stay with my sister for a while."

*I will not cry. I will not cry. I will not cry.*

Pippi put one foot in front of the other, mindlessly propelling herself forward. With each step she took, she repeated her mantra: I will not cry.

She had starved herself enough over the years to know her teariness stemmed from low blood sugar, but she doubted *he* would understand.

She raised her head to glare at Jeremy's back.

Nothing bothered him. The lack of food, of fresh water, of rest, seemed to give him strength; he strode across field after field without faltering, moving his head from side to side, continuously monitoring his surroundings. Not once did he turn around to see if she still trudged along behind him.

If she blubbered, though, she knew he would glance back and give her one of his withering looks.

Or maybe not. Maybe he had forgotten all about her.

The vision she had once had of them—king and queen of all they surveyed—had evaporated along with her belief that she would be embarking on a new career when they arrived in Hollywood. Since Jeremy didn't think she could succeed, maybe he wouldn't even try to help her. Might even dump her and go back to his wife.

At least she'd be away from Colorado and the red death.

But she'd be alone.

She brushed away an errant tear and put one foot in front of the other.

*I will not cry.*

Jeremy stopped and waited for Pippi to catch up.

"I need the binoculars," he said when she drew near.

She gave him a swift glance, then turned her head away.

Blowing out his pent-up breath, he held out his hand. In the stern but reasonable voice he employed when his wife got in one of her moods, he said, "Give me the binoculars."

Without looking at him, Pippi pulled the strap from around her neck and handed over the binoculars.

He focused on the horizon, relieved to see that a long row or two of pine trees—a windbreak, perhaps—lay ahead of them and not another cornfield maze where menace could hide.

He studied the countryside for a minute longer, but did not see anything to worry about.

Except the break in the weather.

He lowered the binoculars and tilted his head to look at the sky. The oppressive clouds that had darkened the morning had thinned to a bright silvery gray by early afternoon; now they were so wispy he could see patches of blue behind them.

The cloud cover had made the previous two nights bearable. Without it, the relative warmth of the day would escape into the atmosphere, and the temperature would plummet to a deadly low.

Perhaps if they could build a good enough fire they would be okay, but a fire big enough to warm them throughout the frigid night would announce their presence to the human wildlife for miles around.

A couple of hours of daylight remained; maybe the sky would cloud over again before nightfall.

Or maybe not, he thought, as the white wisps parted and the sun broke free.

He was looking off into the distance, considering the possibility of camping among the pine trees where there would be some shelter and plenty of firewood, when he saw a bright flash.

He raised the binoculars to his eyes.

A gust of wind rippled through the trees, parting the branches, and he saw it again.

Metal gleaming in the sunlight.

Jeremy tramped toward the row of pine trees, stopping every now and then to peer through the binoculars, but it wasn't until he was within a hundred yards of the trees that he could identify the source of the sporadic metallic flashes.

A small, involuntary groan escaped his lips.

"Let me look," Pippi said.

He turned to her, surprised to see that for once she had managed to keep up.

"I want to look," she insisted.

He handed her the binoculars. With a sidelong glance, she slipped the strap around her neck.

She lifted the binoculars to her eyes. "I don't see anything but those trees."

"If you look closely, you can see a fence with barbed wire at the top."

"What's the big deal about a fence? We've climbed over lots of barbed wire fences."

"Not ones like this," Jeremy said. "The barbed wire is much too high to have any effect on livestock, and if it's not a fence to corral livestock, there's not much reason for all that barbed wire."

"Except to keep people out."

"I know, but it feels wrong. Look at it. It's a ten-foot-tall fence topped with barbed wire, sandwiched between two concentrated rows of pine trees. It's too much. I mean, we're in the middle of nowhere."

"What are we going to do, go around it?"

"Probably. But before we go out of our way, I think we should check this place out. For all we know, it could be a Christmas tree farm owned by someone who likes privacy."

They walked the remaining distance to the trees, then fought their way through the pine branches. At the fence, they still couldn't see into the property; the trees on the other side obscured their view.

"There's a sign," Pippi said, pointing to a placard hanging on the fence several yards away. "I'm going to see what it says."

"Probably the name of the manufacturer," Jeremy grumbled, following her.

He read the sign, blinked, and read it again.

*KEEP OUT,* it said. *THREATENED AND ENDANGERED SPECIES.*

He looked from the sign to the top of the fence. Then he unrolled the bundle of their meager possessions, pulled out the extra bloodstained coat, wrapped the bundle again, and belted it to the small of his back. The coat he slung over a shoulder.

He started to climb the fence. "Come on," he said to Pippi.

"Are you nuts?" she exclaimed. "There's endangered species in there."

A faint smile curved his lips. "What are you expecting? Lions and tigers? This is southeastern Colorado. All we'll see, if we see any animals at all, is frogs and toads and lizards."

"Lizards?" she yelped.

"Tiny, harmless lizards."

He climbed a little more and looked back. She stood on the ground, looking up at him, wide-eyed.

"Come on," he said impatiently. "I know it's high, but it's a chain-link fence. Anyone can climb a chain-link fence. And I'll throw this coat over the barbed wire so you won't get hurt."

She still made no effort to move.

Amazed that he had to explain something so obvious, he said, "We need food and a place to spend the night. There must be a caretaker's cottage in here we can use."

She nodded and clambered up the fence behind him.

On the other side, they paused to catch their breath, then pushed their way through the pine branches.

They stood and stared.

In front of them lay a wide expanse of empty ground. On the other side of the expanse, about a tenth of a mile away, was a high double fence topped with concertina wire. Inside the fence stood a guard tower, and beyond the tower stretched many long, low buildings, like army barracks. A few people listlessly paced the patch of bare earth in front of the barracks. Two half-heartedly played catch. Most stood beside the buildings or leaned against them, doing nothing.

"I don't like this," Jeremy said. "Let's get out of here."

"What is this place?" Pippi asked. "A military prison?" She raised the binoculars to her eyes; then, gasping for breath, she dropped them to her chest. She turned and charged through the trees; scrambled over the fence; thrashed her way through the trees on the other side; took off running.

When Jeremy finally caught up to her, she was stumbling around, blinded by tears. He folded her in his arms and patted her on the back until her sobs subsided.

"What happened, honey? What did you see?"

"Children. Women with babies. Old people. And men, too." She started to cry again. "A small child was lying next to the fence. Vultures were eating its eyes, and nobody cared."

Jeremy stiffened. Then, placing his hands on her shoulders, he gently pushed her away from him and asked in a low, urgent voice, "Do you know where we are?"

She shook her head, but after a moment she said, "Near Granada, I think."

Bile rose to his throat. "Oh, my God."

She gazed up at him, her aquamarine eyes still swimming with tears. "What?"

"We have to get away from here. Right now."

Without checking behind him to see if she followed, he headed for the road. They would be able to move quickly on that smooth surface, and he wanted to put as much distance as possible between them and the so-called endangered species habitat before it got too dark to travel.

He kept to the road until the sun hung low in the sky, then he angled away from it, looking for a safe place for them to camp.

So far, no one had come after them, but he couldn't let down his guard. Surveillance cameras might have been concealed among the pines; perhaps, at this very moment, their pictures were being studied, copied, circulated.

At dusk, still not having found a place to hide out for the night, he climbed a small hill to survey the area. Except for a cluster of buildings, the land looked empty. A single leafless tree grew in front of the tall, rectangular house.

A bright light on a pole in the yard illuminated the property. He could see several vehicles parked by the house, but he saw no people, heard no dogs.

He did see, lying not far from his feet, two mounds of freshly turned earth, both about six feet long and approximately two and a half feet wide.

He was studying the house, looking for signs of habitation, when Pippi finally caught up to him.

"Hey," she said, panting, "there aren't any lights on in that house."

"I know. I'm going around back to see if those windows are dark, too. Maybe you should wait here."

She curled her hands into fists, and when he started down the hill, she trudged along.

"If we see somebody, let me do the talking," Jeremy said, though he didn't expect to encounter anyone. The place felt deserted.

He tried the doors and windows on the lower level of the darkened house. He found them locked, but he rammed the butt of a rifle through the small window in the back door. The sound of glass falling onto the floor inside the house resounded in the stillness. He waited for a minute. When no one came to check out the noise, he reached in through the broken window and opened the door.

The distinctive smell of death lingered in the stale air.

He shuddered at the thought of meeting with yet another dead body, but he steeled himself and stepped into the house. Pippi followed close on his heels.

They had entered by way of a kitchen. All was neat and tidy except for a half-eaten sandwich and a glass of milk on the chrome and Formica table.

Hunger cramped his midsection, doubling him over. He forced himself upright. With a volition of its own, his hand reached out, but he managed to haul it back.

Pippi darted around him and grabbed the sandwich. She let out a small cry of despair when it crumbled between her fingers. She snatched the glass of milk, but set it down again, wrinkling her nose.

"We need to check out the house first," Jeremy said, "then we'll see about finding something to eat."

They left the kitchen and stepped into a large living/dining room area. The dining room table was piled high with rolls of brightly colored paper, ribbons, and bags full of gifts waiting to be wrapped. In the corner, by an old rocking chair, stood a partially trimmed Christmas tree. The unhung ornaments lay in a heap on the floor as if someone had abruptly abandoned the decorating.

Pippi sucked in a quick breath, then mumbled something that sounded like, "I will not cry."

"What did you say?" Jeremy asked, scanning the room.

"Nothing."

He shrugged and peeked behind the sofa for lurkers; piles of wrapped Christmas gifts filled the space.

They checked out the rest of the house—the family room, the basement, the bedrooms—looking in each closet, under every bed. No live person inhabited the dwelling; no dead one, either. Jeremy still could not let down his guard, but he finally admitted to himself that he felt tired, so very tired.

And hungry.

"Let's find something to eat," he said, smiling faintly at Pippi's enthusiastic, "All right!"

They returned to the kitchen, which had been left well stocked. They finally decided on bacon and eggs to start, then later, if all went well, they would defrost a couple of steaks and make a salad with the wilting vegetables from the bin in the refrigerator.

When they had finished their ambrosial meal and were sipping cups of instant coffee, Pippi said, "Now will you tell me what that place is?"

Jeremy sighed. He wanted to forget it, and he'd hoped she'd forgotten it, too.

"Gabriel Weiss told me that everybody who lived along the Colorado border had been evacuated and taken to a detainment center left over from World War Two." He rubbed his forehead. "I thought he meant some kind of temporary housing, but that looked like a prison or a concentration camp."

"What did a place like that have to do with World War Two?"

"I don't know what it was like back then—it's obviously been renovated recently—but it's where they kept the Japanese-Americans during the war." He held up a hand to silence the question he saw forming on her lips. "Let's not get into that now. We have problems of our own."

Pippi nodded and looked down at herself with a rueful twist of her lips. "Will it be safe to take a shower?"

"I think so," Jeremy said, hoping his own desire to scrub

160

away the accumulated filth wasn't clouding his judgment. "Tell you what. You go first, and I'll keep watch. Then you keep watch while I shower. Deal?"

"Deal," Pippi said with the first real smile that had brightened her face in days.

When Kate noticed the lights shining cozily through the curtained windows of her modest frame house, she smiled to herself and quickened her pace.

So Dee had decided to stay after all.

Kate ran up the porch steps, unlocked the front door, and eagerly stepped inside. The smell of lemon furniture polish greeted her. Her smile faded. Did Dee think she wanted her for a housekeeper? Then her face brightened again. The woman was here; they could straighten out any misunderstandings later.

"Dee," she called out. "I'm home."

She stopped to listen and heard a faint clanking sound.

"Dee? Is that you?"

Another clank.

Following the sound, Kate moved through the living room, the dining room, the kitchen, and into the basement, which smelled of urine and mildew.

A shabby man, the source of the pungent odor, crouched in front of her dryer, bits of metal strewn about him.

"Who are you?" Kate asked. "What are you doing?"

Instead of the commanding tone she had intended, her voice came out sounding weak and tentative; even so, the man ducked his head and scuttled away from her.

Dee materialized out of the shadows. "It's okay, Siggy," she said soothingly. "She's not going to hurt you." She caught Kate's eyes and waved her back up the stairs.

A few minutes later, Dee joined Kate in the kitchen. "That's Siggy, a friend of Totter's. He's not much for people, but he's a wizard with machines. He says he can fix your dryer, but it won't last long. You need a new one."

"I know. It hasn't worked for months. I've been drying my laundry on a clothesline I strung in the basement." She laughed sheepishly. "It sounds so pathetic, but I didn't have the energy to cope with repair persons or salespeople."

Dee nodded. "I know what that's like." She went to the refrigerator, removed a large covered bowl, and dumped a hefty portion of the contents into a saucepan.

Kate breathed deeply. "Mmmm. Smells wonderful."

"It's a stew I made with things I found in your refrigerator." She set the pan on the stove, then turned to Kate. "Siggy's going to join us for supper, if you don't mind."

"Not at all. How much do I owe him?"

Dee made a dismissive gesture. "We already worked that out."

When Siggy finished his repairs, they gathered around Kate's newly polished dining room table. Dee and Kate sat at one end; Siggy huddled over his bowl of stew at the opposite end. He ate with small, compact motions. Occasionally one of his hands darted out to grab a piece of buttered bread from the platter in the center of the table, then returned immediately to the huddle.

As Kate ate her own stew, which tasted even better than it smelled, she pondered the strange turn her life had taken.

It had been years since she had eaten in the dining room. When Joe began to lose his coordination, he chose to eat in the privacy of his own room. Without him, the dining room seemed lonely and gloomy, so she had adopted her present habit of eating in front of the television set or in bed with a book.

But here she was, back in the dining room, eating at the heavy oak table she had once found at a yard sale and spent months refinishing.

The silence lay uncomfortably on her shoulders, and she cast about in her mind for something to say. Remembering the strange phone call earlier in the day, she mentioned the woman whose children had thrown her out of house.

"There's a lot of that these days," Dee said. "Some people are so terrified of the red death that when a family member gets sick, they dump them out in the street. One woman even dumped her baby."

"Oh," Kate said in a small voice and made no more effort at conversation.

When Siggy finished eating, he stood and, making a wide detour around Kate, shuffled toward the back door.

Feeling like an ogre, Kate said defensively, "He can use the front door."

Dee shrugged. "He prefers the back."

Kate watched Siggy open the door and disappear outside. "He's wearing a thin jacket. Doesn't he have a coat?"

"I don't think so."

Kate jumped up. "Tell him to wait."

She hurried to the second bedroom, yanked open the door, and entered. Going directly to the closet, she grabbed Joe's overcoat and dashed out of the room, leaving the door wide open.

She thrust the coat into Dee's arms.

"Here, give this to Siggy."

Pippi felt almost human again. The meal had taken the edge off her hunger and raised her blood sugar levels; the long hot shower had pelted away some of her aches and pains, and an antiseptic cream from the medicine chest had soothed her blistered feet.

She wore her own underwear, which she had washed in the sink and dried with the hair dryer. She'd also slipped into jeans and a heavy sweater she had found in one of the bedrooms, and a pair of suede slippers with inch-thick foam rubber soles she had found among the presents on the dining room table.

While Jeremy shaved, then showered, she prowled through the house, looking out the windows for anyone approaching, and listening for the slightest noise. She saw no one, and all she heard, besides the sound of water running in the shower upstairs, was an owl hooting off in the distance and a branch scraping against a window whenever the wind gusted.

She wandered into the living room, which was lit, like the rest of the house, by the floodlight outside. She gazed at the Christmas tree; it still seemed unbearably sad, though she didn't know why.

Thinking how nice it would be if she and Jeremy were in their own home, preparing for Christmas, she picked a shiny silver ball from the muddle beneath the tree and hung it on a bare branch.

As she stood back to study the effect of the ornament, she heard the shower shut off and the faint scrabbling sounds of Jeremy getting dressed.

She knew he was putting his filthy camouflage fatigues back on, but she imagined him dressing in a tuxedo, getting ready to escort her to an exclusive party in Beverly Hills. She would be attired in a fabulous gown by an up-and-coming designer, and would be standing by the tree waiting for him.

Listening to Jeremy descend the stairs, she picked another shiny ball, a gold one this time.

She reached out to hang the ball on the tree—their tree. He entered the room.

"What the hell do you think you're doing?" he demanded. He didn't raise his voice, but that low growl somehow seemed louder than any bellow.

Pippi jumped, dropping the ornament.

She turned to face him.

The force of his fury propelled her backward; she collapsed onto the sofa. She felt herself cringe as he loomed over her, searing her with his blazing eyes.

"You were supposed to keep watch," he said in that same deadly tone, "but you didn't even notice me come in."

"I heard you," she said, marveling that the words managed to squeak through her constricted throat.

"An army could have tramped through here, and you wouldn't have looked up."

She was opening her mouth to explain, to give him a play-by-play recital of all she had done and heard and seen—or rather, not seen—while he showered, when

164

suddenly the hot lava of her own anger welled inside her. Snapping her jaws shut, she pushed herself up from the sofa and stood glaring back at him.

He grabbed her arm, gripping it with a strength she found surprising in an old man. Shocked by the thought, she stared at him, wondering when he had gotten so old. Dark bags sagged beneath his eyes, deep furrows scored his brow, and the gray pallor of someone rotting away in a nursing home shrouded his face.

But he still radiated power—star power.

Pippi remembered that at their first meeting she had sensed something dangerous about him. It had thrilled her then, but now . . .

She averted her eyes. God help her—it still thrilled her even as it terrified her.

Jeremy let go of her arm, drew a long, ragged breath, and stomped out of the house.

Pippi dropped to the sofa and buried her face in her hands, but she did not cry.

Pippi was thawing two thick T-bone steaks in the microwave when Jeremy returned.

"I checked everything out," he said calmly. "Still no sign of anyone."

"Good," she said, trying to match his even tone.

He took a deep breath. "Look. I'm sorry. I shouldn't have spoken to you the way I did."

Pippi inclined her head, then went to the refrigerator and hauled out vegetables for a salad.

"Anything I can help with?" he asked.

"Yes," she said stiffly, reaching into a drawer and pulling out a box of keys. "You can see if these fit any of the cars."

His eyes widened. "Where did you find them?"

"Right here in the drawer."

He sorted through the keys, palmed several, then headed outside.

When he came back in again, the salad was sitting on the

table and the steaks were sizzling under the broiler.

"Well?" Pippi asked when he didn't speak.

"None of the vehicles has any gas except that old pickup truck. It has a full tank."

"That's good, right?" she said, puzzled by his indifference.

"Could be." He took a Colorado map out of his back pocket and tossed it on the table. "Found this in a glove compartment. Looks like we're about fifteen miles from our rendezvous point."

"Great," she exclaimed. Then, when he remained silent, "Isn't it?"

"Could be," he said again.

"I don't get it. What's the problem?"

"The problem is we're still fifteen miles away from the plane. The problem is we're still in Colorado."

"I know, but—"

"We can't count on anything," Jeremy said. "Too many things can go wrong, and I, for one, haven't come this far to end up dead because I celebrated too soon."

Pippi's elation faded, but did not die. They were only fifteen miles from the border. Even if something did go wrong and they had to walk all the way, they could still be leaving Colorado tomorrow afternoon.

After eating the salad and steaks, they leaned back in their chairs and nibbled on the Christmas cookies Pippi had found hidden away at the back of a cupboard.

"Why did you act mean to me today?" she asked.

His lips tightened into a straight line. "I told you I was sorry."

"Not that. I mean earlier, while we were hiking."

"What are you talking about? I wasn't mean to you."

"Yes, you were. You wouldn't walk with me, and you kept wincing at me."

He snorted. "You call that being mean?"

"Yes."

"You don't get it, do you?" he said harshly. "This isn't

some Hollywood romantic adventure where no matter how careless and stupid you are, everything comes out all right in the end."

Stung, Pippi said, "I'm not stupid."

"No, but you act stupid. You stroll along with your head in the clouds, not paying any attention to what's going on around you, and you don't even try to keep up."

"I pay attention."

"Okay, if you're so observant, tell me where the graves are."

"What graves?"

He jerked his head toward the door. "The ones right outside."

"I didn't see any graves."

"That's my point. You walked right over them and never even noticed."

Pippi shuddered. "I walked over graves? Oh, ick."

Jeremy winced. "That's not the issue here. The fact is, you're not observant and that can get me—us—killed. Let me tell you something. I am going to get out of Colorado if it's the last thing I do, and nothing is going to get in my way. Not you, not the red death, not homicidal teenagers."

"I'm not trying to get in your way," Pippi said with a catch in her voice.

Jeremy sighed. "I know. But you're too inexperienced."

He stood and held out his hand. "Let's go find someplace to sleep."

Pippi had visions of snuggling against Jeremy in the big bed upstairs, but he gathered a handful of blankets and comforters out of the linen closet, and made a pallet on the floor in the family room.

He must have seen the unasked question in her eyes, because he pointed to the sliding glass doors leading to a wooden deck and said, "Escape route. We stand less of a chance of being trapped if we sleep here than if we slept upstairs. Also, being on the floor, we probably won't sleep heavily, so we might be able to hear if someone comes. We should take turns sleeping, with one of us keeping watch at all times, but we're both tired—neither of us would be able to keep our eyes open."

*He means me. He doesn't trust me to keep watch.*

Lying beside him, she pondered what he had said about her. She had done the best she could that day, but it hadn't been good enough for him. Maybe he thought she herself wasn't good enough, either.

"Jeremy?" she whispered. "What's going to happen between us?"

His lips parted as if to answer, but all that came out was a gentle snore.


"Who was the old woman I saw you with today?" Jim asked.

"What woman?" Greg glanced around The Lucky Star. "I don't believe it. This place is as crowded as last time I was here. It looks like nothing has changed, except it was never this quiet."

"Believe me, there are plenty of changes. Check out the big table."

Greg scanned the bar again, letting his gaze fall casually on the occupants of the large table in the center of the bar.

Army officers.

"Jeez."

"Exactly. Kind of puts a damper on things."

"I need a drink," Greg said, "but I don't see any waitresses."

"There are no waitresses or bartenders here anymore. Some died. Others stopped coming to work. Zack, the owner, is taking care of things all by himself."

"How can he make drinks and wait tables too?"

A gleam appeared in Jim's eyes. "You haven't been here for a while, have you? We have to go pick up our own drinks now." As Greg pushed back his chair and got to his feet, Jim added, "I hope you have plenty of cash."

"I have enough."

Nodding to a few acquaintances, Greg ambled over to the bar top where Zack filled mugs with beer from a tap.

"I'll have a whiskey and soda," Greg said.

"No liquor."

"What about bottled beer?"

"No bottles."

"Well, then, give me whatever you have."

Zack pushed one of the filled mugs toward him. "Twenty dollars."

"Good one," Greg said, chuckling.

"Twenty dollars," Zack repeated, without cracking a smile.

Greg gave him an incredulous look, then took out his wallet and removed a twenty-dollar bill. Zack plucked it from between his fingers, stuffed it into a pouch tied around his midsection, and turned to his next customer.

Dazed, Greg returned to the small table in the corner he shared with Jim. He set the beer down carefully; at that price, he couldn't afford to spill any.

"Jeez," he said, dropping into the chair. "How can he get away with that?"

Jim shrugged. "Supply and demand. To be fair—which, in this case, I don't want to be—I don't think all the money goes into Zack's coffers. I heard that both breweries in the area had to pay certain people enormous amounts of money to get the gas necessary to transport their beer within the state. They pass the charge on to the bar owners, who pass it on to us along with a hefty profit."

Greg took a tentative sip of his beer and barely managed to swallow it. "Ugh. It's been watered."

"I know. It's enough to make a teetotaler out of me."

"Yeah, right. That'll be the day."

"Nice bit of evasion," Jim said, "but you're not getting off that easily."

Greg wiped his mouth with the back of his hand. "I have no idea what you're talking about."

"The old woman you were with today."

Greg shook his head. "Nope, still don't know what you're talking about."

Speaking with exaggerated patience, Jim said, "I stopped

for coffee at The Black Forest today, and I saw you with an old woman."

Greg laughed. "You'll have to be more specific."

Jim drew back and raised his eyebrows. "Hell, Greg, how many old women were you with?"

"Well, there was Lottie, the owner, who *didn't* raise her prices though The Black Forest is the only restaurant still open in the neighborhood. Then there was her daughter Elspeth, who waited on Kate and me."

"Uh-huh. Now we're getting somewhere. Who's Kate?"

"Kate? Is that who you're talking about? She's not old."

"But older than you. She's more my age."

"So?"

Jim let out a long sigh. "Marriage is hard enough as it is without adding generational differences to the mix."

Greg whacked himself on the side of the head with the heel of his palm, then looked around. Nope, he hadn't fallen down a rabbit hole. He was still in The Lucky Star, talking to his friend Jim who wasn't making any sense whatsoever.

"I have no intention of marrying Kate. I'm not in love with her. I barely even know her."

"Oh? You two sure looked wrapped up in each other."

Greg smiled to himself, wondering what Kate would think about all this. "I like her and I like who I am when I'm with her. She's kind, has a quiet strength, and is easy to talk to. Until I met her, I never noticed how attractive a mature woman can be. The things younger women seem so frightened of, like crinkles around the eyes and extra fullness in the face, are the very things that give older women character and beauty."

Jim laughed. "If you're trying to convince me you aren't in love with her, you're not doing a good job of it."

"You're forgetting one thing," Greg said.

"What?"

"I'm engaged to Pippi."

"Are you?" Jim asked softly.

Greg frowned. "What does that mean?"

"Well, she did leave you."

"She'll be back."

"Maybe. Look, did she ever actually say she'd marry you?"

Greg thought back to that last conversation with Pippi. "She called me on my cell and said, 'If we're going to get married, we have to set a date so I can start making plans. I'll meet you at The Lucky Star tonight and we'll talk about it. Gotta go. Love you.'"

Jim ran his hand over his balding head. "Not exactly a firm commitment."

"I never got a chance to give her the ring she picked out."

"You want to know what I think?"

"No, but I'm sure you'll tell me anyway."

"I think her career wasn't going the way she planned. Since it stopped giving her the fulfillment she needed, she took the standard female fallback position."

"Which is?"

"Marriage and children, though marriage is optional nowadays. When it looked like a done deal, she got scared knowing she didn't really want it."

"Why couldn't she have told me?"

"Because, as I said a week ago, she doesn't know what she wants. She doesn't want to marry you, but she doesn't want not to marry you, so she took the easy way out."

"For her, maybe." Greg drank a mouthful of beer, then pushed the mug over to Jim. "Want this? I can't stomach any more of it."

Watching Jim down the beer, Greg asked, "Are you and Letisha having problems?"

Jim banged the empty mug on the table. "No. Why?"

"You sound anti-marriage today."

A muscle bulged in Jim's jaw, then relaxed. "We found our mass mutilator this afternoon."

"You did?" Greg reached into his pocket for his notebook. "Who is he?"

"She."

"A woman beat those corpses?"

"Yes."

"Jeez. Did she say why?"

"Oh, yes. Once she started talking, we couldn't get her to stop. We told her a dozen times she had the right to remain silent, but she wouldn't take the hint."

"So, why did she do it?"

"Her husband bought her flowers."

"He what?"

"Bought her flowers. Apparently, it was the last straw. She and her husband both worked, but he seldom helped around the house. And when he did help, he acted like such a bumbler, she wished he wouldn't. They have four kids. They were too much for her to handle alone and, of course, he didn't have a clue how to help. He was either too severe with them or too lenient, and somehow always managed to get them riled. On top of all that, they had money problems, caused, in part, by his profligate ways. One morning they had a long talk. He promised to help her more and to curb his spending. That evening, he brought her flowers, expensive flowers and said, 'Here, this should help.' She wanted to beat him over the head with the flowers, but instead she arranged them in a vase and went out for a walk. She happened to find a piece of pipe, and she banged it against traffic light poles, wrought iron fences, anything that wouldn't protest such treatment. Then she stumbled on a corpse. She said beating that corpse felt so good, she kept pounding on it until she couldn't lift her arms anymore."

"Did she happen to mention what kind of food she eats?"

Jim gave him a puzzled look. "What does that have to do with anything?"

"Well, she was obviously exposed to the red death, but she didn't get sick, so I wondered what she's been eating."

"You want me to find out?"

"That would be great, unless I can interview her myself."

"She's not being allowed to talk to anyone except for cops. It's the strangest thing. She's this little bitty woman, yet she managed to turn those corpses to mush. Today, when they found her in the act, she had a great big smile on her face, as if she'd never had so much fun in her life. She still doesn't know why we arrested her. 'It's not like I killed them,' she said. Then she went on and on about how she loved her family, she really, really did, but since her kids couldn't go to school on account of the red death, and since she and her husband couldn't get to their jobs—she works at the Denver Tech Center, and he works in Broomfield—they all got on each other's nerves. So today she went out in search of another corpse. And, even though there aren't that many anymore, she managed to find one."

Greg looked up from his note taking. "How come there aren't as many corpses?"

"People are staying home, away from other people, so there's not as much contagion. Also, since they're staying home, they die inside, not on the streets."

Jim got to his feet. "Speaking of home—I should get going. Maybe for once I can kiss my wife while she's still awake."

"Don't take her any flowers," Greg said.

Jim shot at him with both index fingers, and headed for the door.

Greg continued to sit, reviewing his notes. All at once he remembered he hadn't told Jim about eating unmodified fats, the main reason he had come to The Lucky Star.

He jumped to his feet and hurried after his friend.

# 18

*Tuesday, December 13*

"Hey, boy!"

Hearing that trumpeting voice, Greg thought of slinking away, but he forced himself to turn and face the approaching Valkyrie.

She waved the leather-bound book in front of his nose and demanded, "Where did you get this?"

Greg flinched, but immediately he drew himself up to his full five-feet-ten and three-quarters inches. As daunting as Clara D'Onofrio appeared, she was a reporter, the same as he.

"I asked you a question, boy."

"My name is Greg," he said quietly. Then, wondering why he was trying to alienate the one person who could tell him about the book, he added, "What did I ever do to offend you?"

She took a step backward and gaped at him.

He had already put one foot in his mouth, might as well try for the other. "You treat me with disdain, and I would like to know why. Is it something I did, or is it just the way I look? Would acne scars and homely features make me a more worthy colleague? A better reporter?"

She let out one of her loud brays that passed for laughter and clapped him on the back, practically knocking him off his feet. "Didn't know you had it in you, boy. Now, let's go find someplace where we can talk."

She led the way to the financial editor's empty office and closed the door behind them. Seating herself at the desk, she asked, "Where did you get the book?" Though she had lowered her voice, it still sounded overly loud in the confined space.

Greg sat in one of the chairs in front of the desk. "A woman I interviewed gave it to me."

"Does she know what's in it?"

"I doubt it. She said she couldn't read Japanese. Did you get a chance to go through it?"

"Yes, and it gave me the creeps."

"Why? What is it?"

"It's a journal kept by a doctor named Takamura, detailing various experiments. Human experiments."

Greg leaned forward. "What kind of human experiments?"

"Biological warfare."

"I knew it," Greg said. "I knew Dr. Takamura was the key to the red death."

"Do you think this journal has some relation to the red death?"

Suddenly confused, Greg searched Clara's face. "Doesn't it?"

"I didn't come across any mention of it, but I haven't managed to translate all the names of the diseases they experimented with. But I doubt they'd have called it the red death."

"What names have you translated?"

"Anthrax, cholera, tuberculosis, small pox, typhoid, bubonic plague, dysentery, tetanus, gas gangrene, tick encephalitis, salmonella."

Greg leaned back and blew out his breath. "Jeez. John sure researched a lot of different diseases."

"John? John who?"

"John Takamura. Isn't he the scientist who kept the journal?"

"This scientist's name was Kiichiro, not John."

Greg stared blankly at Clara; then he realized Kiichiro must have been John's father.

"The journal is old," Clara said. "Takamura was one of the scientists conducting experiments in occupied China for the Japanese Imperial Army in the late 1930s and early 40s. I haven't translated the entire journal yet, but I've looked at enough of it so I can give you a rough overview, if you wish."

"I'd appreciate it."

"General Ishii was the leader of the Japanese germ warfare program, and Takamura's commanding officer. It's ironic, but the Japanese had no interest in biological warfare until the Geneva Protocol's 1932 ban on biological weapons. Ishii concluded the ban meant they were an effective means of fighting a war, so he persuaded the imperial army to let him establish a biological warfare installation. The army granted permission in 1937.

"They built the installation in Manchuria near a village called Pingfan, forty miles outside of Harbin, and it was huge—a town in itself, actually, and self-supporting. In addition to living quarters and the research facilities, which included a separate compound for plague research, there was a school, a railroad siding, an administration building, a crematorium, a powerhouse, a hospital, an airbase, and farms for raising food and livestock. A high wall topped with barbed wire hid the facility from view. A moat lay beyond the wall to trap any intruders, and an electrified fence surrounded the inner perimeter to prevent escapes.

"Three thousand doctors, scientists, technicians, and soldiers worked there. The output was staggering. They grew and experimented with all kinds of diseases and bio-weapons. And they had the capacity for producing twenty million doses of vaccine annually.

"Radiating out from Pingfan were eighteen other biological warfare stations, each staffed with three hundred people. Many of those stations were on mainland China.

"The whole program was administered by an organization with the innocuous name of *Boeki Kyusuibu*, which means—"

"Anti-Epidemic Water Supply Unit," Greg said.

Clara raised her eyebrows. "That's right. How did you know?"

"A man at the Buddhist temple downtown translated some papers for me. He said they were requisitions for logs and lumber."

Clara stiffened, then sat very still as if she had turned to stone. Finally, she passed a hand over her eyes and said in a barely audible voice, "I'll get to that in a minute."

She took a deep breath. "The Japanese conducted their

experiments on Chinese villagers and POWs—mostly
Chinese, but also some American, British and Australian
prisoners.

"Hundreds of American POWs died torturous deaths,
and if by chance any of them survived one experiment, they
were immediately put to use in another.

"Thousands upon thousands of Chinese were also
killed—at least a hundred thousand, perhaps as many as a
million—but the Japanese admitted to only a thousand.

"They conducted all sorts of experiments.

"Using planes, they scattered rice and wheat mixed with
plague.

"They dropped anthrax bombs designed to shatter into a
thousand pieces of shrapnel. A single scratch from one of
those fragments caused death in ninety percent of its victims.

"They injected their victims with diseases, fed them
cultures of diseases, exposed them to clouds of diseases in
gas chambers, then killed them at various stages of the
diseases, and performed autopsies on them. They performed
some autopsies while the victim still lived.

"They poisoned thousands of wells in Manchuria with
cholera, typhoid, and dysentery. Interestingly, a regiment of
Japanese soldiers unknowingly drank from one of those
wells. Thousands died.

"They also infected fleas with botulism, put them in
balloons, and let them go, hoping they'd reach the United
States. Many of the balloons did reach the western coast, but
luckily the fleas had all died."

Clara fell silent. "I need a cup of coffee," she said at last.
"Want me to get you one, too?"

"No," Greg said, wondering how she could ingest
anything after that gruesome recital.

"What happened to Ishii and Takamura?" he asked when
she returned.

"I don't know what happened to Takamura. He stopped
writing in his journal in August of 1945. The last entry stated
that since the Russian army was a few miles away, they were
destroying the Pingfan Institute—smashing every piece of

machinery, burning every scrap of paper. Getting rid of the remaining human guinea pigs."

The image of all those Japanese scientists rushing around trying to obliterate the evidence of their dreadful experiments rose in Greg's mind, but he pushed it away.

"All I know about Takamura is that he died in Denver when his son was young," he said, "but I don't know how he got here."

"Maybe he made a deal. Ishii did. After the war, Ishii ended up in the custody of the United States. He told them about his germ warfare program in exchange for immunity. The U.S. concluded that the potential benefits of the research outweighed the demands of justice. No war crimes were ever brought against Ishii, and the whole thing was covered up. Ishii retired to a village named Wakamatsu-cho, where he lived on a pension provided by the U.S. government until his death in 1959."

"How did you find that out?"

"The Internet."

"I haven't been able to gain access for days."

"I have a satellite up-link. I found out one more interesting tidbit. After World War II, while the U.S. was occupying Atsugi, a town near Yokohama, they found an entire underground city the Japanese had used for storing records, including all the documentation for Ishii's experiments. So even though Ishii's papers were supposedly destroyed, and even though Ishii hedged with his confession and didn't tell everything, the U.S. government still ended up knowing all that went on at Pingfan. I shudder to think what they've been doing with that information all these years."

"I don't understand. Those experiments tested existing diseases. If Takamura had continued with his father's research, how did he produce something as sophisticated as the chimera?"

"What chimera?" Clara asked.

"The red death is a chimera—an amalgam of a virus, a bacterium, a fungus, and a few human genes."

Clara opened her mouth, but Greg didn't give her a

chance to speak.

"Don't give me any of that crap about the red death being just a virus," he said.

Clara held up her hands. "I was going to mention that technology doubles every seven years. It's entirely possible that after half a century, anthrax bombs and botulism balloons have given way to man-made organisms."

While Clara sipped her coffee, Greg reviewed his notes. "You didn't tell me about the logs and lumber."

"That's how the Japanese referred to the subjects of their experiments. If they needed more human guinea pigs, they'd requisition a certain number of logs. Soldiers would go to the villages and either capture that many Chinese, or entice them to Pingfan with job offers, then turn them over to the doctors."

Pippi stood with her hands on her hips, surveying the ancient pickup truck. What she had taken to be rust-colored paint was rust. Not a speck of paint remained anywhere on the vehicle to show what color it had once been.

Jeremy finished packing away their provisions, hopped into the driver's seat, and turned the key in the ignition; it started on the first try.

A good omen, Pippi thought with rising excitement.

"Well," Jeremy said, revving the engine. "You coming or not?"

"Coming." She opened the door and climbed into the truck, which smelled of stale hamburgers and dirty socks. Even before she pulled the door closed, Jeremy headed for the road.

When he didn't respond to her attempts at conversation, she looked out the window, watching the mile markers pass by.

Fourteen miles to go. Then thirteen. Twelve.

She bounced in her seat, ignoring Jeremy's wince of disapproval; she refused to let him dampen her elation at nearing the end of their ordeal.

Another marker. Now there were eleven miles to go.

Six miles from their rendezvous point, the truck's engine sputtered. Sputtered again. Then died.

Pippi glanced at Jeremy who was staring straight ahead with no expression on his face, though his knuckles turned white on the steering wheel.

After a moment, he took a deep breath. Let it out slowly. He turned off the ignition then turned it back on. The engine cranked and cranked, but did not turn over.

Pippi scooted over and peeked at the gas gauge; she was reassured to see that it still registered a full tank.

"What's wrong?" she asked.

He waved away her question and tried to start the truck again; still no luck. He rested his forehead on the steering wheel for a second. With a jerk, he straightened, made a fist, drew it back, and punched the dashboard.

Pippi heard a click. She saw the gas gauge wobble, then slide to the left until it rested on empty.

She sat in stunned silence, as did Jeremy. Then, still silent, he got out of the truck and removed the food, sleeping bags and bottles of water they had found at the house, and the rifles he had taken from the teenagers.

He did not say "I told you so," but he did flick one look her way that clearly showed her he thought it.

If only she had kept her mouth shut. When he had spent an hour that morning going through the house gathering supplies, she thought he acted way too cautious, and she had foolishly mentioned it. Well, how was she to know the truck didn't even have enough gas in it to go fifteen miles?

She sighed, climbed out of the truck, and grabbed the bundle Jeremy had prepared for her.

They had traveled a half a mile or so, when Pippi saw horses grazing in a fenced field not far from a barn. She ran a few steps to catch up with Jeremy. Clutching his arm with her free hand, she said, "Maybe we could ride a horse the rest of the way."

He looked at her, then at the horses. A faint smile tugged at the corners of his mouth.

They walked over to the fence and leaned against it

while they eyed the horses.

"Get away from those animals!"

Startled, Pippi took a step back. At first she couldn't tell where the shout had originated, but then she noticed a man in a tee shirt and bib overalls standing outside the barn. He had a shotgun in his hands, and he aimed it right at them.

"I don't believe this," she said, dropping her bundle. "Give me a gun."

Jeremy frowned at her.

"I said, give me a gun."

"What for?"

"Get the hell away from my horses!" the man yelled.

"I want to shoot the son of a bitch," Pippi said.

Holding the rifles out of reach, Jeremy backed away from her.

"Come on," Pippi said. "Give it to me."

"I'm not going to give you a rifle. You can't go around shooting people for no reason."

"Why not? They do it."

"You can't, that's all."

Pippi stamped her foot. "But he's pointing that gun at me. I'm sick and tired of people pointing weapons and shooting at me."

"He's not shooting at you," Jeremy said, oh, so calmly. "He just doesn't want you stealing his horses."

The man in the overalls pumped his shotgun and shouted, "Get away from the horses, I said."

Jeremy waved at him and nodded, then grabbed Pippi's arm and dragged her away from the fence. He darted back to retrieve her bundle. "We're leaving," he called out. "Don't shoot."

He returned to where Pippi stood, glaring at him, and handed her the bundle. "We have to get away from here now. If we don't, he probably will shoot us."

"Then you'd only have yourself to blame," she grumbled. "If you'd have given me a gun, we wouldn't have to worry about that."

Unexpectedly, Jeremy let out a hoot of laughter.

She frowned. "What?"

"Do you even know how to shoot a rifle?"

"No."

He shook his head, still chuckling. "Good thing I didn't give you one of them, then. You'd probably have shot your foot off."

Pippi scowled at him. "As if you'd care."

Jeremy stuffed their supplies into a small culvert that seemed to have once been part of an irrigation system, piled a few tumbleweeds in front of the opening to camouflage it, then grabbed his rifles and headed across the field.

Encumbered only by the purse slung across her shoulders and the binoculars hanging from her neck, Pippi followed him.

They hadn't gone far when she noticed a small plane standing before a long, narrow dirt road less than a quarter of a mile away.

"That must be it," she exclaimed.

"Keep your voice down," Jeremy said. "We don't want them to know we're coming until we've had a chance to reconnoiter."

She spread her arms wide. "This is all there is. Open land, the plane, and that house and barn over there."

"You still don't get it, do you?" He sighed. "Oh, never mind. Give me the binoculars."

Pippi handed the binoculars to him, then watched him position them and take a long look around. When he lowered the binoculars, his face showed no expression, but she could detect a stillness in him like the tensed calm of a cat before it pounces.

She grabbed the binoculars but, peering through them, she could see nothing wrong. Maybe the plane did look smaller and older than she had expected, but since they only needed it to fly a half a mile, what difference did it make? As for the farm itself, it looked like all the others they had seen—no better, no worse.

"I don't like this," Jeremy said. "It feels like a set-up to me. All this open space and that old Piper Cub in the middle, like bait."

Pippi moistened her lips. "What are we going to do?"

"I don't know." Jeremy continued to study the layout of the land for several minutes, then he shrugged. "Well, it can't be helped. We'll have to cross that open field. I would have preferred a more clandestine approach, but since there's no cover, we'll have to take our chances. Stay alert."

He walked toward the plane, turning his head from side to side. For once he moved slowly enough that Pippi could keep up with him. She too moved her head from side to side to scan the terrain since that's what he wanted her to do, but she couldn't see the point. There was nothing to see, and they moved so quietly they would be able to hear anything before it drew near.

When they reached the plane, Jeremy circled it, swearing under his breath.

"I can't believe they had the nerve to charge me a hundred grand for this piece of shit," he said at last. "It's a junky crop duster, for cripes sake."

"Looks to me like it's held together with baling wire," Pippi said. She had no idea what baling wire was, but she knew it held together decrepit aircraft in old movies.

"We should be so lucky. This thing is being held together with duct tape."

"You Jeremy King?"

Pippi turned her head toward the shout.

An old woman in a faded dress stood in the doorway of the house. Beside her, an even older man dressed in dusty coveralls cupped his hands around his mouth.

"You Jeremy King?" he shouted again.

"Yes," Jeremy yelled back.

"Thought so. You look like him, only shorter. Plane's ready to take off. That's the runway, there."

The two old people stepped back into the house and slammed the door. Seeing the twitch of a curtain, Pippi knew they were standing at a window, watching them.

A distant sound caught her attention. She tilted her head,

listening. Then her breath lodged in her throat.

A helicopter. Coming closer.

Jeremy's eyes widened, as if he had just become aware of it.

"Get down on the ground," he yelled. "Under the plane."

Pippi scrambled under the plane and lay on her belly next to him. As the sound of the helicopter grew louder, she trembled. So it had been a set-up after all. The old couple had informed the border patrol they were trying to escape, and now soldiers were coming.

She stifled a moan. This was the end.

She raised her head, trying to catch a glimpse of the helicopter; when she did, it increased her fear—it was one of the insect-looking things with the narrow cockpit she had seen in war footage.

She buried her head in her arms and tried to still her panic.

The sound of the helicopter grew louder.

Almost imperceptibly at first, the noise faded.

When all grew quiet, they crawled out from under the crop duster.

"Must have been a routine patrol," Jeremy said. "Well, now we know this is a good time to cross the border, but I doubt this trash heap can do the job."

He opened the door to the cockpit, laid his rifles inside, and climbed into the seat.

Pippi raised her arms. "Help me up."

"I want to give it a trial run first," he said, studying the instrument panel. "There's no point in both of us getting hurt if this crate falls apart on take-off. I'll be back in a few minutes."

He closed the door and started the engine.

The plane rattled ominously as it taxied down the dirt runway, but it took off without any trouble. It headed away from the border, gaining altitude. A few minutes later, it turned around and swooped toward the runway.

As it descended, it wobbled.

Pippi held her breath, watching.

By the time the plane reached fifteen feet off the ground, it was shaking so much she felt certain it would crash.

But it didn't crash.

Nor did it land.

It kept going.

"Come back here, you bastard," Pippi screamed when she realized Jeremy was heading for the border without her. "You can't leave me here. Come back!"

The plane bucked as if Jeremy were having a hard time maintaining the necessary altitude, but he kept going.

Seconds later, the plane took a nosedive and crumpled into the ground.

Pippi froze, unable to look away.

After what seemed like hours, but had to have been minutes, she saw something move. She fumbled for the binoculars and lifted them to her eyes. Jeremy staggered away from the downed plane.

She listened, but heard no sound of the patrol helicopter returning. So he hadn't tripped the ground sensors. That meant he was safe in Kansas, the bastard.

Watching Jeremy stagger, she wondered if he had been hurt. No. He regained his balance and hurried toward a group of people who waved enthusiastically as they ran to greet him.

Pippi refocused the binoculars and squinted through them. Now she could see that the group consisted mostly of men, but also a woman or two. They were not waving in welcome, as she had thought, but were waving tools. Hoes, it looked like.

She could hear shouts, but could not make out any words. She saw Jeremy stop and gesticulate, as if introducing himself.

The people kept advancing.

Jeremy turned, but before he could run more than a few steps, they pounced on him.

A low keening escaped Pippi's lips. She stood frozen in place, watching Jeremy King, world-renowned actor, being hoed to death.

\*    \*    \*

Greg searched the newspaper's database, but could find no mention of either Pingfan or Japanese biological warfare.

He did find a few articles about the March 1995 release of Sarin nerve gas into the Tokyo subway system and the subsequent deaths of twelve people.

He found another article, which mentioned that in June 1994, Sarin had killed seven people in Matsumoto—a mountain resort one hundred miles west of Tokyo.

Yet another article described Sarin as remarkably potent; a single drop can kill within minutes of inhalation or upon exposure to the skin.

If Sarin was so lethal, he wondered, why had so few died? Then he realized he got sidetracked. Since Sarin was a chemical warfare agent rather than a biological one, it had no bearing on the red death.

Still unable to log on the Internet, he called the main library downtown and most of the branches. All were closed except for the University Hills branch, but they had no books about Pingfan and few about biological warfare.

Would it be worth going to University Hills to look at the books? University Hills reminded Greg of Takamura who had lived in that neighborhood, which reminded him of the papers stacked in his apartment, which reminded him of the journal, which reminded him of . . .

Feeling as if he were running in circles, chasing a tail that didn't exist, he decided he'd better think of something else before he drove himself crazy.

He picked up the phone and called Pippi's number at the television station. He heard her cheerful voice announcing he had reached the voice mail of Pippi O'Brien, but he hung up before the beep.

Would she think that by checking on her he was invading her privacy? Probably. But didn't he have a right to know where he stood?

He debated with himself for a few more seconds, then pressed redial and left a message, asking her to call him.

He called her home phone and left the same message.

Then he called Jeremy King's hotel.

The phone rang a long time. Finally, a sleepy-sounding male answered it.

"Jeremy King?" the man said. "He's not here. He left."

"Do you know where he went?"

"No."

"Do you know if he'll be back?"

"Maybe. His stuff is gone, but he didn't check out."

"He was with a young woman—Pippi O'Brien."

"The weather girl, right?"

"Yes. Do you know if she's still with him?"

"Probably. I don't know."

"Can I leave a message in case she returns?"

"I guess."

"Tell her Greg Pullman called."

"Yeah, sure."

Greg hung up and tapped his fingers on the desk. Jeremy King and Pippi were probably waiting out the quarantine in a plush mansion somewhere. Aspen, perhaps, or Telluride.

He pushed himself away from his desk and put on his coat. He thought about going to the Bowers Clinic to see if Kate wanted to go to lunch with him, then he noticed the time: mid-afternoon.

Maybe he should go home and finish sorting out Takamura's papers. Now, more than ever, he was convinced they held the key to the red death.

All at once Pippi's legs grew too weak to hold her. She dropped to the ground, pulled her knees to her chest, wrapped her arms around them, and rocked herself. She heard a high-pitched wailing sound, and though she knew it came from her own throat, she did not understand how her body could be making so much noise all on its own.

The wailing gradually diminished, but she continued to rock.

In an endless loop, her mind kept replaying Jeremy's awful end.

It hadn't happened. It couldn't have. Any minute now,

187

he'd return from his trial flight, stop and pick her up, and they'd soar into happily ever after.

But Jeremy didn't return. And a tiny voice inside her said he was never coming back.

She was alone.

Oh, God. What was she going to do?

One thing for sure, she couldn't stay here. A few yards away, hidden behind the curtains of their house, were the old people. Murderers, both of them. Maybe they hadn't been directly responsible for Jeremy's demise, but they had purposely sold him that death trap for an outrageous price. They couldn't be trusted. And soon a helicopter would be passing by for another routine check. The pilots would probably notice Jeremy and the crashed plane on the other side of the border. Would the helicopter stop? Would she be questioned?

She staggered to her feet. She had to leave. Now. Before it came.

She hobbled across the field, heading for the culvert where Jeremy had cached their supplies. "To be on the safe side," he had said.

Her mind filled with the sound of his voice giving her instructions, telling her to observe, warning her to stay alert.

She had been staring at her feet, but now she straightened her shoulders, raised her head, and looked from side to side.

*Stay alert.*

She stopped abruptly. What did she see? A man huddled close to the ground, waiting to spring?

She snatched up the binoculars to take a closer look, and sagged in relief. Nothing but large rock.

She walked a few more steps and stiffened. What was that up ahead?

Oh, a clump of weeds. Nothing to worry about.

She took another step, glancing all around her. The field she had traversed so blithely a short time ago now radiated menace.

Anything could happen.

She had to stay alert.

Kate was putting on her coat when Dr. Hart strode into her office.

"Leaving so early?" the doctor asked.

"That's okay, isn't it?"

"Sure, no problem. In fact, I was coming to tell you to go home. We haven't had a patient for the past hour. I'm surprised I don't have to pry you away from your desk."

Kate laughed. "Not tonight."

Dr. Hart winked. "Mustn't keep your gorgeous young man waiting."

Kate thought about explaining that she planned to spend a quiet evening with her new friend, a former bag lady, but she knew Dr. Hart would not understand, would, in fact, be appalled, so she smiled without saying anything and headed out the door.

When Kate arrived home, she heard the sound of cutlery clinking against dishes and smelled the appetizing aroma of garlic, onions, and herbs.

She entered the dining room to find Siggy, snugly buttoned into his new coat, sitting at the table, huddled over his food, apparently still afraid someone would snatch it away from him.

On the other side of the table sat a man dressed in layers of filthy clothes. An acrid stench oozed from his pores and his breath smelled of feces, as if he were rotting from within.

Trying not to gag, Kate smiled at him. A phlegm-rattling cough grabbed hold of him. When it passed, he gave her a wide, toothless grin.

"That's Hooch," Dee said from her place at the head of the table, "but I don't know who this is. He hasn't told me his name yet."

Then Kate noticed a fourth person sitting at the table—a small, solemn-faced boy with a shock of dark hair falling over red eyes.

A fist squeezed her heart. Oh, no. Not another soon-to-be victim of the red death. Would it never end?

"Hello," she said. "My name is Kate."

The boy stared at her for a moment, then, hunching his shoulders protectively, turned his attention back to his food.

Kate went into the kitchen, filled a bowl with the stew bubbling on the stove and sat next to the little boy.

He tensed as if preparing to bolt, but after a quick sidelong glance at her, he seemed to relax.

Kate caught Dee's eyes. "Who is he?" she mouthed.

Dee pointed her chin at Hooch.

"What's your son's name?" Kate asked Hooch.

Hooch choked and coughed and hacked, then shoveled more food into his mouth.

Glancing at the bowed head of the little boy, Kate thought that whatever else fate had in store for him, tonight he would have a full belly.

She tasted the stew. "Delicious." She took another bite. "I didn't think there was any meat left in the house."

Dee shrugged. "There wasn't. Siggy brought it."

Kate spooned out a piece of the meat and chewed it slowly. "It's good. Tastes like chicken." She thought about asking what it was, then changed her mind. Maybe it would be better not to know.

Hooch finished his stew, stuffed the rest of his bread and butter into his mouth, and left the table. Seconds later the back door slammed.

Kate and Dee exchanged glances. Dee jumped up and took off after him.

"Hooch," Kate could hear her calling. "You forgot the boy!"

Siggy rose, made a wide circuit around Kate, and went out the back door.

The little boy stole a look at Kate, then quickly turned away.

When Dee returned, she had a dazed look on her face. She beckoned to Kate. "Can I see you a minute?"

"I'll be right back," Kate said to the boy, but he acted as if he didn't hear.

Dee leaned against the kitchen counter. "That's not

Hooch's son. This morning Hooch was crossing Colfax at Broadway, when an old pickup truck pulled up to the stoplight. The driver, a woman, reached over, opened the passenger door, gave the boy a push. She told him to get out, he had the devil disease, and she didn't want him giving it to the rest of the family. As soon as the boy climbed out of the truck, she slammed the door and took off, leaving the poor kid standing in the middle of the street."

Kate sucked in a swift breath.

"Hooch didn't know what to do," Dee continued. "He knew a child that young couldn't survive on the streets alone, but he didn't want to be saddled with the kid, either. He went looking for Siggy, thinking Siggy would know what to do since Siggy once had a son. Siggy suggested bringing him here. So, for better or for worse, it looks as if we have a child, at least until . . . well, you know."

"Poor kid," Kate said softly. "Did he talk to Hooch at all? Tell him his name or anything else about himself?"

"No. The boy hasn't uttered a word all day."

"Do you know how old he is?"

"Three or four, I think."

Kate went to the doorway connecting the kitchen with the dining room and gazed at the little boy. He had pushed his empty bowl aside, laid his head on the table, and slept. The pinched, old-man look faded, and he looked relaxed, as if somehow he knew he'd reached a safe haven.

# 19

*Wednesday, December 14*

Last night after Kate laid the sleeping boy on her bed, he had awakened and scooted away from her, staring at her with wide, red eyes. No amount of cajoling had enticed him back on the bed, so she had brought the cushions from the living room couch into the bedroom for him to sleep on.

When she awoke and found him curled on the edge of her bed, she lay still to keep from disturbing him, but she couldn't help smiling.

Gradually her smile faded. He seemed too quiet, too inert; the only sound of breathing she heard was her own. She sat up and slowly reached out to check his pulse, but before she could touch him, he stirred and let out a long, soft sigh.

She got out of bed and stretched.

*Oh! What a glorious day!*

She took a shower and put on her pink quilted satin robe. The robe was several years old, but it looked brand-new. The last Christmas present Joe had ever given her, it had been too precious to wear. She smoothed the luxurious fabric, thinking of that Christmas. Soon afterward, Joe had taken a turn for the worse and had withdrawn from her, secluding himself in the second bedroom, but that year they had still been hopeful. They had laughed and joked and hugged and kissed and eaten way too much.

They had gone to bed early, planning to make mad, passionate love; instead they had fallen asleep in each other's arms. But the next morning . . .

Smiling at the memory, Kate went to prepare breakfast. She was sprinkling raisins and cinnamon on the oatmeal when the boy padded into the kitchen, still wearing the jeans and flannel shirt he had worn yesterday. Last night he had finally removed his jacket, but he had refused to take off his clothes.

"Are you ready for breakfast?" Kate asked, setting a bowl of oatmeal on the kitchen table.

Without speaking, without even looking at her, he climbed onto one of the wooden chairs and began spooning the oatmeal into his mouth.

Kate poured a glass of orange juice and set it on the table in front of him. "All I have is powdered milk, but I can make some if you want."

The boy made no response.

Dee materialized in the doorway, wearing one of Joe's bathrobes. She glanced at the boy, then at Kate.

The two women smiled at each other in congratulations, as if they, personally, had managed to keep him alive during the night.

Dee poured herself a cup of coffee, then sat opposite the boy and peered into his face.

She wrinkled her brow. "His eyes are still red."

"I know. I want to take him to the clinic so one of the doctors can examine him, but I'm not sure he can walk that far."

"My grocery cart's in your garage. You can take him in that."

"Hmm. Not a bad idea."

When Kate was ready for work, she handed the boy his coat and led him outside where Dee waited with the cart. She extended her arms to pick him up, but he moved out of reach and stared at her.

"We'll have to walk, then," Kate said, holding out a hand.

He put his hands behind his back, but when she walked away, he trailed along.

Though his steps dragged at times, he followed her all the way to the clinic and then into Dr. Hart's office.

"Who's your shadow?" the doctor asked.

Kate desperately searched her mind for something to say, knowing she couldn't tell the doctor the truth. Dr. Hart, being a stickler for rules, would probably turn the poor kid over to social services.

"A friend," she said at last. "Could you examine him sometime today? His eyes are all red, but he survived the

193

night, and he doesn't show any of the twitchiness of the red death victims."

"I have time now. Go ahead and put him on the table."

"He doesn't like being touched."

Dr. Hart raised her eyebrows, then hunkered down in front of the boy. "So, Little Shadow, what seems to be the problem?"

The boy stared at her.

The doctor stood. "Looks like he might have an eye infection, but I won't know for sure until I examine him."

"I'm sorry, Shadow," Kate said. "I have to pick you up."

He flinched as her hands encircled his waist, but he didn't pull away.

"I'll need you to take off his jacket and unbutton his shirt," Dr. Hart said when the boy was settled on the examination table.

He sat still while Kate undid his clothes, but as soon as the doctor touched the stethoscope to his chest, he squirmed.

"It's okay, Shadow," Kate said, moving closer. "I'm right here."

He gave her a sidelong glance, then the tension in his body slackened.

After the doctor listened to his heart, and examined his eyes, ears, nose, and throat, she reached into a drawer for a vial of eye drops. "One drop in each eye three times a day should clear that infection."

She sighed and raked her fingers through her hair. "I should take a throat culture and a blood sample, but there's not much point. The labs aren't sending us test results."

Kate buttoned the boy's shirt and lifted him off the table. He edged around behind her legs.

"Has he been abused?" Dr. Hart asked. "There's no physical evidence, but he has a lot of the mannerisms displayed by abused children."

Kate glanced at the boy, wondering what he had endured. At the very least, being abandoned by his mother had to have been traumatic.

"He's safe now," she said.

Dr. Hart shot her an inquisitive look but, to Kate's relief, didn't make an issue out of it.

"Do you mind if he stays with me today?" Kate asked.

"If he's not a hindrance."

Shadowed by the boy, Kate went to the waiting room, gathered a handful of toys and children's books, then headed for her office.

She had just dumped the toys on her desk when her phone rang.

"Kate?" said Dr. Hart's voice. "Joan's not here yet. I need you to answer the phones until she arrives."

Kate gathered the toys and returned to the waiting room. She settled the boy in a corner behind the reception desk where he played quietly, seemingly unaware of everything going on around him, but every time Kate had to leave the desk for any reason, he rose and trotted after her.

Greg was sitting at his computer, trying unsuccessfully to access the Internet, when he heard someone plop down in the chair behind him. Assuming Olaf had stopped by for his morning chat, Greg smiled as he swiveled his chair around.

The smile faded when he saw Clara D'Onofrio regarding him with red-rimmed, feverish eyes that glowed against her abnormally pale skin.

"Are you okay?" he asked, hoping she wouldn't take offense.

She made a small gesture with her hand as if to brush away his concern, opened her briefcase, and removed a sheaf of papers.

"I spent most of the night researching biological weapons," she said. "You would not believe the stuff I found. Did you know that the entire genetic code for the Black Death has been mapped, and the genetic sequences have been posted on the web?"

Greg blinked, then shook his head no.

"Also cholera and smallpox. Smallpox! Who in their right mind would mess around with smallpox? It has killed more people over the ages than any other disease, claiming at least three hundred million victims in the twentieth century alone. Why did the World Health Organization spend ten years eradicating smallpox from the face of the earth when scientists all over the world now mass produce it?"

"If they eradicated it, where did the smallpox come from?" Greg asked.

"They eradicated it in the wild, but a lot of research facilities retained samples, including Ft. Detrick in Maryland."

Clara riffled through her sheaf of papers and plucked one from the bunch. "It says here the Russians built an underground facility capable of growing eighty to one hundred tons—tons!—of the smallpox virus every year. Get this—they modified it genetically, combining the smallpox with Ebola and Venezuelan Equine Encephalitis, a brain virus."

"Jeez," Greg said, feeling sick to his stomach. "As if smallpox by itself weren't lethal enough."

"Tell me about it. What's even worse, the collapse of the Soviet Union left hundreds of biological research scientists unemployed. Many of them took the smallpox with them when they went to work for other countries like Libya, Iran, Iraq, North Korea, India, and maybe even Israel and Pakistan. And of course, the United States.

"Can you imagine what would happen if any of the new strains of the disease escaped from the laboratory? They'd travel around the world so fast and kill so many people, it would make the red death appear inconsequential."

"No, I can't imagine it," Greg said. "To be honest, I have a hard time imagining the red death, even though it's happening now. It's too big. Too many have died. I think that's why I focus on the puzzle aspect—who created it, and why. It's something my mind can comprehend."

Clara nodded slowly. "I know what you mean. Last night while reading the information on the screen, I'd be detached, then all at once the implications of the words would hit me like a paralyzing blow to the midsection, and I wouldn't be able to breathe."

She pulled out another paper from the sheaf and waved it under Greg's nose. "And some things, like this, I had to double and triple check with other sources because I couldn't believe it."

Greg tried to focus on the paper, but she was moving it around too much for him to make out the words. He reached for it, but she snatched it back and stabbed at it with a short, neatly trimmed fingernail.

"The CDC—the Centers for Disease Control and Prevention—sent all sorts of virulent biological materials to Iraq in the late 1980s. No wonder the U.S. believed Iraq had been manufacturing bio-weapons. They—we—sold them the raw ingredients. Also, some two point eight billion dollars in U.S. grants were funneled through Italy's National Labor Bank in the late 1980s to help finance Iraq's military build-up. Has the world gone totally insane?"

"All my life I loved finding out secrets—I loved knowing things other people didn't—but I'm fast losing my taste for it. There are too many secrets of a vile nature, secrets I would rather not know."

"In that case," Clara said briskly, "I'll be going."

Greg stared at her. When he noticed her lips twitching on one side of her face, as if she couldn't manage a full smile, he realized she had made a joke.

"Ha, ha," he said, amazed to be bantering with Clara D'Onofrio.

Clara consulted her papers again. "In the late 1980s, the United States sent more than one hundred different biological agents and assorted materials to Iraq. These included anthrax, bubonic plague, various Clostridia bacteria, West Nile fever antigen and antibodies. Iraq also ordered potential biological warfare materials from private firms and corporations in the United States, but I couldn't find out what they bought since those businesses aren't subject to the Freedom of Information Act."

"Did the United States sell just to Iraq?"

"Oh, no. The U.S. sent most countries whatever they

wanted." Clara held up another paper. "Here's a 1969 study on the cost effectiveness of biological warfare. For a full scale operation against a civilian population back then, it would have cost two thousand dollars per square kilometer to produce casualties with conventional weapons, eight hundred dollars with nuclear weapons, six hundred dollars with nerve gas weapons, and one dollar with biological weapons. It's easy to see why governments are interested in biological warfare—it's cheap—but I don't understand why the scientists would go along with it."

"A paycheck, of course."

"I know. But they can still get a paycheck without being so innovative. In addition to shuffling the genes of existing diseases, they're creating new ones, like combining the venom-producing genes from scorpions and cobras with harmless bacteria. Once inhaled by a victim, they produce paralyzing toxins within the body."

"Doesn't surprise me." Greg gave a small, humorless laugh. "Nauseates me, frightens me, but doesn't surprise me."

"I'm no stranger to depravity," Clara said. "No financial reporter can be, considering the criminal behavior rampant in the business community, but I don't understand why scientists would do these things."

"Because they can."

She tilted her head, studied him for a moment, then nodded. "You could be right."

"Ever since I started researching the red death," Greg said, "people have been telling me that biological warfare experimentation has been banned, but I know it's still going on. For one thing, the red death is evidence that someone is experimenting. For another thing, you can't stop progress. Once science had the technology for developing bio-weapons, no ban could stop it. It has to keep going forward. It's the nature of the beast."

"Sounds like you've been giving this a lot of thought."

"It's all I think about these days."

"I can understand why. Now that I've begun translating

the journal from hell, it's all I can think about, too." She rotated her shoulders. "I keep getting the creeps, as if I can feel all those diseases out there, waiting to come whooshing out of the research facilities and flood the world. I hate the idea of being at the mercy of something I can neither see nor control."

"Like the red death."

"Exactly." Clara handed the sheaf of papers to Greg. "These are for you. They're my bio-weapons research notes and what I've translated of the journal so far."

Greg leafed through the papers. Noticing that everything seemed familiar, he asked, "Have you discovered anything new in the journal?"

"Just more than I ever wanted to know about growing bacteria. The Japanese grew the various diseases in aluminum tanks. At the end of each growing season, the bacteria were scraped from the surface of the tanks with a small metal rake. Some diseases, like dysentery and typhoid, were harvested after twenty-four hours. Other diseases, like plague and anthrax were harvested after forty-eight hours. Still others took a week.

"One consolation I have is that a lot of Japanese got sick, too. Some of the lab workers contracted infections, some of the soldiers were killed by the blowback from the bombs when the wind shifted, and Ishii suffered from chronic dysentery."

"Anything else about Takamura?"

"He primarily did anthrax research. In one of his experiments, he tied his subjects to stakes, exposed their buttocks, then exploded an anthrax bomb about a hundred yards away."

"Nice fellow," Greg said, wondering how much John took after his father.

Clara stood, gesturing to his computer. "Looks like you're busy. I'll let you get back to work. I wanted to give you a progress report."

"To be honest, I'm not all that busy right now. I've been trying to log on the Internet, but so far I haven't had any luck."

"Maybe I can help."

Greg shook his head. "You have your own work to do."

Clara put her hands on her hips. "Don't be coy. Tell me what you need."

"Anything pertaining to John Takamura."

"Done. What else?"

"I have a stack of documents with the Anti-Epidemic Water Supply Unit letterhead. Would you mind taking a look at them?"

"Drop them on my desk. I'll see what I can do."

After Clara left, Greg read the papers she had given to him. When he came across the comment that Pingfan was forty miles from Harbin, he checked his computer, wondering if the newspaper had an atlas in its database; it did.

He found Harbin in Manchuria, but not Pingfan; probably too small, he figured. He leaned back in his chair, his focus narrowed onto the spot where Pingfan was located and thought about the misery the Japanese had manufactured there. His eyes watered from staring at the screen too long; he looked away. When his gaze returned to the map, his mouth dropped open.

Bending forward, he touched the dot marked Harbin, then ran his finger straight down the screen to South Korea, where the Hanta virus had originated.

Pippi lay curled in the sleeping bag until the sun climbed high overhead.

She hadn't slept, partly because she had been unable to relax and partly because the sound of helicopters had kept her awake all night, and she felt too tired to move. Not that it mattered; she had no place to go.

Finally, needing to relieve her bladder, she dragged herself from the safety of her nest and crouched behind a prickly shrub.

Hurrying back to the warmth of her sleeping bag, she was shocked to see her rudimentary camp so exposed. She had laid her sleeping bag in the shallow ditch that lead away from the culvert, thinking it gave her some protection, but the two trees standing on either side of the ditch drew attention to it. Which, come to think of it, had helped them find the culvert in the first place.

Suddenly frantic to get away, she rolled all the supplies into a single bundle and strapped it on her back. She staggered under the weight of it, but she couldn't leave anything behind. Her survival might depend on it.

Pippi walked along the road. The few times a vehicle drew near, she ran and hid. Mostly, though, she was alone.

Alone, that is, except for Jeremy's voice in her head. "You're doing it all wrong," he told her. "You have to stay off the road, and if you can't, you have to be more careful. You didn't even notice that last car until it got close. So what if nothing happened? You were lucky. Maybe next time you won't be. Open your eyes. Look. Feel. Be alert. And where do you think you're going? Back to the truck we abandoned yesterday? Lot of good that's going to do. There's no gas, remember? Besides, I have the keys. Oh, you thought it would give you protection? I'll tell you what protection it's going to give you. None. Absolutely none. It's too open, too obvious. Think, woman, think!"

Finally, she clapped her hands over her ears and screamed, "Shut up! Shut up! Shut up! You're dead, you hear me? Dead!"

She took her hands away from her ears. She heard one more "Stay alert." Then nothing.

Toward sunset, she neared the house where she and Jeremy had spent the previous night. She lay on her belly on top of the little hill and surveyed the area; it looked deserted.

She got to her feet and trudged down the hill, carefully stepping around the two graves. She made a circuit of the property, checking the outbuildings, then went to the back door of the house. The broken window gave her easy access.

After checking out the entire house, which looked exactly as they had left it, she went in search of tools and a piece of wood to nail over the broken window. No way was she going to sleep alone in the house when anyone who felt like it could walk in.

She fixed the window and blockaded both the front and back doors with furniture, then went to the den, stuck a long, thin piece of wood in the runner of the sliding glass doors so they couldn't be opened from the outside, made certain she could remove it easily if she needed to make an emergency exit, then closed the drapes. The room was dark, but she didn't dare turn on the lights.

Desperately needing a shower, but remembering all the shower scenes in all the horror movies she had ever seen, she went into the downstairs bathroom and took a sponge bath, then put on a sweat suit she had found among the bags of presents to be wrapped.

Too tired to eat, she lay on the pallet in the den. She tried to sleep, but whenever she closed her eyes, her mind projected hellish scenes onto her closed lids.

Soldiers gunning down Jeremy's fans in Denver.

The teenagers shooting at her; Jeremy bursting out of the leaves and knifing them.

Jeremy flying the plane over her head, leaving her behind.

Jeremy's plane crashing; Jeremy running from the mob; Jeremy being beaten.

Jeremy . . .

When Kate and Shadow arrived home that evening, a dozen unkempt persons were sitting around her dining room table. Most ate silently, but an old woman and a younger man waved their forks and argued vociferously.

Shadow moved behind Kate and clutched her skirt.

"It's okay, Shadow," Kate said soothingly. "No one's going to hurt you."

The boy relaxed his grip but remained so close he kept bumping into her as she headed for the kitchen where Dee was taking biscuits out of the oven.

Dee straightened, put the pan on the stove, then brushed her hair away from her face with an oven-mitted hand.

"What's going on?" Kate asked.

"We ran out of bread."

Kate shook her head. "No, not that." She pointed to the dining room. "Who are all those people? Do I have a mark on my back fence or something?"

"You mean like the hobos used to make when they found a soft touch?" Dee chuckled. "No. You just have more friends than you know."

Dee put the biscuits on a plate, took it into the dining room, and set it on the table. Arms flashed out; the biscuits vanished.

"Some of them helped Siggy bring your new dryer," Dee said when she returned. "Two of them cleaned your gutters, and the woman, Rose, brought some clothes for the boy. I thought the least we could do was feed them."

Sensing a slight defensiveness about the other woman, Kate gave her a reassuring smile. "Good idea."

She took off her coat and bent to help Shadow remove his. With both coats draped over her arm, she walked away.

She stopped abruptly and turned, almost tripping over the boy. "Wait a minute. What dryer?"

Dee shrugged.

Kate yanked open the basement door and clumped down the stairs with Shadow close on her heels and Dee trailing behind.

An aqua dryer nestled next to her white washer.

"It's not new," Dee said, "but it works perfectly."

"Where did Siggy get it?"

"Don't ask."

Kate sighed. If Siggy had stolen the garish machine, he hadn't committed a major felony on her behalf. It couldn't be worth much; no one had manufactured a dryer of that color for many years.

"Take it in the spirit it was offered," Dee said. "Siggy's glad to have eaten a few good meals. The soup kitchens are closed now."

Stricken, Kate stared at her. "I never thought of that. What are they going to do?"

"I don't know. It's a sad situation."

"Well, a few of them aren't going hungry tonight."

Kate took one last look at her new dryer, then started back up the stairs. "You coming, Shadow?"

"Who's Shadow?" Dee asked.

"The boy. I can't keep calling him 'the boy' and somehow the name Shadow fits."

Back upstairs, Kate found the guests in an uproar. The rest of the diners had taken sides in the argument; even Siggy ventured a few comments in a rusty-sounding baritone. They made more noise than Kate liked, but she preferred the raised voices and flailing arms to the eerily silent meals of the previous nights.

Listening to the argument, of which she could not make out a single word, Kate barely heard the doorbell.

When it rang again, she froze.

Greg.

In all the commotion, she had forgotten she'd invited him for dinner.

He had called that morning to see if she wanted to go to lunch with him. Although she had wanted to, wanted it very much, she had to turn him down—Joan still had not shown up for work, and Kate had no one to relieve her at the reception desk. Kate had hesitantly, hopefully, invited him to dinner; he had accepted.

And now he was here.

When Kate opened the door, he peered around her, looking confused. She held her breath, wondering if he were going to leave; she wouldn't blame him if he did.

Instead, he smiled at her and said, "Are you sure I have the right house?"

She laughed, huffing, as she let out her pent-up breath, and stepped aside to let him in.

"Apparently Dee and I are running a soup kitchen," Kate said, smiling radiantly.

Greg's heart seemed to miss a beat as he gazed at her in wonder. The woman seemed so alive, so luminescent, he felt sure that any moment now she would be transfigured into pure energy.

Recalling how sad and troubled she had been as they had exchanged life stories, he said, "Where's Kate? What have you done with her?"

Kate laughed. "She died. Remember? And you met the new me on Monday when we went to lunch together."

"How could I have forgotten?" he said, though he only recalled that she had seemed happy to be alive.

He studied her a moment longer, feeling enveloped by her warmth, then he noticed two red eyes staring warily at him from behind her skirt.

"Who's your friend?" he asked.

"Shadow." She turned around and addressed the boy. "Shadow, this is Greg. He's a friend of mine, and I'm sure he'll be your friend, too."

"Hello, Shadow," Greg said, holding out his hand.

Shadow ignored the hand and stared gravely up at him. Greg let his hand drift down to his side so as not to alarm the boy, and returned his gaze, man to man. Shadow might be young in years, but he had the bearing of one who'd lived a lifetime.

Kate smiled at both of them and led the boy into the kitchen.

"Dee? Will you mind looking after Shadow for a while?" Greg heard her say. "Maybe fix him something to eat?"

He stood, hat in hand, wondering if he should leave. Kate had enough to do without entertaining him.

She returned to the living room, gave him a rueful look. "Sorry I left you standing here. I'm not good at this hostess stuff. Let me take your hat and coat."

"I'm fine, really."

"At least sit down."

He sat at one end of the couch, balancing his hat on his knees. Kate perched at the other end, gave him a brief explanation of her involvement with the homeless people, then told him about Shadow.

"I have a friend who's a cop," Greg said. "Would you like me to have him look into it? Maybe check missing persons?"

Kate's radiance dimmed. "I guess. Even though his mother threw him away, she is his mother. Maybe she's remorseful and wants him back. Don't let the cops know where he is, okay? I don't want him disappearing into the system."

"I'll be discreet. I promise."

"Even if they do find out who he is, I want to check things out before I decide what to do. It's possible he's been abused."

"In that case, we won't send him back. There's enough abuse in the world as it is," Greg said, thinking about the horrors of biological warfare and the even greater horrors of human experiments.

Some of what he felt must have shown on his face, because Kate asked, sounding alarmed, "What's wrong?"

He hesitated. Maybe he should keep his thoughts to himself.

"If it's that bad," Kate said, reading his mind again, "You should tell me. There's no point in carrying the burden by yourself."

Not sure he was doing the right thing, he recounted both conversations with Clara D'Onofria. Unlike Clara, he did not need notes to refresh his memory; every word she had spoken fused to his brain.

When he finished, Kate drew in a long, ragged breath, scooted closer to him, and held out a hand.

He grasped it, glad of the contact.

They sat silently while the argument in the dining room rose to a crescendo then trailed away as, one by one, the wranglers rose from the table and left the house, banging the back door behind them.

Dee, with Shadow's help, cleared the table. "Are you two going to eat?" she called out. "The chicken à la king is gone, but there's a little pot roast left."

Kate turned to Greg. "You hungry?"

"Not really."

"Me neither." She gave his hand a squeeze, then let go. "We'll eat later, Dee. If you want the roast, go ahead, I can fix something else."

"That's okay. I'll save it for you."

Watching the woman clear off the table, Greg said, "I didn't recognize Dee in her new clothes."

"Poor Dee. Her clothes fell apart when we washed them. We couldn't buy her any new ones since the stores are closed, and mine don't fit her, so she's stuck wearing Joe's clothes."

Greg raised his eyebrows. "Joe's clothes?"

Kate laughed. "It has been a while since you've been here, hasn't it? She sleeps in Joe's room, too. I saw no point in her continuing to sleep on the couch when I have a perfectly good bed she can use."

He searched her face. "You okay with that?"

"Surprisingly, yes. I'll admit it felt strange at first, particularly seeing her in Joe's clothes, but I've gotten used to it."

"You are an amazing woman, Kate Cummings."

Kate blushed and averted her eyes.

Before he could elaborate, he heard a distant thud and the screech of a cat. He sat up straight. "What was that?"

"It sounds like Mrs. Robin's cat. I better go see what's going on."

She dashed out of the house. Shadow dropped the plate he held and ran after her. Dee followed. Greg brought up the rear.

By the time Greg got outside, Kate had opened her gate and was hurrying down the alley to the gate of the house next door.

Greg vaulted over the wooden fence connecting the two properties. An old woman lay face down on the back stoop. Her feet propped the door open. Her arms, clutching what looked like a bag of trash, were crushed beneath her body.

Greg touched the side of her neck. No pulse. When Kate came, he stood aside to give her room.

She crouched over the woman. "It looks like she died of a massive heart attack or a stroke. She must have died instantly, didn't even have time to drop the bag and put out her hands to try to break her fall."

A black cat, which had been staring balefully at them, sprang over the woman's feet and entered the house. Shadow scrambled after the cat. Dee grabbed for him, but missed. She glanced at Kate, shrugged, then climbed over the old woman's body and went in search of the boy.

"What now?" Greg asked.

Kate sighed. "I don't know. Are we supposed to call two-two-two when anyone dies, or just red death victims?"

"No one ever said. Maybe we could call a relative."

"She didn't have any. It was the one thing we had in common. We were both only children of only children, and we both married only children of only children. She had a child, a daughter named Jill, but Jill died 'without issue,' as they say."

"Kate?" Dee called. "Can you come here a minute?"

Kate stepped over the old woman and stood inside the door. "Where are you?"

"In the basement."

Feeling like the tail end in a game of crack-the-whip, Greg followed Kate.

"Where are you?" Kate asked again when she reached the bottom of the stairs.

"Over here. To your right."

Greg trailed after Kate and stopped in amazement when he entered a small room lined with shelves. Two shelving units ran down the center of the room. Food crammed every single inch of shelf space. Home-canned fruits and vegetables. Store bought canned fruits, vegetables, meat, fish, soup. Packages of pasta and dried beans. Cans of chili and ravioli. Coffee. Boxes of macaroni and cheese. Bags of powdered milk, flour, sugar, nuts.

"It's like a tiny grocery store," Kate said, sounding awed.

After the first shock wore away, Greg laughed. "Looks

like the storeroom in my grandmother's basement. She grew up in the depression when food was hard to come by, especially on the western slope. Since she didn't believe banks were safe, whenever she got extra money, she bought canned goods. That was the kind of savings she understood. Drove my mother crazy."

Dee spread her arms wide. "Now we won't have to turn anyone away. About all that's left of your food, Kate, is oatmeal, flour, yeast, and all that butter in your freezer— plenty to keep you, me, and Shadow from going hungry, but not enough to share."

"All that butter?" Greg repeated. "How much butter do you have?"

"A little," Kate said at the same time Dee was saying, "A lot."

Kate flushed. "I stock up on butter when it goes on sale. Before the quarantine, the red death distracted me and I kept forgetting I had already stocked up, so I overbought."

Dee hooted. "Overbought! That's putting it mildly. But it's a good thing. Pretty soon bread and butter will be all we have to eat." She showed Kate the back of her hand. "Today I went to the grocery store—I mean, the Commodity Distribution Center—and got chipped, but my ration for the week is already gone. Siggy and those guys ate it for dinner tonight."

Kate looked around the storeroom. "So what are we going to do? There's no way we can carry all this stuff over to my house without being seen either by nosy neighbors or by the military patrols."

"We'll have to get Mrs. Robin away from the house," Greg said. "If one of those fluorescent marks appears on the door, it will be too dangerous for you to come again. Without proof you live here, you could be gunned down on the spot."

Kate looked at Shadow playing with the cat, then at Dee nodding in approval, then at Greg.

Understanding her hesitancy, Greg took hold of her hands. "I know it sounds cruel, but it won't bother Mrs.

Robin any. You have to think of the living. This way you can continue to feed people. You'd like that, wouldn't you?"

"You're right. I know you're right," Kate said, sighing. "I don't like the person this quarantine is turning me into."

Greg smiled at her. "Well, I do. I like her very much."

# 20

*Thursday, December 15*

"Seems like we're going steady," Greg said when, once again, his day began with a visit from Clara D'Onofrio.

One corner of her lips curved in a faint half-smile, but she didn't say anything.

Noting that her pallid cheeks of yesterday had brightened to a rosy glow and the fire in her eyes had died down to a becoming sparkle, he said, "You're looking good today."

She shook her head, frowning. "I'm surprised at you, boy. Flattery is such cheap currency."

Greg opened his mouth to protest that he spoke the truth; then, shrugging, he closed it again. If the woman didn't like compliments, that was her prerogative.

Clara dumped a stack of papers a foot high onto his desk.

"What's this?" he asked.

"Articles from various research journals. You wanted whatever I could find on Takamura. This is it."

"He wrote all this?"

"Some of the papers were written by other people, but since they cited Takamura, I printed them out anyway. Charged it to the newspaper."

With one hand, Greg riffled through the stack of paper. "Wordy fellow."

"And this isn't all. I only went back fifteen years. Let me know if you want the rest of it."

Eyeing the papers, Greg said, "This is plenty for now. Thanks for the help."

"No problem. I had other things to do last night, so I didn't get a chance to work on your journal, but I haven't forgotten about it."

Greg handed her a cardboard box about the size of a ream of paper. "These are the documents you agreed to translate for me."

Clara tucked the box under her arm then, with a swirl of

her flowered skirt, she turned and hurried away from Greg's cubicle, almost running into Don Olaf.

The two nodded at each other as if strangers but, as they passed, their hands happened to touch.

"How's the research coming, Greg?" Olaf asked, a shade too heartily.

"I feel as if I'm drowning in paper."

"So I see," Olaf said, laying a hand on the stack of Takamura's articles. "Mind if I look?"

"Help yourself. They belong to the newspaper."

Olaf settled himself in his customary chair with a handful of the papers. A minute later, he raised his head.

"How do these guys get anything printed? If my reporters turned in work as incomprehensible as this, they'd be out of here so fast they'd think they were flying." He glanced at the papers and shook his head. "Even the titles are incomprehensible. 'Imitating Organic Morphology in Micro-fabrication.' I don't even know what that means."

"Me neither," Greg said, thinking if he had to wade through this sort of stuff to learn about the red death, the earth would fall into the sun long before he read half of it. He put his hands together as if in prayer. "Please tell me it's not written by John Takamura."

"It isn't. Doris Stefano, Melanie Levy, Andrew Forbes, and Lee Nishimura collaborated on this particular gem."

Good. That meant he had to scan it for Takamura's name instead of reading the entire thing.

"These two are by Takamura. 'Self-Dispersement of Genetically Enhanced Corn,' 'Deviant Behavior in Recombinant Plant Parasitoids.'" He tossed the sheaf of papers back onto Greg's desk. "Better you than me."

"What do these guys do?" Greg asked. "Take a course in obfuscation?"

"Probably. Convoluted writing and obscure terms are a way of intimidating the uninitiated, keeping the profession closed to non-scientists, and adding to the scientific mystique. Just think, if diseases had names like Bob and Carol and Ted and Alice, doctors wouldn't make anywhere near the amount of money they do now."

Greg laughed. "That's an idea. They do it for hurricanes, why not everything else?" He mimed seizing the phone and dialing. "Mr. Olaf? I can't come in today. I've got the Bob." He hung up his imaginary receiver and looked inquiringly at his boss.

Olaf nodded. "Works for me."

After an uneventful day at work, Kate hurried home through the silent streets. More than half the houses she passed had fluorescent orange dots splashed on their front doors. Beside some of those doors were small shrines or memorials—artificial flowers, crosses, dolls, teddy bears. Other houses were unlit, mute testimony that entire families had died.

A white unmarked delivery van stopped in front of a house that already had one fluorescent dot on the door. When two men jumped out of the truck and ran up the porch steps, she knew that soon another orange mark would appear next to the first.

She could hear the men lamenting the loss of the Broncos while they waited for someone to answer their knock. It seemed strange that they spoke of such a prosaic matter. Shouldn't they be crying, "Bring out your dead. Bring out your dead," as their counterparts during the Black Death had done?

As she neared the house, she could see the door open. An old woman with bowed head and trembling shoulders stood aside to let the two men enter.

She had passed the house by the time the men emerged with their burden, but she could hear the thud of the body when they threw it into the van.

She thought of Greg and how he had cradled Mrs. Robin in his arms as he carried her down the alley and how he had gently laid her under a tree in the next block.

And how he had said he liked her, Kate, very much.

Halfway home, she caught sight of two men in the driveway of the next house up ahead.

She angled away from them.

When they moved toward the sidewalk, she could see the military vehicle parked in the driveway behind them, and the silhouette of their shouldered rifles.

She cut between two parked cars, and stepped into the street.

Before she could cross to the other side, a deep, authoritative voice rang out.

"You! Stop right there!"

She froze.

With a thudding heart and quaking knees, she watched the two soldiers advance. Though one had a round, babyish face with a pug nose, and the other had a long, thin face with black eyebrows that almost met over a hooked nose, they seemed much alike. Both were young, of medium height, with stocky bodies, aggressive postures, and a look of arrogance in their cold, staring eyes. The baby-faced one might have been a female, but because of the bulky uniform and because he or she didn't speak, Kate couldn't tell for sure.

But, male or female, the creature was a soldier. A soldier who poked Kate in the side with a rifle.

*Stop it*, Kate screamed silently. *Stop it!*

The soldier with the hooked nose still had his rifle slung across his back, but his hands were not empty. He carried a piece of equipment that looked like the wand the grocery store clerk had used to check the computer chip implants.

"Hold out your hands," he commanded.

Kate held out her trembling hands.

He grabbed her right hand, jerked it toward him, then ran the wand over the back of it.

"Nothing," he said.

He motioned with his head. Baby-face stepped away, but continued to keep the rifle trained on Kate.

Hooked-nose shoved Kate against a parked car and shouted, "Hands on the vehicle!"

As soon as Kate had placed her hands on the hood of the car, he kicked her legs back until she leaned at a forty-five degree angle. He kicked her legs again, moving them far apart.

Reaching inside her coat, he pressed his hands against her breasts, between them, under them. He ran his hands down her sides and back up to her chest. He dug his fingers into her breasts, then he pinched her nipples so hard tears stung her eyes.

He ran his fingers down her belly and across her back. Taking his hands out of her coat, he brushed them under her arms.

Kate thought he had finished with her, but then she felt his fingers on her right ankle. Biting her bottom lip to keep from crying out, she tried to will his hands away, but they slowly crept up her leg and under her skirt, lingering for a time at her crotch.

He removed his hands. A second later she felt them on her left ankle.

Her arms shook so violently she thought any moment she would collapse against the car. If she did, would the soldiers consider that a reason to shoot her?

"She's clean," Hooked-nose said at last.

Kate turned her head to look at Baby-face, but saw no acknowledgment in the impassive expression that anything untoward had transpired.

"Eyes front!" Hooked-nose shouted.

Kate stared down at the hood of the car.

He yanked at her purse, which still hung from her arm. It didn't come loose.

He yanked it again, pulling Kate with it. The purse slipped off her arm; she fell to the ground.

He upended the purse on the hood of the car. Snatched her wallet. Opened it. Looked through it.

"Name?" he barked.

"Kathryn Cummings."

He glanced at her wallet, apparently checking her driver's license.

"Address?"

Kate recited her address.

"What are you doing here?"

"Walking home from work."

"Where do you work?"

"The Bowers Clinic on Seventh Avenue."

"Who's your boss?"

"Dr. Winfield Bowers."

He dropped the wallet on the hood of the car. "Go directly home. If we see you on the streets again tonight, you will be arrested."

Kate lay on the ground, waiting for the soldiers to back away, but they continued to stand over her.

"Go!" Hooked-nose ordered.

She reached for the door handle of the car and pulled herself to her feet. She picked up her purse, stuffed everything back into it except for the lipstick and the few coins that had rolled under the car, then turned toward the soldiers.

They still did not move.

Though the rifle was no longer aimed at her, resting instead on Baby-face's cocked hip, both pairs of eyes continued to bore into her.

Trying to make herself as small as possible, Kate squeezed between the two soldiers. She flinched when she brushed against them, but they did not blink.

She left, reeling on wobbly legs. The soldiers pivoted, keeping their eyes on her.

Even when she moved well away from them, she could still feel those eyes on her back, those fingers poking and prodding her body.

She shivered at the thought that they knew where she lived.

But she didn't have to go home to an empty house. Dee would be there, and so would Siggy and the other lost souls in need of a meal. Shadow would be there, of course, along with his new friend, Ebony, Mrs. Robin's cat. Perhaps even Greg would stop by for supper.

She wondered what she should cook, then realized Dee would probably have already prepared a meal.

Her stomach rumbled, reminding her she was hungry. Ravenous, in fact.

Maybe Dee had made one of her delicious stews.

She quickened her steps.

# 21

*Friday, December 16*

"Is Clara around?" Greg asked when Don Olaf stopped by his cubicle. "I haven't seen her this morning."

Olaf sat and leaned back in the chair. "No. She's at a meeting."

The casual remark seemed so normal, so pre-red-death, that it hung in the air between them like a half-remembered scent.

Olaf gave a shake, as if sloughing off a momentary nostalgia. "She's out interviewing Harley Reese."

"Any particular reason?"

"None that I know of. He called her, said he'd be willing to give her an interview. With the red death and all, the media hasn't been giving him enough attention. Clara hates the little weasel, but she felt she ought to see what he had to say. Besides, he's feeding her brunch, and nowadays a person can't afford to turn down a meal. Have you decoded any of Takamura's papers?"

Greg snorted. "You know that one about Self-Dispersement of Genetically Enhanced Corn? It distilled down to the fact that genetically modified corn escapes its boundaries and shows up in distant cornfields, sometimes many miles away. And the one about deviant behavior in plant parasitoids said genetically altered parasitoids, which are parasites that kill their host, behave differently from ones that haven't been altered. Big deal. But none of the articles I've managed to decipher have anything to do with the red death."

"What did you expect?" Olaf said. "A paper explaining how Takamura created the chimera?"

"No, but it sure would be nice."

After Olaf left, Greg tried calling Jim at the police station. He had called several times yesterday, but each time his friend had been away from his desk and he had felt awkward leaving a message about a non-emergency situation.

To his surprise, Jim came on the line.

"I need a favor," Greg said.

"This isn't a good time. Army brass are crawling all over the place. Go to The Lucky Star around three o'clock. I should be able to stop by for a few minutes."

"I'll be there."

Greg replaced the receiver and contemplated the stack of papers on his desk. Sighing, he grabbed one of Takamura's articles, "Biotechnology: Gene Synthesis and Molecular Dynamics," and began the laborious process of decoding it.

Toying with the twenty-dollar mug of beer, Greg studied the patrons of The Lucky Star while he waited for Jim to arrive.

He found it interesting that once he had wanted to be as hard-eyed as these men and women, but now that he could feel an edge being honed somewhere deep inside of him, he didn't like it.

"I only have a minute," Jim said, appearing as if out of nowhere and sliding into the seat opposite him. Indicating the beer, he asked, "You going to drink that?"

Greg nudged the mug across the table. "I hope you like it warm."

Jim chugged half the beer. "Doesn't matter. Warm or cold, horse liniment is still horse liniment. So, what do you need?"

"A friend of mine is taking care of a boy, three or four years old, whose mother dumped him on the streets. Will you check with missing persons—unofficially—to see if his mother filed a report?"

Jim stared at him for a moment, then threw back his head and let out a loud guffaw. "You're always good for a laugh, Greg."

"Why? What did I say?"

"So many people were reported missing during the first days of the epidemic, that no one keeps track any more."

"No one?"

"In the beginning, the vast majority of people who got

219

the red death died in their cars, on the streets, in the stores, at work. When they didn't come home, their families filed missing person reports. There were too many. The system broke down. Plus, we didn't have the resources to track down and contact the next-of-kin of everyone who died—we still don't—so most people have no idea what happened to their loved ones, though I'm sure they've guessed by now. The personal effects of the victims have been saved, so perhaps after the quarantine is lifted, it will be sorted out, but it will take years."

"It keeps getting worse and worse, doesn't it?" Greg said.

"A regular bureaucratic nightmare. I hope your friend wants a kid, because by the time we figure out who he is, if we ever do, he'll probably be ready for college. If your friend doesn't want the boy, there's Child Protective Services, but I wouldn't wish that on my worst enemy. Well, maybe my worst enemy, but that's all."

Jim finished the beer and stood, ready to leave. "I asked our mass mutilator about her diet. She didn't eat anything special, but she loved pumpkin seeds. That's what set her off this last time. Her husband found her stash of seeds and ate every single one."

"Is there any chance I can talk to her?"

"No. She died this afternoon from the red death."

Greg leaned his bicycle against the wrought-iron fence surrounding what he had come to think of as Peter's tree, and paced while he waited for the man to arrive. Peter had left a cryptic message on the answering machine hinting at further developments, which could only mean more bad news.

He was checking his watch for the third time when he heard a car that rattled so much it sounded as if it would fall apart at any moment. He looked up to see a small, boxy green car with a white roof pull into a parking space along the street. Well, not exactly into—the car stopped two feet away from the curb.

A driver emerged from the car. Greg's mouth fell open when he realized it was Peter Jensen.

"You told me you didn't know how to drive," he said.

"I told you I *couldn't* drive. I don't have a driver's license. I can't pass the eye exam anymore."

"So why—" Greg stopped, not knowing how to phrase his question without sounding rude or insensitive.

"So why am I driving?"

Greg nodded.

"Because I want to. I can't see well enough to drive in traffic, but I don't do too badly now that the streets are practically empty. And I like driving."

"What's going to happen if one of those gung-ho army types stop you and you don't have a license? Some of them don't need much more provocation than that to shoot."

"I don't see the point of obeying their rules anymore. I don't even know what the rules are. It seems as if they're inventing them as they go along. You could say that by driving I'm staging my own private rebellion."

Greg squinted at him. "I can't tell whether you're being brave or foolhardy."

Peter shrugged. "Same thing. But I have no choice. The buses aren't running and my legs don't work well enough for me to walk or bike very far."

"I thought you lived around here."

"No."

Greg shot him an inquisitive look; when Peter didn't elucidate, he began circling the green and white vehicle, studying it from all angles.

"Whose car is this?"

"Mine."

"What kind is it?"

Peter raised his eyebrows. "I didn't take you for a car guy."

"I'm not. But I never saw one like this before."

"It's a 1962 Corvair."

"I thought a Corvair was a sports car."

"You're probably thinking of a Corvette. This is a

Corvair, Chevrolet's answer to the Volkswagen Beetle. Like the bug, the engine is in the back. As far as I know, this is the last one left in Denver, and I haven't driven it for several years."

Despite the impatience Greg detected in Peter's voice, he couldn't drop the subject. "Have you had it long?"

"Since I was sixteen. I bought it from the guy next door when he moved to Alaska. And no, I don't know how many miles it has on it. The odometer froze over a decade ago. Anything else?"

Greg wished he could think of a zillion more car questions so they wouldn't have to discuss the red death. Finally, resigning himself to the inevitable, he asked, "What do you have for me?"

"Primary stage infections, liposomes, and zombies."

"Primary stage infection? That doesn't sound good."

"It's not. I told you the chimera mutates rapidly?"

"Yes."

"Until today, people's bodies have all reacted the same to the red death, either getting mild flu symptoms or vomiting blood and dying. But the disease being passed from person to person today is vastly different from the original chimera. The thing is, some people are still dying from the primary stage of the organism."

"So some of the chimeras aren't mutating?"

"The ones being passed around are all mutating."

Greg stared at him in horror. "Are you telling me some of the original organisms are still alive? In the air?"

Peter nodded.

"I didn't realize diseases could live in the open that long."

"Sunlight and ambient temperatures do destroy most organisms rapidly, but not all. Cholera lasts three days. Plague lasts a week, so does dysentery. Anthrax lives for three months unless it turns into a spore, in which case it lasts indefinitely. Gruinard Island, off the coast of Scotland, remained infected with anthrax for forty years after biological warfare tests there in the 1940s. It would still be infected today if they hadn't made a concerted effort to clean it up."

Greg thrust his hands in his pockets to keep them from trembling. "The quarantine is never going to be lifted, is it? Even if the red death mutates into something benign, it could start all over again."

"Looks that way."

Greg had to clear his throat before he could speak; even so, all he managed to get out was a long, low, "Jeez."

Reminding himself that as a reporter he needed to remain emotionally uninvolved with his story, he took a deep breath and let it out slowly.

"What about if we all wore surgical masks?" he asked.

"People have died while wearing them. The chimera found other ways of entering those bodies—through a scratch or any other break in the skin, perhaps even by ingestion."

"Maybe someone will discover a cure."

"I doubt it."

"The other day a friend and I discovered an interesting pattern. People who eat foods containing unmodified fats seem to have a temporary immunity to the red death, but once they stop eating them, they're as susceptible as everyone else."

After Greg had recounted his conversation with Kate at The Black Forest, Peter gave him a long, considering look.

"It's possible," he said at last. "One of the things I planned to tell you is that the doctors at the lab have discovered a liposome attached to the chimera. A liposome, in case you don't remember your high school biology, is a globule of fat suspended in the cytoplasm of a cell. The liposome, in combination with the human genes in the chimera, makes the organism appear as if it belongs in the body. Because the immune system doesn't recognize the chimera as a foreign invader, the disease is able to take over without any resistance whatsoever.

"Because the entire organism has been bio-engineered, it's not too farfetched to think that the liposome has also been genetically altered, perhaps to allow it to combine with some fats and not others."

"And then what?" Greg asked.

"I don't know. Maybe the whole thing exits the body without doing any harm, or maybe the fat somehow detaches the liposome from the chimera, allowing the immune system to see it for what it is."

"And maybe Kate and I are wrong."

"That, too. I can mention this to one of the doctors I work for. He thinks I'm something of an idiot savant ever since I passed along the information about the red death originating at a Broncos game. He took the credit for it, of course, which added to his stature, so I'm sure he won't object to another tip."

"I'd be interested in knowing what he finds out," Greg said.

"I'll be sure to keep you informed."

"Do you know anything about Harley Reese?"

If the abrupt change of subject took Peter aback, he didn't show it. He merely lifted his shoulders in a slight shrug and said, "Some, why?"

"No reason. It's that his name keeps popping up, and I don't like coincidences."

"Are you thinking he might be responsible for the red death? Well, if you want my opinion, I think he's capable of it. He's a true psychopath."

Greg blinked. "A serial killer?"

"Not a serial killer. Most psychopaths don't kill. There are probably twenty to thirty thousand non-violent psychopaths for every murderous one."

"Then why are they called psychopaths?"

"I'm not sure. For a while they were called sociopaths, which is probably a better term, but psychopath is the one that stuck."

"I'm not sure I even know what a psychopath is."

"Someone who has no conscience, lacks empathy, and has shallow emotions. They don't care about other people and don't understand why they should, though most learn to act as if they do. They're excessively neat and organized. They're irresponsible—they see no need to fulfill commitments—and they lie for no reason, but they're also smart and very charming. But the main thing is that they have no conscience.

"I have a theory, entirely unproven, that a lot of psychopaths gravitate to the sciences, biology especially, where they can hide behind that famed scientific detachment. They can also torture animals in the name of science, and no one calls them insane."

"I get the impression you don't like Harley Reese."

"I don't. I think the only reason he isn't a serial killer is that he's not angry. As far as I know, he has no reason to kill, though at one time some thought he killed his partner, the brains behind the Reese Institute. No one could prove a murder had ever taken place since the body never showed up, so nothing came of it."

"I didn't know that."

"It happened a long time ago, and Reese's lawyers managed to keep the whole thing quiet."

"Then how do you know about it?"

"Reese bragged about it once. He didn't say he killed his partner, just that he could have if he had wanted to and no one would ever have known."

Greg stared at him. "This is so weird. You've told me a lot of strange things over the years, but this—"

"If you knew Reese, it wouldn't seem strange."

"It's not that. I don't mean to be disrespectful, but you and Reese? It doesn't make sense to me."

Peter waved a hand dismissively. "We're not friends or anything. In fact, his bragging about being a potential killer was not meant as a confidence, but as a threat."

Greg shook his head. "Weirder and weirder."

"It's simple, really. He used to go to the local art shows, hoping, I think, to find something he could buy for pennies that would eventually be worth millions. Every once in a while, he'd stop by my booth and pick out several of my carvings. We'd chat a few minutes, then he'd drop the figurines on the table and say, 'Maybe next time.'

"One day he handed me the carvings and said, 'I'll buy these,' as if doing me a big favor. I was so surprised, my brain stopped functioning and I took a check."

"So? I mean, he is a rich guy."

"He's notorious for bouncing checks. And, sure enough, the check bounced."

"What did you do?"

"Kept calling the bank to see if it would clear. Kept calling Reese, who insisted the money was in the bank. Finally, I decided to take matters into my own hands. I found out how much he had in his account—"

Greg couldn't help interrupting. "How?"

"Well, the check was for nine thousand dollars—"

Greg gasped. "How much?"

"Nine thousand dollars."

Greg stared at him as if he'd never seen him before. When Peter once mentioned he used to make his living by carving figurines and selling them at art shows, Greg had not envisioned that kind of money. He still couldn't, but he could better understand Peter's anger at fate; the man had lost so much when he started losing his eyesight.

"I called the different branches of Reese's bank," Peter continued. "The first time I said I had a nine thousand dollar check written by Reese on such and such an account. They said he didn't have sufficient funds to cover the check. The second time I called I said I had an eight thousand seven hundred and fifty-dollar check. Still insufficient funds. The third or fourth time, when I asked about eight thousand two hundred and fifty, they said the check would clear. So I went to one of the branches, deposited seven hundred and fifty dollars of my own cash into Reese's account using one of the bank's deposit slips, drove immediately to another branch, presented the bounced check. I got my seven hundred and fifty back, which, incidentally, Reese still owes me, and I also got the eight thousand two hundred and fifty from the account."

"I had no idea—" Greg stopped, not sure what he meant

to say. I had no idea you were so smart? So devious? So crazy?

"No idea what?" Peter prompted.

"That it was legal," Greg finished, though he realized it sounded lame.

"I know one thing," Peter said. "Writing bad checks isn't legal."

"Reese bounces checks and maybe he's a psychopath who killed his partner. Outside of that, do you have any reason to think he's responsible for the red death?"

"Not particularly. I just think he could have. He's smart enough to have created it, careless enough to have let it escape from his lab, and detached enough not to care about what he did. But I don't think he had anything to do with it."

"So we're back to Takamura," Greg murmured, more to himself than to Peter.

"Who's Takamura?"

"A biogeneticist who taught at the University Extension down at Auraria campus, which isn't far from the Broncos stadium. He also worked at a research lab in the Four Corners area. And he was one of the first to die."

Peter looked at Greg as if waiting for him to continue. When Greg remained silent, Peter raised his eyebrows.

"That's it?" he said. "That's all you have linking him to the red death?"

Greg squirmed under the other man's sardonic gaze. "I know it sounds sketchy. I had no reason to suspect him, but I needed a starting place for my investigation. The thing is, once I got the idea into my head, I haven't been able to get rid of it. Every time I think I'm being silly to suspect him, something draws me back."

"Like what?"

"I found out his father did research for the Japanese Imperial Army during World War Two at a place called the Pingfan Institute, near Harbin, in Manchuria."

Greg gave Peter a brief synopsis of the journal's contents.

Peter nodded.

"You know about Pingfan?" Greg asked, wondering why it surprised him.

"I read about it. They often infected a village with a particular disease, then sat back and watched the disease run its course."

"Sounds familiar," Greg said. Then, remembering, "A biogeneticist I interviewed told me the quarantine gave scientists a rare opportunity to see an alien organism moving freely through a human population."

A sudden chill crawled up Greg's spine. *No. It couldn't be. Could it? Nobody could be that cruel.*

Swallowing hard, he asked, "Could John Takamura, or whoever, have released the red death on purpose, just to see what would happen?" Even as he shied away from that unthinkable prospect, part of his mind told him that if John resembled his father, he would be capable of it.

Peter shrugged. "It's possible. It's been done before."

"But here? In the United States?"

"Oh yes. In the 1950s and 60s, all sorts of experiments were performed on unsuspecting citizens. One, called Operation LAC—Large Area Coverage—was the largest test ever undertaken by the U.S. Army Chemical Corps. They dumped Zinc Cadmium Sulfide, a toxic and potentially carcinogenic agent, over a dozen states, but the dispersion of particles covered the country from the Rockies to the Atlantic Ocean, from Canada to the Gulf of Mexico. During one flight of four hundred miles, they released five thousand pounds of the chemical. The thing I find interesting is that they did not study the effect it had on those people. Only the pattern of disbursement and the proper functioning of their equipment interested them.

"And that was only one of the tests. During Senate hearings in 1977, the Pentagon admitted it had conducted two hundred and thirty-nine biological warfare tests over populated areas in the U.S. between 1949 and 1960. The true figure is probably closer to a thousand. Keep in mind, this doesn't include tests done by the CIA or any other government agency.

"I'm allergic to mosquito bites the way some people are allergic to bee stings, so one test I find especially repugnant is the six hundred thousand mosquitoes released in Florida in 1956 to see how insects might spread disease-causing agents. Supposedly the mosquitoes were uninfected with disease, but they greatly increased the pool of potential disease carriers."

Greg blew out his pent-up breath. "How do you remember all that?" he asked, needing to focus on something other than what he had heard.

Peter looked away. "Some mornings when I wake, I can't remember my own name, but this stuff is with me twenty-four hours a day. I can't get rid of it. At first I enjoyed the research, I had an affinity for it, but I found out more than I ever wanted to know, and now, no matter how hard I try, I can't forget any of it, but I can't stop learning, either."

Greg nodded. The same thing was happening to him. "I know they experimented on cattle," he said after a moment, "but I didn't realize they experimented on people, too."

"I have some books you could read, if you'd like."

Greg didn't like, but on the off chance he could find pertinent information, he knew he had to look at them.

"I'd appreciate it," he said, then added, "Do you think the government could be behind the red death?"

"It's possible. The government is a beast without conscience and is capable of anything."

"I hate to admit it, but I think you're right. This whole thing is driving me so crazy, I'm starting to see conspiracies everywhere. I've even been wondering if some sort of biological warfare attack that got out of control caused the 1918 flu pandemic. After all, it did happen while the world was at war."

"Some historians agree with you. In 1932, when biological weapons were first banned, little had been done in the way of biological warfare. Back then, they mostly engaged in chemical warfare, which, by all accounts was horrific. So why, they ask, were biological weapons banned?

The answer is, of course, to make certain another pandemic didn't result."

"I had another strange idea. The other day I noticed that South Korea, where the Hanta virus originated, is due south of Harbin."

Peter stiffened, then closed his eyes as if consulting an internal map. After a moment he opened his eyes and nodded. "So it is. How interesting."

"I know you think the Hanta virus was man-made. Maybe the Japanese created it, and it drifted downward."

"There's another possibility. With all the biological agents the Japanese dumped in Manchuria, perhaps a couple of them infected the same creature, say a rat, and combined to form a new organism. Rats are great incubators of disease."

"Or maybe it evolved naturally from one of those diseases?"

"Could be. Any way you look at it, it's provocative."

"See what I mean about not being able to discount John Takamura? As far as I know, the Hanta virus exists in two places—Korea, which is directly south of Harbin, and the Four Corners area here in Colorado, and both places can be linked to him."

They were silent for a minute or two, then Greg looked at his watch. "I'd better go."

"Do want to stop by my place to pick up the books? We could tie your bike to the car, and I could drive you."

Greg hesitated. Deciding he'd still have time to go see Kate, he nodded. "That'll be fine."

"Good," Peter said. "I haven't told you about the zombies yet."

For the third day in a row, Kate had been pressed into reception duty. The day passed with few calls but, typically, as she was leaving, the phone rang.

She hurried back to the reception desk to answer it.

"I need to know how to kill a zombie," a man said, sounding frantic.

"A what?" Kate asked.

"A zombie," the man repeated, his voice rising. "My wife is dead, but her eyes are open."

"That's perfectly natural," Kate said. "If it bothers you, run your hand over her face to close them."

"I did, but they popped open again. Now she's staring at me." His voice became even more frantic. "She moaned."

"That's natural. It's caused by escaping gases."

"Now her legs are twitching."

"That's natural too," Kate said, "nothing to worry about."

"Oh, God. Now she's sitting up."

Well, that wasn't natural. "Apparently she didn't die."

"She vomited blood, then fell down. I couldn't find a pulse, so I called two-two-two. Oh, no. God, no! Now she's standing." The man's voice rose to a screech. "She's coming after me. Do something!"

Then, abruptly, the line went dead.

"You weren't joking about the zombies?" Greg said.

"No." Peter leaned over the steering wheel and peered through the windshield. "I worked at the morgue yesterday getting body fluid samples from one of the victims of the red death, when suddenly the cadaver sat up and looked around."

"Jeez."

"It gave me a turn, let me tell you."

"What did you do?"

"Called the pathologist, told her she needed to come see something. As she walked in the door, several other dead guys sat up. The pathologist gave me a withering glance and said, 'Oh, puh-leese. I thought you were above this sort of prank, Peter.' Before I could protest that I had nothing to do with it, one of the zombies staggered over to her, grabbed her arm, made a rattling noise in his throat, then died again.

"We ran out of body bags at the beginning of the epidemic, so the corpses were laying on gurneys and piled on autopsy tables, which was a gruesome enough sight in itself, but with all those zombies moving around, the scene came straight out of the worst horror movie you ever saw."

Greg coughed to mask a snort of involuntary laughter. "What did you do?"

"Nothing. Watched. Stayed out of their way. They were too weak to do much harm. In the midst of all this chaos, one of the truckers hired to collect cadavers came in and said something appeared to be wrong with his bodies. As he unloaded one of the cadavers at the disposal site, it struggled. He dropped it, and it slithered away from him. While he and his partner were trying to get it back into the truck, another one crawled out. They finally got both bodies back in the truck, slammed the door so none of the other corpses could escape, then called their dispatcher who told them to bring the bodies to the morgue.

"While he was telling us this story, several more trucks arrived with undead bodies. Since there was no room at the morgue for all those corpses, they were taken to the old meat locker on Wazee Street. I spent most of the day down there helping to sort it all out. The cadavers that remained dead were loaded back on the trucks. The ones that came to life and died again were stored in the locker until someone could decide what to do with them. The other false lifers were taken to a locked ward at Denver Health Medical Center to be tested."

"False lifers?" Greg asked.

"You know doctors. They have to create their own names for things. Can't use a perfectly respectable word like zombie. But the false lifers aren't really zombies since they didn't die.

"As near as anyone can figure it, this new mutation of the chimera doesn't kill. It leaves the body in a state of suspended animation for a while, then there's one last kick of adrenaline, which gets things going again. The trouble is, the people are so debilitated from loss of blood and internal damage caused by the disease, that most die right away. There are some who are hanging on, but their prognosis isn't good."

Greg was reflecting on this latest development when

Peter parked in front of a large house not far from Cheesman Park and turned off the engine.

Puzzled, Greg looked from the house to Peter. Hadn't Peter once told him he lived in a one-room apartment?

"I thought—" He broke off his query when Peter led him to a basement entrance.

"Thought what?" Peter asked, unlocking the door and pushing it open.

"I thought you lived near Washington Park since that's where we meet," Greg said, pleased with his quick recovery.

Peter moved aside to let Greg enter. "It seemed safer."

Greg took a few steps into the room and waited for Peter to turn on the lights. Blinking in the sudden brightness, he gazed at his surroundings.

For the most part the room was as he had pictured it: a kitchenette along one wall, an open door leading to an immaculate bathroom, sparse furnishings, small windows, but he had not imagined the sheer number of books it contained.

The books did not sit on shelves but had been stacked against the walls from floor to ceiling, like three-dimensional wallpaper. Not one inch of wall remained uncovered.

Greg reached out and ran a finger down the spines of the nearest books. "It's like an Aladdin's cave for bibliophiles," he said.

Peter looked around and shrugged, as if he seldom noticed it anymore.

"Where did they all come from?" Greg asked, unable to imagine the time it had taken to amass such a collection.

"Library book sales, garage sales, estate sales, used book stores."

Greg roamed around the room, reading titles at random. No wonder Peter knew so much. He had books on history, science, art, philosophy, health, even one on opals. Also the whole gamut of fiction from mysteries to science fiction to westerns.

"Have you read all these?"

"Most of them."

Still eyeing the books, Greg stumbled into a table. He gave it a curious glance. Three gooseneck lamps stood in the center of the table, all focused on a book with inordinately large print. Then he realized that a rectangular magnifying glass the size of a standard sheet of paper rested on the open book. A pair of magnifying eyeglasses lay next to it.

He swallowed hard at this evidence of Peter's rapidly dimming sight.

"Here are the books I mentioned," Peter said, coming up behind him, making him start.

Clearing his throat, Greg turned around to accept the armload of books. "Sure you don't mind me borrowing these?"

"Not at all. I felt frustrated not being able to talk about what's really going on in the world—it gave it a strength it doesn't deserve—so I've enjoyed having someone to discuss these things with, someone who can contribute to the conversation. Most people are smarter than me and more successful, but they are so arrogant, I find it embarrassing to listen to them. They have learned a trade in life, but they haven't learned life. At times I feel sorry for them because they don't live up to their potential as thinking human beings. They accept the easy platitudes and refuse to look at the big picture. There's no pride in being more knowledgeable than people who embrace ignorance."

Greg gave him a considering look. "I'm having dinner tonight with a friend of mine. I'm not sure how much she knows about so-called conspiracies, but she knows more about life than anyone I ever met. I think you'd like her. Why don't you come?"

"Thanks, but no."

"It's not like she and I are going on a date. We're just friends."

"I'm not exactly dressed for dining out."

Greg chuckled. "Believe me, you will be one of the best-dressed men there."

"What is it? A party? I don't go to parties."

"It's not a party. Tell you what. If you aren't

immediately captivated, you can come right back. I'll make your excuses for you. But I know you'll have an interesting time."

Peter hesitated for a moment. "Sure. Why not?"

Pippi woke and glanced around, trying to recall where she was, and why. Slowly, as if they had to travel a long distance, the memories surfaced. She turned them this way and that, trying to make sense of them, but soon gave up. They didn't seem to have any connection to her.

What was the date? After awakening and falling back to sleep many times, she didn't even know how long she'd been at the house. Two days maybe.

She dragged herself out of her makeshift bed, trudged to the downstairs bathroom to wash, then went to the kitchen and searched the cupboards for something to eat. What about that can of spaghetti with the lift-off top? It wouldn't take any effort to prepare. She leaned against the counter, spooned the food directly into her mouth from the can, and washed it down with tap water.

Back on her pallet, she turned on the television and clicked through the channels. The pretty people on the shows and in the commercials looked odd. Plastic. Studying the perfect face and figure of a model caressing a new car as if it were a lover, Pippi wondered what that woman knew of life. What did any of them?

Click. The raucous sound of a laugh track blared out of the television. Click. The Weather Channel. She sat through detailed descriptions of weather in Utah, Wyoming, Kansas, New Mexico, and heard not one mention of Colorado.

She clicked the remote again. The president's face, carefully arranged in an expression of sincerity, stared out at her. "Shop," he said in mellifluous tones. "Have fun. Enjoy Christmas. Everything is under control."

She turned off the television, lay back down, and listened to the distant rumble of military helicopters until she fell asleep.

# 22

*Saturday, December 17*

Kate opened her drapes and bit back a scream. An unshaven man with bristly eyebrows stared in at her. She hastily pulled the drapes shut and clutched at her chest.

"Dee," she called out. Hearing the quaver in her voice, she breathed deeply, then tried again. "Dee!" This time her voice held strong and steady, but Dee did not respond.

When Kate's heart settled down into its normal rhythm, a sudden pounding on the roof made it beat furiously again.

She slipped out of her nightgown, dressed, and went in search of her roommate. She found her next door in Mrs. Robin's back yard.

"Oh, you're awake," Dee said, meeting her by the fence. "I went into your room this morning to let you know what's going on, but you were dead to the world."

Kate smiled and stretched. "I slept well last night." Then, looking around, "What is going on? What's that man doing at my window?"

"That's Jake. He and Delmar are putting up your storm windows."

"I forgot I had storm windows. Hey, wait a minute. How did Jake and Delmar get them? They were locked in the garage."

"Siggy found them. He's been sleeping in your garage." Dee held out a placating hand. "Before you get upset, keep in mind that if he wasn't there, he wouldn't have heard the guy trying to break in."

Kate stared at her in bewilderment. "What guy? What break-in?"

"At Mrs. Robin's house. Siggy thinks someone who saw me carting food over to your house yesterday at dinnertime came back last night to help himself. Siggy heard the breaking glass and went to investigate, but the guy ran off before Siggy could get a good look at him. Siggy and some of his friends are fixing the window and installing a new lock, but he thinks I should sleep there to keep it from happening again."

"By yourself? Do you think that's a good idea?"

"Siggy will sleep on the couch. And if I cook over there, maybe I won't attract as much attention."

"You're not afraid of getting caught?"

"After all that I've been through the last year? No."

"Whatever you want to do is fine with me. Where's Shadow? I haven't seen him this morning."

Dee gestured toward Mrs. Robin's back door. "He's helping Siggy put in the new lock."

Kate glanced at the little boy hunkered beside Siggy.

"Screwdriver," she heard Siggy say. Shadow, acting as if he had been entrusted with a sacred task, picked up the screwdriver, and handed it to the man.

"He seems more relaxed," Kate said, "but he still hasn't spoken."

"Maybe he has nothing to say."

With her gaze still resting on the boy, Kate asked softly, "What are we going to do about him?"

"Nothing." Dee sounded surprised at the question. "Just take care of him."

Kate nodded. She had come to the same conclusion last night when Greg told her there was no way to find the boy's mother.

A man called down from Kate's roof. "There's some missing shingles up here."

"I'll get some later," Siggy called back.

Before Kate could ask where Siggy got his materials, Dee shook her head. "Don't ask." Then, with a proprietary air, she headed back to her new lodgings.

Glimpsing movement out of the corner of her eye, Kate turned and saw someone peering over her back fence.

She felt a sinking sensation in her belly when she recognized Mr. Crowley, a prim, almost prissy man who lived several houses down from her on the other side of the alley. For years, he had done nothing but nurse his elderly mother, but after her death six months previously, he had made a nuisance of himself by prying into his neighbor's affairs.

Wondering how she could keep Mr. Crowley from finding out what they were doing, Kate ambled to the fence to confront him.

"Is there something I can help you with, Mr. Crowley?" Hearing the sharpness of her tone, she smiled, trying to soften the impact.

Mr. Crowley shuffled his feet and jingled the coins in his pocket. "I wondered . . ." His voice trailed off and he backed away. "Never mind. It was foolish of me to think . . ."

Deciding she'd better find out what he wanted, Kate said, "I haven't had breakfast yet. Why don't you come join me."

"I already ate."

"How about a cup of coffee?"

His eyes lit up. "You have coffee? I finished my ration days ago."

Kate ushered him into the house and poured him a cup of coffee from the pot Dee made earlier. He sipped it reverently, while she fixed herself a cup of tea.

She sat across from him at the kitchen table. "So, tell me, Mr. Crowley, what's on your mind?"

He stole a quick glance at her. "I've been watching you," he began.

Kate tensed.

"I see people coming and going all the time now," he continued. "I see all these people fixing your house and Mrs. Robin's."

He paused.

Kate held her breath.

"And I want to help," he finished, all in a rush.

Kate's breath escaped, leaving her feeling limp.

"Ever since mother died . . ." He toyed with his cup of coffee.

He's shy, Kate realized. And lonely. Perhaps what she had perceived as prying were ill-conceived attempts at neighborliness.

He looked up. "And then this epidemic . . ."

"I know," Kate said softly.

He threw back his shoulders and stiffened his spine. "I'm tired of being afraid. Tired of death. If I don't start living now, I never will. I need to get involved. To help."

"What can you do?"

His shoulders sagged. "Nothing. I'm not good with my hands."

"You took care of your mother, didn't you?"

"Of course."

"So you must be able to do something."

"Basic stuff like cooking and cleaning."

"Do you mind doing dishes?"

"I've washed my share."

"Then come to dinner tonight. You can help with the dishes afterward. Maybe later we'll be able to find something else for you to do."

He reached out and clasped her hand. "Thank you. You have no idea how much I appreciate it."

Kate smiled. When he drew his hand away, looking hurt, she said, "I wasn't laughing at you, Mr. Crowley. I thought of something that happened last night.

"People who come to eat here have been working around the house or bringing something to contribute. Dee and I have made no such stipulation, but Siggy—you'll meet Siggy tonight—has become protective of his private soup kitchen and is determined no one is going to ruin it for him.

"Last night a kid in his twenties came and ate everything in sight. When Siggy told him to help with the dishes or don't come back, the kid ran out of here so fast you'd have thought a posse was chasing him. Yet here you are, thanking me for that same job."

Mr. Crowley gave a polite little titter as if he didn't see the humor, then rose, repeated his thanks, and headed out the back door.

A second or two later, the front door bell rang.

Kate glanced regretfully at her now cold tea and went to answer the door.

"Sorry to bother you," said Anna Brinkley, a retired

schoolteacher who lived down the block, "but I have a problem."

"Yes?"

Anna leaned toward Kate and spoke in a loud whisper. "My toilet is clogged." Then, in her normal voice, she added, "I've called practically every plumber in the book, but no one will come out and fix it. I see you've managed to get people to help you. Can I borrow someone?"

Wondering if she had awakened in an alternate universe, Kate stepped outside and walked around to the back of her house with Anna following close behind.

"Dee!" she shouted when she didn't see her friend.

"What?" Dee shouted back.

"I need to see you a second."

Dee came trotting out the back door of Mrs. Robin's house. "What?" she said, sounding impatient.

"This is Anna Brinkley. She needs someone to unplug her toilet."

Dee shot Kate a bewildered glance; Kate shrugged in response.

Dee went over to where Siggy still worked on the door and conferred with him for a moment. Siggy pointed at one of his helpers, then jerked his thumb toward the schoolteacher.

When the man, who had a thin white scar stretching from his ear to his chin, shambled toward them, Anna backed away and let out a moan. She must have decided a clogged toilet was worse than having to deal with the scarred man, because after a moment's hesitation, she gestured for him to accompany her.

"Very strange," Dee said when she and Kate were alone.

"Obviously, people are spending a lot of time staring out their windows. We'll have to concoct a story about why you're living in Mrs. Robin's house in case anyone questions us."

"Long lost relative, maybe?"

"Long lost *distant* relative, unless we can think of something better. Oh, I found someone to help with the dishes."

After Kate had recounted her conversation with Mr. Crowley, Dee shook her head, looking as befuddled as Kate felt.

Greg felt like throwing the book against the wall. Instead, he carefully laid it on the table with the others he had borrowed from Peter, then he quickly averted his eyes; the very sight of them made him sick to his stomach. How could anyone perpetrate or condone the acts he'd read about? Was everyone in the world a psychopath? No, not everyone, but if he continued with his present research, he would come to believe it.

Some of the books had mentioned Pingfan. In addition to bacteriological experiments, the doctors had conducted experiments on frostbite. Victims were taken outside in the coldest months of the year and forced to immerse their hands and feet in barrels of cold water. They were kept outside until their extremities froze, then were taken back inside so the doctors could investigate means of treating frostbite.

Feeling an empathetic chill, Greg stuck his hands in his pockets to warm them.

The doctors had also done blood work experiments. In an effort to discover if blood other than human could be used to treat wounded soldiers, prisoners had been drained of their own blood and infused with horse's blood. All died.

Equally bad, Greg thought, was how the United States had been so avid to get their hands on the research that not one of the doctors had ever been charged with war crimes.

The pathology squad leader who had conducted live autopsies became a professor at Kyoto University. He later became a professor emeritus of the university and a medical director of the Kinki University at Osaka.

The doctor who had fed typhoid germs in milk to prisoners, and who had been responsible for certain types of germ bombs, became a professor of bacteriology at Kyoto University.

The frostbite expert joined the faculty of Kyoto

Prefectural Medical College and later became its president.

The premier germ bomb expert joined the Japanese National Institute of Health, where he continued his bacteriological research.

The hematologist opened a blood bank that eventually became one of the most successful multi-national medical supply and pharmaceutical companies in the world.

Greg found no mention of Kiichiro Takamura. Either the man had been relatively insignificant and had entered the United States as an ordinary immigrant, or he had been important enough to be brought in with the help of the OSS as many German scientists had been.

Greg rose and paced. The books confirmed what Peter told him; some factions of the United States government, like the military and the CIA, had performed experiments on its citizens.

In 1945, a super-secret experiment conducted by the army and the navy set out to test the effectiveness of airborne viruses as a bio-weapon. U.S. warships off the coast of California cranked open a valve on a large pressure tank resting in the stern. Within seconds, a hissing stream of air, contaminated with influenza viruses, rose into the atmosphere and drifted ashore. For the next few weeks, they monitored the outbreak of flu at various surveillance stations along the coast and up to two hundred and fifty miles inland.

In 1953, the CIA had ordered ten kilos of LSD—enough for thirty million doses—from the original Swiss manufacturer; when the manufacturer refused the order, the CIA contacted an American company who duplicated the formula and made it available to them by the ton.

The CIA established clandestine operations and fronts in both the United States and Canada. One such front was the Society for the Investigation of Human Ecology at Cornell University, which gave grants to institutions for LSD experimentation. One of the grants had been given to the University of Colorado. Although the CIA had conducted experiments on many unwitting and reluctant human guinea pigs, the college students eagerly embraced the new drug culture, and CU became known as a party school.

In the early 1960s, the CIA opened a lab for underground chemists in the San Francisco area. In 1967, they released the formula for STP to the scientific community. Within weeks, STP, a chemical compound more powerful than LSD, became available on the streets of America.

Remembering the chimera's first, euphoric stage, Greg wondered if the red death had been a mind control experiment that had gone terribly wrong.

He knew one thing: it could have come from anywhere. Many countries, both large and small, had experimented with biological warfare. The surprising thing was not that the red death had happened, but that it hadn't happened sooner.

Greg gazed down at the paper littering his living room floor.

Despite what he had learned, he still felt that Takamura held the key. A compass or a divining rod in his mind kept pulling him back to these papers. He stooped, snatched a handful of the yellowed receipts, and let them flutter back onto the pile. The receipts seemed worthless, but he couldn't throw them away until he had found what he sought.

He arched his back, heaved a noisy sigh, and paced again.

What he wanted was to get drunk, but he had finished his small stock of beer and liquor, and he couldn't bear the thought of going to The Lucky Star and drinking horse liniment, as Jim had called it.

What he needed was to be with someone.

He stopped short when he realized Kate's face came to mind, not Pippi's.

*Kate.* The thought of her washed over him like a cool breeze on a hot summer day. Her radiant smile and quiet good sense would be the perfect antidote for the poison coursing through his mind and body. He checked his watch; she'd be serving dinner right about now. He hurried to his bedroom to get changed.

* * *

Kate smiled radiantly at Greg as she drew him into the house.

"I hoped you'd come," she said.

Greg returned her smile. "You couldn't keep me away."

Even after she shut the door, they continued to smile at each other, but then, like a light on a dimmer switch, her smile faded.

"There's something wrong, isn't there?" she asked, searching his face.

Striving for lightness, he shrugged nonchalantly. "The usual."

Kate laughed. "If you're trying to soothe me, it isn't working. For you, 'the usual' generally means something dreadful."

She caught his hand and led him to the couch. "Tell me about it. Unless you'd rather eat first."

Greg glanced into the dining room, which seemed packed with people shoveling food into their mouths, and shook his head.

"So many came tonight, we had to start serving early," Kate said. "There's still more people waiting out back."

Greg hadn't noticed them, probably because he had gone to the front door and rung the bell. Unlike the others who came to this house for food and solace, he didn't feel comfortable drifting in and out of the back door unannounced.

A sudden burst of laughter caught his attention. Greg saw Dee talking to one of the diners as she spooned vegetables onto his plate. The man was looking up at her and laughing. He seemed so young and carefree that Greg felt a twinge of envy.

Greg turned back to Kate, then it dawned on him he knew the man. He whipped his head around to take a second look. *Peter? What was Peter doing here?*

Greg stared at him in wonder, thinking how in all the years he'd known Peter, he'd never heard him laugh.

As if reading his mind, Kate said, "Peter came early to help Dee cook. Looks like she's made a conquest." She laid a hand on Greg's arm. "Don't tease him, okay?"

Without taking his eyes off Peter, Greg said, "I won't. I'm having a hard time getting my mind around it, is all."

Dee moved away from Peter to serve the others at the table. Peter's face didn't fall back into its normal state of impassivity, but continued to be animated. He turned his attention to his fellow diners and engaged in a loud but good-natured argument.

Greg smiled at Kate. "You really are amazing."

"Me? I didn't do anything."

"You started it all. You're like 'a spark of heavenly fire.'"

Kate gazed at him wide-eyed. "What a lovely thing to say. I didn't realize you were so poetic."

"Not me. Washington Irving. 'There is in every true woman's heart a spark of heavenly fire, which lies dormant in the broad daylight of prosperity, but which kindles up, and beams and blazes in the dark hour of adversity.'"

"That's how you see me?" Kate asked, sounding awed.

Greg took her hand and kissed it. "It's not how I see you. It's how you are. You're brightening the world for all of us."

Blushing, Kate averted her gaze. After a moment she turned to him and gave him a shrewd look. "Oh, I get it. You're trying to keep from talking about what's bothering you."

Greg laughed. "You know me so well, but it doesn't make what I said any less true."

Kate edged closer to him until their bodies almost touched. Feeling her heat, he had an urge to gather her in his arms and let her burn away his distress. Instead, he told her everything he had learned.

At the end of his recital, he said, "I feel as if I've lost my way. Even worse, I feel as if I'm being purposely led astray."

"You think you're being given false information?"

"Not just me. All of us. And not false information—as far as I know, it's true. It's more like a smokescreen to obscure a greater truth. It started with the journal. I thought I had uncovered a shocking secret, but it turns out the

Japanese experiments are common knowledge. Most books I go through mention them. Last night I couldn't sleep, so I decided to read a novel. I couldn't believe it when I found out that a pivotal character had been a POW at Pingfan.

"Then there's all this information about the things the Americans had done. People assume there can be no conspiracies because no one can keep a secret, but some of these things were covered up for decades before being brought out in the open. Like MK-Ultra, the CIA mind control experiments in the 1950s and 60s. The CIA destroyed most of those records, so if any information is still available, it means someone wants it to be.

"Between 1955 and 1975, thousands of American soldiers were used as unwitting guinea pigs in various tests. They were gassed, maced, hypnotized, tortured, and drugged in the search for the ultimate mind control weapon.

"The question I keep asking myself is, 'Did they find it?'"

"Did they?" Kate asked.

"I don't know, but I feel fingers poking and prodding at me, as if I'm being herded. There's a saying on the street, 'No one gives away anything of value.' If they're giving up secrets, you have to wonder why.

"A woman at the News told me technology doubles every seven years. If this is true, why don't we see the results of this research? For the most part, new products are sophisticated versions of archaic ones, like the internal combustion engine. Why don't we see anything truly different, anything light years ahead of what we already have?

"I'll tell you why. Because they don't want us to see it.

"I think this proliferation of information about past offenses is nothing more than a sleight of hand to keep us focused on what they want us to see, like old methodologies and outdated technologies, so we don't see what's really going on."

"Sounds like mind control, doesn't it?" Kate said.

Greg nodded. "That's the feeling I've been getting. My

sister once had a poster, 'Life is like an onion. You peel it off in layers, and sometimes you cry.' The way I see it, there's an outer layer most people generally accept as the truth. The whole 'God's in his heaven, the president's in the White House, all's right with the world' philosophy. The ones who can't accept it peel off the first layer and find an entirely different philosophy, one based on so-called conspiracy theories. But an onion has many layers, and somewhere beneath all of those layers is the truth."

"What truth?"

"I don't know and, frankly, I don't want to know. When I first started to research the red death, I lost my enthusiasm for my job because of all the terrible secrets I uncovered. Now I'm losing whatever enthusiasm I have left because I know if I discover something, it's because they want it discovered and if, by some strange quirk of fate I happen to discover something they don't want discovered, it won't get into print. Which means I'm nothing more than a purveyor of gossip. I might as well be writing about movie stars and million dollar athletes. It's all the same in the end.

"I'll tell you something else. That poster had it only partly right. Sometimes I feel like crying, but mostly I'm angry. And scared."

The words stopped flowing out of Greg. After a long while, he said, "Listen to me. I'm talking the way Peter used to. And look at him, laughing and joking. Does it ever seem to you that life plays tricks on us?"

Kate squeezed his hand. "All the time. You know what I think?"

"No."

"I think you should come over tomorrow and help me make bread. There's something basic and decent and com-forting about kneading dough."

Greg smiled. "How did you ever get so wise?"

"Not wise," Kate said quietly. "Whenever I have a problem that cannot be resolved, I bake bread, and I've baked a lot of bread in my life."

# 23

*Sunday, December 18*
Pippi sat bolt upright in bed. *Who buried them?*

She pictured the two neat graves lying a few yards away and realized she couldn't remain at the house. Whoever had dug those graves might return.

But where should she go?

A sudden longing tugged at her heart. Home.

She pictured her beautiful loft and the view of the mountains framed by her front window, and fantasized about long, foamy baths in her soaker tub, cozy nights in her pillow-laden bed, elegant meals in her ultra-modern kitchen.

Why couldn't she make it home? After all, she had managed to get herself back to this house, hadn't she?

But that was fifteen miles. Denver was two hundred and twenty-five miles away. Her feet ached just thinking about it.

What about riding that old one-speed bike she had seen in the shed? It might not get her far before it broke down, but it would give her a head start.

Excited by the possibility of going home, she fixed instant oatmeal and gulped it, having no time for such trivialities as chewing.

After she had rinsed her bowl and spoon, she ran upstairs and systematically searched the bedrooms, looking for anything that might make her journey easier. While ransacking one closet, hoping to find a pair of boots that would fit, she found a small hunting knife. She slipped the sheath on a belt, then buckled it around her waist, not wanting to take a chance on losing it.

She carried armloads of clothes and toiletries down to the kitchen, then searched the rooms on the lower floor.

In the afternoon, she cooked a hamburger and began eating it while eyeing the mound of supplies she had collected. She would be well prepared; no wandering around the countryside eating snow and dried corn for her.

She froze with her hamburger halfway to her open mouth. Oh, God. She would need a pickup truck to carry all that stuff.

She dropped her hamburger back on the plate and slumped in her chair.

What was she supposed to do now?

She closed her eyes, unable to look at the evidence of her foolishness, but after a minute or two, she opened them, sat up straight, and forced herself to finish eating.

When she had swallowed the last tasteless bite, she rose and sorted through her provisions. As a mental exercise, she told herself.

Even after she had discarded all but the most indispensable items, she still had way too much to carry.

She plopped down in a chair, folded her arms on the kitchen table, and laid her head on her arms.

Now what?

Greg moved behind Kate, who stood at the kitchen table kneading bread dough.

Putting his arms around her, he said, "You smell good." He rested his cheek on the top of her head. "You feel good, too."

Kate laughed. "I thought you came to help bake bread."

"I did. When I was young, I loved helping my grandmother. She smelled all yeasty like you."

Kate craned her neck and twinkled up at him. "So I'm a grandmother substitute to you?"

Feeling himself grow hard, Greg said, "I don't think so."

As he continued to hold her, she relaxed against him.

His breath quickened.

Brushing her hair to the side, he bent and kissed the nape of her neck. When he kissed the curve between her neck and her shoulder, she let out a sigh, reached up her arms, and cradled his head.

His hands, with a volition of their own, cupped her straining breasts.

She gasped.

He moved his hands away, but she put her hands over his and held them in place.

He laid his cheek against hers. She turned her head. Their lips touched.

Then all at once they were face to face, clasped in each other's arms, mouths locked together. As he crushed her to him, he could feel her heart beating against his, beating in time with his.

When they finally broke apart, she leaned back in the circle of his arms, and gazed up at him with shining eyes.

He drew in a long, ragged breath, then kissed the hollow at the base of her throat. He felt her pulse fluttering wildly beneath his lips and the answering throb of his own body. The timer went off, but he kept his arms around her, not wanting the moment to pass.

"I hear bells," she murmured.

"The timer."

"Oh."

After another kiss, she disentangled herself. "I have to get the bread before it burns."

"You women are all alike," he said in a husky voice. "You invite a guy over to knead your dough, then you leave as soon as someone else rings your bell."

Her eyes widened. She giggled and threw her arms about him. "Oh, Greg, I do love you."

Deep inside of him blossomed something he'd never felt before. He gently grasped her shoulders and held her away from him to search her eyes. "What did you say?"

"I don't know. You've got me so addled I'm not thinking straight."

"You said you loved me."

She lowered her head, blushing. "I didn't realize I spoke out loud."

"You love me?"

Without responding, she went over to the oven and removed the golden loaves. In an obvious attempt to distract him, she cut off a piece of the bread, slathered it with butter, and handed it to him. Although the bread smelled wonderful, he wouldn't let himself be sidetracked.

"You love me?" he asked again.

She sighed. "Forget it, okay? It's not relevant."

"Not relevant? How can it not be relevant?"

"You're engaged, remember?"

"Oh, right." Suddenly deflated, he dropped onto a chair. "I forgot about Pippi." He nibbled on a corner of the bread, then set it on the dish Kate had placed in front of him.

"The thing is," he said, "I don't know if I'm engaged or not. Remember our first lunch at The Black Forest when Pippi called me?"

Kate nodded.

"I never talked to her again. When I got to The Lucky Star that night, all set to give her the ring, I found out she'd run off with Jeremy King, the actor. It seems she's no longer interested in me, but until I can talk to her and make sure she's okay, I don't feel right about getting involved with anyone else."

When Kate reached out and laid her hands over his, he realized there would be no awkwardness over her declaration. Their friendship would remain the same.

But he didn't want it to be the same.

He wanted more.

When all their guests had gone, when Mr. Crowley and two inept draftees had cleaned both kitchens and disappeared down the alley, when Siggy had left to prowl the streets, Kate and Greg, Dee and Peter, Shadow and Ebony, relaxed in Kate's living room.

Kate listened to Dee telling Peter they weren't using the food in the storeroom as fast as she'd expected. Most of their guests brought small offerings: dented cans of food; mysterious hunks of meat (probably pigeon, Dee said hopefully). Some had even registered at the Commodity Distribution Center and donated the part of their rations that needed to be cooked.

Shadow sat on the floor next to Kate's chair, playing with the cat. Watching him, Kate thought it was a good thing she and Greg had stopped kissing when they did. Moments later, Shadow had quietly entered the kitchen and remained at her heels the rest of the day.

Kate glanced at Greg, who seemed unnaturally quiet. Did their encounter rock him as much as it had rocked her?

Until she had blurted out the words, she hadn't realized how much she loved him, wanted him. She had thought that part of her life was over. She'd never been sexually attracted to anyone but Joe, and after his illness had killed their love life, she'd become so used to being without sex that she had thought she didn't want it or need it.

As if aware of her musings, Greg turned toward her. Their eyes met. Desire swept through her in a warm rush.

She lowered her head to hide her burning cheeks.

"What do you think, Kate?" Dee asked.

"About what?" Kate said, hoping Dee didn't notice the quaver in her voice.

"About serving dinner at my house. That way we won't have to drag the cooked food over to yours."

"Good idea. Greg, yesterday Dee and I inventoried the larder, and we discovered a case of expensive brandy. You interested? We'd as soon get it out of there. Most of these people have been without a drink for some time now, and we don't want to tempt anyone."

"I have a friend who drinks brandy," Greg said. "I'm sure he'd like it. I've been meaning to ask you—Jim, my friend, has four children, and since they're only allowed rations for two, I'm not sure they have enough to eat. Would it be okay if I bought some of the food from you?"

"You can have the food," Kate said, wondering how Pippi could have walked away from this man. "You don't have to pay for it. It belongs to all of us."

"I'd better go," Dee said, without moving from her place on the couch next to Peter. "There's a kid over at my place sleeping off a drug withdrawal. I didn't realize it, but the quarantine is so tight, illegal drugs are no longer coming into Colorado. And the local Methamphetamine labs are closing down. Since the hardware stores aren't open, they can't get the ingredients they need, like anti-freeze."

"You're not afraid to let someone stay over there alone?"

Greg asked. "What if he gets into the food supply?"

Dee laughed. "Siggy has the placed locked so tightly, even I have a hard time getting into it. He and Shadow spent all day yesterday installing locks on the storeroom, closets, and cupboards."

Kate glanced down at Shadow, who studied each of them in turn, his expression unreadable.

Shadow gave Ebony a hug, then scrambled to his feet and padded over to Greg. He stood in front of Greg, staring at him with wide, solemn eyes. Then he climbed into Greg's lap and nestled into the crook of his arm.

Kate stopped breathing. Since she heard not even a whisper of a sound, she thought the others had, too, but she didn't turn to see. She couldn't take her eyes off the little boy; although Shadow had come to tolerate their hugs, this was the first time he had willingly touched any of them.

Several minutes passed. Shadow let out a long sigh and went limp.

"He's asleep," Greg mouthed. Cradling the boy in his arms, he rose.

Kate rose, too, and motioned for Greg to follow. They went into the second bedroom, which now belonged to Shadow. Since the boy was already dressed for the night in an old tee shirt of Joe's, they did not need to disturb his slumber. Greg laid him on the bed. Kate tucked him in and kissed his soft cheek.

Greg put an arm around Kate's shoulders. She snuggled into his embrace and, together, they watched the silent rise and fall of the little boy's chest.

# 24

*Monday, December 19*

Greg sorted through the greeting cards Takamura's mother had saved, but he didn't give the task his full attention. His eyes kept wandering to the bag of children's clothes setting by the door of his apartment.

Last night when he and Peter had dropped off the case of brandy at the Clayton's, along with a box of groceries that included shelled walnuts, two loaves of freshly baked bread, and a pound of butter, Letisha had given Greg the clothes.

"Jim mentioned that a friend of yours is taking care of an abandoned child," she said. "Maybe some of these would fit him."

He could hardly wait to take the clothes to Kate, to see her eyes light up at the unexpected gift.

Thinking of her, he almost missed the note stuck inside an envelope containing a birthday card. Though the note itself appeared unimportant, merely a promise that John would be home for Christmas, it had been written on a piece of paper printed with the message: *From the desk of Richard J. Murdock.*

Wondering who Richard J. Murdock was, and why John used his notepaper, Greg set the note aside. When he got to the newspaper, he would try to track the man down.

Greg found a single article about Murdock in the newspaper archives, a filler in a May 1995 issue announcing Richard J. Murdock's retirement after thirty-five years of teaching biogenetics at C.U. The announcement also mentioned that the professor had once taught Harley Reese, which was probably why the publishers had considered it newsworthy.

Murdock now lived in Lakewood, Greg discovered. He called and talked the professor into giving him an interview.

If Professor Murdock had shrunken with age, he must have been a massive man, because he was still immense. He had a big head, too, made even larger by the fluff of his thick, wavy hair. His voice boomed, as if he had become so used to speaking in lecture halls he had forgotten how to modulate it.

"Sure I know John," the professor said. "He started out as a student of mine, became one of my research assistants, and ended up as a colleague. I haven't seen him since my retirement party. How is he doing?"

"He passed away almost three weeks ago," Greg answered. "He was one of the first to die from the red death."

The professor passed a hand over his face. "Sorry to hear that. He was a good man. He was also a good teacher, but he got more and more disillusioned with each new crop of students, so he devoted his time to research."

"Do you know where Takamura did his research?" Greg asked.

"At ARC in the Four Corners area."

"Do you know what he worked on?"

"Blight, I think, and other cereal grass diseases."

"Anything else?"

"Genetically altered produce. Trying to make vegetables impervious to pests."

"You mentioned he'd been your student research assistant. Can you tell me about the projects he worked on?"

"Not specifically, no."

"Generally, then."

"He helped with one, a classified project for the army. Of course, at the time I didn't know of the army's interest. Like many university scientists, I took money believing my work entirely independent, but I found out later my grant came from a foundation linked to both the CIA and USAMRIID."

"USAMRIID?"

"United States Army Medical Research Institute for Infectious Diseases."

"So you worked on human diseases?"

The professor held up a hand. "End of discussion."

"I have a few more questions. Do you know if Takamura worked with chimeras?"

"I'm sure he did," the professor said. "Chimeras have particular applications to agriculture. To what, specifically, are you referring?"

"A disease—a human disease—combining a genetically altered virus, bacterium, fungus, and human genes."

One of Murdock's hands shook. He grabbed hold of it with his other hand, but that didn't still the tremor.

"Who are you?" the professor rasped.

"I told you," Greg said patiently. "I'm a reporter for The Denver News. I'm researching the red death."

The color drained from the professor's face. "Get out," he said, pointing a trembling finger at the door. "Get out, now. I have nothing more to say to you."

Although Kate arrived at the clinic early, the phones were already ringing. By the time she had handled five or six distraught callers, she realized the red death had taken yet another turn. Now people were getting sick, very sick, with typical flu symptoms, and they were staying sick.

One frightened husband called to say that his wife had developed a violent headache followed in rapid succession by chills, high fever, nausea, and diarrhea. Since the wife was too ill to make it to the clinic, Kate suggested that he call an ambulance and get her to a hospital.

She hung up, ready to answer another call, when the door to the clinic opened and, all at once, it seemed, the waiting room was full of coughing, shivering, moaning patients.

Besides Dr. Bowers, two doctors were on duty. Patients soon swamped them. Dr. Bowers, who concerned himself with administrative tasks and tending to Denver's elite, ungraciously agreed to see a few of the walk-ins.

In between answering the phones and trying to take quick medical histories of the waiting patients, Kate called Joan Wheeler, the receptionist, to see if she planned on coming in to work. Joan whined that she didn't feel well, though she didn't sound sick to Kate.

In the midst of this chaos, Dr. Hart entered, towing her two children: Barth, an overweight six-year-old boy, and Mattie, a skinny, scowling eight-year-old girl.

"You won't mind taking care of them for me today, will you, Kate? Analiese, my au pair, died of the red death Saturday morning. When she rose and stumbled around that afternoon, my housekeeper screamed and ran out of the house. I haven't seen her since."

"My baby, my baby," cried a woman, face blotchy with tears. "Something's wrong with my baby." She held up the infant, whose skin had the color and texture of paraffin. "I can't stop the diarrhea."

"I'll be right with you," Dr. Hart said. She pushed her children toward Kate. "They'll be no trouble. They're sweet children." Looking around the waiting room, she added, "Call Doctors Chen and Forbes. Tell them to get their gluteus maximi down here right this minute. They've been slacking long enough."

Gesturing for the woman to follow, she walked away. Turning back, she asked, "Where's the baby's history, Kate?"

"I didn't have a chance to talk to the mother. They just got here."

Dr. Hart rolled her eyes. "Oh, all right, I'll do it."

As soon as she left, Barth punched Mattie, who let out a loud shriek and pulled his hair. He pinched her. She stamped on his feet.

"Why don't you two get some books and sit back here with me," Kate said, reaching for the ringing phone.

Barth stuck out his tongue. "Why don't you—"

The frantic voice of the woman on the other end of the receiver drowned out the rest of Barth's words.

After fifteen minutes of answering the constantly ringing phone, pacifying the waiting patients, and getting kicked and bitten when trying to separate the two children, Kate called Dee.

"Is there any chance you can come help? We've got a

mess over here."

"What do you want me to do?"

"Your choice. You can either answer the phones or baby-sit two little—" She glanced up. The children had stopped fighting and were regarding her intently. "Charming children," she finished.

"I understand," Dee said, chuckling. "Let me see what I can do."

Half an hour later, Anna Brinkley, the retired schoolteacher who lived down the block from Kate, approached the front desk.

"Dee said you needed someone to answer the phones for a while."

Kate jumped out of her chair. "Come on around. You have no idea what a Godsend you are."

Anna smiled faintly. "I don't think God had much to do with it. That friend of yours can be pretty persuasive."

Kate laughed. "I've noticed."

She explained how the phone system worked, ending with, "Do the best you can. If a patient insists on talking to a doctor, take a message, but let them know it will be a while before anyone would be able to get back to them. If a patient is ambulatory, you can make an appointment for them. If they're not, suggest they go to the emergency room. If you need anything, holler. I'll be working out here for the time being."

She sent the children outside to play, then sat in a chair facing the window so she could keep an eye on them.

While she talked to a man so weak he couldn't even hold up his head, she noticed a woman about her own age and size approach the fighting children. Taking each by an arm, the woman separated them. Barth kicked her in the shin, but after she talked to him for a minute, he hung his head and shuffled his feet.

Kate took a closer look at the woman and recognized Rose, the homeless woman who had brought clothes for Shadow. She looked neat and clean, and wore Kate's best suit.

Kate shook her head, smiling. That Dee sure was something.

A minute later Rose walked into the clinic, head held high, an arm wrapped around each child.

"Is there someplace we can go play?" she asked in her soft, whispery voice.

Kate took them to a small conference room. "How about this?"

Rose looked around, nodding in satisfaction. "Perfect."

"Who is that woman with my children?" Dr. Hart demanded, stalking into Kate's office.

"A friend," Kate said mildly.

"And what about the woman answering phones. Another friend?"

Kate nodded. "They're helping out. Don't worry, I'm not hiring people behind your back."

Kate's tone must have been sharper than she intended, because Dr. Hart peered at her in consternation.

"You've changed," she said accusingly.

Kate smiled. "Maybe."

The doctor put her hands on her hips. "Do you know what that woman has those kids doing? Jigsaw puzzles." Awe tinged her voice. "I can't get them to sit still for even a minute, and she has them so enthralled they didn't even look at me when I came into the room."

Later, Dr. Hart returned to Kate's office. "Who's Dee?"

"A friend."

"I should have known." She gave her head a shake. "You and your friends. When I asked Rose if she would come work for me, she said I had to talk to Dee. What does Dee do? Run an employment agency?"

Kate laughed. "Apparently so."

"I have a favor I need to ask you," Greg said, propping himself on the corner of Clara D'Onofrio's desk.

She gazed warily at him.

"I need the rest of John Takamura's articles, specifically the ones from the early seventies."

She looked relieved. "I can handle that."

"Thanks. So how was your brunch with Colorado's youngest billionaire?"

Clara snorted. "He hasn't been the youngest for a long time—he's a lot older than he looks. Isn't it amazing what surgeons can do these days? But he likes the title, so he pays reporters to call him that."

"I take it you're not one of them," Greg said, smiling.

"Hmmph. If he paid me not to mention his name, then I'd take his money."

"You're the second person I've met who doesn't like him."

Clara raised her eyebrows. "I thought I was the only one."

"No. My friend Peter thinks he's a psychopath."

"Peter's probably right," Clara said. "Reese has all the typical characteristics of a psychopath: the glibness, the lack of empathy, the captivating body language, the deceitfulness." She gave a laugh. "Of course, those are also the characteristics of a successful business person. I once read a book detailing the psychopathic profile and found that except for the psychopath's inability to concentrate, every single characteristic mentioned fit the people I come across in my work. That book did more to help me understand people than any other book I ever read."

"Speaking of psychopaths," Greg said, "did you get a chance to look at the Japanese writings I gave you?"

A pained look crossed Clara's face. "From what I could see, some of them were requisitions for supplies, including logs and lumber, but most were official communications and progress reports. After reading about them leveling entire Chinese villages because the inhabitants were all dead of various diseases, I couldn't force myself to read further."

She indicated a neat stack of papers, with the journal resting on top. "If you're still interested, I can give you the name of the man who taught me Japanese. He should be able to recommend a translator."

Greg folded his arms across his midsection. "No. I've lost my stomach for it, too. And I no longer think it has any bearing on the red death."

Frowning at the stack of papers, Clara said quietly, "I'm thinking of retiring."

"Oh? I would have thought you were too young."

She shook an admonishing finger at him. "What did I tell you about flattery?" The corners of her mouth twitched, robbing the reprimand of its sting. "Technically I am too young, but I'm sick of psychopathic personalities. It's not just that," she added, giving an exaggerated shudder. "Because of this epidemic and everything I've been reading, I've come to the conclusion it's too dangerous being around people anymore."

"What are you going to do?"

"I have an Internet investment counseling business I've been playing with. I'm planning on doing it full time."

"Good for you." Greg rolled his head around his tense shoulders. "I've been thinking I'd like to do something different, too. I'm not interested in exposing the dark underbelly of humanity anymore."

Clara leaned back in her chair and put her hands behind her neck. "Don't tell Olaf. It will break his heart. He's impressed with you."

"Yeah, well, it's not hard to appear impressive when you're one of the few who come to work every day."

"That's one of the things he likes—your dedication. But he also thinks you have such a good nose for news, you could be one of the great ones."

Greg smiled sardonically. "Didn't most of the great ones become alcoholics? I think I'll pass."

Dr. Hart plopped wearily into a chair in Kate's office.

"I talked to John Jacobs." She shot an inquiring look Kate's way.

Kate nodded; she knew John Jacobs—a long time patient of the clinic who was single-handedly raising two adorable

Pat Bertram

little girls, Jennifer and Juliet.

"He said Jennifer is sick and needs to be hospitalized. When he called an ambulance, no one came, so he bundled her up and took her to St. Luke's. They turned him away, even though he has insurance. Denver Health turned him away, too. I called a friend of mine who works at Swedish Hospital. She said they did not have one more inch of space for even one small person."

Dr. Hart raked her fingers through her hair. "She said even if they did have space, they couldn't do anything but give rudimentary care since there was a shortage of personnel and basic supplies, and no drugs. I called the other hospitals in the area. They all told me the same thing."

She heaved a sigh. "At first we doctors weren't needed, and now that we are, there's nothing we can do. It's not right."

"I know," Kate said softly. Nothing about the red death was right.

"I better go back. There are still people waiting to be seen." Dr. Hart struggled to her feet. "I talked to your friend Dee. Rose will be working for me for a while, and Anna will come back tomorrow." She shook her head. "That Dee sure knows how to drive a hard bargain."

Kate laughed. "In other words, she's making you pay a fair wage."

Besides flexing her jaw muscles as if she had swallowed something unpleasant, the doctor had no comment.

When Pippi heard the distant rumble of heavy machinery, she hopped off her bike and wheeled it away from the road. She laid it in an irrigation ditch, pulled tumbleweeds over top, then flattened herself next to it and waited until the cavalcade of military vehicles drove out of sight.

As she was rising, she heard another vehicle approaching. She dropped to the ground and lifted her head to take a peek.

She felt a stab of pain beneath her sternum at the sight of

262

the silver truck. It looked like the one Jeremy had.

Jeremy . . .

*No. Think of something else. Anything else.*

The image of her loft flitted through her mind; she grabbed it and held on tight.

*Home!*

She couldn't remember making the decision to go back to Denver. Waking early after a restless night, she packed all she and the bike could carry. Laden like an old peddler doll she had once seen in a museum, she had wobbled away, but an hour after that shaky start she found her balance, and now she peddled like a pro.

When the truck had passed, she raised her head. Looked around. Listened. Deciding it was safe to continue her journey, she pushed aside the tumbleweeds, righted the bike, and headed back to the road.

Nervous about spending the night in the open by herself, Pippi began searching for a place to camp while the sun still hung high above the horizon.

It wasn't until twilight that she saw the perfect spot—a thicket of bushes and reeds about a tenth of a mile from the road. She wheeled the bike across the field, hid it behind a bush, and set off on foot to explore. The vegetation grew along the banks of an icebound creek and seemed dense enough to give her some security.

Even so, when she finally bedded down, her belly full of frankfurters and beans, she couldn't sleep.

She gazed at the stars, feeling small in the vastness of the night.

An owl hooted, making her heart jump, and a far away coyote howled. She shivered and scrunched further into the sleeping bag. She thought about breaking camp and travelling some more but, contemplating that possibility, she drifted off.

Suddenly wide-awake, she sat up. *What was that?*

The air crackled and tiny ice particles stung her cheeks. She glanced at the clear sky. Where was the ice coming from? When she saw snowflakes materializing before her eyes, she realized the moisture in the air was freezing.

She lay back down. After a minute, she became aware of a distant reverberation that grew louder as it drew closer. She tensed. Stifling a whimper, she lay still until the helicopter passed.

Gradually she relaxed enough to doze, but the sound of a snapping twig jerked her awake. She grasped the hunting knife, still belted around her waist. Holding her breath, she listened, but she didn't hear the noise again.

She told herself she had imagined it, but she didn't let go of the knife, and when she finally fell asleep, she dreamt of brightly glowing eyes and softly padding feet.

# 25

*Tuesday, December 20*

Greg kept shooting surreptitious glances in Professor Murdock's direction. He found it hard to believe that one human being could have changed so much in such a short time. Murdock's hands shook, his head sank into his bowed shoulders, and his hair hung straight and limp over his ashen brow.

An hour previously, Greg had received an urgent phone call from Murdock requesting his immediate presence, but when he had arrived at the professor's house, Murdock had greeted him in a thin, quavering voice, then had lapsed into silence.

He looked up now, pale blue eyes blazing with such fury that Greg recoiled, as if from a blow.

Glad he wasn't a hapless student whose grades and academic career depended on this interview, Greg breathed steadily and waited for the professor to speak.

"We gave the project the code name Atropos," Murdock said. "In case you don't remember your mythology, three fates controlled the birth, events, and death of every person. Clotho held the distaff, Lachesis spun the thread of life, and Atropos cut the thread when life ended.

"Atropos seemed a fitting name for the ultimate killing machine. Wars aren't an efficient way of decimating human populations. Disease has killed far more people than wars ever did, and we designed Atropos to be the deadliest killer of all."

Greg kept his eyes fixed on his notebook. He feared that if he looked at Murdock, his obvious revulsion would stem the flow of words.

"Not only did we try to combine the most lethal virus, bacterium, and fungus, we tried to add human genes to the organism, thinking the body would see the chimera as part of itself and wouldn't mount a defense.

"Most flu symptoms are not directly caused by the disease, but are a side effect of the immune system's efforts

265

to fight off the disease. We thought if we could bypass the immune system, we could infect an enemy territory and no one would know until people started falling down dead.

"When the ban on biological warfare experimentation went into effect, the army did not renew our grant. We continued working until the money ran out, then the army came and took everything—the papers, the computers, the mice, the samples."

"Who worked on the project besides you and Takamura?" Greg asked.

"Some army guy. I don't remember his name. And he didn't do any work. He acted as a liaison with the military."

"So you knew from the beginning your work belonged to the army?"

"At first I thought my grant came from an independent foundation. Originally, my research had nothing to do with biological warfare. I wanted to find out if I could combine different organisms into a single, symbiotic unit. When I reapplied for my grant, that's when the army paid me a visit. Why can't I remember his name?"

The professor fixed his gaze on Greg. "Let me give you a piece of advice, young man. Don't ever grow old. It's hell when your memory plays tricks on you. Now, where was I?"

"The army visited you when you reapplied for your grant."

"Right. He said my grant would be renewed, would even be substantially increased, but I would have to change my focus from benign organisms to lethal ones."

"And you agreed?"

"I needed the money," Murdock said with a shrug. "Except for having to take extra precautions, it made no difference to me."

"Who decided to add human genes to the mixture?"

"The army. Those genes caused us problems from the beginning. At that time, the human genome hadn't been completely mapped, so we didn't know which gene sequences to use. Also, the technology didn't exist to allow us to add the requisite genes to the chimera."

"Yesterday you wouldn't tell me anything except that the project was classified," Greg said. "Why are you talking to me today?"

The professor buried his face in his hands. When he looked up, he had tears in his eyes. "I didn't know. How could I? It happened so long ago."

"Didn't know what?"

The professor seemed unaware of Greg's question. Staring at his hands, which he twisted together as if applying lotion, he continued, "About two weeks ago a man and a woman came to see me, said they were from USAMRIID. They questioned me about the red death. I felt flattered to think that after all these years the army thought enough of me to want my help. I didn't realize they considered me a suspect. Before they left, they warned me that Atropos remained classified.

"Shortly after that visit, my wife died of the red death, so did my son-in-law, and now my grandson is gravely ill. Until you mentioned it yesterday, I had no idea the red death was anything more than a terrible flu. Last night I took a blood sample from my grandson and managed to isolate an organism that looks remarkably like Atropos. My Atropos."

Murdock buried his face in his hands again; his shoulders shook with silent sobs.

Steeling himself against an involuntary pang of compassion, Greg concentrated on filling out his notes.

"Can it be stopped?" he asked when Murdock lifted his head.

"No. We never found a way of controlling it. If the ban on biological weapons had not shut us down, the army would have. Without an antidote, they could not use Atropos. It killed indiscriminately, friend and foe alike."

"A woman I know discovered that foods containing unmodified fats, such as walnuts, flaxseed, and sardines, offer protection against the red death, but that other fats, such as vegetable oil and margarine, aggravate it."

"Atropos did have certain lipophilic qualities."

"Lipophilic?"

267

"An affinity for fatty tissues. It's possible this effect you mentioned rose spontaneously. A bio-engineered organism, like any organism, takes on a life of its own and becomes subject to evolutionary forces. That's one of the reasons biogenetics is such a fascinating field."

He tapped his chin with an index finger for a moment, then he nodded. "I've been on a high Omega-3 diet for my heart, so I've been eating lots of fish, primarily mackerel, sardines, and Alaskan salmon. My wife, son-in-law, and grandson, all hated fish. I have some Omega-3 capsules. I wonder if I can get my grandson to swallow them."

Murdock rose and stared pointedly at Greg.

Refusing to take the hint, Greg settled himself more firmly into the uncomfortable armchair. He opened his notebook to a new page.

Sighing heavily, Murdock sat back down.

"Could the army have continued your research?" Greg asked.

"I doubt it."

"Why not?"

"We had some problems during the last week before the army took possession of the project, so they didn't get everything we had been working on."

"What kind of problems?"

"One of the computers crashed, destroying vital data."

"But they still had samples of the chimera. Could they have reverse engineered it?"

"No." The professor took a deep breath. "The samples corresponding to the missing research disappeared."

Greg stared at Murdock. "You lost samples of a deadly organism?"

"Yes."

"How?"

"I don't know. At the time we assumed they got mislabeled and that we would find them, but we never did."

"Even without the missing samples, the army could have continued your work. Or started from scratch."

"It's possible, but they would have produced a different

268

organism. This one is related to the missing samples. All I can think of is that someone downloaded the data from the computer, crashed it so no one would know who had done it, then stole the samples, and continued the project on his own."

"Who?" Greg asked, though he knew the answer.

"Since it wasn't me," Murdock said, voice trembling with suppressed anger, "it had to have been John Takamura."

When Kate kissed Greg hello, she could feel a difference in him, a resignation almost, as if his internal fires burned low, but it wasn't until after dinner that Greg finally told her, Dee, and Peter, about his conversation with Murdock.

"You must be proud of yourself," Dee said, "to have found the truth about the red death when no one else could."

Greg gave her a bleak look. "Not proud. Empty. Tired. What's the good of knowing when nothing can be done about it? Since Atropos is classified, the paper can't print the truth. And Takamura is beyond human justice. Though there is poetic justice in him dying from his own creation."

"So it was Takamura all along," Peter said. "I got the impression you didn't think he did it."

"I didn't. I did think he held the key to the red death, but for him to be its creator? I don't know—it seems too pat. I mean, I had his name at the beginning, and all through my investigation, wherever I turned, there he was."

"Weren't you the one who said life plays tricks on us?" Kate asked, striving for a light tone.

Greg gave her a questioning look, then he smiled. "You're right. I did. And it does." His smile faded. "I wish I could look Takamura right in the eye and ask him why. Why did he do it? Why did he unleash the red death?"

# 26

*Wednesday, December 21*

In the gray of not quite dawn, Pippi awoke and snuggled deeper into the sleeping bag to absorb the warmth.

Maybe she was finally getting the hang of this camping thing; she had slept all night long. It helped that she had been able to find another secluded camping spot in a thicket of bushes by a creek. She had still felt nervous at first, but after she had curled her fingers around the hilt of the hunting knife, she had immediately drifted off and nothing had awakened her.

Deciding to get an early start, she quickly unzipped the sleeping bag before she could change her mind. Shivering, she put on the voluminous parka she had taken from the house, belted it to prevent the cold from creeping up her back, and fastened the hood around her head. Then she pulled on a pair of boots.

Amazing how quickly you can get dressed when you sleep in your clothes.

She relit last night's fire, which she had extinguished to keep from drawing attention to herself, and put on a pan of water to boil.

After a breakfast of instant coffee and instant oatmeal with raisins, she smothered the fire and packed.

As she wheeled the bicycle away from her campsite, she noticed that she left footprints and tire tracks on the frost-covered ground, but she wasn't worried. They would disappear as soon as the sun rose.

Besides, she felt too pleased with herself to worry.

She was leaving the cover of the bushes, glancing all around with a diligence that had become habit, when she stopped short.

Her face slackened with horror. No. It couldn't be. It was not possible.

Feeling a sick draining of confidence, she stared at the double row of footprints passing within yards of where she had slept.

Tuesday had been as hectic as Monday, but by Wednesday afternoon things slowed down at the clinic, which confused Dr. Hart, but not Kate.

"The red death mutates quickly," Kate explained, "but we couldn't see it because at first each mutation produced the same results, but now each succeeding generation produces weaker symptoms than the last."

"So it might mutate itself out of existence," Dr. Hart said.

"I think there's a good chance of that."

Dr. Hart blew out a breath. "The sooner things get back to normal, the better I'll like it."

That evening, as she always did now, Kate practically flew home. She paused for a moment outside her house to enjoy the warm glow of the illuminated windows, then ran up the porch steps. She opened the door, feeling like a child unwrapping a much anticipated present.

When she saw Greg sitting on the couch reading to Shadow, tears stung her eyes. She wanted the red death to end, but she could not bear the thought of her life going back to the way it was.

Greg set aside the book and welcomed her with a toe-tingling kiss. Shadow came and stood before her, gazing at her expectantly; his face lit up when she hugged him and kissed him on the cheek.

A loud burst of laughter from the dining room drew her attention. Although they had decided to serve meals at Dee's, so many people came now, they still used Kate's house, which pleased her. She had lived alone, haunted by ghosts, for too long.

Noticing Shadow scratching the back of his hand, Kate crouched in front of him to examine it.

Finding a tiny black spot, she looked questioningly at Greg. When he shrugged, she went in search of Dee. She found the woman in her kitchen, stirring a big pot of spaghetti sauce.

"What happened to Shadow's hand?" Kate asked.

Dee took a deep breath. "I stopped by my cousin's place today." She swallowed and blinked rapidly. "There were seven orange fluorescent dots on the door."

"Oh, I am so sorry," Kate said, with a catch in her voice.

"Yeah, me too." Dee dragged a forearm across her eyes. "I broke into the house, went to the den where he kept his important papers, and took the birth certificate for his youngest son, who's about Shadow's age. Also the son's social security card and my cousin's will. Since my cousin lived in subsidized housing, he owned nothing but an ancient station wagon that always needed repairs, but he made a will, naming me guardian, to make sure his children wouldn't be separated if he and his wife both died."

Dee paused for a moment, then said briskly, "I thought we could pass Shadow off as my cousin's boy."

Kate gave her a dubious look. "Do you think it will work?"

"I don't see why not. It has so far. I took Shadow to a Commodity Distribution Center today, showed them the documents, and introduced Shadow as Karl Allenby, my nephew. I wasn't Karl's aunt, of course, but that's what my cousin's children used to call me since we couldn't figure out if we were second cousins or first cousins once removed or what."

"And the people at the distribution center fell for it?" Kate asked.

"Sure. Why wouldn't they? I had the proper documentation. I'll admit my palms sweated since I didn't know if they had chipped the real Karl, but everything went smoothly. Now, for all practical purposes, Shadow is Karl Allenby. If it's in the computer, it's the truth."

Haunted by the image of the footprints—boot prints, actually, man-size boot prints—Pippi forced herself to be extra vigilant. Every time she heard a sound that seemed the least bit out of place, she would stop, cock her head, and strain her ears. Even when all appeared quiet, she stopped often to peer through her binoculars.

She thought she was becoming more alert, more attuned to her surroundings, but she had the uneasy feeling she was fooling herself. If two men—big men, judging by the size of their boots—had come so close without her being aware of it, what other dangers escaped her notice?

At sundown, she wheeled her bicycle into a cluster of trees. Too exhausted to make a fire, she leaned against the massive trunk of an old cottonwood and nibbled on some trail mix she had prepared back at the house by combining a package of granola with nuts and dried fruit she found stashed in a cupboard of baking supplies.

She nodded off. A flurry in the bare branches above her head startled her awake. A crow let out a loud squawk and flew from the tree with a powerful thrust of its wings.

Watching the bird glide on an air current, she wondered what it would be like to be able to soar so effortlessly above the petty concerns of humankind. She wrenched her thoughts back to earth, ate more of the trail mix, then rose to unpack the sleeping bag. Still wearing her parka, she crawled into the bag, zipped it, and laid her hand on the knife. She fell asleep a minute later.

A noise penetrated into her dream. She awoke. Unsnapped the sheath, pulled the knife partway out. Lifted her head. In the moonlight, she could see nothing but shadows. She heard faint, whispery sounds, sounds that weren't loud enough to have awakened her.

She drifted again. Another noise jerked her awake.

How the hell was she supposed to get any rest with all the noise? She tried to go back to sleep, but an odd garlicky smell tickled her nose.

She opened her eyes, and for one heart-stopping moment she stared at a face hovering a scant two feet above hers. Before she could blink, he dropped down on top of her.

She thrashed her legs, straining to get away, but his weight pinned her and the sleeping bag bound her.

A second weight immobilized her ankles.

Oh, God. There were two of them.

The man lying on top of her grinned and lowered his face to hers. She whipped her head from side to side. He pushed back her hood, grasped her hair, and held her still.

She inched the knife out of the sheath, but could not move her arm enough to use it. What difference does it make? By the time the knife penetrated through the sleeping bag and through his heavy outerwear, it probably wouldn't even scratch him.

She scrabbled about in her mind, trying to think of what to do. Trying not to think of those bruising lips, that probing tongue.

After what seemed like a very long time, he raised his head, shifted his weight, and began unzipping the sleeping bag.

She gripped the knife.

As soon as he unzipped the bag to her elbow, she yanked her arm free and jammed the knife into his eye.

She heard a high-pitched squeal at her feet. The weight lifted off her ankles; the unseen person jumped up and went crashing through the undergrowth, still squealing.

The man she had knifed struggled to his feet. Whimpering, he reeled away from her, staggered into a tree, then crumpled to the ground.

Pippi kicked her way out of the sleeping bag and ran off. She crouched behind a tree, gasping so loudly she thought her attackers might hear. She forced herself to take deep, quiet breaths, counting off one minute. Two minutes. When neither of her attackers came looking for her, she stood and sidled around the tree. No one was in sight.

Torn between wanting to run away and needing to return for her provisions, she hesitated. Gritting her teeth, she slipped back to her camp.

All was as she had left it.

After one glance at the man lying motionless at the base of the tree, she kept her face turned away from him.

She packed quickly and wheeled her bicycle through the trees to the road. An itch between her shoulders told her she forgot something, but she had carefully checked the campsite and left nothing behind.

Except the hunting knife.

She stopped and looked behind her, then marched forward again. No way was she going back for that knife.

Now that she knew what was missing, she grew intensely aware of the empty knife sheath. She caught her lower lip between her teeth. How could she ever make it all the way back to Denver without any means of protection?

*You have two other knives.*

Paring knives. What good are they?

She parked the bike, inhaled deeply, and turned around. Took one step. Then another.

Maybe the paring knives would work after all.

No. She needed the hunting knife. Without it, she felt naked. Vulnerable.

Steeling herself, she headed back to the fallen man. When she caught sight of the hilt sticking out of his eye, she gagged and averted her gaze. Without looking, she groped for the knife, but at the last moment she turned to stare the man in the face while she yanked the knife out of his eye.

He shuddered, and lay still.

She bent, wiped the knife on his sleeve, then stuck it back in the sheath where it belonged.

Without once looking behind her, she went to retrieve her bicycle.

# 27

*Thursday, December 22*

Toward early morning, Pippi stopped her headlong flight and found refuge behind a pile of boulders. She took a single sip of water, needing to make what little she had left last as long as possible, and chewed on a handful of trail mix while she unrolled her sleeping bag.

Her breath caught when she saw the bloodstain. She turned the sleeping bag over but, unable to forget how it had bound her when she most needed to be free, she could not force herself to climb inside.

In the end, she wrapped it around her like a shawl, and huddled against a boulder.

After sleeping for a few hours, she opened a can of roast beef hash, the last of her food except for the trail mix, and ate it cold.

She was tying the bedroll behind the seat of the bicycle when she noticed that the rear tire was flat and the front one was spongy.

A broken sob escaped her. This could not be happening. What was she going to do now?

Reminding herself that the bicycle had lasted longer than she had expected it to, she shouldered her backpack, tied the sleeping bag to the small of her back to help support the pack, and hiked toward home.

Journalism might be literature in a hurry, but Greg took his time writing the story of the red death.

Yesterday Olaf had sent him to do a follow-up on his article about how hospitals were coping with the epidemic. Because Olaf had told him to check out several hospitals, and because medical personnel could only talk to him in bits and snatches, it had taken him all day to do the story.

After he had filed it, he had gone to Kate's house, so he didn't start writing the story of Takamura and Atropos until this morning. He sat hunched over his keyboard hour after hour, not even taking time out for lunch. Although he knew the piece would not see print, he wanted this last story he would ever write to be perfect.

And it was perfect—simple and succinct.

Now, perhaps, he could get it out of his mind, out of his dreams.

Sensing a difference, Pippi jerked herself awake. It had been snowing heavily when she stopped for the night, but now the skies were starting to clear.

She rose to her feet and moved around in a circle, gazing wide-eyed at the bright landscape. The moon reflecting off the iridescent snow made everything look blue, like a black and white movie filmed through a blue filter.

All was silent. Still.

Without thought, she slipped the backpack on, wrapped the sleeping bag around her shoulders for extra protection against the bitterly cold air, and resumed her journey.

She walked down the center of the road, feeling as if she were the last person left alive on a strange new planet. The snow lay several inches deep but, light and powdery, it didn't impede her progress. Instead, it energized her and awakened her. It seemed to her that before this very moment, her whole life had been a dream, and now it was real.

She had traveled only a mile or two when she felt a presence. Someone. Something. The awareness vibrated in her body, jangled her nerve endings. She stopped. Looked around. Although she didn't see anyone, she knew she was no longer alone.

On full alert, she walked farther, and suddenly, there he stood, silhouetted on a hill.

A coyote.

Pippi froze, afraid that if she made a single move, he would spring on her. She thought of the knife, but it didn't give her any comfort; the knife was so small and the coyote so large.

She tried to remember what you were supposed to do in a situation like this. Look the animal in the eyes? Look past it? Look at the ground?

Too late. Her eyes locked onto the coyote's.

As she looked into him and he looked into her, she could feel her fear draining away.

They stood motionless, staring at each other for a long time—eons. Then the coyote's ears pricked up. He cocked his head as if listening to something in the distance.

Pippi cocked her head, too, but all she heard was a quickening breeze.

Casually, as if he had more important things to do than to stare at this insignificant human, the coyote trotted off.

He turned to give her one last look, then he was gone.

# 28

*Friday, December 23*

Kate woke to find Shadow's small, warm body curled against her. Half asleep, she lay still, savoring the moment. A loud snore from the living room, along with a whiff of sour, unwashed bodies, brought her to full consciousness.

Last night, Dee's house had quickly filled with people needing refuge from the snowstorm, so Kate had also opened her house, including Shadow's room, which explained why he slept in her bed.

As if aware that she was thinking of him, Shadow lifted his head and gazed at her with solemn, dark eyes. Then, slowly, like the rising sun, his face lit up, and his arms stole around her neck.

Blinking back tears, Kate hugged him and kissed the top of his head.

He hopped out of bed and waited for her to follow. Hand in hand, they made their way around the slumbering bodies to the kitchen. Siggy, who had spent the night as a self-appointed sentinel, sat at the table, nodding over a cup of coffee.

Starting awake, he glanced up at her. Then he staggered to his feet, gulped the last of his coffee, and slunk out of the house.

Kate was wondering what to feed her guests who, from the sound of it, were awakening, when Dee popped her head in the back door.

"Good, you're awake," she said. "I've made breakfast." She held the door open while three of her helpers carried in a heaping platter of biscuits, a big pot of hot cereal, and a plate of thinly sliced and fried canned luncheon meat.

"Coffee's already on the stove," Dee said over her shoulder as she left.

Kate fixed a glass of powdered milk for Shadow, which made her gag, though he didn't seem to mind it. After making sure he had enough to eat, she went into the bathroom to get ready for work; by the time she came out, a line had formed.

She glanced at all the people, wondering if her old plumbing would survive the onslaught. Then all at once it occurred to her she no longer needed to worry about such things. If anything went wrong, Dee would find someone to fix it.

When Greg appeared in Kate's office a little before noon and asked her to have lunch with him, she jumped up out of her chair.

"Sounds great," she said. "I've been shuffling papers around, trying to look busy."

On the way to The Black Forest, they skirted several small children having a snowball fight, a woman shoveling the snow off her sidewalk, and a man walking his dog. They also had to wait at a corner for a few cars to pass before they could cross the street.

"Things seem to be getting back to normal," Greg said.

"People can get bored with anything," Kate responded. "Even fear."

Lottie greeted them at the door, grasping one of Greg's hands and one of Kate's in both of hers, and smiled at them as if in benediction, then led them to their same table by the window.

Before they had a chance to say anything to each other, Elspeth hurried over to them, hugged them both, then hugged Kate again. Holding Kate at arms length, she said, "Your mother would be so proud of you."

"What was that all about?" Greg asked when they were alone.

Kate gave a choke of laughter. "I thought these people knew everything that happened in the neighborhood, and now I know they do. Apparently they've heard we've been feeding people."

"I never met your mother," Greg said, "but I'm certain she would be proud of you. And so am I."

Even if the proliferation of isolated subdivisions

promising country living hadn't told Pippi she neared the Denver metro area, the increased traffic—both military and civilian—would have.

But she felt as far away from home as ever.

She had finished the last of her food and water that morning. Snow still lay in patches on the ground, but this close to the city it was too filthy to ingest. She also hadn't slept for more than a few hours at a time since Tuesday night. Used to dieting, she thought she could get by without eating, but she feared that if she didn't drink something soon and get some rest, she'd be in no shape to confront the dangers of the city.

Remembering the barn where she and Jeremy had slept the first night of their journey, Pippi headed in that direction.

Maybe the woman would take pity on her again.

If she didn't stone her to death first.

Pippi approached the farmhouse cautiously, but she heard no sounds, saw no movement.

She knocked on the front door. When the woman didn't answer, she knocked louder.

Still no response.

She stood on the porch, staring at the closed door. It had never occurred to her the woman might not be home.

Finally, she turned to leave. As she lurched down the porch steps, her knees buckled. She grabbed for the railing, but her hands were too weak to hold onto it; she sat down with a teeth-jarring thump.

She rested her head in her hands for a moment, then struggled to her feet, circled the house, and knocked on the back door.

While waiting for a response that didn't come, she noticed the outside faucet. Tripping over her feet in her haste, she ran to it and turned it on. The frigid water stung her cupped hands, but she didn't care. She drank her fill, wiped her hands on her parka and stuck them in the pockets to warm them, then proceeded to the barn where she intended to take a nap.

Thinking she was seeing an exhaustion-induced mirage, she gazed at the small pile of canned goods she had left last week in payment for the use of the barn; they hadn't been touched.

Her hands shook as she grabbed a can, opened it, and scooped the food into her mouth.

When the wind gusted, she noticed a swaying shadow on the floor.

More curious than afraid, she glanced around. Gasping, she took an involuntary step backward, but immediately got hold of herself and approached the woman hanging from the rafters.

The woman's foot felt horribly cold.

Pippi bowed her head for a moment, then left the barn and plodded to the garage. She peeked through the window into the dark interior. One vehicle. Perhaps two.

She scurried to the back door of the house, certain she would find it unlocked. Who would bother to lock a door when they're set on committing suicide?

The house smelled of death. Thinking how odd it was to know what death smelled like, she quickly searched the kitchen. No keys. No food, either, except for a dried orange in a bowl on the kitchen table and an opened box of cold cereal.

Realizing that the woman's keys would probably be in her purse, Pippi glanced through the downstairs rooms, then climbed the stairs to search the bedrooms. She hesitated outside the closed door of the room where they had laid the woman's husband, then pushed it open.

Gagging on the overwhelming stench, she quickly pulled the door closed, but as she did so she caught a glimpse of a black patent leather purse on the dresser.

Holding her breath, she dashed inside the room and grabbed it.

She upended the purse on the kitchen table; the keys fell out with a satisfying clatter. So did the garage door opener.

A Ford Escort and a Chevrolet pickup truck were parked in the garage, but only the keys to the Ford were on the woman's key ring.

The car started right away. It had almost a half a tank of gas, enough to get her close to downtown Denver. She drummed her ragged fingernails on the steering wheel. She ought to rest first. What if she fell asleep at the wheel?

But home was so close.

Suddenly energized, she filled her water bottles, made a quick stop at the barn to scoop up the remaining cans of food, and hopped back in the car.

*Denver, here I come.*

When Kate returned to the living room after putting Shadow to bed, she found the others strangely silent.

"What did I miss?" she asked.

"There's talk of the quarantine being lifted," Peter said. "There hasn't been an epidemic-related death for three days, and people who are getting sick now are getting a mild case of flu. They think the original chimera has finally died out."

Kate looked from Greg to Dee to Peter. The only illumination in the room came from the silk Christmas tree which someone—Dee, perhaps, or Siggy—had found in Kate's basement and set up. The colored lights reflecting off their faces gave everyone an unearthly glow.

She pressed her knuckles to her mouth, wondering what was going to happen to them. Surely, after all they had been through, they would remain friends? They had to, for Shadow's sake if not their own.

"Just think," she said brightly. "We'll be able to get fresh produce again."

"And unwatered beer," Greg added, smiling at her as if to say two could play this game.

Kate returned his smile. "Ice cream."

"Eggs," Dee said wistfully. "And bacon."

"Orange juice," Peter chimed in.

"Pizza," Greg exclaimed.

Then suddenly they were all talking at once, and laughing.

# 29

*Saturday, December 24*

Pippi awoke and glanced wildly about her. Still groggy from sleep, it took her a moment to realize it wasn't a dream. She really was home.

*Home!*

She arose and tiptoed through her loft, touching first one thing and then another. The racks of clothes in the walk-in closet. The framed museum prints adorning the brick walls. Furniture, appliances, electronic equipment, CDs, DVDs, books, kitchenware. Did all this belong to her?

She went into the bathroom, took a long soak in jasmine-scented water—her second since arriving home late last night. By the time she was dressed again, her pos-sessions no longer loomed over her, but had settled comfortably into the background.

While eating a belated breakfast of oatmeal sprinkled with flaxseed, she remembered she hadn't checked her machine for messages. Well, no wonder. Although she'd encountered no problems on the drive to Denver—besides running out of gas a mile from home, that is—she'd been so exhausted she had practically fallen asleep while unlocking her door.

There were fewer messages than she expected; her friends and colleagues must have thought her another victim of the red death. First thing Monday morning, she'd set that record straight. She imagined walking into Channel Ten. Her friends would stop and stare, then rush to her, thrilled to have her back. Julie, the young production assistant who had taken her place, would turn green, realizing her time in front of the camera was over.

Pippi doubted she would have to explain her absence. As haggard as she looked, people would readily believe she'd been lying in bed all this time, wrestling with the grim reaper.

Playing back her messages, Pippi heard the voices of two of her friends saying they missed her. There were several hang-ups, then a man's voice. Greg's voice.

"Call me when you get a chance," he said.

Though he sounded dispassionate, almost cold, a feeling of warmth stole through her body. She had forgotten how much she loved him.

She remembered telling Jeremy that Greg was so nice she feared getting bored. But boredom didn't sound so terrible now. And Greg would not treat her as badly as Jeremy had.

She reached out a hand for the phone, then drew it back. Maybe it would be better to talk to Greg in person.

Thinking about how good it would feel to pour out all the details of her experience, she grabbed her coat—one of her own coats, not that wretched parka—and took the old freight elevator to the garage level.

She stepped off the elevator and stopped cold.

Nothing but a spot of oil occupied her parking space.

After taking a deep breath and blowing it out to calm herself, she remembered leaving her car at work.

She hurried outside.

First she would get her car. Then she would go talk to Greg.

Feeling oddly restless, Kate left Dee and her army of workers to their preparations for tomorrow's feast, and went out for a walk.

Despite her relief that the quarantine would soon be ending, she couldn't help wondering what was going to happen when Pippi returned to Greg.

And she would return. How could she not? Greg slipped into a woman's heart and remained there forever.

Kate was strolling along a path in Cheesman Park when Greg himself coasted to a stop in front of her.

He smiled. "I was on my way to see you."

A pain stabbed her chest at the thought of never again seeing that slow, sweet smile.

He peered at her. "What's wrong?"

"Nothing." She tried to give a carefree laugh, but it came

out sounding more like a sob.

He raised his eyebrows.

She sighed. "It's silly, really."

He reached out and touched her hand. A jolt of electricity shot through her, turning her insides to mush.

"Do you want to go back to your place and talk about it?" he asked.

She shook her head. "No. There's so much commotion back there I can't hear myself think."

"Oh?"

"Siggy unearthed a huge box full of Christmas lights from somewhere. He and Shadow are busy decorating both houses. I'm sure when they're done the houses will be visible for miles. At least our guests won't have a hard time finding us tomorrow.

"People have been running in and out all day with contributions for tomorrow's feast. Lottie Untermeyer sent over an immense turkey with all the trimmings, plus two Black Forest cakes. Wasn't that sweet of her?

"Dee's commandeered my kitchen. One isn't big enough since she has tonight's meal to prepare as well as tomorrow's. I should have stayed home to help her, but . . ."

"But you needed to think," Greg supplied when her voice trailed away.

Kate nodded.

"About what?"

She felt a blush rising to her face. "Us."

"What's to think about?"

"Well, for one, what's going to happen to us when things get back to normal?"

Greg laughed. "I'll tell you—we'll be able to be alone once in a while. We haven't had a moment to ourselves since Sunday."

"We were alone yesterday at The Black Forest."

"Yeah, right. With the way the Untermeyers hovered over us, we barely got a chance to say hello."

Twinkling at him, Kate spread her arms. "We're alone now."

Two boys on skateboards whizzed passed them, so did a jogger talking on a cell phone.

"This is not my idea of being alone," Greg said. Then, looking at her with half-lidded eyes, he added softly, "We could go to my apartment."

Kate felt the blush spread throughout her body, and her breath caught in her throat.

"That would be nice," she said huskily.

"I like what you've done with the place," Kate said, glancing at the papers spread out on the floor.

"Takamura's papers," Greg explained. "I hate looking at them, but I can't bear to touch them to clean them away."

"Want me to help?"

"No." He traced her lips with a finger. "We have better things to do."

A buzzer sounded, making Kate jump. "What's that?"

"Someone's downstairs wanting to be let in."

"Aren't you going to answer it?"

"No." He unbuttoned her coat and helped her out of it.

The buzzer sounded again. He smiled down at her as if oblivious to it.

Then the phone rang; the machine answered it.

Kate's heart sank when she heard that familiar voice.

"Greg? This is Pippi. I'm calling from the phone in the lobby. Buzz me in, okay?"

While Pippi climbed the stairs after Greg buzzed her into his building, she tried unsuccessfully to figure out what to say to him. How could she possibly explain why she had stood him up that night at The Lucky Star when she didn't understand it herself?

He waited for her, as always, at the open door to his apartment. Though still movie star handsome, he looked older, harder. Unapproachable.

She moistened her lips. It must have hurt him badly, her running out on him. Well, she'd make it up to him.

Greg ambled toward her. Suddenly shy, she stopped and

waited for him.

"Pippi," he said, holding out his hands.

Remembering the last time someone had touched her, she shuddered and took a step backward. Oh, God. Would she ever again be able to touch anyone?

The smile died out of Greg's eyes, and his hands fell to his sides.

They stared at each other for a moment, then Pippi looked away. Although she had planned to tell him everything that had befallen her, she now knew she never would. She couldn't bear his sympathy, but more than that, her experiences belonged to her alone.

Greg gestured to his open door. "There's no need to stand out here in the hall."

Pippi nodded and followed him into his apartment. Gazing at the piles of paper littering his floor, she realized he had changed even more than she had thought; the Greg she knew didn't tolerate chaos.

Neither of them spoke. The silence stretched out awkwardly, as if they were strangers on a blind date rather than long-time lovers.

"I've met someone else," Greg said at last.

Pippi blinked and looked away. So, he hadn't been sitting at home alone eagerly awaiting her return, after all.

Greg raised his voice slightly. "Kate? You can come out now."

A woman stepped out of the kitchen, hesitated, then smiled and moved to Greg's side without offering Pippi her hand to shake.

Appreciating the woman's perspicacity and mildly amused by her unconscious show of possessiveness, Pippi's lips twitched in response.

When the woman's smile broadened, Pippi could see why she had attracted Greg. The woman—Kate—wasn't pretty, wasn't young, but she radiated a vitality that seemed electric.

Kate gestured to a chair. "Please sit."

Pippi made her way through a path in the papers on the

floor and perched on the edge of one of the recliners. Kate sat in the other. Greg stood behind Kate's chair, leaning over the back of it.

Pippi remembered how a thousand years ago, when she was young, Greg had knelt before her on one knee, taken her hand, gazed at her with a hopeful look in his eyes and said, "I love you, Pippi. Will you marry me?"

She had felt a moment of triumph—after all, that was what she had wanted—but even as she opened her mouth to say, "Yes. Yes. Yes," she had wondered what that look in his eyes meant. Was he hoping she would say yes? Or hoping she would say no?

Either way, he had asked, and she had no intention of letting him off the hook, so she had been as surprised as he when the words, "I'll think about it," had come tumbling out of her mouth.

At the last moment, she had sensed he did not love her the way she wanted to be loved, but what she had meant by that she had never been able to figure out.

Until now.

Watching Greg and Kate together, Pippi could see that even though they weren't touching, weren't even exchanging glances, were, in fact, focused entirely on her, they were still somehow aware of each other, as if their souls were in perfect accord.

So, she had been right all along. Greg hadn't really loved her; but then, she hadn't truly loved him either, not in the same way Kate did.

She tried to summon a pang of sadness for her lost love, but only managed a fleeting twinge of nostalgia.

"We have to talk," Greg said.

Pippi eyed him curiously, remembering how once those very words had made him panic. Now she was the one who didn't want to talk.

"No need," she said softly. "I already know."

Kate rose. "You look exhausted. Why don't you rest and I'll find you something to eat."

Pippi rose, too. "I think I'll go home."

"Are you on foot?" Greg asked. "Would you like me to walk with you?"

Pippi shook her head, feeling suffocated by their concern. She had made it all the way back to Denver by herself; she could manage to get home alone.

Strange. She used to hate being alone; now it was all she wanted.

She became aware that both Greg and Kate were looking at her expectantly.

"Did you say something?" she asked.

"We're having Christmas dinner tomorrow at Kate's," Greg said. "We want you to come."

"Oh, no. I couldn't intrude."

Kate laughed softly. "No intrusion. To be honest, you'd probably get lost in the crowd."

"What time?" Pippi asked, knowing she would not go.

"Anytime. People will be coming and going all day."

Greg took his notebook out of his pocket, tore out a page, wrote on it, and handed it to Pippi. "Kate's address. Please come. We'd love to have you."

Pippi shrugged, the briefest hitching of her shoulders, then strode to the door. Kate and Greg followed.

"It was nice meeting you," Kate said.

Unable to unearth the requisite civilized response, Pippi nodded.

Kate discreetly absented herself, leaving Pippi and Greg alone.

A furrow appeared between his eyebrows as he gazed at her. "Will you be okay?"

She touched his face, gently smoothed away the furrow, and smiled.

"I'll be fine."

# 30

*Sunday, December 25*

All day Kate had felt as if there were two of her. One Kate had taken care of Shadow, and had also laughed and joked with the dinner guests while serving them. The other Kate had been aware only of Greg—of his nearness, of his clean masculine scent, of the heat emanating from his body.

Now that they were alone (except for Shadow sleeping soundly in the other room) there was one of her. The her focused on Greg.

They stood about two feet apart, gazing into each other's eyes. The air between them sizzled with electricity, like right before a storm.

"What are you doing way over there?" he asked softly, his voice cracking with emotion.

She searched his face. "Are you sure you want to do this?"

He drew back slightly. "Don't you?"

She hesitated. Yesterday, when Pippi's arrival had ruined their romantic moment, she had been unexpectedly relieved. She didn't know if she was ready, but even more than that, she didn't know if she could give Greg what he needed.

"It's been a long time since I've been with anyone," she said at last. "What if it doesn't work out?"

He smiled at her with heavy-lidded eyes. "Then we keep doing it until we get it right." After studying her for a long, unnerving moment, he said, "You're beautiful."

She turned away. "Don't mock me."

"I'm not. You're downright luminescent."

Stepping closer, he took her in his arms. She snuggled against his chest for a minute, then raised her face to his. When his lips touched hers, the electricity crackling between them ignited, sending a flash of heat through her body. Letting out a moan, she arched toward him. He pulled her closer.

His mouth locked on hers, he unzipped her dress. When

his hands touched her bare skin, her knees gave out, and they tumbled onto the bed. He rose to help her remove her clothes, then he took off his shirt. Seeing his well-defined chest and the line of dark hair disappearing beneath his waistband, she sucked in her breath.

He dropped his pants and lowered himself onto her. She wrapped her arms and legs around him, hefting her hips to meet his.

They were both too eager, and it was over quickly.

Afterward, she lay with her head on his chest while he ran his fingers through her tousled chin-length curls.

"Did I ever tell you how lovely I think your hair is?" he murmured. "It's the same color as wildflower honey."

She raised her head to smile at him. He cupped her face with his hands, skimmed his thumbs over her lips, then drew her to him.

They kissed softly, and this time when they came together, it was long and slow and achingly sweet.

# 31

*Monday, December 26*

Kate felt like crying.

She sat at her kitchen table watching Greg and Shadow eat the breakfast of toast, cereal, and canned fruit she had prepared. Her heart ached with love for them. Life was so fragile, how could she ever keep them safe?

As if aware of her thoughts, Greg reached out and grasped her hand.

Blinking away tears, she held on tightly. Whatever the future brought, today, this minute, they were together.

Shadow crammed the last bite of his toast into his mouth, jumped off his chair, and ran outside without remembering to put on his coat. The door slammed shut behind him.

When Kate rose to get Shadow's coat, Greg also got to his feet. He wrapped his arms around her and rocked her gently.

She hiccupped once, then let out a long sigh.

He leaned back and smiled at her. "We'll be okay. Wait and see. We're going to have one of the world's great romances."

She widened her eyes in mock dismay. "I sure hope not. Have you ever noticed that all the great romances end tragically? Romeo and Juliet. Lara and Dr. Zhivago. Scarlett and Rhett."

He chuckled. "So, we'll have a not-so-great romance and be together forever."

She struggled to keep the lump in her throat from turning into tears. When she gained control of herself, she kissed him. She had meant it to be a light peck, but it deepened until she could feel the tug of it curling her toes.

Gasping, she pulled away. "Hold that thought."

"Why?" he asked, running a hand up her leg and under her dress. "I can take the day off."

Laughing, she batted his hand away. "Well I can't."

"The clinic can do without you for once."

"I know. But I was there at the beginning of the red death. I should be there for the end."

Greg nodded and stepped away from her. "Did I ever tell you how much I love you?"

Her heart seemed to stand still, then it beat wildly.

She searched his eyes. "You do love me?"

He gazed steadily at her. "Yes."

She hesitated, wondering if she was crazy leaving this man for even a moment. Then, sighing, she straightened her shoulders. "I better go before I change my mind."

After retrieving both her coat and Shadow's, she went out to the backyard to say good-bye to the boy.

Greg followed.

While Kate buttoned Shadow into his coat, Dee and Peter came outside and entered her yard through the gate in the fence that Siggy had installed.

All four stood silently, watching Shadow run back and forth between the two yards.

"I can't stay over there when the quarantine's lifted," Dee said at last. "What's going to happen to Shadow when I have to leave?"

Kate bit her lip and looked away. She had been wondering the same thing but had been too afraid to mention it. On paper, Dee was the boy's aunt and so had legal custody. He even treated her as if she were his aunt, but he treated Kate as if she were his mother. As long as the two women could live next door to each other, everything would work out okay. But what if they couldn't?

"Why can't you stay there?" Peter asked.

"It's not my house," Dee said.

Peter settled his glasses more firmly on his nose. "Whose is it?"

"I don't know," Kate said. "The old woman who owned it died a couple of weeks ago. We've been borrowing it."

"Did she have any relatives?" Peter asked. "Maybe you could buy the house from them."

Kate shook her head. "No family. No relatives."

"Did she leave a will?"

"I doubt it. She hated lawyers. Her husband was a lawyer, and from what I could gather, he didn't treat her well."

"Could the husband have tied up the house somehow, in a trust or something?"

Kate laughed. "No. According to Mrs. Robin, he was one of those attorneys who seemed so convinced of his immortality he didn't bother to make his own will."

"So who gets the house?" Dee asked.

"The government, probably," Peter answered.

In the ensuing silence, Kate watched Shadow playing with Ebony.

Shadow looked up and smiled at her. "Kitty," he said.

Kate's heart skipped a beat.

"He spoke," Dee whispered. The two women exchanged delighted glances.

"We have to do something." Kate said. "We're his family. All of us. What will happen to him if we have to separate?"

Peter shrugged. "So, we keep the house."

"How?" Dee asked.

"Make a will."

Peter's words echoed in the silence. Then Kate heard herself say, "Joe has software for a do-it-yourself will, including a self-affidavit so it can go through probate quickly."

Dee laid a hand on Peter's arm. "I still have the key to the trucking company where I used to work. They have notary seals there. I'm sure I can find out if any of the notaries died recently, and use that seal."

"We'll use the names of dead people for witnesses," Peter said, "plus Kate's, since she knew the old woman. That way if there's ever a question about the will, she can swear to its veracity."

Hope flared in Kate, then died. "I don't know if I can do it. Except for using the food in Mrs. Robin's house, I've never broken the law in my life."

"Whose law?" Peter asked harshly. "The governor's?

He's gone. The court's? They've abdicated in favor of martial law. The army's? FEMA's? If you give them any consideration whatsoever, then you've learned nothing from this whole experience."

"But they're the government," Kate said feebly. "We have to take them seriously, don't we?"

"Government?" Peter sneered. "I've never met a government, only government employees, and not one of them has done more for the people of this city than Dee. By all rights, the house belongs to her."

Kate glanced at Greg. "You're quiet. What do you think?"

"I agree with Peter. If we give any consideration to the law, to other people's narrow sense of morality, to anyone or anything but what's right for us, we've learned nothing from these past weeks. I say we do it."

Dee nodded. "Me too."

"Me," Shadow said, laughing.

Kate smiled at the little boy. When she spoke, her voice held strong and steady.

"Then we do it."

Wanting to shout his love from the rooftops, Greg settled for telling Jim Clayton. Besides, Jim deserved to be the first to know since Jim had already figured out that he loved Kate.

Halfway to his destination, Greg remembered Jim's disapproval, but he kept on peddling. Letisha would be happy for him.

Greg hopped off his bike at Jim's house and carried it up the stairs to the porch. His knees buckled when he saw the fluorescent orange dot on the front door. He raised a hand to knock, let it drop back to his side. Maybe he shouldn't intrude on the Clayton's grief.

He dragged his bike down the stairs, then stopped and looked back. Shouldn't he find out who had died? Let the family know he shared their sorrow? See what he could do to help? After a moment of indecision, he retraced his steps.

No one answered his hesitant knock. He knocked louder.

He was heading back down the stairs, thinking no one was home, when he heard the door open.

He turned around.

Jim stood in the doorway, squinting in the sunshine.

If Greg hadn't known who he was, he wouldn't have recognized his friend. The man looked ancient, shrunken. He peered at Greg through eyes as lifeless as black onyx and about as hard. Without a word or any other acknowledgment, he turned and shambled back into the dark recesses of the house.

But he left the door open.

Taking that as an invitation, Greg entered and followed Jim into the living room.

Stiffly, like a rheumatoid old man, Jim lowered himself onto the couch. He sat there, feet flat on the floor, back straight, hands in his lap, and stared straight ahead.

Greg sat on the opposite end of the couch. He also gazed straight ahead, not needing to look at his friend to feel the waves of grief emanating from that wasted body.

"It happened so fast," Jim said finally. "Letisha acted fine. Happy. She kissed me. Told me she loved me. Then she vomited blood, and died."

"But I brought butter and walnuts," Greg said thickly. "What happened?"

"She fed them to me and the children. She was like that. Thinking of us. Not of herself." Jim fell silent again.

Bleeding for his friend, Greg lowered his head and stared at his hands. He wondered what it would be like if it had been Kate who died. He took deep heaving breaths, feeling as if he had been socked in the stomach.

After a long while Jim said quietly, "I was wrong when I cautioned you about falling in love with an older woman. If you find love, no matter what form it takes, grab on to it. Love is too precious to waste."

Thinking of Kate, Greg nodded.

They lapsed into silence again.

"Do you have enough food in the house?" Greg asked

when he realized Jim had nothing more to say.

"I guess."

"Do you have someone to take care of the kids? Do the laundry? Clean house?"

"The children are at my sister's. I want them home with me, but I can't take care of them and continue to work, too."

"Don't worry about it," Greg said. "I'll find someone to help you."

He stood and placed a hand on Jim's shoulder. Jim didn't say anything, but some of the tension left his body.

Greg let himself out of the house.

When Kate saw Greg leaning against the open door to her office, she ran to him, wondering what could have happened in the short time they'd been apart to make him so pale and shaken.

She put her arms around him. He held her tightly. Though she could barely breathe, she did not protest. When his grip loosened, she drew him into the office, closed the door behind them, and led him to a chair.

Crouching in front of him, she held one of his hands and surreptitiously touched his pulse. His heart raced. She brushed the hair off his forehead; his brow felt cool to her touch.

"What happened?" she asked.

"Letisha's dead."

"Your friend's wife?"

He nodded.

"I'm sorry. I know how much she meant to you."

He drew in a short, unsteady breath. "She was good to me. Made me feel like one of the family. Invited me over for the holidays. Baked me birthday cakes. Yet sitting there with Jim, all I could think of was how I'd feel if you died."

Not knowing what to say to comfort him, Kate cradled his hand next to her cheek.

All at once he pushed the chair back, stood, and pulled her to her feet. He grasped her shoulders and stared at her long and hard, his mouth tight.

"Promise me something."

"Anything," Kate said. Even though she said it to pacify him, she meant it.

"Promise me you won't pull any of that self-sacrificing shit on me. Promise me you will always take care of yourself."

She held herself still, half-afraid of his wild intensity.

"I promise," she said.

He stared into her eyes for a moment longer, then he nodded and released her.

He sat down heavily in the chair and buried his face in his hands. It sounded as if he were sobbing, but when he looked at her his eyes were dry.

"Letisha got the red death. She vomited blood and died. Turns out she wanted to make sure there was enough butter and walnuts to protect Jim and the kids, so she didn't eat any herself. Jim is devastated. One of the worst things about it is that Jim can't work and take care of his children at the same time, so they're staying with his sister. He needs them at home with him. I told him I'd find someone to help. Do you know anyone?"

Kate didn't even have to stop to think. "Mr. Crowley."

"I'm not sure I ever mentioned it, but the Claytons are African-American."

"So?"

"Making sure there are no surprises."

"I'll mention it, but I don't think Mr. Crowley will care. Doing dishes for us isn't helping him get over his mother. He wants to be needed, wants to take care of people. I'm sure he'll jump at the chance to help out."

"Good."

Something Greg had said echoed in Kate's mind.

She stared at him in horror. "You said Letisha vomited blood and died."

He nodded.

"I thought the deadly strains of the chimera had mutated themselves out of existence."

"Apparently not."

Kate swallowed hard. "The quarantine isn't going to be over any time soon, is it?"

Whatever comfort Greg had found in talking to Kate evaporated as soon as he left her.

Somehow he had gotten it into his head that Letisha's death had been her own fault, but Kate's mention of the quarantine had reminded him who was really to blame.

John Takamura.

Greg held himself in check while he pedaled home, but when he walked into his apartment and saw Takamura's papers spread out all over his floor, the blood rushed to his head.

He kicked a stack of the scientist's articles, scattering them all over the floor. Then he kicked another stack.

"God damn you, Takamura," he screamed, kicking and kicking. "God damn you to hell!"

He seized a handful of papers, ripped them in half, and threw them at the leering clown hanging on the wall.

Chest heaving, eyes burning with unshed tears, he hauled his arm back, then punched the clown as hard as he could.

Dazed from the shock, he staggered, but managed to keep his balance.

He shook his head to clear it. Gradually it dawned on him he hadn't hit Takamura's jaw but a solidly built wall.

"Fool," he whispered.

He looked around at the mess he had made and felt sick to his stomach.

"Shame on you, Pullman," he said aloud. "You're a grown man. Stop acting like a spoiled child."

He seized one of the papers he had torn and stared at it as if he had no idea what had happened to it. Searching through the litter on the floor for the other half of the page, he thought about another time he had lost his temper.

Shortly after his father had developed breast cancer, a kid had jeered at Greg. "You're father's a pansy."

"Take that back," Greg yelled.

The kid laughed. "My dad says your dad has a girl's disease. Means your dad's a pansy."

Greg remembered how his father had made him save his allowance until he could replace the kid's shirt that had become torn during the fight. "It doesn't matter if he was in the wrong," his father had said. "A man keeps his temper under control."

"A man keeps his temper under control," Greg repeated now, picking up a piece of paper and smoothing it out.

He lost track of time as he concentrated on putting things right. Some of the papers, like the receipts, he put in the trash; he should have done that weeks ago. But others, like the research papers the News had paid for, he sorted and put in proper order. The torn papers he set aside to tape later. He'd finished more than half of his self-imposed task when he picked up a sheet of paper, the first page of one of Takamura's earliest articles, entitled "Self-Optimization of Recombinant Ectogenic Bacteria." He smoothed it out, and set it aside with the rest of the articles, then realized what he had seen. He snatched it back and stared at the name of the co-author.

A chill ran up his spine, and suddenly he knew, with an absolute certainty, who had created the red death.

He scrambled to his feet and rummaged in his desk drawer until he found the notebook containing Professor Murdock's phone number.

The professor sounded old and frail, but he seemed eager to talk.

"You're right," he said. "Takamura wasn't my only student assistant on the Atropos project. I had another who worked part time. How clever of you to have figured it out. What was his name? Give me a moment. I'm sure I'll remember it.

"Takamura had little interest in Atropos, as I recall—he gravitated more toward plant research—but the other student appeared devastated when the army cancelled the project. Strange how I forgot all that. I know it will sound silly to a layman like you, but I think he fell in love with our little organism. Scientists, like artists, do sometimes fall in love with their creations. What was his name? Oh, yes. Now I remember."

All the way to the Reese Institute, Greg had kept turning over in his mind the questions he wanted answered, but now that he stood before the man who had caused the red death, he had just one.

"Why?" he asked.

Looking into the impish face with the twinkling eyes, he felt a twinge of doubt. After all, it had been such a small lie, insignificant, really; the kind anyone would tell.

The kind a psychopath would tell, he reminded himself.

The man stared back at Greg with a slightly quizzical look on his face, but in the end he did not even pretend to misunderstand.

He grinned—the happy, unselfconscious grin of a mischievous child—and said, "Because I felt like it."

"You killed more than a half a million people because you *felt* like it?"

"Sure. Why not? I knew I would be safe."

"Because of the unmodified fats, you mean."

The grin broadened. "You're smarter than you look. But you're wrong. I didn't kill those people. It was a side effect. I didn't plan it."

"If you didn't plan it, why didn't you let anyone know you had a cure?"

"It would have defeated the purpose of letting my baby go, now wouldn't it?"

"Your baby?"

"My offspring. He contains my genes. He's part of me. I am part of him."

"You're nothing but a Frankenstein," Greg said, swallowing his bile.

"How refreshing to meet someone who knows that Frankenstein is the name of the creator, not the creature. Most people miss the point of the story. It's not the story of a monster, but the story of a god. Frankenstein created life. I created life."

Feeling as if he were being drawn into the man's delusions, Greg turned away and breathed evenly. After a moment he turned back and looked directly into the man's glittering eyes.

"You might have created the red death, the actual epidemic," he said, "but you didn't create the disease. You stole it."

The would-be Frankenstein stamped his foot. "Don't call him a disease. Humans are the disease. Why should my baby be doomed to a test tube when humans are allowed to go free? And I didn't steal him. I rescued him. Maybe I wasn't there for his inception, but I did create him—I brought him to life. And anyhow, what makes you think I'm the creator? When you were here a couple of weeks ago, you didn't have a clue."

"You lied to me," Greg said. "You told me you didn't know John Takamura, but I found a paper you co-authored with him."

Jack Thornton let out a loud guffaw. "That's all you have?"

"That, and your confession," Greg said.

Sometime during the interview, Thornton must have pressed a call button, because the door burst open and two huge men, bodybuilders by the look of them, stepped into Thornton's office.

"You need help, Dr. Thornton?" the one with the shaved head asked.

Thornton gestured to Greg. "See if he's wired. He's a reporter, trying to steal company secrets."

Greg stepped back, but since Shaved Head still blocked the door, he had no place to go. The other bodybuilder, who had a wisp of a beard on his dark chin, moved toward Greg.

With a cold, watery feel in the pit of his stomach, Greg gritted his teeth while The Beard patted him down.

"He's clean, Doc."

Thornton took possession of Greg's notebook. "I think

this belongs to me."

"You want us to rough him up?" Shaved Head asked.

Thornton slapped the notebook against his palm. "No need. He has nothing to show anyone."

"You sure?" Shaved Head asked, eyeing Greg. "I'd be glad to do it. Pukes like this make me sick."

Thornton hesitated.

Greg held his breath, wondering how he could deal with the two thugs. Each one alone was more than he could handle.

"No," Thornton said. "Get him out of my sight, but if he ever returns, you can do whatever you wish."

Greg let out his pent-up breath. As he turned to leave, The Beard grabbed his upper left arm in an iron grip and yanked him to the door.

Shaved Head stepped aside to let them out, then grabbed Greg's other arm. They dragged him down the long corridor, opened a door at the back of the building, and tossed him out on the blacktop.

They glared at him for a moment, then they laughed, high-fived, and went back inside.

Greg gingerly picked himself up and limped to the front of the building where he had parked his bike.

As he rode away from the Reese Institute, he pushed his aches and pains to the back of his mind and thought about the article he would soon be writing.

Atropos might be classified, but Jack Thornton's "baby" sure wasn't.


Greg was finishing the last few sentences of his story when a hand reached passed him and touched his keyboard. His article vanished.

"What the hell do you think you're doing?" he shouted, swiveling his chair around.

A tall, black-suited man regarded him with unsmiling eyes. Though the man was not broad, he had such an unmistakable aura of power he seemed to fill all available space.

"Good evening, Mr. Pullman," the man said, inclining his head.

"Who the hell are you?"

"You can call me Mr. Smith."

"That's no answer."

"Let's say I'm—" Mr. Smith paused. With a mocking half-smile, he continued, "a government employee."

Greg wiped his sweaty palms on his pants. He stared at Mr. Smith, wondering if he had misinterpreted the man's remark. There was no way Mr. Smith could know Peter had used those very words that morning.

When Mr. Smith cocked his head and raised one eyebrow, Greg's blood seemed to turn to ice.

"How . . . how did you . . ."

The mocking half-smile returned. "An onion has many layers, Mr. Pullman, and somewhere beneath all of those layers is the truth."

Greg tried to breathe, but all in an instant he had forgotten how.

"I'm not playing games with you, Mr. Pullman. I want you to be aware that we know everything—everything—you've been doing and saying so I don't have to waste valuable time with unnecessary explanations."

Greg sucked in one short breath, then another.

"Oh, come, come, Mr. Pullman. This can't be a surprise to you. You're the one who wondered about technology that was light years ahead of what is generally known."

"How . . ." Greg managed to get out.

"We didn't use bugs, if that's what you're wondering. Talk about your out-dated technologies. We can now pluck voices right out of the air at great distances. And we can see through walls at even greater distances. You're right, Mr. Pullman. Your woman does have lovely hair."

"Who are you?" Greg asked, finding his voice. "Army? CIA? NSA?"

Mr. Smith looked pained. "Please, don't insult me."

"Tell me," Greg demanded.

"I can't. I work for an agency so secret even its name is

classified."

"What do you want? Are you here to arrest me?"

"Arrest you? Whatever for?"

"You tell me," Greg said with some asperity. "You're the one who knows everything."

Mr. Smith smiled benignly, as if at a favored pupil. "Very good, Mr. Pullman."

Greg glared at him. "You still haven't told me what you're doing here."

"Let's say I'm here as a friend." Mr. Smith nodded toward Greg's computer. "You did a good job. I'm sure you'll go far if you follow orders and forget that story."

"Why should I?"

"Do you think the American public can handle knowing that this—What do you call it, Mr. Pullman? The red death?—is the result of one man's megalomania? It is in the national interest for everyone to believe it a naturally-occurring flu epidemic."

"So Jack Thornton goes free?"

"No. Thanks to you, he is in custody."

"I wouldn't have thought you had probable cause."

"In case you've forgotten, Mr. Pullman, martial law is in effect. But even if it weren't, we still would not need probable cause. There won't be a trial. Jack Thornton will quietly disappear."

Greg narrowed his eyes. "What do you mean, 'thanks to me'?"

"We've been watching you closely, hoping you would find the creator of the chimera if we couldn't. Hedging our bets, so to speak."

"I don't get it. Why did you need me? Why didn't you pluck him out of the air?"

"We don't have the resources to keep tabs on every single person. He never came to our attention."

"And I did?"

"When you wrote the article about the red death as a bio-weapon."

"Which the paper didn't publish."

"True, but it still came to our attention. By leading us to Jack Thornton, Mr. Pullman, you have earned your country's gratitude. Now all you have to do is forget about both him and me."

"What if I don't want to forget about him?" Greg asked. "What if I pursue the story?"

"Then we pursue you."

# 32

*Spring*

Greg stood and watched Shadow sleep and felt some of his tension ease. He tucked the covers more firmly around the boy's shoulders and kissed his rosy cheeks.

He closed the door part way, then went into the other bedroom. Lying on the bed, he watched Kate brush her hair. The rhythmic strokes eased more of his tension. By the time Kate had finished getting ready for bed and had come to lie next to him, he was as relaxed as he ever got these days.

It had been more than three months since his meeting with Mr. Smith, but the man's words still haunted him.

He looked up. Though all he saw was the ceiling, he knew they could see him.

Were they watching him? Now? This minute?

When he drew Kate close, his skin prickled, as if he could feel those unseen eyes focused on him.

Much as he hated the thought of being under constant surveillance, he hoped they were watching; that way they would know he was keeping his end of the bargain. He had told no one, not even Kate, about either Jack Thornton or Mr. Smith. He hoped Mr. Smith kept his promise.

"If you keep your mouth shut," Mr. Smith said before he left that night, "everything will go as you and your friends have planned."

Those innocuous words, spoken in that quiet, controlled voice, had been more chilling than any overt threat could have been. Thinking about them made him shudder.

A lump of unshed tears settled in Kate's throat when she felt Greg shudder. She remembered how mischievous he had acted when she first met him. He seemed so different now, withdrawn at times. He no longer liked to talk, and when he did speak, he seemed nervous, as if afraid someone would overhear.

She wondered, not for the first time, what had happened to him the day he had learned of Letisha's death. He had left her office grief-stricken but still himself; he had returned to her that night pale and clammy, as if in shock. When she had opened her mouth to ask what troubled him, he had placed a finger on her lips and had shaken his head.

Kate rested an ear on his chest and listened to the sound of his heart beating. He was alive. So many weren't.

The Bowers had established a therapy clinic for survivors of the red death, and Amanda had asked Kate to run it. She found it challenging but heartbreaking. So much trauma.

And it wasn't over yet.

Although the quarantine had been lifted, the military still patrolled Colorado. According to Peter, once FEMA assumed control, there was no protocol for the restoration of constitutional rule. If so, the military would be with them for some time to come.

Almost as bad were the tourists roaming the streets, staring about with wide eyes and open mouths, as if visiting a theme park. Quarantine World.

Worst of all were the carpetbaggers, the people who had come to make their fortunes in "the new frontier," as the president had called it in a recent speech. It was a real estate bonanza for development companies. They acquired large tracts of property for pennies. Their main expense came from payoffs to the government employees who were taking possession of any house they deemed abandoned and condemning others that were still occupied.

The lawyers, of course, were making a fortune.

One good thing, with business creeping back to normal, Dee's employment agency was doing well. She ran it out of her living room in the house next door. Both Peter and Siggy worked for her. Peter seemed happy, though now legally blind. He often mentioned he loved being able to solve simple problems like finding jobs for people and people for jobs, rather than reading about the big problems and finding out there are no solutions.

And Shadow—

Kate felt a rumble of laughter beneath her cheek. She

lifted her head to give Greg an inquiring glance.

"You're thinking so hard I can hear the wheels spinning," he said.

She sighed. "Shadow still doesn't talk much."

Greg planted a kiss on her forehead. "He talks whenever it suits him. He's one of those strong silent types who prefers to listen."

Kate smiled at him. "You always know the right thing to say."

"Not always." She felt him start to withdraw from her, felt his effort to drag himself back.

"How was your dinner with the Claytons?" she asked.

"Very good. Mr. Crowley is an excellent cook. The kids like him, treat him like their Grandpa. Even Jim treats him like one of the family, though he does find the whole thing ironic."

"And Jim? How is he?"

"As well as a man can be after losing the love of his life," Greg said with a catch in his voice, "but he's surviving."

Kate gently touched his cheek; he turned his head and kissed her palm.

After a moment, he said, "I saw Pippi today. She stopped by the paper this morning to tell me goodbye. She's been working as a local liaison with a film crew from the New York station that came to document the ending of the quarantine, and they've offered her a job."

"Does she miss you?" Kate still found it hard to believe any woman could have walked away from Greg for any reason.

"She's too busy getting to know herself. She told me this is the first time since she was thirteen that she didn't have a boyfriend, and she's never been happier."

*Neither have I.* Kate nestled into his arms.

"Has Mr. Olaf ever gotten over your defection?"

"No." Greg laughed. "He still can't believe I applied for the job as the book section editor, and he's furious with the publisher for hiring me. He humphs at me and growls, and says I'm wasting my talents."

"Are you?" Kate asked softly.

"No." Greg smiled, teeth gleaming in the dim light. "I looked at a new romance novel today, and I learned a lot. Here, let me show you."

He kissed her eyes, her nose, her throat, then took possession of her lips, all while his hands were doing delicious things to her body.

"Before we get carried away," Kate murmured breathlessly, "I have something to tell you."

Propping himself on his elbow, Greg searched Kate's radiant face.

"You mean it?" he asked, grinning so hugely his jaw ached.

"Yes."

"We're going to have a baby?"

"Yes."

Greg pulled the covers down and reverently kissed her belly.

"Hello, in there," he whispered. "You must not be very bright to want to be born into this world, but I'll love you all the same."

Kate giggled and gathered him into her arms.

Remembering Thornton's claim that he had created life, Greg silently told the man: *You created death. Kate and I created life.*

His last thought before succumbing once again to Kate's embrace, was that no matter what other horrors awaited his child, Jack Thornton and his deadly organism would not be among them.

# Epilogue

Dr. Jack Thornton stared out the small, barred window and watched the armed guards patrolling the perimeter. The fence, topped with razor wire, was electrified, he had been told, but he'd never had occasion to test the allegation. Nor did he have the opportunity; he seldom went outside.

He smiled briefly, thinking of the day he had released his baby. The weather had been perfect: blue skies, unseasonably warm temperatures, bright cumulus clouds on the horizon. He had felt such a rush when he had pressed the plunger on the small spray bottle.

And his baby had done him proud.

It was all over now. With as empty and as lifeless as he felt, he found it hard to care what lay in store for him.

"Everything okay here?"

Dr. Thornton turned.

"Let us know if you need anything," said the man he knew as Mr. Smith. "Equipment, assistants, whatever. Money is no object."

Dr. Thornton glanced around his state-of-the-art lab. It was perfect, the sort of place he had dreamed of for himself. No more sneaking lab time, no more appropriating materials from other projects. But now that his baby was grown, he no longer needed such a laboratory.

"Tell me one thing," Mr. Smith said. "Can you really modify Atropos so it becomes more deadly as it mutates, rather than less?"

Dr. Thornton gave him a wan smile. "Already done."

"And what about the synthetic fat, one not available through diet, so we have greater control of the outcome?"

"That's done, too."

Mr. Smith raised one eyebrow. "You seem down. Are you still worried about the guards and security cameras? You shouldn't be. It's nothing personal. This is a highly classified installation. We can't have strangers wandering in and out."

Dr. Thornton sighed. "I've become used to them, but I feel as if it's all over for me."

Mr. Smith presented him with a vial. "Maybe this will help. It's an unfinished project we would like you to look at."

Dr. Thornton cradled the vial in the palm of his hand. It felt warm, as if what it contained were alive. He held it up to the light. Vibrant metallic colors swirled together, like a liquid rainbow.

Gazing at it, his eyes dilated, his breath quickened, his stomach muscles contracted.

A smile lit his face.

It was love at first sight.

Other Titles available from Pat Bertram and Indigo Sea Press.

### More Deaths Than One
### Pat Bertram
Bob Stark returns to Denver after 18 years in SE Asia to discover that the mother he buried before he left is dead again. At her new funeral, he sees . . . himself. Is his other self a hoaxer? A doppelganger? Or is something more sinister going on?

### Daughter Am I
### Pat Bertram
When twenty-five-year-old Mary Stuart inherits a farm from her recently murdered grandparents -- grand-parents her father claimed had died before she was born -- she becomes obsessed with finding out who they were and why someone wanted them dead.

### Light Bringer
### Pat Bertram
Thirty-seven years after being abandoned on the doorstep of a remote cabin in Colorado, Becka Johnson returns to try to discover her identity, but she only finds more questions. Who has been looking for her all those years? And why?

# Excerpt from Light Bringer

Tracks led to the house where a small gray creature huddled against the door.

She clapped her hands. "Shoo. Shoo."

The creature did not stir.

"Go on. Get," she shouted.

The creature still didn't move. Was it dead? This wouldn't be the first time a dying animal had been attracted to the warmth seeping from beneath the front door.

She approached gingerly, relaxing when she saw what appeared to be an old gray blanket that had somehow ended up on the stoop. She bent over to collect the wad of fabric, then straightened. Bad idea. Who knew what vermin had taken refuge in the folds.

Before she could figure out what to do, the blanket moved. She jumped back and stared at it. The blanket moved again, giving her a glimpse of a coppery curl.

She lifted the bundle, cradled it in her arms, and drew back the blanket. Two dark eyes, shining with intelligence, gazed at her.

She sucked in a breath. An infant, no more than nine months old.

As the infant continued to gaze at her, its eyes brightened to gleaming amber. Then it beamed at her—a welcoming smile, both joyous and knowing, as if it had recognized a dear friend.

Helen's face felt tight. "Who are you?"

The baby chortled in response.

"And who left you here?" She glanced at the tracks. They led in only one direction—toward the house.

Feeling dizzy, she crouched to examine the tracks more closely.

They were footprints. Tiny footprints in the snow.